River Pines

To Denise,
Have a wonderful
visit at River Pines!

Enjoy,
Patrice Garfield
Grossman
1/1/02

River Pines

by
Patrice Garfield

Northwest Publishing Inc.
Salt Lake City, Utah

River Pines

PRINTING HISTORY
First Printing 1994

ISBN 1-56901-487-6

NPI books are published by Northwest Publishing Incorporated,
5949 South 350 West, Salt Lake City, Utah 84107.
The name "NPI" and the "NPI" logo are trademarks belonging to
Northwest Publishing Incorporated.

PRINTED IN TNE UNITED STATES OF AMERICA
10 9 8 7 6 5 4 3 2 1

To Eddie, my own wonderful hero,
who has a way of making all
my dreams come true.

To my sweet Mai-Ann,
who brought me uncountable cups of tea.

And to my handsome Buddy,
who brought the cookies to go with the tea.

Prologue

April 6, 1886
Pennsylvania

Early morning mists hovered above the earth and the sun's first rays filtered through the white fog. The horse's hooves pummeled the soft green turf of the Pennsylvania countryside as it cantered over lush rolling hills and farmer's fields.

The rider, with her pale hair lifting in the wind and curling around her face and neck, sped through the dew-heavy air, which clung to her cheeks and glistened on her creamy skin.

For the moment, shrouded in the privacy of early dawn, when there was no one to watch or to judge her, she pursued the course of an unharnessed creature, free . . . fast . . . impulsive.

Jumping over stone fences and recklessly hastening her horse faster when she came to vacant pastures, she rode with the urgency of a courier bearing important news. The message was for her alone and it aroused a mixture of apprehension and gladness, for she ran a race with time, not knowing if she ran toward or away from the changes life held out to her.

Eventually the horse grew tired. She could feel it straining beneath her thighs, so she relented, letting it slow to a soft gait. She guided the horse into a line of trees, knowing that there was a stream ahead, where the horse could drink and she could dream. The water's scent called to her.

The rider slipped from the saddle, dropped the reins, and the animal's graceful neck stretched down, its muzzle touching the water's surface where ripples marred its glassy finish.

She watched the arcs widen and move outward, drifting toward the center of the stream where they met semi-circles traveling from the bank on the other side.

Looking up in surprise, she saw him squatting on the stream's edge across from her, his hand in the cool water, cupping it, then letting it drip from his large fingers.

He lifted his head and studied her. There was a vulnerability and sadness in his expression, as though he looked at an illusion instead of a flesh and blood woman. Then he stood and left the spot, disappearing into the trees, without looking back, as though he had not seen woman or horse on the other side.

Colorado

So, it is time.

The bronze-skinned man with intense black eyes sat astride his horse and looked down from the mountain into the direction of his friend's ranch.

Long awaited, it was finally upon them.

The moon had not yet disappeared, though the sun was beginning to brighten the sky. His white hat looked luminous and its silver and turquoise ornaments winked when the first rays of sun appeared.

He heard it in the blowing wind; he saw it in the formation of the clouds. His heart beat to the cadence of the message.

Rone Daniels awaited destiny.

PART I

CHAPTER ONE

With his large frame cramped in a delicate chair, Jack Drummond stretched out his long legs, crossed his arms over his chest, and let his green eyes look around the sitting room of his aunt's house. There was nothing masculine in the room, nor in any of the other rooms of the Dawson home, except for his cousin David's study. After two weeks of pretty china vases and floral chintz, Jack was eager to leave Benton, Pennsylvania.

He closed his eyes and pictured his ranch house with its large living room, warmly paneled, and filled with sturdy, comfortable furniture. Not a woman's house, but suited to his way of life. *I suppose that's why she hated it.* The notion snaked through his thoughts before he had a chance to stop it. Although he had come to pride himself on catching any dark thoughts like it, occasionally they slipped through his guard.

Jack sprang from the chair and walked to the window. *I have to think of a way to keep the place, despite that damned mortgage. There's got to be a way to raise the money.* Jack ran his fingers through his black hair. *I'll steal before I'll let anyone else have that ranch.*

A carriage stopped in front of the house and the driver jumped down and opened the door. Jack's eyes widened when he caught a glimpse of a slender ankle beneath the skirt of a blue wool suit. His gaze traveled upward toward curved hips and a tiny waist, and he delighted in the hint of a full bosom covered in white silk.

Jack's appreciative smile froze, however, when the young woman was in full sight. His eyes narrowed and his lips pressed together as he studied her pale, almost white, hair. He took in each lovely feature of her face—round gray eyes, full lips, and delicately colored cheeks—as his heart pounded faster against his rib cage.

Jack heard the maid scurrying to answer the door, and a light musical voice met that of the maid's Irish brogue, "Is Mrs. Dawson in, Eileen?"

"Sure, won't you wait in the sittin' room and I'll get her, Miss Elizabeth," Jack heard the maid say politely. He looked for an escape, but it was too late.

She entered the room and was busy removing her gloves when she felt his presence. Her head came up and her eyes searched until she saw him, shadowed by the draperies. They stood observing each other in silence, with Jack having the advantage of being able to see her in the light from the window.

"Elizabeth, dear, what a surprise," Grace Dawson exclaimed, coming into the room, her arms reaching to embrace her guest.

Noticing Jack over Elizabeth's shoulder, Grace said, "I see you've met my nephew."

Jack moved from the window toward Elizabeth. When his face came out of the shadows, his mouth was pulled back over straight white teeth in a magnetic grin and his green eyes glowed emerald. *The man at the stream,* Elizabeth thought.

"Didn't I see you . . ."

"I'm afraid I haven't had the pleasure," Jack said in a deep, sonorous voice.

His skin was tanned from the sun and a loose strand of black hair fell on his brow. A slight cleft was visible where his chin squared off. Beth's stomach tensed and she felt herself blush when her eyes met his.

"Well, let me introduce you then," Grace said. "Elizabeth Gerard, this is Jack Drummond." Grace smiled up at her nephew and continued, "Jack, Elizabeth is a neighbor and the niece of my dearest friend."

His piercing eyes stared into hers and though she felt compelled to acknowledge the introduction, Elizabeth was so held in his mesmerizing gaze, she was unable to bridge the silence. "I thought you were a vision this morning," he whispered finally, then frowning added, "or a nightmare."

Elizabeth's mouth fell open and her eyes widened at his impertinence. "I beg your pardon?" she asked, uncertain that she had heard correctly.

Grace, a plump woman with graying hair, pulled Elizabeth down beside her on a delicate settee. "Beth, dear, Jack is my sister Amelia's son. He's visiting us for a short time. So tell me, how are the plans going for your birthday? Are you ready?"

"Yes, I can't believe the ball is only two days away." Elizabeth glanced at Jack who was seated in one of the chairs across the room. "Would you like to come, Mr. Drummond?"

"I won't be here, but thank you anyway," he replied, not sounding as polite as his words were meant to sound, and Elizabeth felt rejected while Jack continued to study her with a charming, crooked grin.

"By the way, Jack, where's David?" Grace asked, as the maid brought in a tray of tea and iced cakes.

Before Jack could answer, David entered the room, smiled brightly at Beth, and taking her hands while kissing her cheek, said, "I saw the carriage out front and hoped it would be you. I couldn't be more pleased to see you, Beth. You'll stay for dinner, of course." He leaned toward her and continued in a mock whisper, "I need some lovely company after spending time with my sullen cousin over there in the corner."

Elizabeth laughed. "I'd love to rescue you, but I'm afraid I can't. I just came for a short visit."

He put his hand over his heart. "I'm crestfallen."

"I think you'll survive," she told him, smiling brightly.

Elizabeth loved looking into David's warm brown eyes, and admired his distinguished good looks, which were polished and fresh. A deep dimple showed in each cheek whenever he smiled, which was often and easy. Elizabeth wished she could touch his face and kiss his full mouth. Just the thought of it brought high color to her cheeks.

"Tell me," he inquired, "how's your sister? Why isn't she here with you?"

"Emily is composing a beautiful sonata and spends most of her afternoons at the piano. She and Aunt Catherine send their love to you both."

Grace patted Elizabeth's hand and asked, "So what brings you here for a visit during such a busy week?"

Elizabeth panicked. Her whole purpose in calling at the Dawson home was to ask David to escort her to the ball. She had waited patiently for weeks for him to approach her, but with only two days left, she had decided that, proper or not, if he did not ask her today, *she* would ask *him*.

Now, as she sat in this room with his mother and cousin, the idea seemed like an exceedingly bad one.

"I'll wager it's to see the colt," David answered for her. Turning to Jack, he explained, "Elizabeth is one of the finest horse-woman in Pennsylvania. The faster the horse, the happier Elizabeth is to mount it." Smiling at Elizabeth, David added, "This new horse is a winner, Beth. You'll be riding him soon."

Elizabeth beamed at David now, thrilled that he had offered her a ride on his prized colt. Doubtless, it was a sign of his love, which made her all the more certain that on her birthday he would ask her to marry him.

David took a chair next to Jack's. "Did you know Jack is from Colorado, Beth? I'm afraid he's a bit lonesome for his ranch there. Apparently, our Pennsylvania cows aren't good enough for him."

Jack grinned at his cousin, "I miss more than cattle, Dave."

Elizabeth could see the men shared a warm camaraderie and wondered how David, with his pleasant temperament and charm, could feel affection for this strange relative. She wasn't sure that she liked Jack Drummond. Yet, whenever his eyes met hers, for even a moment, Elizabeth felt breathless.

"My sister and I love reading about the West, Mr. Drummond. It sounds so exciting. I'd love to see it some day."

"It isn't anything like it's described in those yellow covered novels. Once they come, prissy Easterners usually find it a little too rough for their liking."

Elizabeth knew she had just been rebuked, though for what reason she wasn't sure. Unused to being spoken to in such a rude manner, she glared at Jack now. His answer was to smile broadly, leaving her completely confused.

Grace served the tea, handing each of them a delicate cup and saucer. Elizabeth thought the china looked odd in Jack's large, callused hand and she hid a smile.

When he saw her staring at the violet pattered vessel, he deliberately held up his little finger and drank with great affectation. It looked so out of character for him that Elizabeth stifled a giggle.

"What's this? Is this scoundrel flirting with you?" David asked, pretending annoyance. But when Beth looked back at Jack, he had put down the cup and saucer and was looking at her in that same peculiar way, and, once again, she wasn't certain if he was entertained by her or mocking her.

Elizabeth decided to ignore the oaf and turned to David. "Tell me about Philadelphia, David."

Elizabeth lost herself in his voice as he described the work he was doing in a law firm there. While she carried on polite conversation for almost an hour, she concentrated on none of it, preferring to picture herself in David's arms, dancing at the celebration of her birthday.

"Elizabeth?" Grace interrupted her thoughts.

"Yes? I'm sorry; did you say something?"

Grace laughed, "Why, you're a million miles away."

"I'd say just a few feet . . . to be precise," Jack corrected sarcastically, his eyes twinkling with mischief.

Beth scowled at him, embarrassed that he had observed her, read her thoughts, and then had the audacity to call attention to them. "Actually, I was thinking I'd better be going home." She said with an icy edge to her voice.

"So soon?" Jack asked, feigning surprise.

Elizabeth noticed David hiding a grin behind his hand and it greatly annoyed her. She stood up and absently kissed Grace's cheek. "Thank you for the tea, Mrs. Dawson." When David and Jack stood, Elizabeth turned steely gray eyes on Jack and said coldly, "It was . . . interesting to meet you."

Jack took her hand and squeezed hard and Elizabeth flinched slightly. "We'll meet again, perhaps."

"I doubt that, Mr. Drummond," she answered sweetly, thinking that she would avoid meeting him again at all costs.

David took her arm. "I'll walk you to your carriage."

When they left the house and walked into the late afternoon sun, Elizabeth pronounced, "Your cousin is insufferable, David."

"He usually has a way with women."

"I cannot see how," Beth said.

David chuckled, "You're just used to a man falling at your feet the moment he meets you. I'm afraid Jack considers women a necessary evil." When her eyes flashed with anger, he decided to change the subject. "I suppose that you have an escort for the ball."

Elizabeth's teeth caught her lip. "Actually, I haven't, David."

He gave her a knowing smile. "Ah, so that's the real reason for this unexpected visit."

Elizabeth pretended to be indignant, but his smile was infectious. "Not that I haven't been asked," she told him.

"Oh, I know you've been asked—by a dozen young men no doubt. Still, you would accept no one's invitation but mine so that you can flirt outrageously with every eligible man in attendance. I know the routine, dear Beth."

Elizabeth laughed now. "Stop teasing me. I don't flirt."

David rolled his eyes. Then his smile faded. "And Emily? Who will be escorting your beautiful twin?"

"She claims she does not need an escort to her own party. I don't always understand my sister. She spends hours at the piano composing the most exciting and romantic music I have ever heard, but denies herself the simple pleasure of a gentleman's company."

"I know what you mean," David said seriously.

Elizabeth continued without having heard him. "She rarely smiles anymore. It's as if she is devoid of happiness. I'm very worried about her, David."

Touched by the sincerity of her concern, David said gently, "Emily's just a quiet, sensitive woman, Beth. I wouldn't worry about her. Things are going to change, you'll see."

Then he brightened again and took Elizabeth's chin in his fingers. "Very well, my beautiful Elizabeth, I would be most honored to escort you on the momentous occasion of your eighteenth birthday."

They said good-bye and he handed her into the carriage, blowing her a kiss as it pulled away. Elizabeth was radiating delight, and she wanted to respond the same way but stopped when she saw Jack Drummond watching from the window, his ever-present grin seeming to mock her.

Elizabeth's smile disappeared and she sat back angrily against the leather seat. Never had she met anyone so irritating. She closed her eyes in exasperation and Jack loomed behind her reluctant eyelids—tall, slender, but with massive shoulders, and one rebellious strand of black hair that dipped on his tanned forehead. She pictured his patrician nose, high cheek bones and powerful jaw which ended with that disconcertingly attractive cleft. His green eyes, which seemed drawn on his face with the darkness of his lashes, were sparkling, amused, and always naughty. Elizabeth found those eyes to be exceedingly annoying—and extraordinarily appealing.

With a huff, Elizabeth looked out through the carriage window. Soon a smile touched her lips as she thought, *He may be the most infuriation man I've ever met, but he's also the most handsome.*

CHAPTER TWO

Catherine Gleason looked out from the open doors of the drawing room of her Eighteenth Century stone house and smiled as Glorie, her beloved maid, came storming toward her from the garden.

When the smile was not returned, Catherine knew something was wrong, and she could easily imagine just where the trouble would be coming from. Glorie's round blue eyes flickered with anger and Catherine readied herself for a good scolding, which would be delivered with a hint of Irish brogue.

"I've said it before, and I'll say it again, they're *spoilt* that's what they are!"

"Glorie . . ."

"They've no respect. It's a switch they need to their backsides," the furious woman ranted, her short, bony frame stretched up so that she was almost nose to nose with Catherine.

"Glorie, they're grown women now. We certainly can't start beating them at this stage, can we?"

The tiny old woman in the immaculate blue uniform and white apron grunted. "'Tis niver too late for a beatin', and I would be more 'n happy to deliver it once and fer all."

Catherine controlled a smile that twitched at the corner of her mouth. "In all the years that you took care of Anne and me, you never once laid a hand on us. Why is it that you think I would even consider doing such a thing to my nieces?"

"In all the years that I took care of you and that sweet sister of yours—God rest her soul—I niver felt the need to beat you."

Catherine put her arm around Glorie's shoulders and turned her into the direction of the beautiful young women who were sitting in the sunny garden, their heads together, their voices drifting toward the treetops where the birds' songs met the gaiety of their laughter.

"Look at them, Glorie," Catherine said quietly. "They'll be eighteen years old in two days. They're women now, and we'll be losing them soon to some handsome suitors." She looked down at the maid and smiled gently. "When that happens, you'll miss them and you'll complain that it's too quiet around here."

Glorie's mouth puckered in a pout, even though her eyes softened, and she said, 'Twill be you who'll be cryin'. I'll put on me dancin' shoes and do a jig!"

Catherine laughed out loud and asked, "What were they up to today that has you so vexed, Glorie Murphy?"

Elizabeth Gerard immediately stopped laughing and pushed at her sister when she noticed her aunt approaching. "Oh, no, Aunt Catherine is home, and by the look on her face, she knows."

Emily's gray eyes widened and she was about to say something when she realized her aunt was standing beside the marble bench where she was seated. Catherine's eyes locked with hers. Emily tried to look away but it was too late. Although the girls were dressed identically, Catherine could always tell them apart by looking directly into their eyes, especially when they were in trouble.

Knowing who to address now, Catherine turned to Elizabeth, "Which one of you greased the pig and which one of you hid it in the pantry?"

Elizabeth bit her lip and Catherine could see tears of laughter fill her eyes. "I asked you a question, Elizabeth Gerard, although I don't need to ask whose idea it was in the first place, now, do I?

Elizabeth swallowed hard. "I'll answer your question if I may ask one first—which was the worse thing to do, greasing the pig or hiding it?"

The girls exploded in laughter then, and Catherine had all she could do to control her own amusement. Elizabeth fell back into her garden seat and cackled, her long, slender legs at odd angles, while Emily giggled ladylike behind her hand.

Catherine placed her hands on her hips and shook her head. "Honestly! By this time I should think I could trust you to behave when I'm out of sight. Whatever possessed you to do such a shocking thing?"

Emily sobered enough to say, "We're terribly sorry, Aunt Catherine. We didn't plan it, really. Somehow it . . . just . . ."

"Greased pigs being released in houses don't 'just happen' if that's what you were about to say."

Elizabeth had difficulty bringing her laughter under control when she confessed, "I hid the pig in the pantry, then talked Emily into helping me grease it. I don't know why, except that it has been exceptionally boring in this house lately. Emily pouts and works on her music all the time. I thought it would be good for her to have some diversion . . . Oh, you should have seen their faces when Cook opened the pantry door and the piglet squealed . . ." She covered her face and fell to the side of her chair, laughing again.

"Elizabeth!" Catherine chided.

The girl stood up and raised her arms dramatically. "Don't you see? Hasn't anyone in this house noticed? It's spring. The world has come to life again and we should all be lighthearted and joyful."

"I find it difficult to believe that causing a circus in the kitchen creates joy, Elizabeth," Catherine argued. "From what I understand, it produced bedlam. Glorie tells me the entire luncheon was ruined when the stable boy knocked the table over trying to catch the poor little creature."

"Tonight's chocolate cake fell on his head, actually," Emily offered, which sent the girls into convulsions of laughter again.

Catherine continued, "Glorie is anything but lighthearted at this moment, and Cook is definitely not joyful. Poor Barret is bathing, and the piglet . . . the animal is . . . covered with . . ."

The scene was too much, and although she was trying as hard as she could, it was impossible for Catherine to stifle the laughter that had been bubbling up inside her since Glorie related the story a few minutes before. Elizabeth's and Emily's infectious giggling undid her, and with slow, irrepressible mirth, Catherine finally joined her nieces in relishing the hilarious account of their mischief, making the twins laugh all the more.

Taking her handkerchief from her pocket, Catherine wiped her eyes and swatted at Elizabeth affectionately with it. "Stop that right now! If Glorie finds us laughing, we'll all be in for it."

Catherine was never sure if living with the twins had kept her young or aged her prematurely. She was certain, however, that she couldn't imagine a life without them.

The older woman studied the lovely faces of the girls. They were so much alike. Their long, curly hair was so fair it was almost colorless, and their clear ivory skin was pink from laughter. Their four identical eyes twinkled at her while their full mouths smiled over delicate white teeth.

Though established as a spinster at forty-seven, Catherine, herself, was still exceedingly lovely. Her blue eyes were always animated with intelligence and her creamy skin was still unlined. She could converse on any subject, for she was well-read and finely educated. She didn't live up to the term "maiden aunt," as she was youthful thinking, and the fact that she was an officer in the Benton Savings and Loan, a job that she had inherited upon the death of her father, made her in demand at every social gathering. She accepted very few invitations, however.

Since the twins had come to live with Catherine thirteen years before, after their parents were killed in a fire, she found she enjoyed their company—mischief and all—better than anyone else's.

Sitting amid the fragrant and colorful spring blossoms, a sudden melancholy replaced Catherine's mirth, for she knew her young charges were on the brink of womanhood and she would be alone before long.

"What is it, Aunt Catherine?" Emily asked her. "You look so sad. You aren't still angry with us?"

Elizabeth was contrite now also. "We'll behave from now on, Aunt Catherine," she promised. "After all, we truly are too old to be acting like children." Turning to her sister, she added, "I blame you, Em. You're supposed to keep me in line. I should be able to count on you to be level headed."

Emily winced slightly, then flashing an indignant look at Elizabeth, said, "That is not fair, Beth. I would have been happy sitting at the piano all day. I refuse to take full responsibility for *your* troublesome ideas."

Catherine held up her hand. "Stop arguing. You're both to blame." Pointing to Elizabeth, she added, "You are much too old to be participating in such shenanigans, as Glorie calls it," then turning toward Emily, continued, "and you should not allow Beth to talk you in and out of everything she decides to do— though seeing you laugh again was almost worth the trouble it caused."

Elizabeth hid a smile and Emily glared at her. It was true. Beth could talk her into doing just about anything. She had to admit, however, that more often than not, she had a grand time doing it. Elizabeth was so full of merriment, always feasting on life, making the best of what the world had to offer. Beth had a way of eating a simple meal as if it were a banquet, or, wearing a plain dress, and have it look like an exquisite gown.

"I feel so restless," Elizabeth declared, suddenly. "I think I'll go for a ride. Do either of you mind?" she asked her aunt and sister.

Emily shook her head. "Go ahead, Beth."

Catherine waved a lazy hand at Elizabeth. "I've got work to do so you might as well entertain yourself. Just promise you'll ride that horse like a lady and handle yourself with some decorum. I beg of you not to jump old Farmer Dalton's wagon again. It cost me a fortune to replace the produce that was ruined when the wagon tipped over. And the poor man nearly had a stroke when he saw your horse coming at him."

Elizabeth jumped from her chair. "The old coot was in the way." She kissed Catherine's forehead and patted her sister's shoulder as she started to run toward the barn. "I won't be long . . . unless I meet David."

"It's getting late, Beth. Make sure you're back before dark," Catherine called to her. They watched as she disappeared through the stable doors. When Catherine looked back at Emily, she noticed tears were brimming in the young woman's eyes.

"What is it, dear?"

Emily shook her head and looked down at her hands.

"Was it her reference to David?"

Emily's head came up quickly and she looked at her aunt with alarm. Catherine's smile was sympathetic and knowledgeable. "I've known for a long time how you feel about David. I had hoped by this time you would have spoken to Elizabeth about it—or that she would have seen for herself."

"Am I so obvious?"

Catherine nodded. "I'm afraid so, dear."

"I couldn't possibly tell her, Aunt Catherine," Emily said, looking back toward the stables where Elizabeth had gone. "She's very much in love with him, and I believe he returns her affection. Not that I blame him. She's very different from me. She's poised and lively, while I sit looking uncomfortable and unhappy in his presence."

Catherine wasn't as certain. "I've seen him with you, Emily. He always seems so interested in what you have to say."

"I know that he's kind and attentive to both of us, but . . . ," her voice trailed off unhappily and a heavy tear splashed on her wrist.

It upset Catherine to see Emily miserable and aching for a love she had held secret for a long time. "Please speak to Elizabeth about it, Emily."

Emily shook her head. "It is too late, and I must ask that you never mention it to her. I would never come between them, Aunt Catherine. Can you understand that?"

The situation worried Catherine. "I am not making light of your feelings, for I know that your love is very real, but you're young and lovely. Many men admire you, Emily."

Emily shrugged and tears glistened again in her large eyes. "Perhaps, Aunt Catherine, but David's the only one who matters."

Elizabeth reigned in her horse and stopped on the sloping hill to look at the graceful meadows and fields where her aunt's land met the Dawson's. *Two days until the ball,* she thought.

She breathed in the fruitful spring air, rich in the earth's rebirth after the long winter's frosts, and her eyes scanned the horizon where the sun illuminated the many shades of green which Elizabeth knew belonged to this season alone.

She threw her long hair behind her shoulder and held her face to the setting sun, and smiled, thinking, *On the night of my birthday, David will ask me to marry him. I can feel it in the air.*

Elizabeth exhaled a long, fulfilling sigh. *And I shall tell him that nothing could make me happier.*

Elizabeth's eyes opened wide when she glimpsed a horseman riding toward her. Then her brows knitted into a frown when she realized it was not David, as she had hoped, but his cousin, Jack Drummond.

At first she wanted to turn and ride away before he reached her, but then changed her mind and decided to give him a chance to apologize for his rudeness at the Dawson's.

Jack stopped and regarded her from a distance while his horse stamped impatiently at the soft turf. After a long while, a smile curled his lips and he touched his fingers to his forehead in an offhanded salute.

The gesture incensed Elizabeth. Never had a man treated her this way. She turned her horse around and rode in the other direction, with the memory of his handsome face haunting her.

"Damn, Dave," Jack said later that evening, "there has to be some way I can get that mortgage from him."

David leaned back in the chair behind his desk. "There is, Jack. Pay him the money—or get married."

"I want my ranch, old boy, but not enough to marry again. My father should know that."

David nodded, remembering a wedding a few years earlier, when he stood beside his cousin as best man and watched the beautiful bride walk toward them. When the ceremony had been over and it was David's turn to kiss the bride, he remembered with a shudder how she had clung to him, and how her lips had parted during the congratulatory kiss.

There were many men the beautiful Kristina had kissed besides Jack, and it was no wonder Jack had become embittered after her death.

"I wish I had it to give you, but . . ."

Jack raised his hand to silence David, "I understand, Dave, no need to explain any more." Jack continued, "I think I'll go to New York to see if I can raise the full amount. There must be someone whom he hasn't warned against me. I hate getting myself deeper into debt, but the ranch is worth it." Jack took a swallow of brandy and decided, "I'll leave Saturday night."

A cagey smile grew on David's face when he asked his cousin, "Does that mean you'll be coming to the ball then?"

Jack's eyes turned a deeper shade of emerald when he answered, "I wouldn't miss it, Dave."

CHAPTER THREE

"Mr. Drummond, how good it is to see you, sir."

"It's good to see you, too, Sam," Jack replied as he handed his hat to the tall manservant. "It's been too long, old fellow. Where's . . . ," he turned and saw an older woman walking down the carpeted staircase, arms outstretched to him, ". . . ah, there you are, Paula," he said, kissing her fleshy cheek.

The elaborately dressed rotund woman took his arm, and her shiny silver curls wriggled when she leaned her head closer to his.

"Well, if it isn't Jack Drummond. Tell me you're back in Philadelphia permanently."

Jack smiled as he walked with her into the lushly decorated parlor of the red brick building. "I'm afraid not, Paula. Just visiting my cousin and thought I'd come to see you . . . and the girls."

She laughed and lifted her chin. "We've plenty girls."

"Clarice?" he suggested.

Paula shook her head and her eyes were vague. "I'm afraid she isn't here anymore."

Jack gave her a disappointed frown. "Where is she?"

Paula let go of his arm and poured whiskey from a decanter into an elegant crystal glass. "She left a few years ago. I haven't heard since."

Jack accepted the glass.

"Now don't you fret, Jack. I promise that it won't make one little difference. You just make yourself comfortable and I'll be right back."

When Paula left the room, Jack lowered himself into a chair and thought of Clarice, her flaming red hair and slender body.

She had had a slight European accent which had made her soft voice all the more attractive. Her face had reminded him of a doll his mother had kept in a shadow box. She was intelligent and sensitive and had known just how to make him feel good. He might have married her had things been different. It wouldn't be the first time a cowboy married a whore, and she had been a soothing balm after the fire he'd lived through.

Paula reentered the room and Jack looked up to see a beautiful young woman standing beside her. Like Clarice, she had long red hair that hung loosely around her shoulders and back. A green velvet dressing gown hung open to show a filmy nightdress beneath. He could see the deep pink of her nipples through the bodice of her gown and he was very pleased. Hazel colored eyes looked smilingly into his as she walked seductively to his chair.

"Won't you come with me?" she asked, the huskiness of her voice exciting him further.

Jack took the girl's hand and allowed her to lead him to the door and out into the foyer toward the staircase.

"This is Yvonne, Mr. D," Paula said as they climbed to the second floor.

He followed Yvonne down the long hallway, passing many closed doors, until she stopped and entered a room. He recognized it as the room where Clarice had entertained him years before. A brass bed stood against one wall, and it was covered in satin. A white and gold dressing table stood against the other wall; it was the same dressing table where he had watched Clarice brush her hair before they had made love.

Yvonne took off the dressing gown and stood before him. "I've always said Paula had the best taste," Jack mused while pulling her gently to him. She smiled and walked him to the bed and he sat on the edge of it while she knelt and took off his boots.

"You're new. I don't remember seeing you before," he said.

"I replaced Clarice."

Jack allowed her to undress him slowly and Yvonne smiled when she saw how eager he was for her. She lay beside him and started to touch him but was surprised when he pushed her hands away.

Very slowly and deliberately he excited her. He was considerate and gentle and she felt herself drifting away with him. She moaned when his hands stroked her, which also surprised her, for she hadn't felt pleasure like this in a very long time.

His long lean body came over her and with each gentle
thrust, her hips met his and she closed her eyes and allowed him
to carry her to an unfamiliar and almost painful zenith.

When they were finished, he held her in his arms tenderly.

"You are what they say," she whispered, nuzzling his neck.

"Who say?" he asked.

"The girls who have been here a long time. They remember
you and speak of you among themselves. Clarice fell in love with
you, and that's why she . . ."

"She what?" he asked, pulling himself up on his elbow.

"She went away," she answered quickly.

Jack's eyebrows lifted slightly. "Where did she go?"

"I don't know. She just went away."

He frowned and became lost in thought for a long while.
Then he smiled and asked, "And you? Are you going to fall in
love with me?" His lips found her breast and she laughed.

"You keep that up and I just might."

Jack spent several hours with Yvonne and when he was leaving, he kissed her sensual lips lingeringly, as though she were a
virginal maiden, rather than one of Paula's girls.

"Thank you for a most pleasurable evening," Jack said,
touching her cheek tenderly.

Yvonne felt strangely alone when he parted from her, and she
sat at her mirror, where she found a fifty dollar bill that he had
stuffed under her brush. She knew what it meant, that it was hers
to keep.

Yvonne took out the little box that she had hidden in her
dressing table. She found it the first night at Paula's. The box contained Clarice's journal. Yvonne kept it and would read it from
time to time when there were no customers to entertain. She felt
that she had come to know the young woman who had written
in the little leather covered book.

They were alike in many ways, even though Yvonne had not
emigrated from France as Clarice had. Both were fairly well educated, from good families, but they had made irreparable mis-
takes which left them outcasts and alone in the world, until Paula
took them in. Their profession was an old one, but they were
lucky to be practicing it in the clean, well-visited house of a ma-
dame who cared about her "girls" and paid them well.

This night, with the scent of the strange and wonderful man
she had just lain with still in the room, she turned to the pages in
the journal that were about Jack Drummond.

Thursday, 1 June 1881

"I was frightened tonight. Paula brought me to a very handsome man in the front parlor and I was pleased when I saw him. He was so different from the fat old men who usually come here. But when Paula introduced us, he looked at me—no through me—then he stood and took my hair in his fingers. 'Red,' he said. 'Yes, red. Red is good.' He took a bottle of whiskey and led the way upstairs.

"Then he asked me where my room was and I opened the door. He walked in ahead of me and threw himself on the bed. He drank from the bottle of whiskey for a long time. When I tried to touch him, he pushed me away, saying, 'Leave me alone for now.'

"I sat at my dressing table and brushed my hair. I was afraid of him, afraid he would hurt me, as some of the drunks here have done. My hands were shaking so that I could barely hold the brush. After a long while, he said, 'What's the matter? Are you afraid? Of me?' and he laughed so loudly that I was startled. He stood up and walked over to me, took a strand of my hair in his hand and kissed it.

"'You're beautiful. What is your name?' he asked me. But he didn't wait to hear my name, for he kissed me, softly at first, then hard and demanding. My heart beat so fast that I thought he'd hear it, but I wasn't afraid anymore. I felt calm. I knew suddenly that he wouldn't hurt me. After he kissed me, he left the room."

Monday, 5 June 1881

"He has been here every night. He stays late, but until tonight he has not touched me. He lies on the bed and tells me to brush my hair, which I do, over and over again. He drinks whiskey and talks. He is very sad. He thinks he is angry only, but I feel his sadness. Twice, after he had drunk most of the bottle of whiskey, he cried like a child. My heart ached for him, but he wouldn't let me come to him. He pushed me away. Until tonight. Tonight he was different. He had no whiskey with him when he came to my room.

"Still he asked me to brush my hair for him and I did. Then he said, 'I thought I had been dreaming of this. In the daytime I would picture you sitting at the mirror brushing your beautiful red hair, but I wasn't sure if it was real or just a dream. I decided I had to see for myself. And there you are, just as I see you in the daytime.'

"He knelt beside me and touched my face. 'Have I been cruel to you, Clarice? Have I hurt you in my drunkenness?' He was so gentle and kind that I thought I would cry. I kissed him. He pulled away from me at first, but I told him I knew why. I told him all the things he had said during the nights he spent on my bed. I told him that the horrible woman who hurt him was gone, and no one would ever hurt him that way again. I wanted to show him love as he had never known it; and he let me.

"He let me love him, and when I did, I knew I would never be the same again. He held me in his arms and thanked me. He said, 'Thank you for finding my soul again.'

"I have come to love this very strange man."

Wednesday, 5 August 1881
"He is leaving. He has been with me these many nights and now he is going away. I mean nothing to him. He said, 'You have made me better, my sweet Clarice. I will never be able to thank you. I will think of you always.'

"He told me that if things had been different, he probably would have married me. 'Who would have thought I'd find such treasure in a whore house?' He made love to me as he had never done before. I would not let him know how much I hurt.

"How could I have imagined he'd take me with him? I, a whore, and he a gentleman. He never said he loved me. I knew he couldn't love anyone with his pain so fresh. But I thought he'd take me away with him. I cannot go on without him. I cannot bear to be touched by another man now."

Yvonne put the little book down. She knew the rest of the pages were blank, for she had read the book many times. She knew, also, that Paula had found Clarice dead in the wine cellar the next morning, while a Fifty dollar bill was untouched beneath Clarice's hairbrush.

Two weeks later, a young red-haired girl named Jane came to the door of Paula's house and asked for a job. The plump, kindly older woman brushed tears from her eyes, declared that Jane was now to be called "Yvonne" and showed her to her room where the beautiful Clarice had once lived and worked.

Yvonne put away the little book and looked at herself in the mirror. *He may be a good lover, and handsome in the bargain, but to kill yourself for?* She hid the Fifty dollars in a drawer of the dressing table. "I guess anything's possible with a man like that," Yvonne said aloud.

Jack undressed in his room at the Dawson home. He could still smell the young girl he had left at Paula's. He smiled at the thought of her—so young, so pleasing, so easy to please. He lie on his bed and stared at the ceiling. He thought of her, and her beautiful red hair, and it made him wonder about Clarice again.

He tried to remember the first night he'd been with her, but he couldn't. That entire summer was blurred in his memory. He remembered coming to his aunt's home after days of searching for the truth about Kristina's death. He remembered that all he found out was that Kristina was unfaithful throughout most of their marriage. She had lain with his friends and his enemies alike.

Jack remembered David trying to help him, to console him, but that it was useless. Instead he found solace at Paula's house, a place he'd known about since he was in Princeton. He remembered going to the door that night and asking for a woman—any woman—who didn't have golden hair.

By the end of that summer, he was better, though the black thoughts still smothered him from time to time. Clarice helped, with her sweet smile, her strange, exotic accent, and her passionate lovemaking. He still felt foolish whenever he thought of how he considered taking her away with him. She must have been laughing at him the entire time. Jack had told her the sordid story and knew she must have thought him an idiot.

The last night with her, before he returned to his ranch to recover what was left of it in his neglectful absence, he wanted to ask her to come with him. He didn't. He knew he couldn't offer her marriage, for he would never marry again. In addition, he felt slightly embarrassed that this strange woman knew all his pain, all his failures. In the end, Jack knew she was better off without him. Perhaps she would have learned to hate him, too, as . . .

Jack turned on his side and thought of Yvonne again and was troubled, for he suddenly remembered that at the very moment of carnal pleasure in her arms, it was not Yvonne's face he saw, nor Yvonne's thin body beneath his. It was Elizabeth Gerard's.

CHAPTER FOUR

"Emily, you look beautiful. Absolutely beautiful."

Emily stood in front of her mirror, with Beth behind her, while they looked at each other's reflections. Emily wore a deep rose shaded taffeta gown. The bodice was cut low and showed the delicate mounds of her satiny skin. It hugged her slender waist as it came too a point just below, where the skirt pulled closely around her and over a bustle. Ecru lace trimmed each puffed sleeve. Her hair was pulled back with rose colored ribbons that cascaded through shining curls.

A small cameo surrounded by diamonds—a gift from Catherine—hung from a delicate gold chain around her long, slender neck.

Emily turned from the mirror and her cheeks were flushed with excitement, her gray eyes radiant. Her appreciative smile told Elizabeth that the compliment was returned. "David will be speechless when he sees you."

She held Beth's hands out to her sides and looked at her twin sister fully. The blue damask gown was also cut very low and the shade was exactly the same as the sapphires at Beth's ears. Her seventeen-inch waist met a skirt that draped behind her in layers of damask, trimmed with silk fringe. The sleeves were long and tight.

There were no adornments in Elizabeth's hair, two long curls hung down one shoulder, their pale color striking against the deep blue of the gown.

Catherine entered the room carrying a long green velvet jeweler's box. She offered it to Elizabeth. "Your gift, dear. Happy birthday, Beth."

Elizabeth opened it slowly and her aunt and sister smiled when she exclaimed, "Diamonds!"

Catherine helped her unclasp the sapphire choker and replace it with the single diamond drop. In turn, diamond earrings replaced sapphires. Elizabeth hugged and kissed her aunt.

"Now, wait a moment, Beth. The earrings are from your sister," Catherine said. Beth grabbed Emily into the embrace. Laughing, Emily pulled back again. "They're small, but they are dazzling, Beth."

Elizabeth agreed when she looked in the mirror. "Oh, Em, they truly are. I feel so guilty that I only gave you paper and pens for you to use when you write your music, but I love the earrings, and you—both of you."

They heard voices in the foyer. "That must be David," Elizabeth said, pulling Emily and Catherine out into the hallway. They walked to the carpeted stairway together.

David Dawson stood in the foyer and looked up when he heard them approach. His smile broadened when he saw them.

Catherine reached him first, gracefully extending her hand as she floated to the bottom step. "Good evening, David."

The young man bowed over her long slender fingers and smiled warmly into her eyes. "Good evening, Miss Gleason. You look elegant tonight." Catherine was surprised to find herself taken in by his smile and good looks and could easily understand Elizabeth's and Emily's infatuation with him. She followed his eyes up beyond her to the twins standing together silently.

"Beth?" he asked, not quite sure which was the twin he was escorting.

Elizabeth laughed softly and stepped down, her hand reaching out to his. "So, you weren't certain, and after that long speech the other day about how you could tell us apart and we couldn't fool you."

He laughed now, "I admit at first glimpse it is difficult, but I have only to be in your presence for a moment, and I know who you are." He looked at Emily then.

She was watching them silently. *How handsome you are, my love,* she thought. When he smiled at her, she felt suffocated and immediately looked away.

"Emily," his voice danced to her, "you're beautiful."

Emily managed an uncomfortable smile and murmured a thank you, dismayed at the sound of her shaking voice. Catherine heard it sympathetically. Beth looked puzzled.

"Are you all right, Em?" Elizabeth asked, concerned.

"Of course I am. I'm just excited. Let's go enjoy our special evening," and she walked beyond them into the large drawing room which had been emptied of most of its furniture to accommodate the dancing.

Although it was early in the evening, many guests had arrived and were gathered in groups, chatting and drinking from small crystal cups. Emily mingled quickly, graciously accepting lavish compliments on her appearance. When the dancing began, Elizabeth was surrounded by a group of admirers, leaving David to mingle among the other guests, as was their usual custom. Emily accepted the arms of her own admirers, though her eyes gazed longingly toward David from time to time.

After dinner had been served, Catherine suggested the twins entertain their guests. Emily sat at the piano while Beth took her place as vocalist. Everyone enjoyed Elizabeth's sweet, strong voice, but Emily's talented accompaniment was greatly admired and spoken of. Eventually, Elizabeth complained of being tired and turned to her sister.

"Emily, play that piece you finished composing yesterday," then turning to the audience, she added, "It's brilliant."

Emily blushed a deep red. "Oh, no, it isn't good enough to . . ."

Her protests went unheeded when the guests insisted. She began to play the sonata reluctantly, but as she performed, the audience faded away and she was taken up in her own music. Lost within the chords, her eyes found David's, and there was a subtle change as the notes turned plaintiff and haunting.

When Emily stopped playing, there was a long, silent interval in the room, followed by thundering applause. The guests were shouting "Bravo" and Catherine's cheek was against Emily's while Elizabeth clapped her hands proudly. David's eyes still held Emily's for several meaningful heartbeats. Unable to control the tears that caused an unbearable ache in her throat, Emily left the room quickly.

Grace Dawson, who was among the most enthusiastic admirers, said to Catherine, "My goodness, she's so shy. Another girl would bask in this attention."

Catherine looked back at the doorway where Emily had passed through. "Emily is extremely sensitive about her music." She took Grace's elbow, "Come, let's go talk to Alberta. She's looking perturbed as usual."

No one noticed David Dawson standing alone near the French windows, pensively staring at the empty place where Emily had been, no one but his cousin, Jack Drummond.

Jack was a man who had come to dislike social events. After meeting Elizabeth, however, he had decided to attend the Gerard sister's birthday gala, and was surprised to see that there was not only one Elizabeth, but an exact replica as well. It also surprised—and amused—him to see that Emily was in love with David. He wondered if she was aware of Elizabeth's feelings for his cousin, and received an answer when Emily reentered the room, pale and glassy eyed from freshly shed tears.

Elizabeth also noticed her sister's return when Emily walked to the piano and put away her music, smiling shyly at the musicians who had begun to perform dance music again. While Beth chatted with four young men gathered around her, she saw David walk over to her sister and extend his arm.

They danced a waltz, and it wasn't long before Beth realized that Emily was becoming paler by the minute, while David steadily stared into her sister's eyes as they twirled around and around. When the music stopped, she saw them walk out to the garden.

Beth no longer pretended to pay attention to the young men and one by one they drifted away, finding other partners to dance with, leaving her momentarily alone.

"They sure are a lovely looking couple, wouldn't you agree?"

Startled, she looked up into the direction his voice came from. Drummond leaned against the wall behind her, his arms crossed over his broad chest, the ever-present mocking smile on his lips.

"Mr. Drummond, I hadn't noticed you there. I didn't think you were coming this evening. When did you decide to join us?"

"The day you enticed my cousin to escort you. I thought it would be amusing to watch your wiles at work with David."

Elizabeth flashed a nasty look at him. "Mr. Drummond, I . . ."

"But I must say," he interrupted, "that I'm disappointed. It seems another has caught his eye. By the way, your sister is lovely. There's an amazing resemblance."

"We're twins," she snapped. "Most people can't tell us apart."

He stroked his chin as though thinking about what she had just told him, then said, "Ah, but *she's* beautiful."

Elizabeth stood up. "If you'll excuse me." But before she could step away, Jack swung her into the dance and held her tightly. Her face was red with anger.

"I don't know how gentlemen behave in Texas, but . . ."

"Colorado," he interrupted her again.

". . . But in the East, a gentleman asks a lady if she would like to dance. Apparently your education has lacked appropriate social behavior."

"I was educated at Princeton, Liz," he said.

"It doesn't show," she hissed, "and my name is not Liz."

"I like it though. It suits you."

"Please, let me go. I need some air."

"I don't think so. At least not right now. Let them alone for awhile."

Elizabeth looked up into his face then. "Let who alone?"

"Your lovely sister and David."

"What are you talking about?"

He smiled down at her but did not answer.

"Mr. Drummond, they do not want to be alone. Emily and David are good friends. You have no right insinuating . . ."

"I'm not insinuating anything. I noticed that your sister is in love with my cousin and I think they need a minute together."

Elizabeth lost a step and would have stumbled if Jack hadn't been holding her tightly against him.

"Let me go this minute or I'll make a scene!"

Instead he held her closer and a puff of air escaped her lips with the pressure of his arm. "Scenes don't bother an old cowhand like me," he drawled, expertly swinging her into the circle of dancing couples.

Emily stood uncomfortably beside David and held her hands within the folds of her skirt to hide their trembling. She cleared her throat nervously.

"How is your law firm doing, David?" she asked, searching for safe conversation.

He lifted a brow and smiled at her. "Just fine, Emily, although Philadelphia is too far from home to suit me. As soon as I've gotten enough experience, I hope to start practicing here in Benton."

"That would be nice. We've . . . we've missed you," she whispered, hoping her voice would not betray her.

He leaned his back against a tall oak and took her hand gently. His voice matched hers when he asked, "Have you, Emily? I've wondered. When I'm away, I think of you often."

She tried to pull her hand away, but he held it tightly, his thumb caressing the soft flesh of her hand. "You mean Aunt Catherine and Beth and me," she said, feeling foolish.

"No," he answered.

Emily was embarrassed at how she trembled. Then he said, "Oh, I do think of your aunt at times, and when I need a good laugh, I think of Beth and her antics. It's very different when I think of you, Em."

"We'd better be going in," she started, panic rising in her. He took her shoulders in his hands.

"Why do you act so anxious to get away from me when you know that you love me? Don't look so frightened, Emily, I would never hurt you. I adore you, darling. Not long ago I thought you were starting to feel comfortable with your feelings for me, but then you suddenly turned back. For awhile, I believed you had stopped loving me, stopped caring, but tonight I knew that wasn't so. I knew when you looked into my eyes. I knew by your music."

Emily was crying now. "Stop, David, you mustn't speak this way."

"Why not? Every word of it is true."

She tried to push away from him but he held her closely. "It is *not* true! You love Beth. You and she are going to be married."

"Beth? Emily, I love Beth, but not that way. She's my friend; you are my heart."

David leaned down and his lips pressed gently on hers. Emily stood frozen, her heart pounding. Then she circled his neck with her arms, returning his kiss with a passion that surprised both of them, unable to stop what his words and kiss had unleashed.

"You see," whispered Jack standing behind Elizabeth as she stood and watched her sister in David's arms. I told you they wanted to be alone."

Beth stood motionless, her face ashen. When Jack looked at her in the moonlight, his sardonic grin disappeared. "By God, you *are* in love with him. Liz, I'm sorry. I thought you were playing games with him."

Jack reached out to touch her and Elizabeth turned and struck his cheek. A tiny stream of blood dripped from the corner of his mouth. He seized her shoulder hard and she winced.

"You little witch. I'm not the one who just broke your heart, *he* is."

Elizabeth kicked his leg with a force so brutal he dropped her shoulder and bent down to grab his shin. "Get out of my way," she spat, "you . . . you ugly brute."

David and Emily separated when they heard the scuffle near the house just in time to see Elizabeth run through the doors. Emily gasped and started after her sister but David stopped her. "Wait, Emily, stay here with me."

"She must have seen us."

"She was with my cousin and he probably insulted her in his usual charming way."

"No, David. You don't understand. She loves you." Looking at the house, she continued, "I've betrayed her. She'll never forgive me."

When Emily looked back at David, her face was twisted with pain. "David, why did you always escort her everywhere? If you didn't feel anything for her, why did you do it?"

"So that I could be near you. I thought she wanted me to escort her so that she could flirt, knowing I wouldn't demand her constant attention." David took Emily's arm, "I love you, Em. I'm sorry she found out this way, but I won't allow it to prevent us . . . you love me, too. Your kiss confirmed it."

Her imploring eyes looked into his before she turned away, quickly walking toward the house, past Jack, who was still rubbing his shin.

Emily found Catherine at the bottom of the stairs. "What's wrong with Elizabeth?" her aunt whispered, throwing a nervous glance toward the room where their guests were gathered.

Emily shook her head and ran up the steps. She tried to open her sister's door but found it locked.

"Beth, let me in."

When there was no answer, she rapped harder. "Let me in, I have to explain."

Still, Beth did not respond.

"Elizabeth, open this door now. Don't do this to me."

There was only silence. She leaned her forehead against the cool wood and pleaded, "I'm sorry, Beth. Let me speak with you, please." When the door remained locked, Emily went to her own room.

Catherine breathed a sigh of relief when she closed the front door behind the last guest to leave.

"*Spoilt*, I say," Glorie remarked from behind her. "You've been too easy with 'em."

"Not now, Glorie," Catherine said wearily, dragging herself up the stairs.

She stopped at Emily's door and entered. The young woman sat on the window seat and looked out at the moon. She didn't turn to look at her aunt when she asked, "Do you remember when Beth and I were eight years old, and she brought home a kitten from the barn?"

"What in the world has that to do with . . . ," Catherine started.

"For some reason the kitten seemed to prefer me. It would stay in my room and sleep in my bed. Beth would come to get it during the night, but it always came back in here. Whenever I closed the door, it would cry in the hallway for me."

"Emily, you're making no sense. What happened tonight?"

Emily's eyes were overflowing. "I really loved that little cat but denied it because Elizabeth was so hurt and angry with me. She accused me of trying to steal it away from her, so I had to keep it out of my room and ignore it. After a short time, Elizabeth got bored with it, and the cat wandered away and never came back."

Catherine sat on the edge of the bed now and listened, knowing by Emily's toneless voice and troubled eyes that some catastrophe had befallen her family.

"David and I were talking in the garden. He told me he loved me and before I knew what was happening, we were in each other's arms. Elizabeth saw us."

Catherine groaned, "Oh, Emily."

The girl turned to look at her aunt, her face distorted with anguish. "I feel like I'm eight years old again, Aunt Catherine."

Catherine leaned over to the beautiful girl and kissed her forehead. "You'll feel differently in the morning. We're all overwrought tonight. Beth will understand in time, dear." She kissed Emily's upturned face and smiled reassuringly. "It will be all right."

When Catherine walked out of the room and closed the door gently behind her, she hesitated near Elizabeth's bedroom. She raised her hand to knock, but decided against it. Tomorrow, she thought, we'll settle this tomorrow.

Catherine felt old for the first time in her life. She undressed slowly and put away her dress, then unfastened her bustle and put that way also. She lie upon her bed, without turning down the counterpane, and thought about her nieces.

She loved them beyond words, and felt it deeply whenever they hurt. Their pain was her pain, their sadness, her own. It was all the more intensified when trouble affected both of them.

Catherine's life had changed drastically when she had received a telegram informing her that a fire in her sister's new brownstone home in New York had taken Anne and her husband Gregory's lives. Miraculously, their five year old twin girls had been saved.

When Catherine first brought the girls home to live with her in Benton, she couldn't bear to be with them. They reminded her of her beloved sister too much. She had never had experience with children and they made her uncomfortable. Catherine had buried herself in her work at the bank or in her room. Glorie found herself in charge of two little girls once again.

One night when Catherine was unable to sleep, she had slipped soundlessly from her room to brew tea for herself. She had heard voices coming from the large parlor and looked in. In the moonlight, Catherine had seen the little girls sitting together in a chair. One child was sobbing while the other had held her twin tightly, singing a lullaby. It was a song Catherine had heard her sister sing to them when they had been babies.

Only then did it occur to Catherine that her grief was not exclusive. She had approached the chair and the girls had looked up at her. Without hesitation they had reached for their aunt and included her in their sorrow and tears.

From that moment on, Catherine dedicated her life to her nieces, loving them as if they were her own daughters, and in turn they adored their lovely, vibrant aunt.

For most of their lives with Catherine, there was very little jealousy and, aside from occasional mischief, the girls gave her no trouble. But Catherine had always worried about Emily, for the girl was the quieter of the two and without intending it, Elizabeth overshadowed her sensitive twin. It was easy for visitors to shower attention and praise on Elizabeth, for she dazzled everyone with her zest for life and her winning personality. Emily was content to sit quietly and let her sister entertain, while she herself was more talented.

Catherine had always known that it was a matter of time before Emily would realize she had as much to offer the world as

Elizabeth did, and the older woman wondered, when it finally happened, how Elizabeth would react.

Catherine closed her eyes and turned on her side. There had never been a problem too much for her to handle, but the story Emily had told her about what had happened this evening worried her more than she wanted to admit.

Elizabeth looked around her bedroom, at the discarded blue gown crumpled on the floor and the wrinkled counterpane where she had been crying an hour before. She picked up the diamond earrings her sister had given her just that evening and placed them on her dressing table next to the pendant. Without a sound she left her room and descended the stairs quickly, leaving the house without anyone hearing.

The horses stirred when she opened the heavy stable door and she winced when it squeaked. She knew if Barret, the stable boy, was awakened, she'd never be able to get away.

Beth saddled her mare quickly and quietly. When the task was finished, she leaned her head against its coarse mane. The import of what she was doing hit her suddenly and frightened her. Then she remembered the scene in the garden. "How could they do this to me?"

"Perhaps you did it to them first."

Jack walked out of the darkness of an empty stall.

"What are you doing here?" she hissed.

"Waiting for you."

"How could you know?"

He shrugged.

She brushed past him. "Get out of here."

"Where are you going?" he asked her.

"None of your business."

"Have any money?"

"That's no concern of yours."

"Clothing?"

"Enough to get by."

"A weapon?"

"A weapon?" she echoed.

"A woman traveling alone, at night, without money, without a weapon—you're real easy prey."

Elizabeth's eyes were not as arrogant as they had been, but she said, "I'll manage.

Jack indicated the house with his head, "Your aunt and sister will be worried."

"This is none of your affair."

"I won't let you leave, of course," he said, taking the reins just above where her hand held them.

"Then I'll walk."

"I guess your mind is made up, then, Liz?"

"Yes."

Jack was disgusted. "You're acting like a bad-tempered child. They were probably in love with each other all along."

Beth grabbed back the reins from him and mounted her horse. Jack took hold of the mare's bridle. "I'm on my way to New York. You can ride with me. At least you'll be safe until you come to your senses and realize how unreasonable you're acting."

"This has nothing to do with you."

"Oh, but it has. I feel responsible for what happened tonight."

"You are responsible for your own insufferable attitude, sir, and hopefully, someday it will get you killed, but you are most definitely not responsible for me or my actions."

Elizabeth rode away and within minutes she heard another horse galloping behind her and knew it was Jack.

As he passed her, he changed direction and called over his shoulder, "New York is this way . . . and keep up."

CHAPTER FIVE

"Does the lady have a trunk? A bag perhaps?" the clerk asked, eyeing the young woman and the tall dark man.

"I will be bringing the lady's luggage this afternoon. We won't be staying long." Jack Drummond took the keys to both the suites and led Beth by the arm up the huge staircase. He unlocked the door to her suite and roughly pushed her inside the room.

The trip from Pennsylvania was tiring, and Jack was annoyed that it had taken so long, and he blamed his self-appointed charge. Beth had snarled and snapped at him constantly since they had left Benton. When they reached the Union Square Hotel, their nerves were raw, and they were not speaking to each other.

Elizabeth walked through the beautifully decorated suite and took in every detail. "How do you expect payment from me for all this?" she asked him.

Without answering her, Jack walked to a chair by the fireplace and dropped into it.

"I asked you a question."

"Well, Liz, how do you think?"

"Stop calling me that."

"I'll find a way for you to repay me for all my kindness," he smirked.

"Kindness? Is that what you call it?"

Elizabeth sat down on a needlepoint covered settee. Her riding habit was dusty, and her boots felt tight over her swollen ankles. Her white silk shirt was stained, and she had lost a button during the torturous trip by horse.

Jack laughed to himself quietly. This was decidedly not the way she was used to being dressed, and it showed in the expression on her face.

"Don't leave this room until I come back with some clothes for you."

Elizabeth touched her hair, which was knotted and dirty, and she was alarmed at the impression she must have made in the lobby of the elegant hotel. The thought made her blush. "What must they have thought downstairs?"

"I wouldn't worry about it, Liz. That's why I chose this hotel. It caters to actors and actresses who, at best, are . . . different, shall we say." His eyes laughed into hers. "They probably think you're my mistress." Satisfied with the startled reaction he had solicited from her, he said, "I'll arrange to have hot water for a bath brought up—you stink worse than your horse right now."

Outraged, Elizabeth threw a china vase that had been sitting prettily on a small cherrywood table beside her. It shattered against the wall when it just missed his temple. Jack turned in surprise, but was laughing as he walked out of the room.

A few minutes later, a young hotel maid and two men carrying pails of water walked into her suite. The maid curtsied to Beth. "The gentleman wanted you to have a bath, Miss. Shall I help you unpack your clothing?"

Embarrassed, Elizabeth turned her back to the girl. "I haven't any now; just fix a bath, please."

"Yes, Miss. The gentleman sent up some perfumed oil, too."

Elizabeth frowned and mumbled, "How thoughtful of him."

The hot bath was relaxing after so many hours on horseback, and Elizabeth closed her eyes and enjoyed the restful water and sweet scent of the oil that floated on top. When she was finished washing, the maid wrapped a warm towel around her. With nothing to dress in, and too tired to care, Elizabeth climbed into the large bed and slept dreamlessly for hours.

When she awakened, it took her several long seconds before she knew exactly where she was and from the lack of light from the window, she knew it was evening. She took a quick look around the room, settled back on the soft pillow with one arm cradling her head. Her thick silver-gold hair curled around her pale skin.

"I was wondering if you'd ever wake up." Jack spoke to her from a tapestry covered chair in the corner.

Beth pulled the covers up to her chin.

"Don't worry, Liz, I didn't see anything—anything interesting anyway."

"Get out," she demanded.

Chuckling, he slowly left the room and walked into the parlor of the suite. She looked around for something to wear and found a blue velvet dressing gown thrown over the bottom of the bed. She brushed her hair and joined him in the other room.

Jack, dressed in an elegant black coat and gray trousers, stood beside a table that had been set with china and several covered serving dishes.

"I suppose you're starving as usual," he said, lifting a cover from one of the dishes.

She smiled when she saw the food and began to serve herself, piling her dish with tender slices of beef and vegetables. After pouring red wine into a crystal glass for her, Jack sat at the other side of the table. He shook his head in wonder while he watched her eat. "I have cowhands who don't eat as much as you do."

When she was finished, she felt calm and content and the wine helped to make her feel warm. Jack's face was serious while he smoked a cigarette.

"Have you thought of what you're going to do now?" he asked.

"I'm going back to bed to sleep."

"That isn't exactly what I meant. What are your plans for the future?"

"I don't know. I'll think about it tomorrow."

"You'd better think of it now because I'm leaving in a couple of days for home."

"Good riddance, I say," Elizabeth gave him a nasty grin as she plucked grapes from a fruit compote and popped them into her mouth.

Now Jack was annoyed. "Liz, I'm about as fond of you as you are of me, but I refuse to leave you in New York alone, although it will be sweet relief to be rid of you."

"Mr. Drummond, I haven't asked you to be here, or to trouble yourself with me. If you recall, I have asked you to leave me alone on several occasions."

"Are you ready to go home?"

"No."

"Go home, Liz, before it's too late and you're even more embarrassed."

Beth stood up and walked to the fireplace. She gazed into it for a long time before realizing he was standing behind her.

"Elizabeth, go home and make peace with your sister. I like my cousin, David, but he's not worth all this."

"How do you know what he's worth?" she snapped. "You would not appreciate his fineness, being so coarse and rude yourself. You don't know what love is like with someone like him."

Jack's eyes settled on the fire now and she saw sadness in them which reminded her of when she had first seen him by the stream in the early dawn.

He walked away from her. "I suppose a silly girl like you knows all about love?"

"I know that I love David. You could never understand what it was like for me to see him holding . . . kissing . . . my own . . ."

Going back to her then, Jack gently took her shoulders and his voice was kind when he said, "You'll get over it, Elizabeth."

Jack saw Elizabeth's defenses crumbling and her eyes filling with tears. She allowed her heavy head to drop against his chest. Jack held her awkwardly. He had never intended to get this close to the girl. On the contrary, he had every intention of keeping as much distance between them as possible.

Most of the time it had been easy, for she was an uppity little brat with a fresh mouth and a quick temper. However, just now, when her eyes filled with tears and the corner of her mouth turned down with heartache, she looked lost and vulnerable. How well Jack knew what it was like to be hurt by someone you loved. He knew, also, how lonely it could feel.

His arms tightened around her as his lips brushed her hair, moved to her temple, and down to her cheek. His thumbs wiped her tears away, and she was surprised at how gentle he was, and how breathless she felt under his touch.

The naive Elizabeth wasn't prepared for the sensations that surged through her when Jack's lips found hers again, this time urgently, the heady odor of wine lingering between them, nor was she prepared for the disappointment when he released her suddenly and backed away.

Elizabeth's eyes burned into his. Her heart was racing. She wanted him to come to her again, to hold her and to kiss her in that same way, but Jack spun away and poured himself a glass of wine, drinking it down in one swallow.

When Jack put the empty glass on the table, he turned to look at her again with the old sarcastic grin in place.

"Damn you," she whispered.

"Why? Because I just proved to you that you can enjoy another man's kiss?"

Elizabeth ran into her bedroom and slammed the door behind her, while his laughter rang out through the suite.

The next morning, Elizabeth opened the chifforobe and found an assortment of lovely dresses. Jack had filled it, and the chest of drawers as well, while she had slept the afternoon before. She decided on a black and white striped gown. When she replaced the hanger from her dress, Beth noticed a short black cape and a tiny felt hat decorated with silk violets. She had never worn clothes this sophisticated before. It excited her to see them and know they were for her.

The maid from the day before knocked on the door. "Miss Gerard, your breakfast is here. Are you awake?"

"Awake and dressed," Beth said, opening the door, smiling brightly.

The maid curtsied. "You look lovely this morning, Miss."

"Indeed she does," Jack said. He was seated at the table which was set for breakfast now. Elizabeth's smile faded when she saw him.

"How are you this morning, Liz?" he asked, buttering a roll and handing it to her.

She took and ate the delicious bread while being seated across from him.

"Have any nice dreams?" Jack continued.

Beth ignored him and poured herself a cup of black coffee. "Mr. Drummond, I've decided to go home after all. I hate to admit it, but you've made good sense. I certainly can't stay here alone, without money or family or employment. I've considered the latter, of course, but I'm not suited for anything really."

"No, I can't see you sewing in a manufactory," he agreed, pretending sympathy.

"I don't even know how to sew well."

"That's definitely no good then. I suppose you could be a maid in one of the hotels."

She shook her head. "I don't think I'd do a good job of that since Glorie would never let us clean at home. I did consider being a singer or an actress here in New York."

Jack bit back a smile. "You can hold a tune, but that's about it, Liz."

She glared at him. "I'll just have to go home and face my family and . . . David."

Jack felt sorry for her then. "Now you're talking sense, and it will work out." He placed his hand on hers, sending currents up her arm. "You'll have to leave tomorrow as there's no stagecoach to Philadelphia today. It would be better to send you by coach since it stops in Bucks County and I can arrange to have someone pick you up at the Spread Eagle Inn."

He pulled his hand away from hers. "It looks as if I'm stuck with you for the rest of the day. By the way, those clothes you're wearing are on loan from Strauss's—Abe's a good friend of mine—so be careful with them."

Elizabeth instinctively leaned closer to the table, her eyes glancing down to her skirt to make certain crumbs hadn't gotten on the dress.

Jack hid a smile. "We might as well make the most of your visit to New York. There's no place like it. I have some business to take care of early this morning, then we can do whatever you'd like for the rest of the day. I'll take you to dinner tonight and . . ."

Elizabeth jumped up excitedly. "Could we go to the Metropolitan Opera House? I've always dreamed of it."

"The opera?" Jack asked with a frown of distaste. "I haven't attended the opera since I was forced to do so as a student at Princeton."

When he saw her face fall in disappointment, he said, "I suppose if you've got your heart set on it . . ."

"Oh, I do, Jack. And there is something else that I would like to do today."

Jack leaned his head on his hand and groaned, "Don't tell me, the ballet."

"No," she said, laughing a little. "I was born here in New York," she informed him.

"You were?"

"My parents were killed when our house went on fire. That's how we came to live with Aunt Catherine. Anyway, I would like to go to the place where we lived. It was thirteen years ago, and another family bought the house and renovated it after the fire, but I'd like to see it. I think I remember the address."

Jack stood up and smiled broadly at her. "I'll order a hansom and meet you in the lobby at ten," he said. Taking his hat, he left the suite after saying, "See you then, Liz."

Elizabeth stared through the carriage window in awe. The city was bustling with people. She had never seen such wealth, even in Philadelphia, nor had she ever seen such poverty.

"We must be close by," she said, pointing out of the window of the cab. "There is the church we attended. I recognize it."

Jack looked out beyond her. "That's Saint Thomas' Church."

"Yes, that's it, Jack," she said, excited that she remembered so clearly.

When the cab stopped in front of the address Beth had given him, Jack helped her to the ground. She knew which brownstone it was at first sight, and her eyes filled with tears.

"It seems so much smaller than I remember it," she said.

"Unfortunately, everything in our lives appear smaller after we've grown up," Jack agreed. "But they don't always lose their importance," he added, identifying the poignant look in her eyes.

The door of the house opened and two small children skipped down the steps, followed by a fashionably dressed young woman. Beth was embarrassed that she had been caught staring at the house, but the woman smiled and asked, "May I help you?"

In his most warm and charming manor, Jack said, "Actually, you may be able to. This young woman lived in this house as a child and she'd like to see it again."

For a moment the young mother looked at Elizabeth puzzled, then her eyes brightened. "Is your family name Gerard?"

"Yes."

"This is a pleasure and a wonderful surprise. My parents bought this house after the . . ." The woman colored deeply. "I'm sorry, that was horribly insensitive . . ."

Elizabeth smiled at her. "It's all right. Please go on," she urged.

"My father and yours were friends. They worked in the same law firm. My parents felt compelled to buy the house and repair it, and when it was finished, they decided to move into it. My parents have lived here ever since."

The woman called to her children who had skipped away, then turned to Elizabeth again. "How rude of me. Please come inside and have tea with us. Mother will be delighted."

Elizabeth looked up at Jack and, with a warm smile, he put his hand on her back and guided her into the brownstone.

CHAPTER SIX

Mrs. Reginald Smythe was reading in the library of the brownstone when her daughter brought in the two strangers. Putting the book down and looking up, her hand stopped in mid-air as Elizabeth walked into the room.

"Mother," her daughter began, "this is . . ."

The older woman put her palm up. "Anne," she breathed.

No one spoke when Mrs. Smythe stood and walked over to Beth, putting her arms around her, embracing her as though she'd known her a long time. When she pulled away, she looked into the younger woman's eyes, and said, "No, of course you aren't Anne. You must be one of the twins."

"Yes, my name is Elizabeth."

Mrs. Smythe nodded and touched Elizabeth's cheek in a motherly fashion. "We always called you Beth. You're very beautiful. I knew your mother. She was my dearest friend when we were young married women, both new to this overpowering city. Our husbands were close friends also. I was devastated the night they were . . ." Mrs. Smythe looked at Beth sadly. "You are so like your mother, dear."

Beth took the older woman's hands, "Thank you, Mrs. Smythe. It's very exciting for me to be here in this house again. I remember it vaguely, although it seems very different now that I'm here." She looked around and then at Mrs. Smythe again.

"I'm happy to know people who cared for my parents live in this house. It makes being here feel as though I've really come home."

They stayed for most of the morning. Mrs. Smythe entertained them with stories of Elizabeth's parents as newlyweds, and Beth alternated between laughter and tears as the woman related the promising life the young couple had.

Jack sat quietly, watching Beth intently. A sadness settled over him when he thought of their imminent parting, and although he had been goading her, thinking her a spoiled nuisance, he found himself liking her more as the day went on.

When they were leaving, they thanked Mrs. Smythe and her daughter and promised to visit again.

Elizabeth waved good-bye from the carriage window, and then settled back against the leather seat and sighed. Jack studied her face. Her clear gray eyes were round and fringed with dark lashes, surprising since her hair was so light. Her cheek bones were high and had delicate color in them, and her chin was fine yet strong. It was her full mouth, which was sensual in its sweetness, that intrigued Jack most of all.

Before now, it had caused him too much pain to look at her closely. Her resemblance to his past made him unreasonable and angry, and he wanted to strike out at it, at the memory her lovely face brought him.

At the moment, he saw only Beth, the bright, happy, strong-willed young woman from the Pennsylvania countryside.

"Why are you staring at me that way?" she asked him.

"What would you like to do this afternoon?" he inquired, changing the subject.

She smiled. "I don't know. What is there to do?"

Jack laughed. "We're in New York City, my girl. What isn't there to do? I thought we might go over the new bridge to Brooklyn, where there's a park called Coney Island."

Elizabeth sat forward. "I've read about that bridge. It was finished just two years ago. Do you know a man—a Mr. Farrington—actually made a test trip, hanging on a swing, across the loop of cable that was strung between the towers?"

"Is that so?" Jack contemplated, his mouth twitching to hide his amusement.

"Yes, it *is* so. It was very exciting to read about." She sat back against the seat again. "It would be a thrill to actually see it with my own eyes."

"Well, then, Liz, old girl, you're in for a thrill."

When they approached the bridge, Elizabeth stuck her head out of the hansom's window. Halfway across, she pulled her head in again and closed her eyes tightly, color draining from her face.

"What is it?" Jack asked in alarm.

"The water . . . it's everywhere . . . we're so high," she stammered.

Jack laughed and crossed to her side of the carriage. "Elizabeth, look into the horizon, or beyond the bridge to the other side. Don't look down and you won't feel dizzy."

Very slowly she opened her eyes. Jack pointed out at the panorama where the river met the land and the trees reflected on the water's surface for miles. "There, look over there. It's quite a sight, is it not?"

Beth relaxed. "Yes, Jack, it's mesmerizing. I've never seen anything like it. I never shall again, I'm sure."

"Ah, but there's so much to see in this world—in this country, Liz," he said wistfully, brushing a hair from her face which had become loose from under her little hat.

Elizabeth was gay and animated when they arrived at the amusement park. They walked from booth to booth, playing games of chance and Jack bought her popcorn and peanuts covered in caramel. When she had finished it, he bought her more, shaking his head at how much she had consumed.

"What's that, Jack?" she asked, indicating a large wooden structure. They could hear a thundering noise and shouts from within it.

"That, Elizabeth, is called a roller coaster."

"Can we ride on it?"

He looked at her in surprise. "I don't know. I'm told it's rather rough."

"Don't tell me a Colorado cowboy is afraid of a ride at the fair?" she challenged him.

Jack pulled himself up to his full height and affected a drawl. "There ain't nothin' this cowboy's scared of, Ma'am. It's *you* I'm worryin' 'bout." Then looking beyond her, he pointed to the carousel and asked, "Wouldn't you rather ride on that?"

Elizabeth scowled in disdain. "Absolutely not! I can't think of anything more tedious than going around in circles on a wooden horse." She pulled on his arm. "Please, Jack, let's do it. Let's go on the roller coaster."

When it was their turn, they were seated with four other people on a long bench which faced the interior of the structure. Attached to the bench were large wheels and a foot platform.

The operator winked at Elizabeth. "Better hold onto your hat, lady."

Beth pulled the small violet covered hat down, fastening it to her hair with a pearl-tipped pin. Immediately, the bench began to move very slowly.

She looked up at Jack with a disappointed pout. "This isn't so exciting. It goes rather slow, don't you think?"

They had been climbing steadily, and before Jack could answer her, they reached the top. Jack put a protective arm around her shoulders and shouted, "Hang on to me, Liz," just as the bench pulled to the left and then to the right and fell straight down.

Elizabeth screamed and buried her face in his coat. Up and down they rode the waves of wood, and whenever she looked up, she screamed and buried her face again. Her hair blew into Jack's eyes, but instead of letting her go to brush it away, his arms tightened around her, while the person sitting beside Beth leaned down so far, her head was on Beth's lap.

Finally, the bench came to a stop. Beth peeked out to see the operator again, unhidden laughter in his eyes. She patted the head in her lap and said, "I think it's over."

Elizabeth knees were shaking when she descended a ramp that brought them to the street. She looked up at Jack and noticed his face had turned a pale shade of green.

Grabbing his lapels, she said, "Let's go on again!"

"What?" he shouted, incredulous. "Why you did nothing but hide your face and scream the entire time."

"I know! Wasn't it great fun, Jack? Oh, please, let's do it again."

Jack looked up at the structure made of steel and wood and then looked down at her face. Her eyes were wide with delight, her cheeks a bright pink. She looked like a child.

He shook his head. "I must be mad . . . no, *you* must be mad. All right, let's get back in line."

"Jack."

"Yes?"

"You've been unusually pleasant today. I could almost like you," Beth said.

"Yeah, well, you've been making it easier—you haven't called me a name or bitten off my head in hours." He took her soft hand in his. "But I have a feeling it won't last, so don't get too used to it, Liz," he cautioned with a sarcastic smile.

Elizabeth selected a brown satin gown adorned with pink roses and tulle to wear for the opera. She wove some of the tulle through loose curls fastened with golden combs. She was pulling on beige satin gloves, when the maid opened the door for Jack.

Beth's heart jumped when she heard his voice, and it reminded her of the fun they had had that afternoon. Surveying her image in the wardrobe's mirror, and being satisfied with the results, she walked into the parlor to greet him.

Jack was dressed in formal evening attire, and Beth thought she had never seen anyone so handsome. His own eyes widened with approval when he looked at her.

He circled around her very slowly, then said, "You look . . . presentable."

Insulted by such a simple compliment, she sniffed and looked away. Jack laughed, "I see you are used to more lavish praise, Miss Gerard. Well, my dear, Liz, you look ravishing tonight, absolutely beautiful. You put the moon and the stars to shame. You . . ."

"Shut up," she snapped.

Still laughing, he grabbed her arm and pulled her close to him, giving her a quick kiss on the mouth. Just as abruptly, he released her. "Shall we go?" he said, motioning to the door.

They entered the Metropolitan Opera House and Jack escorted her to a box. "How did you ever manage to get us seats here?" she asked. Jack shrugged, "Someone owed me a favor."

Elizabeth watched the German opera "Tristan and Isolde," while Jack paid more attention to Elizabeth, enjoying her excitement and fascination with the opera. He smiled to himself when he saw Elizabeth hold her handkerchief to her mouth to muffle a sob when the beautiful Irish princess lie down upon her slain lover and died.

They dined at Delmonico's, and Elizabeth's eyes continually glanced around the room. She was astonished by the other patrons, but more so by the fact that Jack knew many of them. Politicians, actresses, and princesses of New York society all seemed to know him and stopped to chat momentarily as they entered or left the restaurant.

"Do you know everyone in this city?" she asked.

"Not nearly everyone. Many are business associates of my father, or friends I made a long time ago."

Elizabeth pointed to a man sitting across the room. "That man looks like one I saw in a picture in the Post today. I think he stole money from the Broadway Surface Railroad."

Jack's eyes widened and he studied the other man. "Yes, I think you're right. He's a member of what they call the 'Boodle Board' and turned state's evidence." Then Jack smiled and said, "This man who is coming in now is Jacob A. Riis. He's a police photographer and a man with a very noble goal."

Elizabeth was fascinated. "What does he do?"

"He photographs the very poor and the homeless in this city and all the deplorable conditions in which they live. He plans to write a book about it in hopes that through his work, the politicians and the wealthy will see the need to build better housing and improve the living of the immigrants and orphans in New York. The future will be very different for the less fortunate here if he's successful."

With this, Jack stood to greet Jacob Riis as he approached their table. The men chatted briefly until Mr. Riis, with a polite smile to Elizabeth, joined another party on the opposite side of the room.

"You didn't introduce me," she complained. "You haven't introduced me to anyone this evening."

"It's better I don't, for your own sake. I have a reputation that could ruin yours for good . . ."

"Jack, old man," the interruption brought Jack's eyes away from hers, "what are you doing in New York?"

Elizabeth looked up to see a middle-aged man approaching, hand extended. He was tall and overweight with a ruddy complexion and a seemingly pleasant face. When Elizabeth looked at Jack, she saw his expression had clouded over and he looked angry. Jack inclined his head in a glacial manner. "Tom." He did not accept the handshake. The gentleman looked directly at Beth and stopped short. He and Jack exchanged a secretive glance.

The man called Tom was visibly shaken, and sat down in the empty chair at their table, uninvited. His pale eyes searched Elizabeth's face.

"Who is she?" he demanded of Jack, as though Elizabeth was not present.

Jack shot a glance at her. "Liz . . ."

She bristled at the name and interrupted, "*Elizabeth* Gerard."

Jack's eyes smoldered when she finished. "Liz, this is Tom Blackwell," he mumbled.

Elizabeth was provoked by Jack's attitude and turned her most flirtatious smiled toward the stranger. "How do you do, Mr. Blackwell."

Jack summoned the waiter.

"Gerard . . . ," Blackwell said, rolling the name over in his mind. "The name is vaguely familiar, although I can easily see you aren't a native of New York. Where . . ."

"We arrived yesterday," Jack said in an unnerving tone.

"Oh? So you're traveling together then?"

Jack counted out money for the bill the waiter had handed to him, while he said, "I'm afraid we can't chat, Tom. We were just leaving."

Elizabeth didn't hide her surprise when Jack led her away from the table abruptly and walked out of the restaurant. "That was rude," she told him.

"Tom Blackwell is a snake."

"He seemed pleasant enough."

Jack stopped walking and pulled her around to face him. "He is not pleasant, Liz. You would do well to remember I told you so."

They walked in silence all the way to their hotel. Jack led her to the door of her suite. Before she unlocked it, he said firmly, "You should leave for home tomorrow. I'll make all the arrangements and leave instructions for you. I'll be leaving for Colorado the following morning myself."

Elizabeth looked into his eyes for a long while.

"Good night, Liz," he said, more softly now.

She opened the door and, still holding his eyes with hers, said, "Good-bye, Jack."

Alone in the empty room, Elizabeth leaned against the door for a long time. She heard him walk down the corridor to his own suite, and listened to his door open and then close again.

She found it remarkable that the thought of never seeing this insufferable cowboy again caused her such misgiving.

CHAPTER SEVEN

The hotel maid rapped lightly on the door of the bedroom early the next morning. "Miss Gerard, breakfast is here."

"So early?" Beth asked, reluctantly pulling herself out of bed.

"Mr. Drummond left this note for you and asked that you be ready to leave by ten o'clock."

Elizabeth realized that meant he had made the arrangements for her return home. She slowly tied the velvet dressing gown around her and slipped her feet into the matching slippers. The sun was just rising, and she could see its first beams make patterns on the carpeted floor. Particles of dust floated in a yellow ray of light.

Stepping to the balcony window, she looked down at the street below. Elegant carriages bearing well-dressed gentlemen mingled with shoddy wagons filled with fruit or dry goods, driven by seemingly downtrodden people. The city was alive, though the sun had barely risen. She loved the buildings, with their grand arches and granite facades.

Many people had told her that this city was ugly, that it couldn't be compared to the beauty of the countryside. Elizabeth didn't agree. She understood now how her parents could have been so happy in a place with so much life going on around them.

As she poured coffee from the silver pot, she heard a knock at the door of the suite and felt excited anticipation thinking it was Jack. The maid opened the door and Beth heard a vaguely familiar voice say, "May I see Miss Gerard?"

"She hasn't yet had her breakfast, sir," the maid started, but the gentleman interrupted her.

"Please tell her Tom Blackwell is here to see her."

Beth knew immediately who it was. She pictured his face and then Jack's face when their dinner had been intruded upon by this man the evening before.

"It's all right, Mary. Please let Mr. Blackwell in."

He stood just inside the doorway and stared at her. His eyes covered her from her hair to the hem of her dressing gown. She blushed under his perusal and regretted she had let him enter before she had dressed.

"I'm sorry," he said as if reading her mind, "how rude of me to stare at you that way. It is just that you look . . . so like . . . you are exceedingly beautiful, Miss Gerard."

She smiled, "Thank you, Mr. Blackwell. Will you have a cup of coffee?'

"I'd like that very much," he said, joining her at the table.
They exchanged pleasantries for a short time, all the while Beth wondering who this man was and why he was visiting her. Finally, she asked him, "What can I do for you, Mr. Blackwell?"

He leaned into the table, his voice almost a whisper now, "I haven't been able to stop thinking about you since we met last night. I needed to see you again, to know that you are real."

She laughed nervously. "I assure you, Mr. Blackwell, I am real."

He didn't laugh with her; his face was very serious, his eyes intense. Beth squirmed under his scowl and clumsily knocked over her coffee cup.

"Oh, I'm so sorry. Has any gotten on you?" she asked, jumping up with a clean napkin.

"No, dear, no harm done at all. Please, don't be so upset," he said calmly and pleasantly to her. She felt ridiculous then.

"I'm afraid my visit has unnerved you, Miss Gerard. Won't you please sit down again and finish your breakfast? I truly didn't mean to intrude upon you so early, but as I have a busy day ahead of me, I thought it would be a good time to stop by to invite you out this evening. That is, if you aren't already involved."

"I'm leaving for home today, Mr. Blackwell, but I do thank you for the invitation."

The expression in his face changed again. "You've only just arrived here in New York. Surely you haven't seen all of our city? There is so much to enjoy. As a matter of fact, the Parisienne Ballet

Troupe is performing 'Black Crook' at Niblo's Garden. I had hoped to escort you there if you will permit me."

Her eyes widened. "I would enjoy that immensely. I wish . . . but it's impossible."

"Nothing is impossible, my dear."

"But I'm supposed to leave this morning."

Tom stood up and took her hand in both of his. "I'll pick you up at six-thirty. You won't regret your decision to stay."

"Well, it would be exciting," she said thoughtfully, "and I can always leave tomorrow. All right, Mr. Blackwell, I'd be delighted to join you this evening."

He winked at her. "Oh, you will be delighted, I promise you that." Then, as he approached the door to leave, he asked, "This won't cause you a problem with Jack, will it?"

Elizabeth thought about Jack then and knew somehow it would indeed cause her a problem. She remembered what he had said to her when they had left the restaurant. Looking at the kind and pleasant face of Tom Blackwell, Beth decided that whatever Jack's dislike for this man stemmed from, it had nothing to do with her. She was not his property, after all, and was free to make her own decisions.

Smiling at Tom, she said, "No, there won't be a problem. We are just friends."

Satisfied, he kissed her hand. "Well, then, six-thirty."

When Blackwell was gone, Beth took the envelope that Jack had left for her and she read it quickly. It informed her that her ticket for the stagecoach would be at the front desk and he would telegraph David to meet her upon arrival at the Spread Eagle Inn on Old York Road. After this, he had written, "It will give you a chance to speak with David. Whatever happens, I wish the very best for you. Jack Drummond."

Beth quickly wrote out a message for him, explaining her change of plans. When she was dressed and in the lobby, she asked the desk clerk to exchange the ticket for the following day. Once that was done, Elizabeth spent the day walking in the city, not stopping to eat, fascinated by the intensity and bustle of each street. She browsed through elegant stores and watched people as if they were actors in a play.

It was late in the afternoon before she realized she needed to return to the hotel to dress for her theatre engagement. She rushed through the hotel lobby and climbed the staircase quickly.

Jack was sitting in the suite's parlor when she entered. By the look on his face, she knew he was in an unpleasant mood.

"Jack," she tried to sound light, "did you get my message?"

He glared at her, but didn't answer.

"What is it?" she asked.

"Why didn't you go home as we planned?" he asked her, his voice low.

"I decided not to, that's all. I wanted to see more of New York. And, after all, it was *you* who decided I go home today."

"Tom Blackwell's visit had nothing to do with it then?" Jack was in a dark mood and she felt trapped, like a little girl caught doing something naughty.

"Tom Blackwell?" she stalled.

Jack stood up then and came close to her. "Don't play games with me, you little witch. I know he was here this morning. What did he want?"

Her anger matched his now. "What is it to you?"

Jack's face was close to hers, and his eyes were menacing, "Answer me, Elizabeth. What did he want?"

"He invited me to the theatre with him this evening and I accepted."

Jack grabbed her arm painfully. "I told you to stay away from him."

She wrenched free and, moving aside, placed a chair between them. "You have no right to tell me whom to associate with, Jack Drummond. You do not own me. You are no one to me."

He raised his hand and raked his fingers through his hair. "Don't go with him tonight, Liz," he asked, his tone changed, almost pleading. She took a deep breath, relieved that his anger had subsided slightly, but she stood her ground.

"I've committed myself already. Besides, I really would like to go."

He shook his head. "Don't . . . I'm asking you not to."

"Jack, please, you have no right to ask me that."

In one swift, sudden movement, he overturned a table, all of its contents spilling to the floor, crashing into pieces. Elizabeth jumped and backed into the wall. He turned to look at her, and in that glance she saw a confusion of pain and hurt and anger. He said nothing more and left the suite, slamming the door behind him.

The musicale was very good, and Elizabeth enjoyed it tremendously, although the scene with Jack earlier that evening lay heavily on her mind. She was distracted at dinner, but Tom Blackwell didn't seem to notice. He talked incessantly, and much of the time sounded as if she already knew what he was talking about. He mentioned people's names as if she knew them, then he'd apologize and explain who they were. He drank whiskey before dinner, then several glasses of wine with his meal, and Port afterward. It annoyed her when she realized he was intoxicated.

During the ride back to the hotel, she was uncomfortable with his attentions and felt he acted all too familiar.

The carriage stopped and Tom helped Elizabeth out. "You needn't see me in, Tom. I had a wonderful evening. I can't thank you enough."

He ignored her and took her elbow, leading her through the hotel doors, up the stairs, and to her suite.

"Thank you again, Tom," she started, but he took the key and opened the door. He entered with her and closed it behind him.

"I'm very tired," she said directly.

"Then why don't you get undressed," he said, smiling slyly.

"Why don't you leave?" she said, angry now.

"I'm staying, Krist . . . Elizabeth." He touched her hair, pulled a curl loose, and allowed the silvery strand to wrap around his large, stubby finger. A chill touched Beth's spine.

"Mr. Blackwell, it is time for you to leave."

Tom wrapped his arm around her waist, pinning her to him, with her wrist in a painful grasp behind her back. She was frightened now. The stench of his breath assaulted her nostrils as she turned her head away. He grabbed her chin and pulled her face to his, kissing her mouth hard. She tried to wriggle free, but he held her immobile. Tom covered her mouth again to prevent her from screaming and pushed her into the bedroom.

Throwing her to the floor, Tom turned and locked the door. Terrified, Beth made an awkward attempt to stand, but her tight corset and cumbersome bustle prevented it, and within moments he was above her, slowly, threateningly lowering himself on her, unfastening his pants as his weight fell on her.

"Don't! Please, let me up. Why are you . . . ?"

He kissed her again, and she felt faint for one terrifying moment as his hands groped beneath her clothing.

Elizabeth tried to scream again, but he slapped her across the face, his eyes suddenly murderous. She knew she couldn't struggle with him, he was insane, and inhumanly strong in that insanity. She tried to reason with him, forcing herself to speak quietly, "Please, Mr. Blackwell, what are you doing? You're drunk, you don't mean to do this . . ."

Blackwell slapped her again, harder this time, and she tasted blood. Her clothing ripped while she fought him hard. It halted him momentarily and she tried to flee, but could not get out of his grip. Then, with a lecherous sneer, Tom tore her chemise and she managed to scream, but it sounded weak.

Elizabeth reached up to the night stand above her, trying to get some leverage. The lace table skirt pulled down, spilling everything on the table with it. Her hand searched for a weapon, as Blackwell was forcing apart her legs. Crying out as her hand touched cold metal, she gripped it fiercely, and lifting her arm, brought it down into his side.

The oak door of the room splintered and crashed open at that very moment and Tom Blackwell was lifted off her. She saw the brass letter opener gleaming from his side as it went by her face. Elizabeth rolled over, pulling her knees up, trying to crawl under the bed, desperate to escape.

She heard scuffling and the sound of flesh hitting flesh, but her only thought was to hide herself. Then, when she felt arms go around her again, she screamed, but her mouth was covered and she looked up frantically into the face of Jack Drummond. He was kneeling beside her, hushing her, telling her it was all right—she was all right.

"Don't scream, Liz. It's over, he won't hurt you. Calm down," Jack murmured. "Calm down. That's right, it's over."

Elizabeth leaned against him then and cried as he whispered comfortingly, rocking her gently. When she stopped crying, she looked around and saw Tom Blackwell lying face down, a stain of blood slowly spreading through the fibers of his clothing.

"He can't hurt you now," Jack said.

"Is he . . . ," she started, but couldn't finish, for she was crying again.

"Listen to me," Jack took her face in his hand making her look into his eyes. "Elizabeth, listen. I want you to calm down and get dressed in your riding clothes. Don't waste any time. I have to get you out of here right now."

He started to let her go, but she clung to him. "No, don't leave me. Please don't leave me, Jack."

Jack pried her arm from his neck, speaking softly, "Liz, it's all right. He can't hurt you now. I'll drag him out of this room while you undress. Do as I say."

He pulled her to her feet and led her to the wardrobe. Then he bent down and lifting the limp body of Tom Blackwell, dragged him through the broken doorway.

Elizabeth closed her eyes, suddenly felt ill and retched into the chamber pot. She dipped a towel into the bowl of cool water next to her bed and wiped her face. Blood stained the white cloth. Then she cupped the water in her hands and drenched her face several times.

She dressed in the clothing she had arrived in two days before. The maid had cleaned and repaired the riding habit, but Elizabeth didn't notice. She stumbled, as if drugged, into the parlor where Jack waited for her. There was an urgent knock at the door.

"Miss Gerard," she recognized the concierge's voice, "Miss Gerard, are you all right?" He tapped again, rapidly. "Open up please." She looked at Jack but he shook his head, whispering, "Tell him you are all right. Say you aren't dressed and can't open the door. Do it."

Elizabeth took a deep breath. "I'm fine. Why are you disturbing me at this hour?"

"Someone said they heard a scream coming from your room."

Her voice was shaking, "No, I didn't scream. I've been asleep. If you don't mind, I'd like to go back to bed."

There was a long silence as the concierge was deciding what to do. Then he said, "I'm sorry I've disturbed you, Miss." They heard his footsteps fading as he walked down the hall.

"Good," Jack said.

"Why did we do that? Why didn't we let him in . . . tell him what this . . . this . . . horrible man tried to do to me?"

Seeing her on the verge of hysteria again, Jack put his arm around her, turning her away from the man lying on the floor.

"This would be a scandal beyond your imagining, Liz. It's bad enough your being here, unchaperoned at your age, arriving with me, then being seen this evening alone with him."

"Oh, Jack, I've killed him. I killed a man. How can I ever face what I've done?"

Jack stepped back from her. "Killed him?"

Beth was shaking her head and crying into her hands again. Jack looked at the prostrate Tom Blackwell a long time, then back at the beautiful young woman.

"Do you want to go home?" he asked quietly.

She grabbed the lapels of his coat then. "No! No, Jack, please, I can't. I could never face them now . . . knowing that I . . . You have to help me, Jack."

He put his arms around her protectively. "We have to leave right now. It's important that you be very quiet. I'll help you, but you must trust me. Will you do that?"

She nodded, and taking her hand, he opened the door. They walked into the empty corridor and he led her away from the main staircase. She started to ask him where they were going, but his look silenced her.

They walked down a dark enclosed staircase which led to an alley. A black carriage waited there and Jack lifted her into it, saying, "You stay in here. Don't move, I'll be right back." Several long minutes later, she felt the carriage move, then the door opened and Jack jumped in beside her, tapping against the roof to signal the driver.

It seemed to Beth that they drove a very long time before the carriage stopped near a small house surrounded by trees. The moon reflected from a river not far from the back of the house. Jack helped her out of the carriage. Elizabeth saw the driver for the first time, and gasped when she realized it was Jacob Riis.

"Let me go in and explain to Mrs. O'Hanlon first," Riis said to Jack.

"I appreciate your help, Jacob." He rested his hand on the other man's shoulder.

When Riis left them and disappeared into the little house, Jack explained to Elizabeth, "Jacob and I had dinner together and he was having a drink with me in my suite when we heard you scream. Mrs. O'Hanlon is a friend of mine. She'll keep you here for the night."

"What will happen, Jack? Where are you going tonight?"

"I'll explain everything tomorrow. For now you'll stay here. Mrs. O'Hanlon works with Jacob in the city. She knows all about trouble. She's had her share of it and she'll understand if you need to talk to her. But don't mention that . . ."

Her voice was strained. "That I killed a man."

The door of the house opened, and they saw the outline of Riis as he waved them in. Beth entered through the door into a large kitchen, where a woman in night clothes stood in the center of the room, looking Beth over with bright, intelligent eyes. Jack walked to her and took her hand warmly. "I'm sorry about this, Mrs. O'Hanlon."

"Enough said, Mr. Drummond. We're only glad we can help you for a change." Then indicating Beth with her chin, she asked, "Is she all right?"

Jack looked at Beth. "Take care of her. She's shook up badly."

Mrs. O'Hanlon nodded and closed the door behind Jack and Riis. "You're a frightened little bird, lovie. Sit down at the table and have a cup." She mashed tea and poured the brew into a cracked china cup. As Elizabeth took a sip, Ellen O'Hanlon said, "How is it that a pretty little thing like you could get into trouble? Never mind. I'm fond of Jack Drummond, but he has a penchant for disaster, I'm afraid."

"How do you know Jack?" Beth asked.

"A long time ago he found me and my family living on the streets of New York. He not only gave me money to feed my babies, but he took me to Jacob Riis and together they found this little house for us to live in. Mr. Riis gave me a job helping him take photographs and writing captions." She smiled then, "There's nothing I wouldn't do to help Jack Drummond."

They talked through the night. Elizabeth found herself explaining all that had happened to her throughout the past week, stopping only when she came to the part where she believed she killed Tom Blackwell.

It was morning when they heard horses. Mrs. O'Hanlon looked through the window, opened the door, and Jack entered the house and saw Elizabeth at the table.

"It's all taken care of. We can leave within an hour. Your clothes are in the carriage."

"But they're not mine," Beth said, confused.

"Never mind that." Jack knelt on one knee to look directly into Beth's face. "You have to make a decision right now, Elizabeth. Do you want to go home to your aunt?"

Alarmed, she shook her head violently. "No, Jack, I can't."

He frowned in thought for a moment. "All right then, Liz, you'll have to come with me."

Elizabeth's eyes widened. "To Colorado?" When he nodded, she sighed, "This is dreadful . . . dreadful . . . but I'd rather go with you than ever face my family after what's happened. I suppose I have no choice."

Jack pulled her to her feet. "It could be worse. I could let you go to jail," he said angrily.

"Now, Mr. Drummond, she's upset enough," Ellen O'Hanlon reasoned.

He glared at the young woman. "Well, Liz, it looks like your vacation is being extended. God help us both!"

CHAPTER EIGHT

They entered the private car of the train, and at Jack's insistence, Elizabeth held her head down so that no one would see the bruises on her face. When they were inside, she looked around at the small but luxurious quarters they were to share until they reached Colorado. A porter put a trunk that contained their clothing in one corner and Jack unlocked it.

She eyed the berths, one above the other, each with their own pair of heavy curtains for privacy. Although not ideal, she was relieved there was more than one bed.

Neither of them spoke as the train pulled away from the station. A waiter came in with a tray of assorted meats and cheeses and placed it on a table near one window of the car. When he left, Jack asked her, "Are you hungry?" Elizabeth shook her head no.

"Well," he said derisively, "that's a change."

Beth's teeth played with her lip, and he looked at the small red gash at the corner of her mouth where Tom Blackwell had hurt her the night before. Jack knew she hadn't slept all night and he offered, "If you're tired, you can use one of the berths."

Again she shook her head, and he shrugged and began eating the meat from the tray.

"How did you arrange for a private car?" she asked.

"It's my family's," he answered, breaking off a piece of bread.

She looked at him in surprise. "You must be very rich."

"My father is." He pointed to a golden emblem hanging on the wall that she had noticed when they had first entered the car. It was an elaborately molded double "D." "That's the name of my father's ranch."

"And what is the name of your ranch?"

"River Pines."

"What's it like, Jack?"

"Heaven," he said, smiling gently. "I'll be relieved to be back there."

Elizabeth looked down at her hands. "You must be sorry to have me coming along. I've been a great deal of trouble."

Jack didn't answer and she continued, "How will you explain my presence when we get there?"

"I'll worry about that then," he answered, looking out through the window.

Elizabeth swallowed hard. "About last night . . ."

"All right, let's get this whole thing straightened out now, then I don't want to discuss it again. By the time they fish Tom Blackwell's body out of the East River, we'll be long gone and forgotten. He was hated by just about everyone who knew him, and he won't be missed, believe me. They'll probably declare a holiday when he's found dead."

Jack's eyes narrowed when he continued, "As for his attacking you, be thankful he didn't rape you, and let it be a lesson to you to find out who you're flirting with from now on."

Elizabeth leaned on the edge of the table. "I didn't flirt with him. I swear it."

"Save it for someone who'll believe you, Liz. I've seen you in action."

She raised her hand to strike him and he grabbed her wrist in midair. "Let's get something else straightened out. If you ever try to strike me again—if you even think of it—I'll break your damned arm. We have a week's trip ahead of us and I'm in a bad temper. I advise you to stay away from me as much as possible until we've decided what to do with you."

Elizabeth met his tone of voice. "And I'll say this and no more. I hate your black soul, Jack Drummond. My life was happy until you crushed it. You're responsible for everything that has happened, and for as long as I live, I will never forgive you. You'll rot in hell for destroying my life as you have."

Jack poured himself whiskey from a decanter and drank deeply, threw the glass against the wall of the car, and walked out, letting the door slam behind him.

Beth could see him through the window of the door where he stood between the train cars. Hoping he would not return too soon, she allowed herself the comfort of tears and dropped down onto the lower berth, sobbing.

Jack attempted to roll a cigarette, but the tobacco slipped from the paper several times, and he cursed aloud, throwing it, unfinished, to the passing ground. He leaned his long, slender body against the side of the car and stared unseeingly at the passing countryside.

Damn her, he thought, *she's right. From the moment I met her, I've wanted to hurt her, crush her spirit, prove to myself she's like Kristina.* Jack closed his eyes momentarily as his thoughts went on. *Kristina, my beautiful wife . . . my beautiful whoring wife.*

He slid down until his spine rested against the metal floor, his head rocking with each movement of the train. *How many men did she have?* he asked himself, as he had over and over again for five years. *When she went to New York and Boston, how many men shared that soft welcoming body with me? Tom Blackwell was one. He saw to it that I knew . . . the son of a bitch.*

Jack turned his head as though to listen for Elizabeth. The constant clacking of the wheels against the tracks drowned out all other sounds. His head nagged him with a dull pain as he brushed soot from his pale gray trousers.

Jack walked back into the car, and Elizabeth was curled up in the berth, sleeping restlessly. He could see she had been crying, and after he watched her for a moment, he took the blanket and covered her. She moved slightly, still asleep, and murmured her sister's name. He looked at the dark bruises on her face and felt his stomach tighten with anger.

He poured more whiskey, sipped it slowly, feeling it flow through his blood, calming him with old familiarity. He sat at the table and allowed himself to remember—something he rarely did.

The soiree was especially tedious, held in the home of one of David's former classmates. Jack had permitted David to talk him into accompanying his cousin because of a promise extracted from David that there would be lovely young ladies of good standing there, and another promise that if they didn't meet anyone interesting, they would go to one of the taverns in town and meet young ladies of lesser character who would certainly prove to be interesting.

Jack had been visiting the East for the express purpose of finding a wife. After graduating three years before, he had gone home to Colorado, where his father showed him the most beautiful acreage of land he'd ever seen.

It was a budding ranch, with only a hundred head of cattle. The owner had decided he wanted to try his hand farther west, and had sold his ranch, cattle and all, to Daniel Drummond. Jack wanted it—as his father had hoped—and had given a small down payment, then had borrowed it back a year later to buy more cattle and to increase the crops. Within a short time, the ranch had started to thrive, and Jack was well on his way to becoming one of the most successful ranchers in the state.

It wasn't enough, however. Jack had decided he wanted a wife and children to fill the ranch house he had built for himself. Colorado was still growing, and there were few families around with eligible young women that had held any interest for Jack.

Although his father was one of the founders of Denver and a successful business man and rancher, and although his mother had been accepted in every social circle, Jack's own reputation preceded him as wild and dangerous. He was not considered good company for well-bred young ladies, and they were all but locked in their rooms when the handsome and notorious Jack was around. As a result, he had concluded it would be best to shop for a suitable wife back East.

Jack proceeded to visit friends in Boston, New York, and eventually Philadelphia, without success. Though he had his choice of fair young women, they all seemed bloodless and too delicate for the hard life of a rancher's wife.

While Jack had sat listening to the boring recitations of an obese sister of a friend of David's, he decided he was ready to return to Colorado and live out his life alone, or with the company of a dance hall girl.

His eyes had searched for David, in order to demand the second promise be carried out, when he had seen Kristina. She was standing alone. Her golden hair shone brilliantly in the gaslight of the chandelier above her.

Her gown was violet, and even in the distance, Jack had seen that her large eyes were also a deep violet blue. His breath had caught in his throat when those incredible eyes had locked with his.

Jack had known he was being willed to approach her, and he did. A faint smile had touched her lips as he had drawn nearer, and though the image before him had been ethereal, he had had the uncomfortable feeling he was being pulled into a black void.

And so it was. From that moment until long after her death, Jack lived in a darkness that seemed unending and unbearable.

Alive, she tormented and destroyed his life, but her death blackened and shattered his spirit. Then whiskey slowly started to destroy his body and mind, until time, and the sensitive touch of a Philadelphia prostitute, helped him fight through the darkness that had enveloped him in his existence with Kristina.

When he had realized he would survive, Jack went back to rebuild his ranch, which had been sorely neglected. He continued whatever life was left from the wreckage of his ill-fated marriage, a bitter and less trusting man.

Now, in the private car of a train headed west, he opened his eyes without seeing the landscape passing before him. Elizabeth was still asleep. Alone, frightened, and thinking she had committed murder, he manipulated her into coming with him for the sole purpose of . . . what? . . . he wasn't sure.

Did he want to use her to get back full ownership of his ranch? The idea was almost too perfect. Or was it also to punish Elizabeth . . . for being like Kristina? . . . for looking so much like Kristina . . . and if that were true, where would it end?

Jack involuntarily shook his head at the thought that Elizabeth's life would possibly end the same way Kristina's had.

The truth of why he had this young woman with him formed in his mind, and he pushed it away, refusing to believe it. *That will never happen to me again.* Jack swallowed the whiskey from his glass. *I'll fight it every step of the way.* His eyes rested on the beautiful woman with the long, silvery hair who looked like a child when she slept. *It won't be easy. This one has the power to wear me down.*

CHAPTER NINE

When they arrived in Denver, Elizabeth looked from the window of the car and was amazed to find that, although nothing like the eastern cities they had passed through earlier in their trip, Denver was built up and more habitable than most of the primitive western towns they had seen. There was a mixture of horses, wagons, and elegant carriages with people who were dressed expensively or in flannel shirts, leather vests, and even buckskins. Elizabeth was wide-eyed watching fashionably dressed women being escorted by men wearing gun belts and wide brimmed hats.

She followed Jack from the train and tried to listen when he made arrangements for the private car to be uncoupled and taken away, but she missed most of the conversation when she saw a towering black man, a good twenty years older than Jack, walk up to them. "Welcome home, Mr. Jack," the man said warmly.

Jack's smile was brilliant and he embraced the man, pounding him heartily on the back. "It's good to be home, Jim, mighty good. How're things at the ranch?"

"Same as when you left, Mr. Jack. Calla's cookin' up a storm, fixin' beds, gettin' ready for you."

Jack laughed for the first time since they had left New York. "Well, I'm glad to hear it. I've missed her cooking for too long, Jim." Jack suddenly remembered Elizabeth. "This is Miss Gerard. She's my guest for awhile."

"Yessa', you mentioned a visitor in your wire. How do, Miss Gerard," he said smiling, and Beth was warmed by his cheerful, easy way.

"How do you do, Jim," she answered.

Jim asked, "Mr. Jack, you goin' to make a stop here in Denver first, or are we goin' straight home?"

"We're going home, Jim. I'll come back another time." Elizabeth had a feeling there was more to the question and answer than she could discern.

There was a buckboard waiting for them and when they reached the wagon, Jack lifted her into the back. "This won't be a comfortable ride, Liz. Buckboards aren't meant for elegant ladies like you. But it's all we have at River Pines." She knew she was being ridiculed, for he was wearing the grin she'd come to know in New York, but she was surprisingly happy to see it replace his cross and distant attitude of the train ride. *Even sarcasm is better than indifference,* she thought. The wagon, pulled by two solid horses, started to move.

Weary, but too excited and too uncomfortable to sleep, Elizabeth watched the countryside as they rode along. She studied the lush green mountains, so tall that they disappeared into the clouds, and she was awed by the beauty of the flower dotted flat terrain in front of the mountains.

Emily would love it here, she thought, and it brought her great sadness that her sister was not with her and that she may never be again. Beth had tried to decide what she was going to do, but could not think clearly for the past few days. She knew one thing only, and that was that she could never go home, not after what had happened in New York.

During the nights on the train, when Beth was sleepless, she longed to be with her aunt, and it was Emily's face, so like her own, that she saw when she closed her eyes.

It will never be the same with Emily, she admitted to herself, *and it's entirely my fault. How could I have been so foolish to leave my home?*

She tried not to think of that last night in New York, but although the bruises on her face were almost gone, the scars remained embedded in her conscience. The senseless twist of fate ensconced her in Jack's begrudging care and she saw no way out of the unhappy situation.

The ride in the buckboard was beginning to seem endless, but not as much so as the train ride had seemed. At different cities and towns, the private car had had to be coupled with another train, going in another direction southwest.

Finally, in Cheyenne, Wyoming, the car had been connected to the Denver Pacific Railroad. This, Jack had explained over dinner at the Tivoli, was the final step in their journey. Elizabeth was relieved, for her sagging spirits had all but consumed her. Jack's moodiness hadn't helped, and she had wondered more than once if there would be some way to escape him when they reached their destination. But in Denver she followed his lead, like a lost and timid lamb, nervous around Jack, yet afraid to be without his grudging protection.

Much later that day, when the sun was setting over the mountain, the wagon stopped and Beth looked up over the side. There was a ranch in the distance. Cattle grazed peacefully behind a timber and stone house, where smoke curled up from a huge chimney. A small white house sat about a hundred feet behind the larger one, and there was another building beyond, in addition to the barn and several corrals.

Jack said, "There it is, Liz, and ain't it the most beautiful place you've ever seen?" Elizabeth didn't answer. She knew he was thinking out loud and not really addressing her. "Hurry up, Jim," he said, slapping the black man's shoulder. "Take me home."

A large, handsome woman came out of the door at the rear of the log house and waved steadily until the wagon stopped and Jack jumped down. He put his arms around her and swung her in circles, hugging her tightly.

"By God, Calla, I missed you. I hope you have chicken pie all ready and waitin'," he said, kissing her cheek.

She pushed him away, laughing, "I ain't got a thing to eat," she informed him haughtily. "You'll have to do your own cookin', Mr. Jack."

"Don't you fool with me, woman. Jim's already told me you've been cookin' and cleanin'."

Calla gave her husband a stern look but turned a radiant smile to Jack again. Then she saw Elizabeth. Her mouth opened to speak but no words came out. The smile vanished from her face, but reappeared quickly as she visibly regained composure. She said, "This be your comp'ny, Mr. Jack? My, ain't she pretty."

She looked at Jack seriously for a moment, then pushing him forward, she prodded, "Go help that girl outta' that wagon. She looks wore out."

Jack smiled as he walked over to the buckboard. "Home just two minutes and already she's ordering me around." He held out his arms to Beth and she let him lift her down.

"Liz, this is Calla. The best cook, the best housekeeper, and the best person in the county . . . the country for that matter," he said proudly.

Calla took Beth's arm in her dark, rough hand. "It's gonna be fine havin' a woman 'round here for a change. Come on in and eat. Then I'll fix you a bath."

She bustled Elizabeth into the large kitchen. "It ain't right bringin' comp'ny in through the back door, but Mr. Jack needs some lessons in polite manners sometimes."

Beth nodded, "That's an understatement, Calla."

After they had eaten, Calla wasted no time filling the tin tub with hot water. She threw the men out of the house so that Beth could bathe by the fire in the kitchen. Despite Elizabeth's protests, Calla proceeded to scrub Beth's skin until it was red, and massaged her scalp with perfumed soap and rinsed her long blonde hair with rain water.

Calla chatted pleasantly and Elizabeth asked questions about the ranch.

"Mr. Jack built this house with his own hands. Those stones around that fireplace in the parlor were carried up from the creek out back," Calla informed her. "Then he helped me and Jim and our boys build that little white house when we came here to work for Mr. Jack eight years ago."

She laughed and shook her head. "I always wanted a little white house, and Mr. Jack took up a paintbrush himself and painted it for me, sayin', 'A woman who cooks the way you do deserves whatever she wants.'" Calla continued to shake her head and chuckle. "He sure been good to us. Makes us feel like this place is as much ours as it is his."

When the bath was finished, Calla said, "I put your clothes in the extra room." She led Beth down a short hallway to where two doors stood opposite from each other.

"You just get in that bed right now and catch up on some sleep," Calla said.

Opening the door to a small bedroom, she told Elizabeth, "I switched Mr. Jack's feather tick with the old one in here. No sense in makin' him too comfortable with all the work to be done." Calla cackled at her own words, bringing her head down near Elizabeth's as if to include her in on the joke, then said, "We'll get you up for a late supper later on."

But when Elizabeth awakened, it was early morning, and she dressed quickly. The water in the earthen pitcher was cool when she washed with it. It smelled faintly of herbs and lemon, and Beth knew Calla had scented it for her. She smiled to herself. It was nice to know she had such a wonderful friend in this strange house, in a stranger land. Jim, with his white smile and warm brown eyes, made her feel welcome and at ease, also. They had asked no questions—not in her presence—so there had been no need for embarrassment.

Elizabeth left her room and looked at the closed door opposite hers. Her heart beat a little faster wondering if Jack was in there, still sleeping. Then she turned and walked down the dim hallway until she reached the large living room. The walls were a rich, dark wood and a stone fireplace took up one wall.

She liked the way it was furnished, with simple, comfortable chairs and cushioned benches. Books lined another wall, which surprised her, as she didn't imagine Jack was a man who had the patience to read. The other walls were decorated with rifles and an earlier oil painting of the ranch hung between two windows. A braided rug covered the shining pine floor.

The room invited her, enticed her to sit down and relax. Elizabeth liked the feeling it conveyed, though it was very different than the home she had been reared in. This house was masculine in every way, and yet, she felt comfortable and welcome in it.

Elizabeth continued into the bright kitchen. Calla was chopping potatoes and turned a happy smile toward Beth. "Y'look like springtime," she said, her wet hand placed on her hip, her eyes appraising the younger woman.

"Good morning, Calla," Elizabeth said shyly.

"You sleep good?"

"I certainly did. I feel refreshed for the first time in days."

Calla smiled, satisfied. "Well, Mr. Jack wanted to wake you to give you somethin' to eat late last night, but I wouldn't let him. I figured you needed that sleep. So he warned me you'd be a hungerin' like a bear this mornin', said you have a fine appetite for a lady."

Elizabeth didn't know whether to smile or be annoyed, but she admitted, "I am starving."

Calla poured her a large cup of black coffee. "You just sit and drink that while I cook up a breakfast fit for a queen."

When Beth had finished eating, Calla poured herself some coffee and sat at the table, her face serious now. "Mr. Jack done explained everythin' to us last night, so there's nothin' to hide nor nothin' to be ashamed about. Mr. Jack won't say it hisself, but I'm tellin' ya that you're welcome to stay here for as long as you want. This be your home until you don' want it no longer."

Calla's little speech brought sudden tears to Elizabeth's eyes. She took a moment, then said, "Thank you, Calla, but I'm afraid you're wrong about that. Jack Drummond is quite eager to be rid of me."

Calla clicked her tongue. "Now I knows Mr. Jack a long time and I knows how he thinks. Oh, he's difficult at times—down right ornery—but he's got a heart in the right place. He's had his share of unhappiness, I can tell ya, and it's made him bitter. But he's a good man. Ain't none better. You just trust what I say, Miz Liz. You make yourself comfortable here. He wants that."

Beth smiled then, especially when Calla called her "Miz Liz." She bristled when Jack said it, but it sounded like an endearment from Calla.

Just then, Jack walked into the room dressed in tight britches and a tan shirt, opened at the neck, and his dark hair was covered by a beige hat. She couldn't tell if his smile was genuine or sarcastic, but he looked different, relaxed, almost happy.

"Feeling better?" he asked her, his green eyes peering out from under the brim of his hat.

"Yes, thank you," she replied, blushing under his gaze.

He took the mug of coffee Calla handed him and leaned against the cupboard, pushing his hat back on his head. "Have you eaten breakfast?" When she nodded, he added, "Did you leave any food in the house for the rest of us to eat?"

Calla laughed in that warm, infectious way she had and Elizabeth found herself laughing also. Then Jack asked, "Would you like to ride around the ranch?"

Elizabeth was still sore from the buckboard ride the day before, but Jack was being so hospitable and agreeable, she decided not to ruffle his feathers in any way. "I'd like that. Let me change my clothes and . . ."

"Wait," he said, "You can't go riding in those fancy clothes I bought you in New York. Calla, go get little Ben's britches and boots for her. She can wear one of my shirts. Dig up a hat for her, too."

"Oh, no," she protested, "I hate hats. I don't mind riding without one."

Jack smiled then. "You're not used to our sun out here, and just about everyone wears hats in this part of the country. You'll have to learn a whole new dress code while you're in Colorado, Liz."

Calla left the ranch house and Jack went into his room. They both returned at the same time, handing her clothing. "Go put those on," Jack commanded.

She had a hard time fastening the blue pants and the high-heeled boots pinched her toes. In contrast, the shirt was over-sized and she shoved its tails into the waist of the tight pants and rolled up the sleeves just above her slender wrists. She felt ridiculous when she went back to the kitchen, especially when Jack laughed aloud while Calla tried to hide her smile.

"Well, they're a bit tight, but they'll do." With a mocking smile, he held out a beat up black hat for her to wear, and she glowered at him as she took it from his hand. "Do I have to wear this?" she complained.

"It's a change from what you usually look like," Jack said as they walked out into the early morning sun. "But I gotta tell you, it becomes you," he added, viewing her from behind.

Jim had a gentle gray dappled mare waiting for her in the courtyard. She mounted the horse refusing assistance from either man. "I've been riding since I was six," she said offhandedly.

Jack whistled into the air and a shiny black stallion pranced over to him. He gracefully jumped astride the animal, which stamped impatiently.

As they rode through the courtyard of the ranch, Jack pointed to the little white house. "That's where Calla and Jim live with their two sons. The boys are in Cherryton today, the closest town to here. They're getting supplies, but you'll see them later. Over there's the bunk house," he said indicating the longer build-ing. "It's almost empty now, but when we start preparing for the cattle drive, it'll be filled. I employ ten to fifteen men then."

Elizabeth was intrigued as he continued to show her his land. She watched the cattle graze lazily in the spring sun. Jack waved to each line rider they passed, and he explained who they were and how they kept tract of his stock and property throughout the year.

They stopped on a hill to overlook the rest of his ranch toward where it met a wide blue creek, almost a river, with its surface glistening and rippling in constant movement. All this was surrounded by the magnificence of the Front Range of the Rockies.

Elizabeth breathed in the fragrant air and closed her eyes, taking off her hat and turning her face to the sun. Her hair had come loose and the breeze lifted it back to expose her long, white throat. When she opened her eyes, she saw Jack staring at her and caught the look of appreciation before he turned away.

"Is all this land your, Jack?"

"All mine . . . well, it will be."

"It's beautiful."

Jack's eyes scanned the horizon. "It can be rough and demanding and unforgiving, but you're right, there is no place more beautiful."

"Don't you worry about it when you go away?" she asked him.

"I've got the right men working for me, and I never go away for long. I did that once and was real sorry for it." He looked at her then, "Still paying for it, too."

They rode on until they reached the creek and dismounted. The horses drank while Jack and Elizabeth sat on the smooth grassy bank and watched the water for a long time. Then he said, "This is a good place for swimming in the summer when it's warmer." He turned to look at her and spoke again, "Liz, I sat up most of last night thinking. I've got a little problem that needs to be settled. We both know what kind of problem you have. I may have a solution to both."

"What is it?" Elizabeth asked cautiously.

"First, we declare a truce. No more fighting. No more screaming matches."

She thought for a moment. "All right."

"Good, now, if you'll agree to marry me, you can stay here for . . ."

"What? Marry you? Are you insane?" She leapt to her feet.

Jack also stood and raised his voice above hers, "Just a minute. Listen to me. I hate the idea as much as you do, but it might work to both our benefits."

"Never . . . I will never . . ."

"Just for a year," he shouted and it silenced her.

"A year?" she asked, her brows knitting together.

"One year. Then we'll get a divorce. You can go home. You can go anywhere you want—to hell for all that I care."

"Why?" she asked him suspiciously. "What kind of trouble are you in?"

"That's my business. Look, Liz, I've helped you out of a mess. Now I'm asking you to do the same for me."

"You're the one who got me into the mess in the first place," she said. "What about my family? What will they think?"

"How is it that you're so concerned about what they'll think now? Seems to me you've already caused them enough pain and trouble to last a lifetime."

Then seeing her wince at his harsh words, he said, "Never mind that, we can tell them you ran away with me because you fell desperately in love with me the night of that damned party. Knowing how your aunt would feel about your marrying the renegade nephew of her best friend, we just eloped. It will clear you, your sister, David . . . and help me."

"What happens when we get our nice little divorce? How will I explain that?"

"It was a mistake marrying me. You were impetuous, foolish . . ."

"Down right stupid?" she added, glaring at him.

". . . You made a mistake and want to come home, that simple. It happens."

"Not in Benton, it doesn't."

"It's the best way to get both of us out of horse dung."

She winced in distaste. "You are a vulgar man, Drummond."

Jack's green eyes flickered in amusement. "Yeah, but I'm one good lookin' fella. You could do worse."

"I doubt that."

"It could work, Liz."

"It can't."

Jack took her hand. "It could if you let it."

Elizabeth pulled away and turned her back to him. After a few minutes, she asked, "Will I have to . . . to . . ."

He read her mind and laughed. "No, this will be a business agreement between us. Separate bedrooms. I won't lay a hand on you, Liz. You'll be as pure as new fallen snow when you go back there."

She thought for a few more minutes, then said, "All right."

"All right what?"

Elizabeth faced him. "All right, I'll marry you."

PART II

CHAPTER TEN

The preacher stood in front of the stone fireplace and declared them man and wife, but there was no kiss, no noisy congratulations from the guests. It was a marriage of convenience, with a borrowed ring from Calla, and no one pretended differently.

Jack and Elizabeth signed the paper the Reverend Adams handed them which stated that the marriage took place on the Twentieth of April, in the year of Our Lord Eighteen Hundred Eighty-six. Ted and Sue Manning, Jack's nearest neighbors, acted as witnesses and signed the paper accordingly.

Calla had a fine supper laid out for the wedding party, which they ate quietly, chatting about cattle, the inconvenience of fences imposed upon them by sheep ranchers, the weather, and the Manning children. When they were finished eating, Jack and Ted settled themselves in Jack's den, a small room off the living room, to discuss business.

"Well, Jack, your problem is just about solved," Ted said, raising his whiskey glass in a toast, "and lucky, too. She's a real beauty. Does she know why you married her?"

"No, and I have no intention of telling her."

Ted nodded slowly and frowned. "She's a nice girl, Jack."

Jack realized that his friend misunderstood. "I haven't deceived her, Ted. She has no notions that I love her, if that's what you're thinking."

Changing the subject, Jack said, "I've been hiring some wranglers. The bunk house is almost full. The drive's not far off, Ted, you almost ready?"

Ted leaned forward now, saying, "I started a little late, but I'm getting there. Won't take long to brand 'em. Seems a shame you have to leave your new bride."

Jack shrugged and looked down into his glass. "That's life on a ranch," he said. They finished their drinks, stood up, and shook hands. "Thanks for being my best man," Jack said.

"My pleasure, though I would have liked to see a happier bride and groom."

The men joined their wives in the living room and Ted put his arm around Sue's shoulder. "Better be gettin' back, Sue. It's dark already."

The small woman brushed a hand over her straight brown hair and patted the knot in back to be sure it was still in place. Her narrow brown eyes darted around the room and her nose seemed to sniff the air. Elizabeth didn't like this wily little woman. She found it hard to be pleasant to her, but at the thought of being alone with Jack, and embarrassed knowing that they must be thinking it was a *normal* wedding night, she insisted, "Please, stay. You needn't leave just yet."

Ted grinned as though he had read her mind. "No thanks just the same, Mrs. Drummond, but we gotta be gettin' back. Don't you worry, now that we're neighbors, we'll be seeing each other more."

Sue Manning's high nasal voice grated on Beth's nerves when she added, "Yes, you must come over for tea one day soon. You can meet our babies then. They're our greatest joy."

"Yes, I'm sure they are," Beth said as politely as she could. She was glad now that they were leaving, for she was sick of hearing about the Manning babies—all eight of them.

When Ted and Sue left, Calla and Jim called good night from the kitchen. Elizabeth and Jack stood looking at each other from across the room.

"If you don't mind, I think I'll have another whiskey," Jack said, disappearing into the den for his bottle. He returned with two glasses. "Join me?"

"I've never tasted whiskey," she said nervously.

"You're a big girl now—a married woman . . . but suit yourself," and he poured himself a good portion and sat looking at the fire.

Elizabeth gingerly took the bottle of amber liquid and poured it into a glass and took a sip. It burned her throat and she wanted to gasp for air, but his sarcastic grin prevented her from showing any reaction, although her eyes teared and two spots of red glowed on her cheeks.

"So, we're married," Jack declared, leaning back in his chair and putting his feet up on a low table near him.

Beth cleared her throat several times before she could say, "Yes."

"A year isn't all that long," he considered reasonably, continuing to say, "We could make it a lot more pleasant, you know."

Beth put her glass down on the table. "We have an agreement and I intend to make sure you keep it."

"Somehow that doesn't surprise me, Liz, darlin'. I just thought I'd let you know that I'm easily persuaded to absolve that part of it."

"Well, I'm *not*." Her gray eyes flashed at him.

"Relax, Liz," he said, showing annoyance now. "I have no intention of going against your wishes. There's plenty of lovely ladies who'll keep me warm this next year—if I so choose."

Elizabeth took another sip of whiskey and studied Jack over the rim of her glass. His face looked younger in the firelight— even boyish—yet there was an aura of masculinity that surrounded him all the time, in the way he moved, and spoke, and smiled. As much as she hated to, Elizabeth had to admit that Jack was the most attractive man she'd ever known.

It wasn't just his looks, it was the way he treated the people he loved, like Calla and Jim, and the way he cared for the ranch, the horses and cattle, everything in his life—except her.

Yet sometimes when they both let their guard down, moments which were few, he'd be friendly and warm. Since arriving at River Pines, Jack went out of his way to be hospitable and make her feel welcome. The very first day, when she had agreed to marry him, he told her that for the duration of her stay at the ranch, she was to consider it her home.

Elizabeth had caught him staring at her several times and she knew men well enough to know by the look in his eyes that he liked what he saw, and whenever that would happen, it was hard for her not to be flustered by his intense green gaze.

Yes, Elizabeth thought, watching him closely in the firelight, she wouldn't be the least bit surprised that there were many willing women who would love to be courted by Jack Drummond.

"What's the matter, Liz? Homesick?" he asked, misinterpreting her serious contemplation of him.

He laughed when she didn't answer but his eyes showed no amusement. "It seems a shame that on your wedding night you're pining away for a man who's in love with your sister."

The statement stung and even though David was the farthest from Elizabeth's thoughts, it hurt her and made her angry that Jack would be so cruel as to mention it. "Mind your own business, you insufferable oaf."

Putting his glass down and placing his elbows on his knees, he said, "I could make you forget him, Liz."

You already have, she thought, and the notion infuriated her. She stood up stiffly. "I'm going to bed now . . . alone."

Jack laughed again. "Good night, *Mrs.* Drummond."

Elizabeth spent her time familiarizing herself with the ranch. She enjoyed the bustle of the day to day work, and got to know the growing number of ranch hands that Jack hired to prepare for the cattle drive. She watched as they repaired bridles and shod the newly broken horses.

Of all the activities on the ranch, horse breaking was the most thrilling to Elizabeth. Jack seemed to enjoy her delight as she sat for hours on the corral fence. He took time to explain each step the men took to prepare the horse for mounting and he would sit beside her and watch with her on occasion.

Before long, the men vied for her attention, each trying to be the one she cheered on. "Now you just watch this, Miz Liz," they'd shout and she would play along, delighted with their efforts as they mounted the wild horse, bobbing and jouncing, usually being thrown, sometimes just below the rail where she sat on the fence. She'd laugh sympathetically and they'd smile sheepishly at her. Beth always encouraged them to try again.

She started to realize that there were really only a few men who were experts at breaking the horses, and they took their work very seriously. One of them was Jack.

It was on the days when Jack would break a horse that Elizabeth became the most excited. There was a different mood altogether around the corral as he pulled the latigo and jumped easily into the saddle.

Elizabeth sensed the horse knew it was being taken by a master, and it would tame quickly or fight harder. She would study Jack's face then and knew he loved the challenge of the broncing horse, the one that didn't want to give in to his mastery.

Jack's nostrils would flare and the muscles in his arms would tighten as the horse bucked and fought. Beth's knuckles would turn white as she held on to the fence, wishing she could know what Jack—and the horse—were experiencing. She was always as breathless as he was when it was over.

Often at the end of these sessions, Jack would jump down from the now quiet horse, look directly into Elizabeth's eyes, and try as she would, Elizabeth could not control the flush of her cheeks and the racing of her pulse. More disconcerting was his smile which told her he knew just exactly how she was feeling.

Early one morning as Elizabeth carried milk from the barn, she noticed a lone horseman approach from the west. When his horse entered the courtyard, he passed the door where she stood, and his black eyes met hers, but he made no attempt to address her. He rode on to the corral where Jack and the other men worked the cattle. He dismounted as Jack walked over to him and they shook hands.

"Who's that, Calla?"

Elizabeth felt the other woman come to look over her shoulder. Then Calla smiled. "That's Rone Daniels. Him and Mr. Jack are best friends. He shows up whenever there's work to be done or someone's in trouble."

Elizabeth studied the two men as they talked. "He's odd looking, Calla."

"He's a half-breed. Father was white, mother Ute Indian. Somehow got hisself adopted by Mr. Jack's daddy when he was young. They raised him, educated him. Took Mr. Jack's father's first name as his last in appreciation for all they did for him. Mostly, he's kept the Indian ways, especially when he's alone in the mountain where he lives."

Calla went back to the stove. "Story is his father left him and his mama when he was a small boy. She went back to her tribe but was already sick. She died, and the boy was trained in the ways of the Ute, though he was never really accepted with his white blood 'n all. A few years later he left the tribe, ending up on Daniel Drummond's ranch. Him and Mr. Jack became good friends and have been ever since."

Elizabeth listened to the story with great interest. She had read about Indians and half-breeds, but never expected to see one, thinking they were all on reservations or dead. She watched him for a long time, until he turned, and his eyes caught and kept hers. She backed into the house and realized she was holding her breath.

Rone Daniels and Elizabeth met for the first time that evening when he entered the kitchen with Jack. The table was ready for them, as Calla had explained that Rone took the evening meal with Jack whenever he was at River Pines. Elizabeth stood in the center of the room, nervously clutching at her dress.

"Liz . . . ," Jack said, as if he'd forgotten she was there.

She didn't answer, but looked at the large bronze-skinned man who stared back at her. His hair was black and straight and it fell on his forehead above his eyes, which turned up slightly at the corners. His cheekbones were high and his face broad, almost flat. Elizabeth was amazed that she was actually looking at an Indian this close up.

She felt paralyzed in his dark stare, held by some primitive fear. His eyes never faltered, and as much as she wanted to look away, she couldn't.

Jack's voice broke the spell. "Liz, this is Rone. He's a good friend of mine. Rone," Jack said with a voice unusually low, "this is my wife."

There was a change in Rone's eyes, though they still didn't move, and she could see in that brief lapse of concentration he was surprised by this news. His face stayed sedentary, but he reached out with his hand and she took it, embarrassed to find she was trembling.

They sat down together at the round table and Elizabeth served herself, then passed the bowls to Rone, each time trying not to meet his eyes for fear she'd be captured again in their depths.

They spoke very little, but she caught several glances exchanged between the men. She felt a struggle—a silent argument—being fought at the seemingly placid meal. Instinct told her to be quiet, let the scene be played out, all the while knowing that she was the cause of it. She was relieved when they were finished and she could busy herself with clearing the dishes from the table and pump water into the basin.

"It's good to have you here, Rone," Jack said, after taking a drink from his mug of coffee.

"I'm late," Rone answered so quietly that Elizabeth wasn't certain she had heard him.

"On the contrary, this is a good time. I'll be going to Denver in the morning to take care of important business. I'll feel more confident knowing you'll be here to take care of things."

There was a long pause before Rone said, "Is this trip necessary?"

"You know it is."

"Will it be a success?"

Jack stood up and went to the stove to pour more coffee into his cup. "While I'm gone I want you to get to know Elizabeth better. Show her a few things she'll need to know. The drive isn't far off."

Elizabeth looked at Jack. "What kind of things?"

"How to keep the ranch going—how to defend yourself."

Annoyed, she sniffed, "I can take care of myself."

"When we're on the drive, there won't be any men left on this ranch but Calla's boy, Little Ben. You and Calla are at the mercy of any rider who comes through here."

She looked over at Rone who sat staring away from them. *He's as disturbed about this as I am,* she thought. "I guess I don't have much choice."

Jack smiled and waved his mug a little, "Guess not."

Elizabeth started to wash the dishes again, then turned, animated now. "All right, Jack, then I want to learn everything."

Jack raised his eyebrows and asked, "What does that mean?"

"I mean that I want to learn how to shoot a rifle. I want to learn how to use a pistol and a knife. Everything, Jack. Then I want to break horses."

Both men looked at her now, and it was the first sign of emotion she had seen in Rone. He was very amused, and Jack laughed aloud.

"I mean it, Jack."

"It's too dangerous, Liz. You'll end up breaking your neck instead of a horse."

"You know that I can ride a horse as well as any man on this ranch."

"That's not good enough," he told her.

She wouldn't be dissuaded. "Everyone has to start somewhere, Jack."

"No, Ma'am."

"Yes, Jack."

"I said no, Liz."

"What's the matter? Afraid I'll be able to do it?"

He stopped arguing now and studied her. "It's too dangerous, Liz. I'm afraid for you." But Jack could see the determination in her face and he threw up his hands and turned to Rone, saying, "She's all yours."

The amusement was gone from Rone's eyes now, but he said nothing. Elizabeth decided it was settled and she bid them good night and left the kitchen to go to her room.

When they heard her door close, Rone asked, "Why did you do it, Jack? There must have been another way."

"I went to Boston, Philadelphia and New York. I couldn't raise the money anywhere. He had them warned and not one of them would budge. Except for some fancy clothes for her and a couple of Opera tickets, I couldn't raise a thing. I didn't intend to do it this way, but the opportunity fell into my hands and I took it. I can't wait to see his face when I tell him about her." He put his boot up against the edge of the table and leaned back in his chair, "and when he hands me that mortgage in a year."

Rone was frowning. "Why her?"

"Why not her?"

"There's a painting in the shed that says why not."

Jack's chair came down hard and he said, "You're the only man who could make reference to that and not be shot."

"The first mistake almost left you insane. This time it could mean death," Rone continued.

"Mind your own business, Rone. It's different this time. There's no love involved. We have an agreement."

Rone stared at his friend for several long minutes. "You're fooling yourself, Jack. You're in this one deeper than you were the last time." He put on his white hat and walked out through the kitchen door, and Elizabeth, watching from her window, saw him move toward the bunkhouse.

She felt Jack's presence before she heard the knock at her door and Jack opened it slowly. Elizabeth didn't turn from the window and the moon shone on her silvery hair and white night dress, silhouetting her in the dark.

"I'll be gone a few days, Liz. If you need anything, Rone will help. You can trust him."

Elizabeth said nothing and he moved toward her. She closed her eyes, feeling the familiar pounding in her chest, the roaring in her ears, enough to deafen her, yet through it, she could hear every breath he took, each quiet step closer.

"Liz?"

"I heard you," she whispered.

"Can I get you anything from town?"

She shook her head. Jack stood there silently, and she willed him to touch her, to take her in his arms, as he had done in New York, and kiss her.

"I'll be back in a few days," he said.

"And I'll be here," she answered.

CHAPTER ELEVEN

When Elizabeth entered the kitchen the next morning, Rone was sitting at the table drinking coffee. He was dressed in a blue shirt covered by a brown leather vest and a green bandana. His white hat, decorated with silver and blue marbled stones, was placed on the table; its color contrasted with the dark skin of his hand, which rested beside it.

He looked up at her when she walked in and she said, "Good morning, Rone."

"Ma'am."

"Have you eaten?" Elizabeth asked him.

"Calla takes care of the bunk house first thing."

Elizabeth nodded while she poured herself a mug of coffee.

"You got work clothes?" Rone asked her.

"What for?"

"You want to learn how to break a horse, you've got to wear the right clothes."

Elizabeth felt breathless and her eyes searched his for any sign of ridicule. Then she said, "I'll be right back."

Rone led the way as they walked from the house toward the area where horses were kept before they were broken for the remuda. He studied them silently for awhile, then called out to one of the hands, "Barnes, get out the bay, and bring him over to the corral."

Barnes' eyebrows lifted. "Whatever you say, Rone."

Following Rone as he walked to the corral, Elizabeth felt dizzy with nervous anticipation. Barnes singled out the horse with his lariat and towed him through the gate held open by another man. Once in the corral, Barnes pulled the animal to the snubbing post, and they hobbled the horse by binding its front legs together so that Rone could slip on the bridle. With expert swiftness, he saddled the animal and released the hobble.

"You gonna' break him, Rone?" Barnes asked, seating himself on the rail.

"No."

"Why you saddlin' him up?"

Rone didn't answer but kept working. Slowly, one by one, the men found their way to the corral, curiously watching the black-eyed man prepare the horse for breaking.

Elizabeth's heart was beating furiously and she wondered if she had made a mistake, but she knew that she had to do this, to at least attempt to break this horse, in order to save her pride after insisting upon it the evening before.

Rone pulled the latigo, finished, and turned to her, saying nothing. All the men's eyes were on her now, and she could see their disbelief.

"Hey, Rone, you ain't lettin' Miz Drummond try breakin' that horse? You gone loco?" Barnes shouted.

Rone still said nothing and his eyes never left Elizabeth. The gauntlet was thrown. She pulled her decrepit black hat low on her head and climbed through the fence rails. Immediately the horse reared, but Rone stilled it, whispering soothingly. When Elizabeth was next to Rone, he said, "I assume you know how to mount?"

"I've been riding since I was a child," she answered.

"Not like this, you haven't."

Calla looked out through the window of her house and saw the crowd of men around the corral. She knew something was up, and walked out into the sunny courtyard, wiping her hands on her apron, just in time to see Elizabeth's body fly into the air above the heads of the men, and then disappear again. Calla's breath caught in her throat and she started running.

Rone helped Elizabeth to her feet from where she had landed against the fence. Her face was red; dust and sweat made smudges on her cheeks. She looked around for her hat, picked it up, and pulled it firmly down on her head again.

The look in her eyes told Rone she was ready to mount the wild, bucking animal for a second time. He took hold of the lead rope and started murmuring to the horse, twisting its ear as he had done before. Beth wiped the palms of her hands on her pants nervously.

"Miz Liz," shouted Calla, "what you think you doin'?"

Barnes answered for her. "She's bustin' the bay, Calla. What d'ya think of that?" There was a ripple of laughter through the crowd of men.

"I don't think much of it. Miz Liz," Calla called again, "It ain't no good for a lady to get all shook up inside like that. It ain't good for her innards. And it just ain't fittin'."

Elizabeth straightened her shoulders, and approached the horse, saying, "I'll be all right, Calla."

"I don't like this one bit. Mr. Jack gonna have all your hides for allowin' this. If that little girl gets hurt, you'll all have hell to pay," she warned harshly.

Elizabeth carefully mounted the horse again, but within seconds of Rone's letting go, she was thrown, this time farther and harder. It took her several minutes to catch her breath and the men looked worried this time. Rone and Barnes worked frantically to get the horse calmed down and away from the prostrate Elizabeth. She heard one of the other men step near her. "You all right, Miz Liz?" he asked, starting to lift her.

She shrugged him away and stood up. Now she was angry. Every inch of her body was tingling with it. "Where's my hat?" she demanded, her eyes narrowed to icy gray slits, her voice hoarse with fury. The scruffy black hat was handed to her.

Again and again she was thrown, but each time she managed to stay on the bronco a little longer. They were battling now, unrelenting horse against determined woman. Beth used the quirt, holding firm with each thrust of the horse's back, her thighs aching with the effort. She thought she had succeeded when the horse quieted suddenly, putting Beth off guard. Then with one bone shattering jounce, she felt herself unseated, the whistle of air in her ears, and the now familiar impact of her body hitting the dirt.

Only this time the horse sighted her and before any of the men could react, it reared up, screaming with victory, and landed with its hooves just missing Elizabeth as she rolled to her left, painfully slamming her thigh against the post of the fence, but away from the horse's hooves.

With her body drawn around the post, her eyes closed, Elizabeth waited for the horse to strike again, waited to feel the violent blow against her side, the blow that would crush her.

She could hear the commotion of men hurriedly getting the horse under control now. She was unable to move, so tensely drawn were her muscles. Beth felt gentle hands lifting her and she opened her eyes to see Rone looking down at her, concern creasing his smooth face.

Calla's voice was shrill when she said from behind Beth, "That's enough! I can't bear no more. You come outta' that corral this minute, Miz Liz. You ain't got no more to prove. You done as good as any man woulda', and *I say no more!*"

Rone's voice was very low when he asked, "What do *you* say?"

Elizabeth wanted to stop. She wanted to leave the corral and go back to the house and lie upon the soft feather bed. She looked down at her leg and saw the bloody gash that the post had left there. It frightened her. She had never been injured before, not even slightly.

But as she looked at the horse, whinnying against the ropes that held it, she knew there was no turning back. This horse was hers, and she wanted it.

"I'm going back up," she said, pushing Rone's hand from her arm.

Rone leaned closer to her. "Now do it my way. Give me the quirt and walk over to the horse's head." Rone threw the quirt aside as he walked with her. "Look it straight in the eye. Don't be afraid, I'll hold him steady. Stroke him, whispering and crooning as you would to a baby. Put your face near his and breath into his nostrils."

Elizabeth put her hands on the velvet muzzle of the horse and flinched when his lips parted in an attempt to bite her. His eyes were rolling back in their sockets. She looked at Rone, but he indicated that she should continue.

Elizabeth whispered, "No, baby, no. You just be nice now. You calm down and let me near you. We're going to be friends, you and I. I'm sorry. I've been going about this all wrong. It's you and me together now. That's right. Be nice, baby. You just be quiet now." The horse was calmer.

"That's good," Rone said, his voice as smooth and soothing to her as hers was to the horse. "Now get back up and this time think of yourself as part of the bay, joined, moving as one."

As she mounted the horse, Beth heard one of the men say, "If she does it this time, she deserves a new hat."

Elizabeth's leg came up and over the horse and she put her foot in the stirrup. She gripped the reins tightly, nodding at Rone. He hesitated a moment, then stepped back from the horse and rider. The bay bucked, but Beth held fast, this time murmuring quietly, "Okay, baby, okay." It bucked repeatedly, but Beth felt a difference as she hung onto the horn, no longer distracted by the quirt.

She rode each jounce, each rolling jolt, until her nose started to bleed. Her spine ached and she was so winded she gasped for air, until, finally, after a halfhearted fight, the horse was spent and trotted gently around the corral several times.

Elizabeth wiped the blood and sweat from her face on her sleeve. Then she saw Rone and beamed at him. She saw a faint smile touch his lips and a muscle twitch in his square jaw as he held out his hand to shake hers. The ranch hands cheered and whistled.

They quieted down when Rone's hand went up to his white hat, its brim shining with silver and turquoise. Taking it from his head, he reached up to Beth and placed it gently on hers. Again the men shouted and cheered, waving their own hats in the warm air, as Elizabeth guided her new horse around the corral in a victory ride. Only one man stood immobile, watching with keen interest. His name was Wilkes.

Elizabeth worked with the horse each day. She loved the feel of the spirited bay under her as she rode around the ranch, training it, touching it repeatedly with a slicker, as Rone has instructed her to do. They were learning each other's moods and Elizabeth felt an acute oneness with this new friend.

She wondered what Jack would have done had he seen her triumph in the corral, and it made her restless and eager for him to return. She wanted to show off her horse . . . and her hat.

Though it was a little too large for her, Beth wasn't seen without it from the moment Rone placed it on her head. She laughed along with the men when, in passing, they'd say, "Fine hat you're wearin', Miz Liz."

Jack had been gone two days when Beth entered the barn to saddle the bay for her morning ride. The horse greeted her with a whinny. Beth thought she heard another noise as well.

"Who's there?" she called out, but no one answered.

She started to walk toward the stall where the bay waited for her when someone grabbed her around the waist.

"Better watch your step, there, Miz Drummond." Wilkes said, holding her in his arms. "You almost tripped."

Elizabeth pulled away, "But I . . ."

"I know, the sun is bright out there and it takes a while for the eyes to get used to the dark." He smiled, showing rotten teeth, stained from tobacco.

". . . Yes . . . I suppose it is," she said, distracted.

"Is what, Ma'am?" he asked, stepping closer to her.

"Hard to become accustomed to the dark. I must have tripped on something."

"Yes, Ma'am," he agreed, stepping yet closer, making her back away. "You're a right pretty lady, be a shame if you fell and got hurt." His offending breath made her feel ill when it reached her.

"Wilkes! You got work to do."

Startled, Beth and Wilkes turned to see Rone open the door a little wider and cast a cold stare at Wilkes. The man gave her one last sickening smile and walked out.

Rone went to her. "You need something?"

"I was going to saddle my horse and go for a ride, and Wilkes . . . well, I'll just finish and leave."

He went over to the bay and saddled him for Elizabeth. She watched Rone closely, studying his face, which showed no sign of a beard. His eyes were fringed with long dark lashes. His neck was thick where his straight black hair ended, and his skin was tanned, but there was no line where his shirt met it, unlike the other men.

"Something wrong?" he asked.

Elizabeth was embarrassed that she had been caught staring at him. "No," she said quickly.

"Where you riding to?"

"Nowhere special. I just like to ride."

"Mind if I come along?" But in the way he asked, she knew it had already been decided that he would.

They trotted off and around the cattle and through the trees at the edge of the ranch. He stopped riding and got off his horse. Putting his finger to his lips, he motioned for her to do the same.

Elizabeth slipped off the bay and walked closer to Rone. He pointed to a buck who was grazing in a clearing. The rays of the sun shone through the trees, leaving patterns on the animal's back. "He's beautiful," she whispered, and with that the buck's head came up to look in their direction, then turned and loped away. She was disappointed, but Rone smiled.

"I'm afraid they always do that when I watch them," Beth said.

"Do you like to watch wildlife?" Rone inquired.

"Oh, yes, I could spend hours just watching and listening. Unfortunately, they always know I'm around."

"I'll make moccasins for you and teach you to walk in silence."

"I'd like that, Rone."

"Then I'll teach you how to hunt them."

"No!" Elizabeth said alarmed. "That I wouldn't like. They're much too beautiful. I would never kill a deer."

"Someday you may need to know how. Are you ready for your first lesson in shooting? I believe you mentioned it was something else you wanted to learn."

She smiled warily. "Now?"

Rone reached up to his saddle and pulled out his Winchester .44 Carbine. He unloaded the weapon and handed it to her.

"I want you to hold it, like this . . . right . . . feel it against your skin. Balance its weight in your hands. Good. Put the stock against your shoulder. Fit it in real good. That's it."

By late afternoon, Beth could load the carbine, square off her target, and shoot. As time went on, she was thrown back less, and although her shoulder hurt, she was becoming accustomed to the feel of the gun.

This was to be the beginning of many such lessons for Beth. Rone took her out and taught her how to use a different weapon every day.

Beth knew he was pleased as she learned quickly and adeptly, and it became important for her to earn his approval. They were becoming friends, comfortable in each other's company. Just as she had quickly learned her new horse's moods, she was learning Rone's.

He taught her how to ride bare back, throw a knife, and how to sneak up on an animal. Then he went on to teach her how to wrestle, Indian style, and how to protect herself if taken from behind. She never complained about the rough lessons, but actually enjoyed them.

One day, as she was walking toward the creek for her daily swim, she saw him at a distance, crouched low, leaning over something. She stalked him, using all the approaches she had been taught.

Elizabeth moved silently in her new moccasins, until she was close enough to jump on his back, but he turned, the blade of his knife glinting in the sun. Instinctively, Beth kicked out, knocked it from his hand, caught it in midair, and then pretended to stab him.

Rone's eyes were cold and his face a deeper shade of brown. Then, unexpectedly, he smiled brighter than she had ever seen him smile before.

"You learn well, Elizabeth," he said, using her name for the first time since she'd met him. "You'll be safe enough."

Elizabeth was puzzled. "Safe from who, Rone?"

He touched her shoulder. "From anyone or anything . . . as long as you remember all that I've taught you, and as long as you maintain your strength and spirit."

He took the knife from her delicate fingers, put it back in its shield, and handed it to Beth. The mother of pearl handle gleamed against the brown leather. "Take it," he directed her.

"But, Rone, this is yours. I can't take it from you."

"Consider it a wedding gift, Liz. A gift from your friend."

The smile had vanished and his face was very serious again.

She kissed his cheek while her hand touched the other side of his face tenderly. Embarrassed, he turned away and walked over to where his horse was grazing.

"Thank you, Rone," she said softly to his back.

He stopped, and turning very slowly, he faced her, more comfortable with the distance between them. "I'm glad you're here," he said.

Chapter Twelve

Jack tied his horse to the post and walked into the large brick building. The lobby was cool and dark and several people stood at the teller's window, transacting business. He approached the marble staircase and took the steps two at a time, quickly reaching the second floor. Brushing dust from his clothing, and taking off his hat, he opened a large oak door with gold lettering that read, "Drummond's Financial Advisory." Jack entered the offices of his father.

A small man sat behind a desk in the anteroom and looked up as Jack closed the door behind him. He pulled his wire-rimmed glasses down on his nose, stared for a moment, then smiled thinly.

"Good to see you, Master Jack," he said in a very nasal, Northeastern manner.

Jack shook his hand and the little man winced slightly. "By God, Allgood, I'm a little old for 'master,' don't you think? Jack will do."

"I'll tell him you're here . . . Jack," Allgood said and tapped lightly at another door. Jack heard a familiar voice shout, "What is it, Allgood?"

Taking a deep breath, Jack pushed the little man aside, saying, "Never mind, I'll announce myself."

He opened the door and stepped in, holding his hat in his hands. *Damn,* he thought, *I still feel like a kid when I come in here.* A quick look around told him the office hadn't changed. Gold velvet drapes hung at the window, and a leather sofa sat against one of the oak paneled walls. A large desk stood in the center of the room, two brown leather chairs facing it. He breathed in the scent of old wood and fresh wax. *Nothing has changed,* he thought again.

"Jack! It's good to see you. Come in, come in."

Jack looked at the lined but still handsome face of his father, and noticed his green eyes were sparkling, his neatly groomed black hair was mixed with streaks of gray and his straight white teeth showed in a dazzling smile.

"It's good to see you, too, Sir," Jack said, shaking hands with his father.

They both sat down and looked at each other cautiously over the hand-carved desk.

"Tell me, Jack, have you raised the money?"

"You don't waste any time getting down to business, do you?"

That's why you're here; it's what you want to talk about, isn't it?"

They were silent for a time, then Jack said, "No, I didn't raise the money. I did think about the alternative, however. I'm married."

Daniel Drummond's eyes widened, his smile gone now, and there was a heavy silence in the room except for the tall clock in the corner that ticked away the seconds.

"When?" Daniel asked finally.

"Three weeks ago. She's at the ranch."

"I don't believe it."

Jack stood up and threw his hat down on the desk. "Have you ever known me to be a liar, Dad?"

Daniel shook his head slowly. "Reckless and careless and irresponsible, maybe . . . but no, never a liar."

"You told me to raise the money or settle down and get remarried. Well, I got married."

The older man stood up, anger flaring in his eyes. "Damnit, boy, I can't believe you went out and found a woman so soon. What whore house did you dig her out of?"

"What the hell do you want from me?" Jack asked. "You told me you were going to sell the ranch unless I paid you in full or settled down and got married. You knew damned well I wouldn't be able to raise the money—all your friends back East saw to it that I could not."

"I expect you to earn the money, not borrow more."

"I'm doing the best I can . . . but that doesn't matter now because I've got myself a wife and that's what you wanted."

"You walk in here only months after I last see you and tell me you've found a wife—very convenient. That proves nothing to me, least of all that you've settled down."

Daniel rubbed his eyes with his fingers, then asked, "Who the hell is this woman anyway?"

"Elizabeth Gerard."

"Gerard . . . Gerard . . . I don't know the name. Where's she from?"

"Benton."

Daniel Drummond sat back in his chair thoughtfully. "I still can't place it."

"She's the niece of a friend of Aunt Grace's."

Daniel's eyes lit up with recognition, then his face went white. "You didn't take an innocent girl from a genteel Pennsylvania family out here just to keep your God-forsaken ranch? I don't believe that even of you."

Jack said nothing.

"Were you married in Pennsylvania?" Daniel asked.

"River Pines."

"Her family wasn't present?"

"I sent them a telegram a couple of days ago."

"How did she come to be here with you at River Pines in the first place?" Daniel questioned him.

"Does it matter?" Jack said impatiently. "She's just the woman you wanted for me. She's from a well-respected family back East. Real good stock!"

Daniel exploded now. "Good stock? She's a woman, boy, not a cow!"

"Stop calling me boy."

"Then stop acting like one. Jack, I've got a lot of money invested in that ranch of yours. I don't intend to lose it because you're not stable enough to handle it. I'll admit, I've seen you make some changes, and it's been a relief, but you have a way of being unpredictable. I thought that if you found a good woman to help you settle down, one that would work by your side and help to build that ranch into what it has the potential to be, you'd . . . Damn it, Jack, what happens when this girl realizes she's not cut out for the rough life of a rancher's wife? Like the last time."

Jack stood up again, knocking his chair over, and walked toward the door. His father's voice followed him, "Wait, son, sit down. I'm sorry I flew off the handle. I only want what's best for you. A good wife, a good mother to your children. I don't want to see you hurt again, Jack."

"Forget it. Sell the ranch."

"Not yet," Daniel said. "I told you to raise the money or get married. I didn't specify to whom, so I'll keep my end of the bargain."

Jack relaxed slightly and turned back to look at his father standing behind his desk. "Then the ranch is mine?"

"Not until you prove to me that you can make this marriage work. In the meantime, you have the cattle drive. See how much money you raise from that. I'll extend your loan payment until you're back. Agreed?"

Jack smiled slightly, "It isn't exactly the deal we had, but . . . agreed." He sat down across from his father.

"Answer me this, Jack. Do you love her?"

It was a question Jack hadn't expected. For the most part, love wasn't needed in marriages in the West. That was for the romantics in the East—for men like David, who had many young women to choose from—ladies from good families with fine manners. In Colorado you took a wife to help on the ranch, cook your meals, have your sons. Love wasn't much of an option to young men out West.

Jack looked at his father and realized there was still much of the Pennsylvanian in him. Yet the question left an odd feeling in the pit of Jack's stomach, as if a raw nerve had been touched, and he couldn't pinpoint where it was paining him.

"Just as I thought," his father said. "How long before she runs off like . . ."

Jack swore and slammed his fist down on the desktop. "Don't keep throwing that in my face. I'm warning you."

The older man stood up, "And don't you threaten me. It's man to man now and I won't hold back."

Jack remembered the last time he and his father had fought. He was seventeen and had swung first, hitting his father square in the jaw. A muscle worked in Jack's temple as he went on to remember how his father had brought up that powerful right fist and knocked him to the ground, and when Jack had stood up, Daniel knocked him down again, this time leaving Jack unconscious.

"Never mind," Daniel said, calming down. "Let's get back to drawing up our new agreement."

Jack left his horse tied up outside the bank and walked over to the saloon across from his father's building. Jack ordered whiskey, drank it down, then ordered another. The meeting with his father wasn't as bad as he'd expected, although Rone had been right about one thing, Daniel suspected a rat where his marriage was concerned. He should have known Daniel wouldn't accept that he'd fallen in love that easily.

A year. It was what he had expected, what he had told Elizabeth. Jack took the bottle from the bartender's hands and walked to a table in the corner. *She'll stay that long. I'll make it comfortable for her,* he told himself, *not that it's going to be easy. She's damned ornery and stubborn.* Then smiling a little, he thought, *Even if she is beautiful."*

He recalled the unexpected question his father had asked him about loving her. He'd never love again. Not that it mattered. *Love is nothing but pain,* he thought. Jack pictured Elizabeth in New York on the roller coaster, and the same evening when she was dressed for the opera. He remembered, too, the way his heart beat unsteadily when he looked at her then. *One minute she's an irritating little witch and the next she's as sweet as an innocent child.*

"Hey, Jack, where you been, cowboy?"

Jack looked up to see a brown haired girl standing by the table. Her face was painted and the dress she wore was cut low, showing the ample mounds of her breasts.

She leaned over and put her face close to his. "Aren't you gonna' buy me a drink, Jack?"

He smiled, pushing the empty chair at his table out with his foot, and she sat down. "Bring us another glass," he called to the bartender. The girl licked her lips and smiled with her sultry and inviting blue eyes.

"I missed you, you know," she whispered.

Jack leaned over and kissed her lips lightly.

"That kiss was for free, Mr. Drummond," she said, still smiling. He poured her a glass of whiskey. "Drink up, Jenny."

They sat quietly for a few minutes, then she asked, "How was it up there?" motioning toward the building across the way. He stopped smiling and answered, "Not too bad. I told him what he wanted to know."

Now she stopped smiling and her eyes widened. "You told him you're married?"

"Yep, it's true enough."

Jenny sighed. "Lucky girl. Did he give you the deed?"

Jack sat back and pushed his hat high on his head. "You sure know a lot about my business."

She smiled again, "You sure were drunk the last time I saw you."

"Well, anyway," Jack answered her, "he gave me a year—just to make sure everything goes all right."

"I see . . . I guess that means you won't be staying."

Jack looked at the woman sitting at his table. His eyes drifted down to the bodice of her dress, to her tiny waist and full hips. "Well, I just might have an hour or so, Jenny."

She took his hand and pulled him to his feet. "Then let's waste no time, darlin'."

When they reached a small room, she undressed quickly and lie on the bed, opening her arms to him. "The first time's a little wedding present."

Jack undressed and went to her, kissing her deeply. Her excitement rose as his hands moved over her body and his lips traveled after his fingertips. She moaned and wiggled under him, and his mouth found hers again and he kissed her more insistently this time. She stroked his back and crooned to him, but his kisses stopped and he pushed off her, swearing. Jenny watched him stand up and start to dress.

"What is it, Jack? You aren't giving me much of a chance to please you. Come on back, honey," she said, patting the bed.

Jack pulled on his black leather boots and threw two large bills on the bed beside her. "Sorry about this, Jenny. It's not your fault."

She stopped trying to coax him and laughed. "You fool, you're in love with her. I don't believe it. After the last time, I'd think you'd have learned . . ."

Jack buckled his gun belt and his eyes smoldered in her direction. "Whores do better when they learn to keep their mouths shut."

He smoothed his hair with his hand and placed his hat on top.

"After a few months, Jack, you'll be ready to have me again," Jenny predicted.

Jack turned to look at her, and his face was serious when he said, "I sure do hope you're right, Jenny, girl."

Chapter Thirteen

Elizabeth and Rone sat on the bank of the creek in the shade of the pines. She watched him while he leaned against a tree and sharpened his new knife. His eyes were hidden by the fringe of his black lashes, as he concentrated on the silvery blade. His black hair shone and a strand of it fell over his brow.

Rone's chest and shoulders were glistening with perspiration and his muscles rippled against the smoothness of his skin when he moved his hands. He was clothed in deerskin pants and his legs were stretched out and crossed in front of him.

When she looked up, Beth found him staring back at her, his face expressionless as usual.

"I'm sorry," she said. "I didn't mean to stare."

He went back to his knife. "You want to ask me something," he told rather than asked her.

Elizabeth brushed dirt from her hands and he continued, "You think me mysterious." He felt the knife's edge for sharpness with his thumb.

"I'd just like to know more about you," she said quietly.

"There's nothing to know," Rone assured her.

She stood up and walked to the edge of the embankment, the soft green moss cushioning her bare feet. She squatted down, put her fingers into the clear water, and let it drip from her cupped hand. "I'm as transparent as this water. Everyone knows what I'm thinking, even when I try to keep my thoughts secreted away; but you're different, Rone. No one ever knows what you're thinking."

He put the blade down into the ground. "I'm a man—half white, half Indian. I work for my friend when I'm needed, live alone in the mountain when I am not. What I think is of no consequence to anyone else."

She turned back and sat across from him again. "That isn't true. None of us are alone in this world. Whatever we think, whoever we are, affects others whether directly or indirectly. And what you think is important to me, Rone."

"For instance?"

"Well, for one thing, I'd like to know what you think *of me*," she said, smiling into his eyes.

He crossed his arms over his chest and considered her. "You're beautiful," he said after a long time.

She frowned. "That isn't what I mean, and I think you know it. I know what I look like, though I do not presume myself beautiful. I'm more interested in what you think of me," she pointed to her chest, "this me—the one inside. It doesn't seem to matter to . . . to some people . . . about this me, but I'm here, not just body, but soul."

"I think you are beautiful—not just your body—your soul."

Elizabeth looked at him with surprise. "Then you are probably the only person alive who does."

"Then you're not like the water as you said you are."

"What do you mean?" she asked.

"If you're so transparent to everyone, then all would know your soul. Perhaps you're more like muddy waters," he finished, smiling.

Elizabeth laughed a little. "We're getting off the subject. We were speaking of you, Rone, not of me."

He smiled that rare smile she so enjoyed seeing. Then she said, "Very well, maybe I prefer not to talk about myself either. I am muddy waters then. And what are you?"

Rone considered a moment, then answered, "A dense forest."

"Oh, but a dense forest can be explored. Isn't that so? If you are a dense forest, all I need do is explore and find out who you are."

Rone's smile faded and he was very quiet then. She felt uneasy. "I'm sorry, Rone. I guess I'm prying. Forgive me."

"I'm not used to having anyone care enough to ask about me, I guess." He stood up and looked out at the water. "My mother was Ute, my father white—from the East. When he came to Colorado to mine gold, he made friends with the trappers and the Indian tribes, including my mother's people. I guess he was lonely and so my grandfather gave my mother to him in exchange for a statue of a stallion made of gold. It was quite an honor for my father, since my people value their daughters greatly."

Rone looked back at Beth. "She left her tribe to live with him while he helped other white settlers found a town. We lived among the white families until I was three. Then he went back to the Front Range to live with his wife—his white wife."

"And you and your mother?"

"He wanted to take care of her secretly, but she wouldn't allow it. We went back to her tribe, and she died a year later."

Elizabeth's throat ached thinking about the sick woman and small child left alone. "He left you just like that?"

"Life is very complicated. There were no easy solutions. I stayed with my tribe seven years, then left to live in the white man's world."

"That's probably where you belonged, Rone," Elizabeth said innocently.

Rone smiled sadly, "A half-breed does not *belong* anywhere. I found a home on Daniel Drummond's ranch, and they were kind to me. Amelia Drummond treated me as if I were her own son."

"She must have been a wonderful person. Is that how you became so close to Jack, too?"

Rone nodded. "That's how I found my good friend."

"You must hate your father very much."

"No, I don't hate him. I can't forgive him. But every man has to answer to himself. It is not my place to judge."

They were silent for awhile, then Beth said, "I'm happy you told me this story, Rone. Somehow it makes me feel closer to you."

He reached down to help her up, and they grabbed each other's wrists in a firm grip.

Beth had come to love looking into his eyes where she found a gentle strength and a warm glow. "I'm very grateful for your friendship, Rone. It has made being at River Pines easier for me," Elizabeth declared, surprising herself.

"You do not know it, but we are more than friends."

Elizabeth wanted to ask what he meant, but he changed the subject quickly. "I have to get back to work. Are you coming?"

He put on his deerskin shirt and placed his new gray hat, purchased in Cherryton, on his head.

Beth had practiced shooting all morning and was tired, her shoulder hurt, and her head ached from the noise. She looked at the inviting water. "No, I think I'll swim awhile. It's peaceful here. Tell Calla I'll be back soon."

Rone nodded and she watched him mount his horse and ride toward the ranch. Alone now, Elizabeth undressed to her chemise and waded into the water. She slipped under the surface and swam into the creek's depths, washing away the heat of the day. When she surfaced again, she heard Jack say, "I understand you've been busy, Mrs. Drummond."

Her heart leapt at the sound of his voice, and she turned around quickly to see him hunkered down, smiling at her from the embankment.

Returning his smile, she said proudly, "I earned myself a new hat."

"So it seems." He picked it up from where she had put it on top of her other clothing. Then he picked up her pants and shirt and turning a sly grin to her, said, "Sure is a hot day. Wouldn't mind a little swim myself."

Elizabeth stopped smiling. "Well, go find yourself another spot to do it. This one's taken."

Jack looked around. "This spot's as good as any. They tell me this is a free state," he said, stripping off his shirt.

"Jack Drummond, don't you dare."

As he started to undo his trousers, she turned and swam away. She heard a splash as he dove into the creek's coolness and she screamed.

"You keep your distance!" she warned him.

Jack stayed several feet away from her when he said, "Tell me about this horse of yours."

Elizabeth laughed. "It sounds as if you already know quite a lot. Oh, but, Jack, it was thrilling. I never felt so proud of myself."

His eyes were dancing at her now. "You ought to be. That's a hard job for a man, let alone a pretty little thing like you. How'd you feel the next day?"

Elizabeth rolled her eyes. "I couldn't walk. I had never known what pain was until then. My whole body hurt, every muscle in me ached whenever I moved. Calla fussed and scolded, but it was worth it. Just looking at the bay and knowing he is mine, that I earned him, makes it worthwhile. Of course,

Calla fixed me up with her horrible liniment," she added, making a face at the thought of it.

"Have you named him?" Jack asked.

"Yep," Elizabeth said smiling broadly. "I call him Rusty Nail—Rusty for short—because of his color and because of what it felt like I was landing on every time he bucked."

She joined Jack in laughter. Then he pointed behind her and they watched as an eagle swooped down toward the water and glided up again, a fish in its claws. She turned back to smile at him.

"It's beautiful here. I never imagined it would be like this."

"I'm glad you like it, Liz. I guess River Pines is as close to heaven as I'll ever come," he said, looking at the mountain beyond him.

Elizabeth closed her eyes and sighed. "I don't know how I'll ever leave it and go back to the placidity of Benton."

Jack looked at her from under his brows. "I'm really pleased to hear you say that, Liz. I want you to be happy while you're here. I want you to feel at home at River Pines." Their eyes locked for a long moment.

He splashed her then, and she splashed back, swimming away laughing. "That's enough of that. You can't goad me into coming up out of this water any further, Jack Drummond. And don't think I haven't noticed you inching closer. You stay where you are."

He floated a little closer, daring her with his eyes, and she felt a strong desire to drift nearer instead of backing away. As she returned his gaze, she wanted to know what it would feel like to have his bare arms around her waist, their bodies touching, his mouth on hers. She quivered at the thought and Jack noticed. "Cold, Liz?"

"Yes, I really must be getting back to the house. I promised Calla I'd let her teach me how to cook. She said I was getting strange notions—like breaking horses—because I was bored. The way to keep her from nagging me was to agree to bake a pie."

"Remind me not to have dessert tonight," he said, wryly.

Elizabeth gave him a gray look, then pointing her finger at him, said, "Now, I want you to promise to close your eyes until I'm out of the water and behind those bushes. I'll call you when you can open them."

"I promise," he agreed, feigning a serious look.

She started to move, then looked back at him. "I can't imagine you being a man of your word, Jack Drummond."

He pretended to be hurt. "If you were a man, I'd pull my gun on you for saying such a libelous thing."

She sighed. "All right, I'll trust you. Close your eyes."

Elizabeth swam to the bank and quickly grabbed her clothing and ran behind the bushes. Without calling out to him as she had promised, she took her time dressing. When she finally came out from around the shrub, she ran into him head first. He was smiling at her, bare from the waist up, beads of water running down his neck and arms, making rivulets through the coarse dark hair on his broad chest.

"Oh . . . you rake! How much did you see?" she demanded.

"Enough to know that I like what I saw," he answered, winking.

Elizabeth pushed at him. "So much for your word. I'm ashamed of you."

Jack's laugh was velvet and warm when he grabbed her around the waist and lifted her so that her face was even with his. "Ah, but I'm proud of you, Liz Drummond."

The nearness of his lips and the feel of his arms around her, made Elizabeth light-headed. She found it exciting that he showed such pride in her, and was thrilled that he was finally giving her the attention and admiration he gave everyone else on the ranch. Mostly, she loved his eyes as they sparkled and danced. She was dangerously close to kissing him.

Elizabeth wriggled out of his arms and ran to her horse as fast as her legs would carry her, mounted and rode away. Jack leaned his shoulder against a gnarled tree trunk and watched until she was out of sight. "This agreement of ours, Liz, darlin', isn't going to be easy . . . for either of us, it looks like," he said aloud, knowing that he had almost been kissed.

Jack's senses suddenly became alert when he thought he heard footsteps. He took his Peacemaker from its holster and scouted around. All he found was some broken shrub.

Several days later, Beth was looking for Rone and knocked on the bunkhouse door. Wilkes opened it, and immediately smiled at her.

"Well, howdy, Miz Liz."

Elizabeth hated the way he leered at her and she glared back at him. "I'm looking for Rone," she said.

"He went into town for supplies. Won't be back for awhile, I'm afraid."

"Thank you," she said, turning to leave.

"Goin' swimmin', Ma'am?"

Elizabeth swung around and looked at him hard. "Why?"

"No reason," he said, giving her his disgusting brown smile again.

She backed away slowly, feeling abused and frightened, but not understanding why.

Elizabeth didn't see much of the men after that. They were busy preparing for the cattle drive and took their midday meals on the range. Dinner was very late and everyone was tired. To ease her boredom, Elizabeth helped Calla around the house and let the black woman teach her more recipes, although it wasn't Beth's favorite chore and usually resulted in good natured ribbing from the men.

In order to avert another cooking lesson, Elizabeth decided to sew curtains for the windows in the living room and asked Calla where she could find some material.

"Well, now, I think there might be some old but usable goods in the chest in the shed. I'll go on in and get it."

Beth stopped her. "No, Calla, you're busy. I'll go find it." She let herself into the small dark building. The shed smelled dank when she entered it and cobwebs caught in her hair. It was cluttered with old furniture and broken tools. It took her awhile before she saw the chest under some picture frames and started working to pull it out, when she came upon a painting of a woman. Elizabeth took it into the light of the doorway to look at it closely.

The woman had fair hair, very like Beth's own, though not as light, and the eyes were painted a deep shade of violet blue. The woman vaguely reminded Beth of Emily. However, Elizabeth came to the conclusion that she had never seen anyone as beautiful as the woman in the portrait.

Jack's voice came, deep and threatening, from behind her. "What are you doing?"

Elizabeth jumped at the intrusion and looked at him. "Nothing . . . I . . . was . . ." she stammered without finishing.

"I asked you what you're doing," he said, stepping closer, his eyes like green ice.

"I was searching for some fabric to make curtains and found this. I was only looking at it, Jack."

"Well, put it away and get what you came in here for."

"Who is she?" Elizabeth asked him.

"None of your business," he answered walking away.

Elizabeth continued to look at the portrait of the beautiful woman for a while, then hurriedly searched for the material. Once she had all she needed, she replaced the painting against the chest with a final glance.

She saw Jack riding back out onto the range on his stallion and entered the house again. Calla sent a nervous look at her when Beth returned to the kitchen.

"Who is that woman in the portrait, Calla?" Beth asked, knowing by the expression on the older woman's face that she had seen what happened when Jack found Beth in the shed.

"Mr. Jack's wife."

Elizabeth slumped down on a chair at hearing this. "His wife?"

"She's been dead goin' on five years. And, God forgive me, it's just as well."

Elizabeth felt weak. "I didn't know he'd been married."

"No, Miz Liz, he don't talk 'bout it."

"Did he love her very much?"

Calla's eyes were sad when she answered, "I guess. It tore him up, what she did."

"What did she do, Calla?"

"Well, now, Miz Liz, 'tain't my business to say."

"Perhaps I would understand him better if I knew."

"That's true enough, honey, but it gotta be him that tells you," Calla said with finality in her voice.

No one had seen Jack for the rest of the day and he didn't come home for supper that night. Elizabeth and Rone exchanged worried glances during the meal, and she ached to ask him the story of Jack's first wife. Elizabeth knew, however, that he'd put her off just as Calla had done.

"You'll be leaving for the cattle drive tomorrow, won't you?" Elizabeth asked him.

"That's what we plan."

"Rone, tell me about . . . ," Elizabeth couldn't complete the question about Jack because Rone stood up precipitously and bid her good night, leaving her alone in the house.

Elizabeth awakened from a restless sleep later and heard Jack in the living room. She was staring at the ceiling, waiting to hear him enter his room. When he didn't, she put on her dressing gown and quietly walked down the hall. Jack sat before the fire, a half-empty whiskey bottle in his hand.

"Come on in, Liz," he beckoned to her.

She walked to the hearth and looked him fully in the face. "Are you drunk?"

He laughed. "Not sufficiently." Then he motioned to the new curtains. "I like what you've done in here. Looks nice."

"I was afraid you'd be annoyed, or wouldn't like them."

"It's your house, too . . . for now. I suppose you hate it."

"No, not at all. I like it. It's a strong house, Jack, warm and secure."

"Not what you're used to, though. No fancy staircases or carpets. Just a plain old ranch house."

"Nevertheless, I do like it."

Elizabeth blushed at the pleased look in his eyes. "You surprise me. I think I have you pegged, and then you turn around and do something or say something contrary to what I thought you'd do or say."

"You just aren't a good judge of character, I guess," she said, smiling at him.

He thought it over. "Maybe not . . . maybe not."

He leaned forward then and took her hand. "You're not all that unhappy, are you, Liz? Can you stick it out, do you think?"

Elizabeth nodded her head slowly. "You're a strange man, Jack Drummond. No, I'm not unhappy. Although I do wish we'd get along better. Whatever happened to that truce we made at the creek that first day?"

"I guess we keep forgetting it," he said, still holding her hand. "Shall we try again?"

"Yes, let's, Jack."

"Okay, then we'll drink to it." He poured whiskey into a glass and handed it to her. "To a new and better truce!" He raised the bottle and tapped it against her glass. They each took a drink. Elizabeth started coughing, and Jack jumped to his feet, laughing. He patted her on the back roughly. "Still can't seem to get the hang of it, can you?" he teased.

Wiping tears from the corner of her eyes, Elizabeth laughed too. "No, but I am getting used to the taste," and she took another drink, this time gasping only a little.

They were standing very close now, his hand still on her back, and he started to rub it, very slowly, circling her shoulders.

Beth looked up at his face and they stared into each other's eyes a long time. Jack brushed her hair back behind her ear. Then cupping her cheek, he kissed her very gently, hesitantly, as if to ask permission. She didn't pull away, but leaned closer to him, and her arms encircled his neck. Their kiss lingered, became stronger, passionate. He pulled her down on his lap and continued kissing her, his hand stroking her silky hair and satiny skin. When the kiss ended, she leaned her cheek against his shoulder, and they sat staring into the fire together, afraid of breaking the spell.

Elizabeth lifted her face to his again, this time initiating the touch of their lips, and he moaned deep in his throat, his hand moving down her arm, stopping to cup her breast as he had done her cheek. Her body responded and she arched slightly toward his hand. Jack stiffened and his breathing intensified.

The smell of whiskey was strong on his breath, and without warning, Elizabeth's mind took her back to the hotel in New York, to another man who kissed her this way, the smell of liquor on his breath.

Behind her closed eyes, Elizabeth could see Tom Blackwell touching her body, demanding the unspeakable, and just as she was being carried away by passion for Jack, fear overwhelmed her. She pushed Jack away and ran to the other side of the room.

The expression on his face would have been comical if Elizabeth were not so frightened. Then his face changed and his eyes showed that he was hurt.

Jack's blood turned cold in his veins as he wondered why it was that every time his lips met Liz's, her love for David intruded. The knowledge that no one had ever loved him that much, and his desperate need to be loved that way, especially by this particular woman, made him reach out involuntarily to her.

Elizabeth raised her hand. "Don't touch me . . . I can't bear it," she cried, covering her face.

Jack got to his feet. The sight of her cowering away from him, and the thought that she was so repulsed by him, fanned his temper. "It's him, isn't it, Liz? Always him," he said. Elizabeth felt the bottle of whiskey *whoosh* past her, its contents splashing on her arm as it crashed against the wall.

Still frightened, but with an anger that matched his now, Elizabeth screamed, "And what about her? What about your precious wife? Tell me about her, Drummond. Tell me what she did to you to make you hate *me* so much."

"You've gone too far." His face was distorted when, in a swift movement he crossed the room and grabbed her throat in his hand, cutting off her breath. "I could kill you right now . . . ," he looked into her eyes, which were shining with tears, showing great fear, as they pleaded with him to release her.

Jack let her go immediately. She slumped against the wall, slid to the floor, sobbing and gasping for air.

"Oh, God, Elizabeth. What did I do . . . ? I didn't mean to hurt you . . ."

She tried to stand. Jack wanted to help but she slapped his hands away, still crying. "You're an animal," she screamed at him.

He shook his head. "You don't understand."

"I wanted to help you, Jack. I wanted to lo . . . to be your friend. But you are a devil. You've seemed so different here on the ranch, I thought . . . but I was wrong. My first impression was right. You are nothing but a brutal egotistical maniac."

Elizabeth saw tears spring to his eyes and her anger dissipated at the pain she saw in his face. His hand came up to cover his eyes while he sat down in the chair again.

"Jack . . ."

"Go to bed, Liz. I'll never touch you again. You needn't be afraid of me."

"Jack . . ."

"Leave me alone! Just leave me alone."

Elizabeth started to walk out of the room, still staggering slightly, when he asked, "Do you think you can stay the year after what happened tonight?"

Elizabeth was crying when she answered, "No."

Jack and the rest of the men were gone when Elizabeth walked into the kitchen the next morning. His used mug sat alone on the table in his place. Calla looked at her sadly, then looked away again. Elizabeth took her cup and poured herself some fragrant black coffee. She stared down at it once she was seated at the table. Calla touched her shoulder gently. "Miz Liz, by the look in your eyes, I can tell you hardly slept atall. Let me git you some breakfast."

"I'm not hungry, Calla. Coffee's enough," she said, and then, putting her head down on her arm, she sobbed as she had throughout the night.

Calla knelt beside Elizabeth's chair and put her heavy arm around her, murmuring, "Aw, honey, don't take on so. It gonna be all right. You jest wait and see. It was just your findin' that paintin' of his first wife. He won't stay like this, not when he sees you smile like you do. When they come home from the drive, honey, ever'thing will be back the same as it was before yistiday."

Elizabeth picked up her head and Calla wiped Beth's unhappy face with her apron. "I won't be here then, Calla. I'm leaving today, this morning, as soon as I can."

Calla was really dismayed now. "You can't do that, Miz Liz. It will kill him. He'll lose this ranch and I don't want to think what will happen again."

Elizabeth stopped crying. "What do you mean? How will he lose the ranch?"

Calla sat back on her heels and looked toward the door, as if she would see Jack standing there.

"Calla, I want you to tell me what you meant. I deserve to know."

The black woman took a deep breath, "Mr. Jack's daddy owns this ranch. Mr. Jack had to borrow a lot of money to get it back on its feet after she—his first wife—died. Before Mr. Jack went away to the East, Mr. Daniel told him he had to raise the money to pay him back or get married and settle down. Mr. Jack couldn't raise the money, so . . . he . . ."

"Married me."

Calla nodded. "But when Mr. Jack went to get the mortgage last week, Mr. Daniel said that you'd have to stay one year before he'd turn it over to Mr. Jack."

"Why? Why wouldn't he expect the marriage to last?"

Calla smiled a little. "Well, I guess nobody knows someone better'n a parent does . . . and because of the last time."

"What last time? You mean his first marriage?"

Calla didn't like the way the conversation was turning, and she stood up, but Elizabeth grabbed her wrist, "Tell me."

She sat down opposite Elizabeth now. "Mr. Jack's first wife only lived here three months. She was a bad one, she was. He met her in Philadelphia, and they had a big weddin'. Then he brought her out here, but it wasn't like she thought it would be. She got unhappier and unhappier—meaner than anyone I ever knowd—until one day, she just left."

Calla's eyes drifted out through the window, "Ain't right, leavin' a man without even tellin' him. Mr. Jack went searchin' for her, all the way back East. When he got there, she was dead already. A ridin' accident. No one could understand how she had a ridin' accident, when she was such a good horsewoman—like you, Miz Liz—but she was gone. Mr. Jack took it real bad."

Calla's eyes misted when she continued. "He come back here and drank most of the time. He got deeper into debt to his daddy. Rone tried to help out, but Mr. Jack just got worse. Then he packed his bag and left again to go back East, sayin' he had to find out somethin'. He was gone from this ranch a long time. He almost lost ever'thing."

Elizabeth thought this over, then asked, "What did he need to find out, Calla?"

"I don't know. But I got my suspicions. Maybe he just wanted to know how exac'ly she died. Anyway, when he come home, he was off the whiskey, and started workin' hard again, gettin' this place back in order."

She shook her head, "It ain't been easy though, and he still didn't have enough money to pay Mr. Daniel all he owed him. Then he got a telegram to go to Denver to see Mr. Daniel. That's when he gave him that there ult. . . ulta . . ."

"Ultimatum."

"That's it. I think he only wants to see Mr. Jack happy again and thought forcin' him to find a good wife this time would help. Now you have the story. Miz Liz, you gotta be blind not to see how he loves River Pines. If Mr. Daniel sells it to a stranger, we'll all be done for, but no one as much as Mr. Jack."

Elizabeth looked at the other woman. Whatever Jack Drummond was, he elicited loyalty from his friends, and that accounted for something.

Knowing the story now, Elizabeth realized how important her being there was. River Pines was in Jack's soul—a part of him no one could ever take away. She knew it would destroy him to have to leave it, and for some reason she couldn't explain, Elizabeth didn't want that. She was having trouble understanding him and struggling constantly with her feelings for him, but she couldn't leave him knowing about this.

Taking Calla's hand, she said, "You're right, Calla. He can't lose this ranch. If my staying will help, then so be it. But once he has the deed to this ranch again, I'm leaving—that very day."

Calla grabbed Elizabeth in her strong embrace. "You're a good girl, Miz Liz. I knowd it the moment I laid eyes on you. I said to my Jim, 'This girl gonna fix Mr. Jack up fine.'"

CHAPTER FOURTEEN

The cattle drive was nearly at an end. The men sat around the fire talking. The position of the stars told them they had awhile before Rone and Jack, who were riding guard, would be back. They felt pretty free while out of the watchful eyes of both men, and they talked and argued and laughed at each other. Barnes took out his harmonica and played a soft, sweet tune.

"That sure is pretty," one of the men said.

With his back to the others, Wilkes took a bottle out from under his blanket roll. It was nearly empty when he swallowed the whiskey it contained.

"What you doin' over there, Wilkes?" Jim asked. "I been watchin' your head go back all evenin'. You ain't got no whiskey here? Mr. Jack tan your hide, you drink on the trail."

Wilkes ignored the black man who served as cook while on the drives each year. "Yeah, that music sure is pretty," Wilkes said, recorking the bottle and hiding it once more. He turned toward the other men again. "It's pretty enough to be a woman."

"Any woman in particular, Wilkes?" they goaded.

"Matter of fact, yeah. One hell of a pretty woman at that."

"We know her?" someone asked.

"Sure do. The boss man's wife."

The group fell silent then, but Wilkes went on. "She's a beauty all right. I wouldn't mind havin' her right now."

Jim threw the contents of his cup into the fire and flames shot out. "You better stop talkin' that way, Wilkes."

Wilkes lay back, his hands under his head, "She's got some body . . . all white and lean. Nice big tits, too. I seen her bathin' in the creek back at the ranch. Soon's I'd see her headin' for it,

I'd run and climb a tree and get an eyeful. Then I'd dream about her for days."

His senses were slightly dulled from the liquor. Barnes started playing the harmonica again, trying to change the mood that was brewing in camp. Wilkes continued, "In those dreams she'd undress for me, just like I seen her done by the creek, then she'd come to me. She wasn't so refined in my dreams, though, like she pretends to be. No sir, not refined 'tall, more like she was when she was up on that bronco. I knew then what kind of woman that gal is. Why I'd take her and rip off what was left of those fancy under clothes and she loved it all right."

Jim stood up, his fists clenched at his sides. "You stop it, now, you hear? That ain't no way to talk 'bout a woman, 'specially Miz Liz."

Wilkes smiled up at him. "Why? You gonna do somethin' about it, old nigger?"

There was a deadly silence in the camp, and Wilkes droned on about his dream, ignoring Jim. "That nude little body of hers would wiggle and squirm under me . . ."

He stopped and sputtered when hot coffee was thrown into his face, blinding him momentarily. He swore and jumped up in time to have a fist knock him back down to the ground. He looked up and saw Drummond standing over him.

"Funny how time gets away from you when you're drunk, isn't Wilkes? Now get up. I'm gonna kill you with my own hands."

Wilkes was angry, too, he jumped up, punching out, hitting Jack in the stomach. The two men threw themselves at each other. They rolled on the ground near the fire, and the group of men, on their feet now, made a circle to watch, sometimes yelling out.

Drummond was on top, then Wilkes, then Drummond again. A knife blade flashed in the firelight, just as Jack managed to jump off and away from the knife's point. Wilkes jumped up, too, the knife in his right hand, lurching out, threateningly. Drummond was able to move out of the way of Wilkes' plunges, until Rone handed his own knife to Jack, now evening the fight.

Wilkes smiled, his rotten teeth showing in an ugly sneer. "Okay, Drummond, okay. You interrupted my story a minute back. You want to hear the rest of my dream? It goes like this," he plunged, missing by an inch. "After I take her once, she rolls over on top of me, and her mouth comes down . . ."

Jack lunged this time. Wilkes moved back quickly, tripped on a stone, and fell back onto the ground. Drummond leapt on top of him with his knee slamming hard onto Wilkes' wrist, and the men could hear the snap of bone.

He screamed and dropped the knife. The men fell silent while Drummond's knife point was at Wilkes' throat. Wilkes' eyes were frantic with fear; Jack's smile was vicious. "You were saying, Wilkes?"

The wild-eyed man looked around. "Get him off me. Get off me, you son of a bitch!"

Drummond moved the knife slightly, drawing a thin line of blood from the skin over Wilkes' windpipe. "I should kill you, but I won't." Jack stood up and turned away in disgust.

With his left hand, Wilkes grabbed the knife that he had dropped moments before. Drummond heard Rone shout, "Jack!" and spun back around with his weapon extended. Wilkes was bent at the waist, preparing to plunge his knife into Drummond's back. As Jack sprang aside, out of the way, Wilkes stumbled and his face glanced against Jack's blade, leaving a bloody gash across his cheek. Wilkes fell again, groaning.

Jack looked surprised, but his anger flared. "You goddamned fool! I'd suggest you make sure you're not drunk the next time you try to stab a man in the back." He took his gun from its holster and held it on Wilkes. "Now get the hell out of here. If I ever see your ugly face again, you're a dead man."

In an afterthought, he put his foot on Wilkes' heaving chest, "And don't go near River Pines. Don't even go to Colorado."

Jack lifted his foot and watched as one of the other men saddled Wilkes' horse. He rode away without looking back.

Jack put his gun back in its holster and handed the knife to Rone. "We pull out early in the morning," he said.

Almost two months had passed, and they were not back yet. Elizabeth would ride a little farther north each day to watch for them, then would return to the ranch house alone. Calla told her, "It won't be long, honey. They'll be back any day now."

Elizabeth would shrug, trying to hide her disappointment. "I really don't care, Calla. It's quite pleasant around here without him." But in spite of what she said, Beth did miss Jack. She missed Rone and all the men, as well. She kept herself busy learning to cook and sew. At Calla's request, she tutored Little Ben and Nathan and taught them how to read and write. She even visited the Manning ranch and put up with the whining Sue and her screeching, misbehaved children.

The heat was almost unbearable that summer, and the only relief from the unrelenting season was the creek and the mountain breezes in the evening. Calla and little Ben tried to keep Beth entertained while they sat on the porch of the ranch house in the evenings, but Elizabeth dreaded the nights when she was alone in the house. As the long summer weeks wore on, she would find herself going into Jack's room in the middle of the night to lie on his bed. Aside from the fact that there was a better breeze through his window, she felt oddly comforted in his bed.

It was on one of those nights, when she climbed into his large bed, dressed only in a cool chemise, and drifted into a deep sleep, that she was awakened by a light. Jack was leaning against the bed post, a crooked grin on his lips.

"Well, what have we here?" he asked.

Embarrassed, she jumped up, her long slender legs showing before she pulled the summer quilt around herself.

"Please don't leave on my account," he drawled.

She stuttered a moment, then managed to ask, "When did you arrive?"

"A few minutes ago. We rode through the night. I was eager to get back."

She stepped around him gingerly. "Was it successful?"

"I made a bundle of money, if that's what you mean."

She nodded and looked around. "Are you hungry?"

"Not for food, Liz." His smile made her blush.

"Well, you must be tired. I'll let you go to bed," she said, moving by him, but he took her arm.

"I've missed you, Elizabeth," he said quietly. She pulled her arm away, and he let it go easily, when he continued, "I'm really glad you're still here. I'm sorry about the night before we left for the drive. I wish I could make it up to . . ."

Elizabeth walked to the door. "Good night, Jack," she said, closing it behind her.

When she left her room the next morning, Jack was just leaving his and they bumped into each other. She apologized and he smiled. They entered the kitchen together and Calla asked him, "Did you tell her yet, Mr. Jack?"

"Tell me what?" Elizabeth asked, sitting down at the table.

Jack gave her a mug filled with coffee then poured one for himself.

"It's going to be busy around here for the next few days, Liz. We're hosting a fandango and barbecue roast. I've accepted the hospitality of my friends and neighbors for a few years now, so I figure it's our turn to have them to River Pines."

Elizabeth was puzzled. "A fandango?"

Calla placed two plates of pork chops, eggs, and potatoes on the table. "That's a dance, Miz Liz."

Elizabeth's eyes lit up. "A dance? That's wonderful."

"I'm glad you think so, darlin'." Jack's eyes crinkled in a happy smile. The endearment made Elizabeth's heart beat faster. Then he said, "And I expect you'll be the most beautiful lady at it, too! You'll be meeting ranchers and politicians from the entire area. People from as far away as Pueblo will be coming and staying at neighborhood ranches." His smile was warm when he said, "There's a lot to do, are you up for it?" When she nodded, he said, "Well, let's get ready then."

The inhabitants of River Pines were indeed busy the entire day and all of the next. Beth helped Calla prepare the food that would be served along with a baby steer, which was already being roasted over an open pit. She plucked two turkeys and pared a bottomless barrel of potatoes. They made punch for the ladies, while Jack and some of the men cleaned out the barn.

Elizabeth had just started washing a mountain of pots, pans, and dishes when she heard Rone call her from the courtyard. "Liz, Jack wants you in the barn."

She wiped her hands on her apron and joined him. The sun reflected on his black hair and his smile was relaxed and warm.

"I'm very busy, you know, Rone, with important work," she said, but her smile told him she didn't mind the interruption at all.

"It'll only take a minute, then we'll let you get back to washing the dishes and all your other *important* work," he said leading her toward the barn.

Elizabeth was amazed when she entered the barn. It smelled clean and sweet with fresh hay. Lanterns were hung on the posts to fill it with light once the sun went down, and the long tables— some from the bunk house and some borrowed from neighborhood ranches—were covered with bleached muslin or white linen. Chairs and stools were scattered in little groups in the corners of the building and a makeshift stage was against one wall where the musicians would entertain at the fandango. The floor was immaculate and ready to accommodate the dancing.

In the center stood Jack, hands on his hips, looking extremely pleased with himself. "What do you think?" he asked her.

Elizabeth held back her smile and sauntered around, very deliberately checking to see that all was perfect. Then she turned to him, raised an eyebrow in imitation of Jack, and said, "It looks . . . presentable."

It took Jack a full second to remember that he had made this same statement to her in New York and he threw his head back and laughed. "Oh, it does, does it?"

Elizabeth dropped the pretense then and laughed with him. "It looks grand, Jack. Just perfect. Who would have ever thought the barn could be so attractive. But I think it's lacking something."

Jack's face fell, "What?" He turned to Rone, "Do you think it lacks something?"

Rone shrugged and shook his head no.

Elizabeth giggled. "Flowers, of course. We need flowers on the tables."

Jack hit the palm of his hand on his head. "Flowers . . . of course," and turning to Rone, said, "Flowers . . ."

Rone's arms crossed over his chest when he said, "Of course."

"You gentlemen wait here and I'll be back with them in no time."

Jack called after her as she started for the garden. "You better ask Calla if it's all right, Liz. I don't want my face eaten off when she sees her garden chopped up to bits."

Liz waved and he saw her bend down and break off a red bloom, then a yellow, and soon her hands were filled with a colorful bouquet.

Rone was watching her from behind Jack. "She's very special, Jack."

"I've noticed."

Rone's eyes were troubled when he looked at his friend and Jack saw it immediately. "What's wrong?"

Rone shook the question off and looked back out at Elizabeth. "I think she's fallen in love with you."

A wave of emotion passed over Jack's face. "You're wrong about that, old friend. She's still in love with . . . someone from her home town."

Rone took a few steps forward, still watching the beautiful young woman in the sun-drenched garden. Her hair fell over one shoulder as she leaned down, and her profile was perfect in the light that fell on her face.

Rone turned to look directly at Jack. "The first night I met her, before I . . . got to know her, I told you I thought that you were in this deeper than the last time. I know it now. I know you were hurt before, and I don't want to see that happen ever again, but you'd be a damned fool to deny how you feel just because you're scared."

Looking back out at Elizabeth, who was approaching the barn again, her smile radiant, her arms filled with fresh flowers, he added, "I could be wrong about how she feels about you, but I don't think I am, Jack."

Elizabeth came into the barn and handed each of them a bunch of flowers. "Now divide these up for the tables and I'll go get some vases to hold them." In a moment she was gone again, and the men looked at each other.

"I'm going to town tonight, Jack," Rone said, looking back where Elizabeth was walking away. "I'm not much for fandangos. I'll be back in the morning."

Elizabeth dressed in one of the new dresses she and Calla had sewn while the men were away. It was made of light blue gingham trimmed in white eyelet lace. The neckline was low, the bodice fit tightly to her slender waist and pulled back over a small bustle.

Her fair skin had been tanned lightly by the summer sun, which had also bleached her hair even lighter than its normal shade. The color of the dress and her darkened skin made her eyes appear a bright gray.

When she walked into the living room that afternoon, Jack whistled through his teeth. "Whoa," he said, "you sure didn't disappoint me."

Elizabeth curtsied mockingly. "Why thank you, sir. You yourself look quite handsome."

Jack wore a white shirt, opened at the neck, with a green bandana knotted at his throat. The usual chaps were missing, and she noticed his black leather boots were new and finely detailed. His face was tanned dark, and tiny lines crinkled at the corners of his green eyes whenever he smiled.

He held out his arm to her. "Shall we greet our guests, Ma'am?"

When they entered the barn, the musicians—some of them ranch hands like Barnes, who played harmonicas and fiddles— called out a square dance and Jack took her as his partner, teaching her as they went along. He held her confidently, twirling her, switching partners, then back again, stepping to the caller's words. They laughed breathlessly when it was finished.

Jack introduced Elizabeth as his wife to all the guests and she liked the sound of it. Most of the people she met were genuine and friendly.

However, she sensed hostility from some of the younger women, surmising they had been vying for the attentions of the widowed Jack before Elizabeth had arrived.

This was especially apparent when Elizabeth was introduced to Darla Stuart, the daughter of a wealthy Pueblo rancher. Older than Elizabeth, the woman barely acknowledged her, but turned a radiant smile to Jack.

"It's been too long since your last visit to us, Jack," she said, kissing Jack's cheek and touching his chest in a familiar gesture.

Elizabeth noticed that Jack looked uncomfortable and excused himself to take care of some detail. It was only when he was out of earshot that Darla turned to Elizabeth and said, "Congratulations on your marriage. You are a lucky lady. There are many disappointed women here. I wasn't the only lady dismayed at the news. I'm sure you'll agree he's the handsomest man around."

Elizabeth looked across the room to where Jack stood talking to a group of gentlemen. Whatever he was saying made the group around him laugh, and Jack's eyes caught Elizabeth's and his smile dazzled her. "Yes, my husband is very handsome."

"What a shame," Darla said, looking critically at Elizabeth.

Refusing to acknowledge the insult, Elizabeth motioned to the table filled with food. "Why don't you have a glass of punch, Miss Stuart, while I chat with some of my other guests."

As she crossed the barn, one of the ranch hands stepped up to her and asked her for a dance, and she accepted. They laughed and talked during the reel, which did not go unnoticed by Jack. He deliberately asked a pretty young woman to dance and held her tightly in his arms as they passed Elizabeth. And so the remainder of the evening went, Elizabeth dancing with other men and Jack with other women.

During one dance, when they switched partners, she found herself in Jack's arms again, and it made her smile. His eyes looked down into hers and he said, "Looks like you're a success, Liz."

"I haven't had this much fun in a long time," she told him.

He put his mouth close to her ear and whispered, "Hey, beautiful lady, I'd like to kill each man who dances with you."

She laughed as he twirled her under his arm. "And kiss each woman who dances with you!" With that they were pulled apart and were in other arms again.

While helping Calla to serve the food, they found there weren't enough plates and Elizabeth offered to fetch some from the house.

The night was warm and the sky was filled with stars while the moon shone bright as day. She thought she heard a laugh but saw no one. She stood listening a moment, and hearing the murmur of voices, decided not to investigate for fear of intruding upon a private conversation.

She continued into the house and pulled some dishes from the hutch. The voices drifted through the open window and again Elizabeth peered out into he moonlight but saw nothing. She took the dishes and moved out into the courtyard. This time the voices were stronger.

"What do you mean, you can't?" she heard a woman say. "Remember the last time—the time you came to visit Papa? It was wonderful. I've been waiting for you ever since. Thinking about it excites me. You excite me, Jack."

Elizabeth dropped the plates to the ground and walked behind the shed and looked into the garden. Her heart was pounding in her ears, and she was no longer able to hear the words that were being spoken. She saw them together, Darla Stuart's dress was unbuttoned to her waist, her breasts showing beneath her chemise. Jack's shirt was also unbuttoned, and the black curly hair on his chest was exposed. He held his lover's shoulders against the shed.

A deafening buzz started in Elizabeth's head. She picked up a stone and expertly hurled it across the garden where it slammed against Jack's temple.

Cursing, he grabbed his head and found blood already oozing from the gash. "What the hell . . . ," he started, then saw Elizabeth and pushed the other woman aside. "Liz!"

"I'm sorry," Elizabeth said sweetly, "have I interrupted anything? Please, don't let me disturb you. I thought I heard an animal . . . two actually." Then, in a voice so cold that it sent a shiver up Jack's spine, she continued, "I'll just go back inside and leave you two alone to rut in the garden."

Not bothering to cover herself, Darla touched his arm. "Let her go. I knew the moment I looked at her that you don't have with her what you had with me."

Jack pushed Darla away again. "I told you then and I'm telling you now, there's nothing between us. That was over the same night it began. I don't even like you. Get dressed and go find yourself someone who won't cringe at the sight of you. And don't ever try to create another scene like this again, Darla."

Leaving the astounded woman in the garden, Jack walked toward the house buttoning his shirt and swearing when he found two buttons missing where Darla had torn his shirt open.

Elizabeth was in her room and Calla was knocking on the door, calling, "Miz Liz, what's the matter? Let me in, honey."

Jack walked over and gently pushed Calla back down the hall. "Go to the barn and keep everyone busy. I'll take care of this."

Calla shook her head. "Mr. Jack, I saw her running in here like she saw . . ."

"Just do as I say."

She walked away hesitantly, then left the house mumbling. Jack banged on the door with his fist. "Open up, Liz, before I take this door off its hinges."

"Go to hell!"

"I'm warning you, Liz."

His tone was fierce but Elizabeth felt equal to his anger and flung the door open. "All right, you want to talk, well so do I."

"Shut up until I've finished," he said

"Oh, no, not this time," she said, pushing his shoulder with her finger, her nose stuck up into his face. "How dare you take your whores right here under my nose. What nerve you have. I'll be a laughing stock. You introduce me to the whole state as your wife, then sneak behind the shed with . . . I won't allow . . ."

"You'll allow anything I choose to do on my own ranch," Jack told her, furious now, pacing back and forth around her. "What the hell do you expect me to do? Live like a padre for a year because we have that Goddamned agreement while you pine away for a man who doesn't want you? You flounce around this house, practically naked, and expect me to read a book?"

"I don't flounce around naked, you imbecile, and I expect nothing from you than the whoremonger you are."

"You've learned some pretty fancy language hanging around the ranch hands. I ought to give you a good whippin'."

"Try it—just try it. You'll get as good as you give, Jack Drummond, and don't change the subject. I'm warning you, Jack. Don't you ever try to take another one of your bitches in heat in my house again."

"Whose house? Whose damned house is this? Why you're only here out of the goodness of my heart. I should have let you go to jail in New York. It's what a dirty-mouthed chit like you deserves."

"I wish you had!" she screamed. "Anything would have been better than living here with you!" She finished by spitting in his face and felt gratified when saliva dripped from his eyelid and mixed with the blood from his temple.

Elizabeth was rewarded by the rage that shone in his face, but was bewildered when it subsided quickly and turned to amusement. He studied her a long time, and she couldn't believe it when a smile touched his lips and he leaned casually against her chifforobe and crossed his arms over his chest. His green eyes danced with secret delight.

"I do believe," he drawled, "that the lady is stiff with jealousy.

Elizabeth's mouth opened and she looked murderous. The comment—accompanied by his cavalier behavior—fueled the temper that had already been ignited to a conflagration almost uncontrollable. She wanted to lash out at him but was riveted in place with frustration. Her face puffed out with anger and her eyes narrowed when she snapped, "You wish!"

"No, Liz, *you* wish. You wish it had been you in that garden with me." He was almost laughing and Elizabeth pictured herself scratching his glimmering eyes out—for the simple reason that he was right. She was jealous and wanted to kill him for even looking at that woman. How could this happen to her twice? Why did she have to find the men she cared for in other women's arms? And to make matters worse, to confuse her even more, finding Jack with Darla was much more hurtful.

Tears filled her eyes and Jack's arms fell to his sides and his smile disappeared. He approached her slowly but she backed away from him.

"Have you fallen in love with me?" Jack asked her. "Is it possible, beautiful lady?" He drew closer faster than she backed away and she could feel the warmth of his breath on her forehead as he continued, "Is it possible, Liz? Because if it is, I want to know."

Her throat was dry when she denied it. "Don't be a fool. How could I fall in love with you when you're so hateful to me? You're nicer to everyone else—even your damned cattle."

Jack's hands touched hers and his fingertips brushed up her bare arms toward the eyelet that fluttered at her shoulders. She had a great deal of trouble controlling her breathing and knew Jack was also, from the way humid air puffed against her hairline. Every nerve in her body was pulsating.

Jack's mouth covered hers, and for a moment Elizabeth thought she'd lose control of her legs. Then the image of Darla Stuart, shamelessly bare chested and preening in the garden under Jack's hands, flashed behind Elizabeth's closed eyes and she pushed Jack away and dodged around him.

"Don't touch me, Jack."

His shoulders lifted in a heavy sigh and his eyes hardened from her rejection. "Then you're not jealous?"

She crossed her arms over her chest now, lifted her chin, and huffed, "Indeed, I am not."

"Good," he told her. "Because I'm not sure you're woman enough for me anyway." Jack stripped off his shirt and left the room to enter his own, where he angrily pulled a clean blue shirt from a hook on the wall and began to put it on.

Elizabeth stormed through her bedroom door, across the short width of hallway and into his room. "Is that so? I'm a lot more woman than you've ever had—or will ever have."

Jack adjusted his bandana over his buttoned shirt and looked down at her when he was finished. "You couldn't prove it by me, Liz. Now if you'll excuse me, I'm going to have myself a few more dances with some *real* pretty women."

He left her alone and she slammed the bedroom door behind him, forgetting that it was his room she was standing in. Her fists clenched and unclenched and she kicked the footboard of his bed, crying out when a stabbing pain shot up through her toe. "Damn you, Jack Drummond. I hate you."

She opened the door and entered her own room again and cleansed her face in the cool water from the pitcher. When she was drying it, she caught a glimpse of her reflection in the tiny mirror that hung above her chest of drawers, and wondered if he were right, if she were woman enough for him or any man. Not long ago, in Benton, she was always the most sought after girl in the area. Her dance card was always filled with boys' names, she had numerous callers and always kept them at bay, flirting and impressing them with her wit and intelligence.

What had happened to that girl, she wondered. Had she left the desirable Beth buried somewhere when she became a woman—or had she never become a woman—only an imitation of one that men could easily see through—men like David . . . and Jack.

"Why do I allow him to hurt me?" she asked her reflection. "What do I care who he was with—or what he was doing with her?"

Elizabeth threw herself down on her bed, and brushed her hair, pulling it neatly into a chignon on the back of her neck. When she looked into the mirror again, she was disappointed. Her hands were shaking when she undid her hair, allowing it to fall down her back, fanned around her shoulders.

Straightening her dress, taking a deep breath, knowing that it would not be easy to show her face again, certain that everyone must know about Darla Stuart and Jack, she left her room and headed for the barn.

Jack had been sulking in a corner until he saw her approach. He immediately started to move toward the first available woman to ask for a dance. Too late. Before he could reach the tiny, birdlike girl standing alone watching the other dancers, Elizabeth marched directly to Jack and placed herself in his arms.

"It will look rather odd if you won't dance with me, now, won't it?" she asked when he hesitated.

Without answering, his strong arms guided her onto the dance floor and she never took her eyes from his. They glided across the barn's floor and Elizabeth moved smoothly like liquid against his body. When the music stopped, she placed her hand on the back of his neck and pulled his mouth down to hers and kissed him there in front of their guests.

"You've just danced with the prettiest woman here, Jack," Elizabeth whispered and gave him a smile that she had perfected as a coquette in Benton. She knew it had driven many young men mad and she used it on Jack with perfection.

When she turned away from him, she saw Darla standing by the barn door, red-faced and wild-eyed, and Elizabeth smiled at her, belying the disgust and betrayal she felt inside.

Through the remainder of the evening, Elizabeth sought out and occupied Jack, making it clear to him and everyone else paying attention, that Jack Drummond was hers. That did not prevent her from flirting with and charming every man who came near her.

It wasn't long before Jack made certain he was by her side to stake claim to every dance. Satisfied, Elizabeth thought, *This might be the West, but in the long run the rules of the game are the same, and played right, get the same result.*

During one waltz, Jack asked, "Not that I'm complaining, but what's this all about? I have a feeling I'm about to be stung by a honey of a bee and it's making me damned nervous."

"I'm up to nothing—except to reclaim some of the face you helped me to lose earlier."

"You're playing games with me. Just take care that it doesn't backfire on you, Liz, darlin'." With that his hand moved to the small of her back and he pulled her closer until they were barely moving to the music. Jack nibbled gently on her neck. He felt all the strength ebb from Elizabeth and he held her tighter. "So, you like that, do you?" he whispered into her ear.

Elizabeth stiffened and pulled back slightly. Suddenly the game had turned on her and Jack was making the rules again. A slow, knowing smile creased his face and he kissed the tip of her nose. "You're playing with fire, little girl."

Elizabeth was not to be out done, and her smile matched his. Leaning into him, so that her breasts were close against his chest, she threw her head back and said, "So far, Jack, all I've seen is kindling."

The Stuarts were the first to depart, Benjamin and his wife unsuspectingly bid farewell. The Mannings left with them since the Stuarts were staying at that ranch until morning. Elizabeth thought it served Darla right to have to sleep in the same house with the Manning "babies." Darla tried to smile at Jack, but he ignored her and stood with his arm possessively around his wife, who said good night to Darla with a victorious smile.

Other guests drifted out then, kissing the beautiful young bride and praising her as a hostess, wishing the seemingly happy couple good luck.

It wasn't long before Calla and Jim stood alone in the barn with the Drummonds. The two women began to clear away the plates and food, but Jack walked over to Elizabeth and took her arm.

"Leave it for Calla. We have some unfinished business."

Calla exchanged a knowing look with Jim and Elizabeth saw the gentle black man hide an embarrassed grin. Beth's eyes opened wide and she protested, "I must help . . ."

"You leave it be, Miz Liz. I'll take care of ever'thing. You and Mr. Jack go on to . . . talk. I'll wash these up in my house." Turning to Jack, she added, "No one gonna bother you anymore tonight."

He leaned down and kissed the rotund woman's cheek. "You're pure gold, Calla." Then he pulled Elizabeth from the barn and into the moonlight, his hand holding hers so tightly that no matter how hard she struggled she couldn't pull away.

When they entered the house, Jack extinguished the oil lamps while Elizabeth stood in the center of the living room watching. She wondered what to do, how to escape him, yet she experienced a quiver of anticipation, not quite sure what was about to happen, but certain that something most definitely was.

When the last light was out, with only moonlight illuminating the room through the windows, Jack turned to her and said, "I have never been seduced like that before in all my experience with women."

"Are you trying to tell me that you've changed your mind and have decided that I'm woman enough for you after all?"

Jack smiled. "I guess that's what I'm saying. There's more to it and it's something that I'm afraid neither one of us can handle any longer."

Now Elizabeth shrugged. Once she had thought there wasn't a man alive that would be too much to handle, but that was before Jack.

When she had entered the barn that evening, placing herself in Jack's arms, she had believed her purpose was to prove to herself that Jack could be enticed by her as other men had always been, and to get back some of the pride she had lost when she found him with another woman. Now she wasn't as sure.

"What are we going to do with this—what is it, Liz, passion?—hate?—love?—that's between us. This thing that's tearing us apart one moment and drawing us to one another the next?" Jack was standing near her now. His hand cupped her face and his callused thumb brushed her lips. "Shall I demand you make love to me the way you seemed to promise every time you looked at me tonight . . . every time you molded your body against mine when I danced with you . . . by the way you played with me like the vixen that you are. Shall I take what you held out to me tonight?"

The thought exhilarated her. She longed to taste his intoxicating kisses, to feel his hands on her. Even through her anger earlier, it was always there—this desire that left her trembling and bewildered.

"I think I'll go to bed now," she whispered, turning to leave the room. Jack took her hand and pulled her back. His head came down, his blue-black hair fell on his forehead, while his hand held her face. "I think I will too . . ."

The kiss was just as wonderful as she knew it would be, and with all reserve melted away, she opened her mouth to his and she heard his breath catch in his throat. He pulled away slowly, looking into her eyes, surprised, uncertain that she wanted what he wanted.

"There's something I have to tell you before you go to bed," he said, his mouth inches from hers.

"There is?" she asked, wanting his lips again.

"Yes . . ."

She had them again, warmer, firmer, more demanding this time, then gone again as he pulled away for the second time.

"I should have told you a long time ago, and I apologize for not . . ."

The next kiss lasted longer and tasted better than all the others and it was with great reluctance that she allowed him to pull away from her.

"Whatever it is, Jack, just say it. It's easier if you . . ."

Almost beyond consciousness now, the fourth kiss buckled her knees and she fell into him and he into her. Her lips held onto his this time when he tried to pull away.

"Listen to me, Liz. I need to tell you that . . ."

Her lips crushed his this time. Jack had never known such heady kisses in all his life. He was drowning in her softness, in the sweetness of her mouth. He forgot what he wanted to say while her tongue teased his. Elizabeth's teeth nipped his bottom lip as her head fell back slightly, parting them again.

With great difficulty, Jack inhaled. "I was saying that . . ."

Sweet . . . sweet and wonderful. Warm, guileless and delicious. If only she would stop kissing him long enough for him to . . . "God, Elizabeth, you're beautiful."

Her body molded against his and she breathed, "Is that what you wanted to say?"

The heat that surged through Jack was almost unbearable and he had no idea how he was going to pull away from her and deny himself everything his body and his mind was demanding.

He looked down into her eyes and knew without any doubt that if he said what he had planned, she would be lost to him forever.

"The hell with it . . . ," his arms pulled her against him and still they weren't close enough as he crushed her lips. When he released her, he looked down into her soft, sensuous face and her gray eyes begged for more.

His conscience told him to pull away now before there was no turning back, but before he could, Elizabeth had claimed his lips again in a kiss so passionate and demanding that his control was abandoned once and for all.

He picked her up and carried her to his room. She sought his lips again and again as he glided down the hall and through the door. Once inside, with the door closed, he placed her on her feet and with one last kiss, asked, "Undress for me, Liz."

Suddenly embarrassed, she pulled away.

"It's all right, don't feel ashamed. I've dreamed of it since the first day I saw you. I promise you, there's nothing to be ashamed of."

Elizabeth knew by the loving lights that danced in his eyes that he told the truth and so she undid the buttons of her dress and let it fall to the floor. Her under garments followed and she stood naked before him, while her heart pounded steadily in her chest.

Jack tore his eyes from her beautiful face to look at her body, from her long white neck, to her firm, full breasts, slender hips and shapely legs.

He started to undress and Elizabeth closed her eyes, but he said, "Look at me, Liz." She did as she was told. Her eyes beheld his face, dark with passion and desire for her, but she dared look no farther. He approached her, and taking her in one arm, lowered her onto his bed.

Jack lie beside her. She felt his hands caress her hair and face. He took her in his arms gently and she felt the warmth from the full length of his body against hers. His lips moved from her temple to her eyes and over the bridge of her nose.

She felt his swift tender kisses near her ears and on her neck and shoulders as he traveled lower and lower. His fingertips left burning sensations over her arms as he stroked them softly.

She felt the heat of his breath on the nipple of her breast, and an involuntary sound escaped her. His teeth teased it gently when his hand stroked her thighs in the same manner it had her arms.

Elizabeth tensed when he placed his lips over her mouth as his fingers found her, where she had never been touched before, moving gently in and out and over. She responded, her hands clung to his back and she moaned with the pleasure he was giving her, opening herself to him, accepting all he had to give with his kiss and his gentle, probing fingers.

His leg came over her as he held himself on stiffened arms, careful not to crush her with his weight, and she cried out slightly when he entered her, then relaxed and enjoyed the feel of him inside her.

She met each thrust and felt herself lost in waves of sensations. Unable to bear the sweet, exquisite ache any longer, her legs encircled him, pulling him close against her, and she felt his body shuddering, as her own was doing, right before his weight fell heavily on her. He rolled next to her and took her in his arms again, covering her tenderly with the quilt.

Elizabeth turned toward him and he asked, "Are you all right?" He sensed rather than felt her nod. "I'm sorry we broke our agreement," Jack said with his lips against her hair.

"I'm not," she said into his shoulder. "I didn't know breaking the agreement would feel so good. We should have long ago."

He pulled away from her gentle lips as she began to nuzzle the soft flesh above his collar bone. "Do you mean that?"

Elizabeth nodded. "Yes, Jack, and don't be surprised, because I've wanted this for a long time. I wanted it that night before the cattle drive, but what had happened in New York flooded my mind and I was frightened."

Jack let out a long breath and let his head fall back on his pillow. "What a simple-minded, half-witted excuse of a man I am. I believed you were thinking of David that night, Liz. I was so jealous I couldn't see straight."

Elizabeth teased his mouth with her own while her hand randomly explored his thighs. "Do it to me again," she whispered.

"What?" he asked, stiffening against her investigating fingers.

"All of it—just like before—don't leave anything out."

Elizabeth didn't bother to dress the next morning. She went into the kitchen in her dressing gown. Jack sat at the table drinking coffee and looked up when he heard her enter.

His smile made her blush, for it communicated how much more he knew about her since their intimate night together.

"Good morning," she said, matching his smile and sitting down beside him. Calla beamed when she saw Jack's large brown hand cover Elizabeth's small fair one. "You hungry, Miz Liz?"

Elizabeth answered, still without taking her eyes from his, "Not at all, Calla."

Jack's eyebrows went up and he said, "What's that? Not hungry? You?"

She leaned into him seductively. "My appetites have changed," and was delighted to see him blush this time.

Calla placed a cup of coffee on the table in front of Elizabeth and asked, "More coffee, Mr. Jack?"

"No, thank you, I have to leave in a few minutes."

Elizabeth stopped smiling now, "Leave?"

"I have to wire my father and make arrangements to see him. Then I have some business in Cherryton."

She was disappointed and drank her coffee sullenly, pulling her hand out from under his. How could he leave her, when all she could think about was being with him?

He left the house to saddle his horse, and Calla turned to Elizabeth. "Now, I don't take to interferin' much, but if I was you, I'd go out there and say good-bye right."

Elizabeth nodded and walked out into the courtyard where Jack was leading his horse. His green eyes searched hers and she smiled. "How long will you be gone?" she asked, as they stood facing each other, longing to, but not, touching.

"I'll be late."

Her lips parted as she looked into his eyes, feeling lost in the green lights that glistened there. He swung up onto the black stallion and, looking down at her, touched the brim of his hat, then rode away without looking back.

The day was unbearably long. She helped Calla put the barn back in order. She could see Jack in every corner, smiling, holding out his hand to her, calling her with his eyes.

She tried to recall when she first fell in love with him, for now she knew that her heart had been his for a long time, long before she succumbed to him in the night. Was it the first day here on the ranch, when she rode beside him as he proudly showed her his land; or on the river bank, when he asked her to marry him?

Could it have been in New York, that night she walked into the parlor of the suite and saw him standing there, dashing and elegant; or was it in the Dawson's drawing room, where he looked too large for the dainty furnishings and the fine china cups?

It didn't matter. All that mattered was that she loved him, and it scorched her soul and sharpened her mind.

She never knew her body could be so awake, and sensual excitement filled her again and again, whenever she thought of him, touching her, kissing her, needing her in return.

Elizabeth ate very little all day. She stood watching at the window, willing the sun to go behind the mountain, knowing that he would come to her then . . . in the dark.

When Calla finally left to go to her own little white house, Elizabeth undressed and washed herself in the sweetly scented water from the pitcher in her room. Then she donned Jack's white shirt, the one she'd worn on her first day at River Pines, which she had kept secretly in her chest of drawers.

She was waiting by the door when he rode up. He saw her in the moonlight against the shadows of the house behind her. "What are you doing?" he asked, still astride the impatient black horse.

"Waiting for you . . . always waiting for you."

Jack reached down, took her wrist in his hand, and pulled her up until she was against his chest. The horse galloped with the urgency of Jack's heels, the wind whipping at their faces, over pastures, through the trees, never stopping until halfway into the creek.

They slipped from the saddle and, as the water engulfed them, they embraced, drowning, not in the watery currents that surrounded them, but in each other.

Her loose shirt floated to the water's surface and Jack's hands caressed the soft white flesh of her breasts. She sighed softly against his shoulder. Lifting her in both arms, Jack carried her to the grassy bank. He placed her on its softness, unbuttoned the soaking shirt and exposed her to his hands, his mouth.

He knelt beside her to undress, and the cool night air touched her wet body and she shivered. He noticed and tenderly pulled the wet strands of hair away from her shoulders, her throat, her breast.

She said, "I love you, Jack. I can't bear how much I love you."

Jack lowered his body onto hers, and her hands moved over his back, exciting her with the feel of his muscles tightening and rippling with each thrust inside her. She could hear him cry out as her own body exploded with the pleasure and pain of the release of their long suppressed passion.

They lie still, gradually returning to the surface of consciousness. He started to move from her, but she stopped him. "No, don't. I want to feel your weight on me, your heart beating against mine."

He took each of her hands, entwining his fingers in hers, and held them against the damp ground. Jack looked into her adoring eyes, and Elizabeth saw his own eyes shining with unshed tears.

"You've made the pain go away. All these years I've searched for a balm . . . some kind of nostrum . . . whiskey, work, cattle . . . even women . . . and all the time it was you, Elizabeth Gerard Drummond . . . you are my salvation . . . for in loving you, I can see that I have never loved before."

CHAPTER FIFTEEN

Catherine was standing with an envelope in her hand when Emily walked into the library. The older woman still wore her cloak and hat.

"Aunt Catherine? Glorie said you wanted to see me?"

Catherine looked at her niece. "A letter from Elizabeth. I received it at the bank and hurried home."

Emily's eyes widened. "Thank God. What does it say?"

"I haven't opened it yet. I wanted to be with you."

Emily pulled her aunt to the window seat. "Read it to me."

"Dearest Aunt Catherine and Emily,

"For months I have tried to compose this letter, and have never finished writing it, for I just cannot explain my behavior. I can only imagine how angry and hurt you both must be. There are no words to say how sorry I am.

"My only excuse is immaturity. I allowed Jack to talk me into running away with him, Aunt Catherine. I was foolish and impetuous and wrong to treat you so horribly.

"As Jack explained in his telegram, we are married and living on his ranch here in Colorado. River Pines is very beautiful, and there was much for me to learn when I first arrived. I love it here, though it is very different from Benton. There is so much I wish I could share with both of you.

"I will pray, as I have all summer, that you will find it in your hearts to forgive me. Please believe that I would never deliberately hurt you. I send both of you my deepest love. I miss you desperately.

Your niece and sister,
Elizabeth."

When Catherine finished reading the letter, she looked at Emily, who had turned pale. "What do you think?" Catherine asked her.

Emily shook her head. "I don't know what to think. Will you write to her?"

Catherine folded the letter and replaced it in its envelope. "Yes, I don't believe the story for a moment, and I want her to know that she can return home if she is unhappy."

Emily nodded sadly. "I wonder if he's kind to her. Do you think he is, Aunt?"

Catherine looked out of the window into the garden. "I don't know, dear. Grace tells me he is troublesome. She said his first wife was killed in a riding accident, and he has never been the same since. Yet, David thinks very highly of his cousin, as you know."

Emily sat quietly, thinking about the past months since Elizabeth's disappearance, which had at first frightened her and then had enraged the usually placid girl. Overnight, her life had been changed drastically. Riddled with guilt at first, she longed to be able to explain to Elizabeth what had happened in the garden the night of their eighteenth birthday.

However, as the days wore on, anger replaced some of the guilt, and she was incensed that Elizabeth could be so heartless, leaving without so much as a note to explain where she was going. Emily couldn't bear to see her aunt so distraught with worry and fear for Elizabeth's safety. Many nights, Emily had lain awake vacillating between ire and self-blame.

David had gone to New York after receiving the telegram from Jack that Elizabeth was with him in New York and then had not found her on the coach at the Spread Eagle Inn as Jack had informed him.

It was he who had realized that she had left for Colorado with Jack. He brought the news to Catherine and Emily, asking if they wanted him to pursue the couple to Colorado. Catherine was frantic, but David assured her his cousin would not harm Elizabeth. Eventually Catherine decided to let them alone. Elizabeth would have to find her own way back, if she wanted to. David had agreed, but Emily had strongly opposed this decision.

Even when the telegram from Jack arrived, announcing Elizabeth's and his marriage, Emily was unconvinced.

"She left because of us, David," Emily had cried.

"I don't believe that, Emily. Jack can be very persuasive. She wouldn't be the first woman he's swept off her feet."

Emily knew the truth and said, "She left because she found out we were in love and she couldn't face it. She is my twin, David, *I* know how she thinks. She's not happy, and I believe we've ruined her life."

Emily refused to see David after that, although he came every day, demanding she listen to reason. Blaming her own indiscretion for Elizabeth's running away, Emily wouldn't allow herself any happiness, thinking her sister was miserable. Then, after many days, David stopped coming to the house, and Emily believed he had returned to Philadelphia.

Catherine asked Emily one evening to get a book for her from the library. When Emily walked in, David was waiting, closed the door behind her and leaned against it.

"David . . ."

"Your aunt knows that this has to be settled between us, for all our sakes," he said, taking her in his arms.

"Let me go, David. I have nothing to say to you."

"Well, I do have something to say, Emily. Elizabeth acted like a child. I'm sorry she was hurt, but *we* must go on living . . . and I cannot go on living without you, Darling."

"There can't be anything between us now, David. I would feel that my happiness was at her sake."

David held her very close, and she stopped struggling, allowing him to kiss her. "I love you, Emily."

"Please don't say that," she begged. "Our love would die very quickly under these circumstances." She placed her fingers on his lips, "No, David, don't say anymore. I've made up my mind, and you cannot change it. Go back to Philadelphia and leave me alone."

He let her go abruptly, his anger flaring. "Obviously both twins are headstrong and stupid. So, that is it? It is finished?"

"There never was anything to finish, David."

"Very well, Emily, as you wish. But I will love you my entire life, and you will go on loving me. Don't you see the futility in our being apart?"

She shook her head, tears brimming in her large gray eyes. Then he moved close to her again. "If you should find out that Elizabeth is happy, will you relent and marry me?"

"She isn't."

"I asked if she were, would it change things?"

Emily looked into his warm brown eyes. "If she were truly happy, yes, David, then I could marry you."

David had returned to Philadelphia the next day. She hadn't seen him since. She spent most of her days at the piano, composing. She refused to go out socially, and would attend no functions after Church services on Sundays.

Emily worried incessantly about Elizabeth, and became reticent with her aunt and friends. In time, Catherine worried less about the absent Elizabeth than she did about Emily.

When word of the letter became known, visitors were seen coming and going frequently from the Gleason home, looking for gossip and news of the runaway twin. Grace Dawson was one of the first.

"When I wrote David about the good news, he came right home. He wouldn't take me to call on you today, though. He asked me to tell you," Grace said, turning to Emily, "that he is available at any time, if you would like to speak with him, dear."

Catherine glanced at her niece. "That's very kind of him, Grace. Tell him we appreciate his concern."

"Oh, he is concerned. He's changed since Elizabeth left. As a mother, I can tell you he is extremely unhappy. Of all things, for Elizabeth to have married my nephew. He was untameable as a young man, and I sometimes think he was the cause of my poor sister's death. I do hope he is better humored now, for your Elizabeth's sake. After his first wife died, he . . ."

Emily came to life then. "Mrs. Dawson, what was his first wife like?"

"Kristina Lamond—that was her name—was a beautiful girl, but spoiled. It turned out to be an unhappy marriage to say the least. Now that I think of it, she resembled you, Emily, especially in coloring. But not in the least in demeanor. We didn't know it, of course, when Jack married her, but she had the most shocking morals of any woman I'd ever heard about. She hated Colorado; left after only a few months. She had a terrible accident in Boston—where her family lived. Her death left Jack changed . . . moody, you know."

Emily left the room without another word and Grace shook her head. "What has gotten into these young people? David is just as uncommunicative and unpredictable lately."

An hour later Emily left the house, and Catherine was waiting for her when she returned. "Where did you go?"

"To get a train schedule. I'm going there to see her, Aunt Catherine. I have to see her, to know for certain she is all right."

"When?"

"I'll leave Friday. There's a train from Philadelphia on Saturday."

Catherine sat thoughtfully for several minutes. "Well, if you're going, you are not going alone. Let's pack."

On Friday morning, David stood in the foyer of the Gleason home and argued with Emily. "I'm going with you. My carriage is waiting outside to bring us to Philadelphia, with my bag on it, and I'm going. This time, *you* will not change *my* mind."

"David, I really don't think it is wise to . . ."

"If she's unhappy, then we'll bring her home together and I'll leave you alone once and for all. But if Elizabeth is happy, Emily, we will be married within twenty-four hours."

Catherine stood halfway down the staircase, a valise in her hand. "Actually, David, you will be most welcome to accompany us," she said, firmly, looking at her niece.

The sign hanging from the eaves of the station building announced that they were in the town of Ogallala. *At least two more days,* Catherine thought with a sigh. She looked at the map in her hands that indicated the Union Pacific route and she counted the towns they would still pass through.

The trip was dragging on unbearably, and she almost wished she had turned back in Chicago. The relentless rocking of the car and the clacking of the wheels on the endless tracks made her head ache.

"Catherine," David said, as he leaned over to her and took her hand in his, "shall we get off and stretch our legs a little? There won't be another stop for quite awhile."

She looked over at Emily, whose lovely profile was silhouetted against the window. The girl had been lost in her own thoughts throughout most of the trip. Try as he did, David couldn't seem to reach her, for she had enclosed herself in a cloak of worry and guilt.

"What do you say, Emily?" Catherine asked her niece.

Slowly Emily's face turned toward her, and Catherine knew by the dark circles beneath her eyes that she, too, was travel-worn and weary. "Whatever you'd like, Aunt Catherine. I suppose it would feel good to move around."

Her lovely gray eyes moved up to David's face. Catherine winced at the longing and hurt she saw in the glance

they exchanged. She wanted to scold them for being so foolish as to allow others—namely, Elizabeth and Jack—to cause
them such pain. She had an urge to admonish them for their
own stupidity and tell them to grow up. Instead, she silently
stood to leave.

The three of them went to the door of the car and Emily descended the metal steps easily while holding the hand of the conductor. Catherine gripped the bar and could feel the cold of the
metal through her black glove as her other hand extended to the
conductor for assistance.

Before she had taken another breath, her foot slipped out and
her hand missed the conductor's, and with a great swish, she fell
onto the splintered wood of the station's platform, a pile of blue
serge and silk petticoats.

"Aunt Catherine!" Emily cried, throwing herself next to the
unconscious woman.

"Don't move her, Emily," David said as he jumped over
Catherine in order to reach the platform. He and the conductor
administered to Catherine quickly. Other passengers milled
about, whispering and asking what had happened. The station
master came out and asked David what he could do.

"Where's the doctor in this town? I think she's hit her head
on the step."

"Is she hurt anywhere else?" the conductor asked, looking at
Catherine's legs and arms. "It doesn't look as if she's broken anything, but her ankle is swelling."

Emily took her aunt's hand. "Oh, David, help her. Please help
her."

"Don't worry, darling. She'll be all right."

Several men had gathered around them now, "The Doc's office ain't far from here. No reason we can't just carry her over,"
one of them said.

"I'll carry her myself." David lifted her into his arms. "Show
me where to go."

Emily picked up her aunt's hat from where it had fallen on
the platform, and hurried after the group. One of the men held
her elbow as they stepped off the boardwalk and into the soft
dust of the street. "You be careful, Miss. These cowboys ride
them horses too fast in this crowd."

Emily wanted to smile at the solicitous old man, but she was
distracted with worry. The doctor was just coming out of the
building when the entourage from the station approached. He
opened the door to his office and motioned to a table where

David could place Catherine. Emily ran to her aunt's side and touched the older woman's forehead.

The doctor pulled open one of Catherine's eyelids to look more closely. He hurriedly examined her, making sure there were no broken bones. He felt behind her head and nodded.

"Here's the bump. I'd say she hit her head on somethin' pretty solid."

"It was the train step."

The doctor smiled. "That'd do it."

"Will she be all right?" Emily asked him.

"I'd like to think so, Miss, but head injuries are hard to judge. There could be bleedin' on the brain. I'd say she's got to have a concussion for sure." Then he smiled reassuringly and patted Emily's hand. "Now don't fret so much. We'll watch her real close. Are you her daughter?"

"Her niece."

David put his arm around Emily's shoulders. "We're traveling to Denver, Doctor."

Just then, Catherine's delicate eyelids fluttered slightly and Emily grasped her hand tighter. "Aunt Catherine, are you all right? Can you open your eyes, dear?"

Catherine did so and stared vacantly at the room's ceiling. The doctor spoke softly. "You had a hell of a fall, Ma'am. Can you see all right?"

Catherine turned her head in his direction and looked at the whiskered old man. His shirt sleeves were rolled up and his hair touched a frayed, though immaculate, collar. She closed her eyes and opened them again to see a pale and tearful Emily looking over her, with David's worried and intense face behind Emily's.

Catherine tried to smile, and found she couldn't. Her head throbbed painfully and she was disoriented. She wanted to ask them what had happened and where she was but couldn't seem to speak at that moment.

"I think she's just shook up," the doctor said. "Isn't that right, Ma'am?" He took his finger and held it in front of her eyes. "Can you follow this?" he asked moving it to one side and then the other. She followed his movement. He smiled and patted her shoulder. "You two young people go out and get yourselves something to eat while I check this lady over. We'll have something more to talk about then."

Emily looked astounded. "No, I couldn't leave her."

"This is my office, young lady, and I'm in charge. You just do as I say and stop worryin'."

He led them to the door and out onto the wooden platform beyond. "The food at Greene's Hotel is passable," he said. "Come back when you're done eating."

"But the train . . . ," David started, but the door had closed already.

"What do we do now, David?" Emily asked.

"We'll got find out when the next train comes through, then we'll get rooms at the hotel and have some of that passable food the doctor told us about."

David looked down at Emily, whose eyes were clouded with worry. She looked vulnerable and lost, and his chest tightened with a combination of love and frustration. He touched her cheek with the back of his finger. "It'll be all right, love. I'll make it all right."

She turned her cheek toward his touch and closed her eyes a moment. "Oh, that you could, David."

CHAPTER SIXTEEN

From atop the summit of a foothill, Jack looked at his land, which was tinged in the warm colors of early autumn. The trees were becoming illuminated with crimson, gold, and purple, while the slopes and valleys were still covered with a lush, green velvet blanket of grass.

Jack had never worked harder or had ever been happier. For the first time in his life, he had everything he ever wanted.

The black stallion beneath him stamped at the ground. Jack patted his neck. "Okay, boy, just a few more minutes. Let me look one more time," he said, squinting against the sunshine. Then the horse moved slowly down the hill, and Jack could see Elizabeth riding toward him. Though she was far in the distance, he could see her prized white hat crowning her golden hair.

His heart beat faster watching her approach. Within minutes they'd pull up their horses, and Liz'd flash her gray eyes at him. It would be hard to resist grabbing her and kissing her perfect mouth.

Each reunion they had now, no matter how short a time they were apart, was a sweetness he looked forward to, made all the more exciting knowing she would respond to him with the same passionate need he felt for her.

Jack loved to watch Elizabeth ride the bay—two wild creatures, pretending to be reigned in, but ready to lope at a moment's freedom. He had laughed until tears glistened in his eyes when Rone had told him about the day she broke that horse, and he knew the look in her eyes as Rone described them, the determination, the fearlessness. He'd seen it often enough, and although it was very frequently the reason for argument and frustration between them, he always felt a hearty respect for it.

Elizabeth let the bay dance around the stallion a moment, with her lips pulled into a devilish grin, her silver-gold hair blowing around her shoulders and chin. Jack stilled the black horse and nonchalantly pushed his hat back on his head. *Let her have her little ritual dance*, he thought, his eyes looking at her, through her, into her soul. She met his look and knew what he was thinking, and she laughed, throwing her head back, showing the delicate length of her neck.

"You're not much better than a saloon girl," he said, shaking his head.

Elizabeth pulled the bay around now so that it was next to the stallion and her thigh brushed against his. "Ah, but I'm much more, Mr. Drummond," she said, seductively, "Much, much better. For I'm yours alone and from what I understand, that's a very heady thing for a man, even one like you."

"Shall we go for a swim?" he asked, his voice matching hers. "It's still warm enough."

"Tempting as it may be, sir, I'm afraid it will have to wait. Rone needs you back at the house."

Jack's gaze went into the direction where the white smoke curled up from Calla's chimney. Elizabeth put her hand on his, wishing she could feel his skin rather than be separated by the leather of her gloves.

"Later, darling, I'm always here for you, no matter when."

He looked back at her and smiled warmly. "I know," was all he said, but it was like an embrace.

They rode side by side to the courtyard and when they reached the barn, Jack took the reins of her horse. Their lips touched briefly with a promise of what they would share later, then he went into the barn where Rone was waiting for him.

Jack knew immediately that there was something wrong by the look on his friend's face. Rone held two letters in his hand.

"Trouble?" Jack asked, taking the envelopes.

"I'm not sure. They were in town when I picked up the supplies," Rone answered.

Jack opened the first envelope, which was from Benjamin Stuart.

"Jack,

"Would appreciate your making plans to visit me at your earliest convenience. There is much to discuss.

"Be advised that I have spoken to Darla, and I am prepared to support your decision.

"Ben Stuart"

Jack handed the letter to Rone, who read it casually, then asked, "What's this about?"

"I'm wondering the same thing," Jack said, as he opened the second envelope, knowing it was from Darla by the feminine script.

"My darling,
    "I believe I have finally devised a way to release you from that loveless marriage and free you to come to me.
    "I have already executed part of the plan, but I must speak with you personally about it."

Jack looked up at Rone, his eyes like slivers of ice, then continued reading:

"Never before have I known such heartache. Oh, Jack, I know you have said our love affair is over, but in my heart, I cannot believe it, especially now, when I need you most. Come as soon as possible. I will explain everything then. If you delay, I will be forced to come to you at River Pines.

Forever,
Darla"

Rone could feel the tension mounting in Jack while he finished reading the letter. He wasn't surprised when Jack threw it to the barn floor.

"She's insane," Jack hissed.

Rone picked it up and read the letter. A grin touched his lips.

"I'm glad you find this amusing, Rone."

"When will you leave?" Rone asked him.

Jack swore and spat into the hay. "I've a mind not to acknowledge them at all, but she's just crazy enough to show up here with dear old Papa. That's the last thing I want right now. I'd like to know what it is she's cooking up and stop it before it goes too far. Something tells me it isn't going to be easy to fix."

"None of your saddle biscuits are, Jack," Rone said.

Jack spun around to look at him. "I didn't ask for this. That one night I spent with her was the sorriest of my life—and the most boring."

Rone shrugged, this time looking out toward the house. Jack followed his gaze when Rone said, "Liz will know."

"It isn't likely. I won't mention the Stuarts. I'll tell her it's business. I'll be back before she can find out."

Rone shook his head. "She'll know. You better tell her."

Jack wondered how his friend could almost predict trouble. He seemed especially in tune with Elizabeth these days, just as he had always been with Jack and, at times, Jack's father.

Elizabeth and Calla finished preparing the noon meal when Jack came in and sat down heavily in his chair. He hadn't decided whether to tell Elizabeth about the letters or not. He knew Rone was probably right, but then, when he looked at the pretty smile Liz gave him, he decided not to say anything that might take that smile away.

"Mr. Jack, you look done in," Calla said, dishing out chicken and potatoes in a creamy sauce. Elizabeth brought a bowl of steaming peas to the table and sat opposite him.

"What's wrong, Jack?" she asked, her eyes searching his.

"I'll have to leave today to take care of some business in Pueblo."

Elizabeth was disappointed and he tried an unconvincing smile. He said to her, "I won't be gone too long."

"May I come?" she asked him.

His face hardened for a moment. "No!"

She felt as though she had been slapped, like a naughty child.

"No, Liz," he said more gently, "I'll travel better without you."

They both started eating silently now. Elizabeth tried to think why Pueblo sounded so familiar and why he would be going there. She felt uneasy and suspicious because of his mood. Then, suddenly, she remembered the significance of Pueblo. Putting her fork down, she asked, "Isn't Pueblo where the Stuart's ranch is?"

Jack's eyes glanced up at her and then down again at his food. He didn't answer.

"Jack?" she persisted.

"Yes, as a matter of fact, it is."

"Why are you going there?" she wanted to know, keeping her voice very calm.

He kept eating and then, after finishing the last forkful of food from his plate, he stood up and looked down at her face, which had lost its lovely smile, after all. "Business, as I said before."

"What kind of business?"

"Damnit, Liz, I told you, I have business there. What are all these questions about?"

She stood up now. "You're acting awfully tense—no, not tense—perhaps guilty is a better word."

Calla left the house unnoticed.

"What would I have to be guilty about?"

She turned away and walked to the window. Everything had been so wonderful since the first time they had made love. She never knew she could love anyone the way she loved Jack.

He was a fever in her and she couldn't get enough of him. Whenever they were together, in their room, or sitting quietly watching the fire, or playing in the creek like children, then making love on its bank, day after day, night after night, she thought she would burst with the sheer pleasure of it.

Yet, sometimes when Elizabeth let her guard down, she'd picture him as she had seen him in the moonlit garden, his shirt open, his hands caressing Darla's shoulders, and Elizabeth would seethe inside. Afraid of knowing the truth, she would not mention it to Jack, and although hard to squelch, she would bury the memory down deep and try to forget it.

She succeeded most of the time, but now, with pangs of uncertainty, the obscenity of what she had seen played out in her mind. Jack's mood was so strange, she was certain Darla had something to do with this trip to Pueblo.

She turned to look in his eyes. "Are you going to see Darla, Jack?"

He returned the gaze and then looked away quickly. "Of course not," he said.

"You're lying. Oh, Jack, you are actually lying to me."

His face turned red. "Elizabeth," he started.

"Was this all part of the plan, Jack? Your unfailing plan to keep me here for a year? You're smooth, Jack Drummond. You declare love for me, knowing that I love you, then make love *to* me over and over again, and when you think I'm solidly in place, you go to her, believing, of course, that your faithful, besotted wife will be waiting with open arms when you return."

"That's not true, Liz," he told her.

"Well, Jack, go to her. Go to your old lover. Then come back and see if I'm here."

"Liz," he said, almost pleadingly, "I'm not . . ."

"Don't waste time," she said, devastated, and brushing by him, slammed the door of the bedroom she had first inhabited when she arrived.

Jack hit the table with his hat and knocked a plate to the floor, where it smashed to pieces. He stormed out of the house, mounted the stallion, and raced away from River Pines.

The September sun was strong and the afternoon was warm as Elizabeth lie on her bed staring at the beamed ceiling, dried tears streaking her cheeks. Her thoughts were chaotic and her emotions were raw. Knowing that Jack was on his way to Darla, Elizabeth had one thought that formed again and again in her mind throughout the rest of the day and night. *I have to go home.*

The next morning, Calla knocked on the door, "Miz Liz?" she called.

"Come in, Calla," Beth said quietly.

"I got a letter here for you, Miss Liz . . . ," Calla stopped speaking when she saw that the younger woman was packing. Miz Liz, what you doin'? You ain't goin' to leave?"

"I have to, Calla. You don't understand how important it is for me to get away from here, away from him." She continued to pack.

"Now, Miz Liz, you can't do it. I ain't never seen Mr. Jack so happy and I know you are, too. There's never been so much laughter and lovin' around this ranch as there has been the last few weeks. Even Rone is whistlin' and smilin' more."

"I can't stay," Elizabeth said with finality.

Calla shook her head and Elizabeth could see she was very angry. "This is wrong, Miz Liz. You can't go. It's just a little spat you've had. You can't just leave him like . . ."

Then remembering why she had come to Elizabeth's room, Calla held out an envelope. "You got a message today. Jim's brought it from town."

Elizabeth looked up from her packing and took the envelope. She read her name—her married name—written in the sloping handwriting she knew well.

"Calla, it's from my sister. She's written me!"

Receiving no answer from the still angry woman, she sat on the bed and opened the envelope. Tears sprung immediately to her eyes when she read the salutation aloud, "My lovely sister."

Elizabeth studied the words and read certain parts to Calla. "'I cannot begin to tell you how much we've missed you,'" Elizabeth read aloud, then looking up, she said, "They aren't angry with me, Calla."

She continued reading silently, then, coming to her feet, she read out loud, "'I must see you. That is why I'm sending this note with Jim, to ask you to meet me here in Cherryton as soon as you can. Please, Elizabeth come to me, or let me come to you.'"

Elizabeth looked at Calla, "She's here? In town? Calla, my sister is here! Jim must go and get her at once. Hurry, hurry, tell Jim . . . no, wait, I'll get Emily myself. Tell Jim to get the wagon ready . . . how did he know she was my sister? . . . oh, it doesn't matter, I'll ask him later. Go get him. Hurry, Calla."

The portly woman walked down the hall shaking her head and smiling. In the confusion, Miz Liz seemed to have forgotten about leaving Mr. Jack, and that was fine. Maybe a visit from her kin would solve this new problem. Calla's face lit up with the thought. "Thank the Lord," she said.

The buckboard pulled up in front of the hotel and Elizabeth jumped down without waiting for Jim's help. She walked from the bright sunshine into the dimly lit lobby. Just as she entered, Emily appeared on the stairs. The sister's eyes met; there they stood, ten feet apart, not knowing what to do. Then they fell into each other's arms, crying and laughing.

Emily took Beth's face in her hands. "Oh, Beth, you look beautiful."

Beth cried, "I've missed you so much. I'm sorry, Emily."

"Sh, it's all right. We have to talk. There is so much to explain."

"Later, I just want to look at you and touch you and know that you are really here," Elizabeth said.

Emily took Beth's hand. "Let's go up to my room where we'll have some privacy."

They ascended the stairs and Emily led the way into her tiny room. Alone, the girls embraced once more. "It's so very good to be with you again, Emily," Elizabeth said, her voice heavy with tears.

Emily searched her sister's face. "How are you, Beth? Are you happy here?"

Elizabeth turned away. "Of course," she said.

Then their eyes met again and Elizabeth could see she had not convinced her twin. "At this moment, Emily, I am anything but happy. Everything has become awful. I hate him."

She covered her face and cried. Emily went to her. "I was afraid of this. Grace Dawson told us he had a violent temper and stormy moods. She said he had had an unhappy marriage and . . ."

Elizabeth looked up, "You know about his first wife?"

"Yes. Apparently, from what Aunt Catherine and I could discern, she was unfaithful to him. She was killed in a riding accident while visiting in Boston, but, of course, you know all this."

"No, I don't know much at all, Emily. I know that she was beautiful because I saw a painting of her, and that's all. Do you know any more?"

Emily shook her head. "Not really. Mrs. Dawson did say that her death seemed to twist his personality. We were concerned and frightened for you. That's why we've come. We had to see for ourselves that you were all right."

"We?" Elizabeth asked.

"Yes, Aunt Catherine and I . . . and David. Let me start from the beginning."

Emily told Elizabeth what had transpired from the time they had received her letter. She told her of David's insistence on accompanying them, and how long and arduous the trip had been, and finished with Catherine's accident.

"She has a concussion and a sprained ankle, and the doctor insisted she not be moved until he was certain she was all right. Her ankle is very painful and he said it would take days to heal. I couldn't wait days to see you. I insisted they let me continue on, although David was quite upset. I wouldn't let him leave Aunt Catherine alone in a strange town, disabled and ill."

Elizabeth took her sister's hands, "You're in love with David, aren't you?"

The question made Emily redden and she started to deny it, but Elizabeth put her finger to the other girl's lips. "You can't deny it, Em. I recognize it too well. All that happened seemed so long ago, and I've had time and reason to look back and relive it in my mind. In doing so, I can understand that you have loved him much longer than I ever thought I did.

"What I felt for David was a deep fondness—a girl's being 'in love'—but nothing of what a woman really feels. You, Emily, felt a woman's love for him. I have asked myself over and over how it was that I didn't see it. In your selflessness you denied yourself that wonderful love . . . and David must have loved you as much."

She stood up and walked to the window. "Am I so selfish and shallow, Emily, that I cannot see what is going on around me? It seems the truth just eludes me, over and over."

"No, Beth, not selfish, and not ever shallow. You are just so full of life. You have always been excitement and happiness personified. That is probably why I could never tell you how I felt about David. I was afraid to see that shining light dimmed, even a little."

Emily crossed the room and stood close to her sister, "Is he very mean to you, Beth? Does he hurt you . . . hit you?"

"No, not that. He's not twisted, as Grace Dawson said."

"And the ranch?" Emily asked.

"I love it there. Life is so different and so wonderful. Sometimes I don't know how I managed to live not knowing Calla and Jim and their sons. And there's Rone who is a wonderful friend."

"I know Jim, and he is wonderful," Emily said smiling. "Did he tell you how we met? It took me fifteen minutes to convince him that I was not you. He was exceedingly upset that you were in town alone, without his knowledge, and it was only after I had him standing with a letter from me to you in his hands that he relaxed. Although, I believe, he still thought he was dreaming."

The young women laughed, then Elizabeth explained, "Calla is his wife. They tend the ranch for Jack. I've never tasted food the way Calla prepares it, and try as she will, she just can't seem to teach me. In the beginning, when Jack first brought me here, I thought I would die of loneliness for you and Aunt Catherine and Glorie, but Calla got me through it. She's become very dear to me."

"You mentioned someone named Rone," Emily questioned.

Elizabeth smiled. "He's Jack's—and now my—dearest friend. Rone's changed me, and you'd be shocked to see how. I can stalk a deer without it even knowing I'm near. I can shoot a rifle like a man, and use a knife like an Indian. I am truly a rancher's wife," and her eyes filled with tears again.

"You are deeply troubled, Beth. I can feel it in my own soul."

"I have to go home . . . forget all this, if it's possible."

"Of course, we'll leave on the next train to Cheyenne and then on to Ogallala. We'll all travel back together."

Elizabeth shook her head. "It isn't that simple, Em. As a matter of fact, I was planning to leave him today, but . . ." she thought of River Pines and all the people on it whom she loved and how Jack's father would sell it if she were to leave Jack. "I have to stay on the ranch for another eight months, then I can get a divorce."

"A divorce?"

"It's difficult to explain. Everything is so complicated."

"How can I help you?"

"You can't," Elizabeth said sadly. Then, in afterthought, her face brightened and she said, "Maybe you can. Oh, no, it's preposterous . . . but it could work, just for a short time."

Elizabeth paced around the little room ignoring her sister's demands to tell her what she was planning. Finally, she smiled, "Em, do you really want to help me?"

"Yes, you know I do."

"Will you take my place? Pretend you are me?"

"Are you insane, Elizabeth?" Emily said, alarmed and walking to the other side of the bed, as if to protect herself from her twin.

"Maybe, Em, but not as insane as I will be if I don't get away from the ranch for awhile. I need to think . . . to figure out what I'm going to do."

"Is it so bad? Yet you want *me* to go there?"

When Elizabeth realized how upset Emily was becoming, she said soothingly, "No, Emily, it won't effect you the same way. As I've said, it's complicated, but you wouldn't be in any danger."

"Beth, you're married to this man. What if he expects me to . . . you know, share his bed?"

Elizabeth sat down again. "He knows I'm furious with him, and knows that there is something between us now that will forbid that. You must avoid him. Naturally, you can always tell him the truth. But don't . . . unless it's absolutely necessary."

"We can't do this, Beth. It just won't work."

Elizabeth looked dejected. "You're right, I suppose. It's too much to ask you to do for me, even for a short time."

Emily sat beside her sister on the bed. "How short?"

"Just until I can get myself together and sort out my feelings. I need to see Aunt Catherine. I need to be away without Jack really knowing. Someday, I'll explain why."

Emily concentrated on her hands a long time. She said, "I'll do it, Beth."

Elizabeth threw her arms around Emily. "It'll work, I promise."

Emily shook her head. "I hope so. I certainly hope so."

The sisters made plans and rehearsed their stories. Emily filled Beth in on what had been happening at home while Elizabeth was away. That was the easy part, as Elizabeth knew the people and could easily imagine the comings and goings in Benton.

Emily was at a disadvantage as she had never seen the ranch or known the people there. If she were to pretend to be a member of the ranch, she would have to know each person by name—recognizing them by description only.

Elizabeth made sketches and mapped out the ranch so that Emily would be more familiar with it. They decided Emily would feign illness and put herself to bed for much of the time. The one person she would have a real problem with would be Calla. That would be difficult, but not as difficult as Jack.

"At all lengths, Em, you must act angry with him. Be as unreasonable as possible. He's easily angered himself, and will storm off to lick his wounds. If he thinks you are ill, you know with your monthly, he'll leave you alone. Men are like that. Don't get into any conversations with him if you can help it. They will just confuse you."

Emily saw Elizabeth blanch. "I forgot Rone. He's supposed to leave today. I said good-bye this morning, but if he should return to the ranch, stay as far away from him as possible. Somehow I feel that he would be able to sense something's amiss better than anyone there."

Emily groaned and put her head down on her pillow. "I'll never be able to carry this off, Beth."

"You must, Em, for my sake and my sanity."

They decided to switch places the next day.

Jack was riding south, following the Goonight Loving Trail toward Pueblo. He had been riding hard, but the stallion galloped smoothly beneath him, showing little sign of the fast pace being forced upon it. Jack's eyes were narrow and his jaw was set in an angry grimace.

The horse came to a wide, shallow stream, and Jack stopped so that the animal could drink and rest. He dismounted and climbed on a boulder, taking off his hat so that the setting sun could warm his face.

Jack tried not to think about his argument with Liz, but it was impossible. To add to his irritation he wondered what he was about to face at the Stuarts.

Darla had turned out to be the most conniving woman he'd ever known—except for Kristina. He wondered why his life was plagued with unstable, unpredictable, selfish women, and Elizabeth was no exception.

Damned her unreasonable little mind, he thought about Liz. He pictured her standing in the kitchen, flinging accusations and insults at him. *How in the name of all that's holy can she think I'd be going to another woman?*

Ever since the first night they had made love, he had professed his love for her. Could she really think him so callous as to believe he was lying? He had never loved anyone the way he loved Elizabeth. He gave everything he had and held back nothing, even in their bed.

It was impossible not to, for she demanded it. Jack had never known lovemaking like it with anyone else—virgin or whore. It was as if he was fresh off his father's ranch, making love for the first time whenever he took Liz. Her sweet, passionate embraces brought sensations to Jack he'd never experienced before. He became lost in her eyes and excited as her voice grew heavy with sensuality.

Jack smiled to himself when he thought, *and she never has enough.* He had no idea what he was awakening in her when he took her to his bed that night of the fandango. *It has been a pleasant surprise, I'll say that.*

It occurred to Jack now that maybe it was because she was in love with him that made all the difference. More importantly, maybe it was because *he* was truly in love with *her*.

It gave him a certain pleasure to know how jealous she was. It occurred to him now that Elizabeth had a right to be suspicious after what she'd seen in the garden that night. He had never explained to her that Darla had stood behind the shed, waiting for him with her dress unbuttoned, and called as if in trouble when she saw Jack leave the barn. He didn't think he'd need to explain anything about Darla once he made sure Elizabeth knew he loved her.

Now he was sorry that he hadn't shown Liz the letters he had received. He should have been honest and explained the story to her. Perhaps he should have brought her with him to convince Darla just how serious he was about his marriage. Instead he had left the ranch, letting Elizabeth think there was more to his relationship with Darla.

It's not too late. Jack mounted his horse and turned it around, riding nonstop through the night until he reached River Pines the next morning, only to find that Emily Gerard had arrived to reclaim her sister.

When he barged into the house shouting Elizabeth's name, and was told by Calla that she was in town visiting her sister, his blood turned cold. He had been afraid that it would happen, a visit from a penitent Emily, full of guilt and contrition, denying her love for David, and giving Elizabeth her blessings to return to him.

Jack knew human nature well enough to know that the naive Elizabeth might have mistaken her carnal passion for Jack as love, and in the long run, she might feel the need to pursue her first love, the love she had run away from.

All at once, Jack realized things had been going too well in his life. It had been almost too good to be true, and Jack admonished himself for becoming too content. He had broken his one rule—not to trust in life again.

On the way back to the ranch that evening, Elizabeth sat next to Jim and considered the situation. She was excited and afraid all at once. She made a mental note of the things she might have forgotten to tell Emily, things her sister would need to know, and the whole idea worried her suddenly. How could she have concocted such a scheme? Then she thought of Jack, and where he was, and the anger flared up in her all over again. It's what he deserves, she thought, deception for deception.

As they approached the ranch, Elizabeth was dismayed when she saw Jack's stallion tied up at the corral. "Damn," she said aloud.

"What's that, Miz Liz?" Jim asked.

"Nothing. I don't feel very well, is all," she answered.

When Elizabeth entered the ranch house, Jack was in the living room and she prepared herself for a confrontation. Calla greeted her pleasantly, but whispered, "He's in a bad way, Miz Liz. Step careful."

Elizabeth took a deep breath and headed for the room where Jack sat staring into the cold fireplace. "You're home then?" she asked haughtily.

"Sit down, Liz, we need to talk."

"I've nothing to say," she answered, glaring at him as she had done so often in the past, before they were lovers.

"I said sit down," he shouted.

"You're in quite a mood," she said, sitting across from him. "Wasn't Darla home?"

He ignored her remark. "Look, I want you to know that I wasn't with her or any other woman."

"This time," she hissed.

Jack rubbed his fingers across his forehead in frustration, then leaned forward, his voice calmer now. "Liz, you know how I feel about you. How can you think . . . after what is between us . . . that I . . . ?"

Elizabeth stood up and walked away. "I wish I could believe you," she said over her shoulder, "but I don't."

Jack's voice was low and cold when he said to her back, "Did you have a nice visit with your sister?" When she stopped but didn't turn around to face him, he continued, "Why didn't you bring her back here with you?"

Elizabeth was quiet for a long moment. "Yes, I had a nice visit with my sister. She didn't wish to stay here."

Jack was leaning back in the chair again, and her hands started trembling when she looked at him and recognized the old sneer—the one that had vanished all those days they were lovers—and the cold-blooded look in his eyes. "Is all forgiven?" he wanted to know.

"We explained everything to each other."

"Everything? Even *New York*?" When his words reached her, she felt as if she had been struck. She couldn't speak.

Jack's deathly calm voice went on. "Your anger over Darla Stuart is quite convenient now that all has been pardoned at home. I recognize the cold reception, your indignation. Your sister has told you that she has nothing to do with David, and now you plan to go back to him, Liz, don't you?"

Elizabeth swallowed hard. It was true in a unique way, but how could she explain?

"Isn't that it?" he demanded. "Well, isn't it?"

She turned to go to her room, but he lunged across the room and grabbed her arm. "I'll kill you first, Liz. I'll not have my wife in another man's arms."

Elizabeth slapped his cheek as hard as she could, and stepped back. "I'm not her, Jack Drummond. I'm not your first wife, the one who had other men, not that I blame her . . ."

Elizabeth knew before she began, that this was the one thing she could say to hurt him, and she wanted to hurt him. She had not expected his reaction, however, when, instead of anger and protestation, he looked beaten and ill.

She was immediately sorry, knowing she had touched some unhealed wound that festered in him, an anguish that this strong, capable man could not seem to overcome. She reached out to touch him, but he flinched and backed away.

His voice was thin when he said, "You were right, Elizabeth. We have nothing to say to each other." He turned and walked from the house through the kitchen. Elizabeth started to follow him, but stopped when she saw the accusing, pain-filled eyes of Calla staring at her.

In the morning, she found Calla quietly sewing in the kitchen. The late September morning was chilly and Calla had a shawl pulled over her shoulders. She didn't smile when Elizabeth walked in. Beth felt heavy with guilt. "Good morning," she tried.

"There's coffee in the pot," Calla said.

Elizabeth poured herself a mug of the rich dark liquid and sat down near Calla. "Where is . . . everyone?" she asked.

Calla did not look up from her sewing. "They's got things to do, I guess. Jim's gettin' the buckboard ready for your trip back to town." Looking up for the first time, she added, "Mr. Jack's left."

She said it so casually, Elizabeth wasn't sure she had heard correctly. "Left?"

"He tol' me he won't be back for a few days. He looked terrible when he went, Miz Liz."

She put the sewing down and looked deeply into Elizabeth's eyes. "I hope you know what you're doin'. He's a good man, and he been hurt plenty already. What you said last evenin' wounded him good."

Elizabeth looked down at her hands. "I'm not leaving him, Calla. He'll get to keep his ranch." Then looking up, tears stinging her eyes, she added, "What else do you want from me?"

Calla was angry, though her voice was still soft. "Seems a wife should trust her husband."

Elizabeth felt her throat ache with tears at this reproach from Calla. Admittedly, she was cruel the evening before when she brought up Jack's first wife to him. She didn't know the whole story and had no right to mention it.

Yet, throughout the night, as she had drifted in and out of a restless sleep, Elizabeth tried to believe he had not been going to Darla Stuart, but she had seen the truth in his eyes when she had asked him directly the day before.

Elizabeth had waited for him to come to her in the night, so that they could talk, and when he didn't, she decided the situation was beyond correcting. It was not her fault, as Calla seemed to believe, but Elizabeth knew that Calla's loyalty to Jack would not allow her to accept he was wrong this time.

Elizabeth's argument with Jack, and the fact that Calla was angry with her, reinforced her need to leave the ranch for awhile. She needed time to think, to sort out her feelings.

Elizabeth looked down at the smooth brown skin on Calla's face that showed no sign of her age or the years she had spent working in the sun. She studied Calla's exposed forearms, round and solid with natural bracelets that formed at each of her wrists. Elizabeth felt an urge to throw her arms around the woman, to ask for forgiveness, and to beg for help in understanding the man she was married to, the man she desperately loved.

But Elizabeth knew the rift between them would be an advantage in that Emily's unfamiliarity with Calla would be construed as a result of the strain between them. It made Elizabeth sad to think that because of it, Emily would not get to know this endearing woman the way she, herself, had.

As she stood to leave the kitchen, Calla said, "I'll tell Jim to bring the wagon 'round. Don' seem right your sister leavin' so soon and not comin' for a visit here to your home."

Elizabeth looked back sadly and the women's eyes met, then for the first time that morning, Calla smiled gently. "Don' be sad, Miz Liz. You'll see her again 'fore too long."

Chapter Seventeen

Jim drove Beth into town that morning. She went to her sister's room in the hotel, where they exchanged clothing, and proceeded to the train station where Beth boarded the train to Ogallala after a tearful farewell to Emily and Jim. Emily, in Beth's place, started home with the black man. To that point, their plans were successfully executed.

Jim suspected nothing on the trip back to the ranch. He mistook Emily's shyness for sadness at seeing her sister leave. In truth, Emily was very nervous about what lie ahead, and she wondered if she could really pull it off. She tried to recall everything Elizabeth had told her about the people, the layout of the ranch, and the day to day schedule. Her stomach fluttered with anxiety.

She was so lost in thought that she didn't notice the three men on horseback, faces covered, riding toward them, until the gun shots startled her out of her reverie.

Jim frantically whipped the horses, but the riders caught up and one of them jumped from his mount onto the sweating team and pulled the horses to a stop.

Jim fought one of the bandits off with the whip, but another jumped from behind and brought his pistol down on Jim's balding head. Emily heard the impact against Jim's skull and screamed.

A dark skinned man told her to sit still and she wouldn't be hurt. She put her arm around Jim and held her other hand to his bleeding wound.

"Mrs. Drummond," said the same voice, "step down off the wagon nice and slow."

Jim held her arm to keep her. In a shaking voice he said, "We ain't got no money, Mister, just on our way back from town. Let us be and we'll . . ."

"Shut up, nigger," the man said. He looked at Emily, "Mrs. Drummond, if you don't mind."

In an unsteady voice, Emily said, "No."

The man laughed. "Then we'll have to kill your man there."

Alarmed, and afraid they would injure Jim again, Emily pulled her arm from his hand and stepped down. One of the other horsemen picked her up and placed her on the saddle in front of him. The dark skinned man rode around to Jim's side of the wagon and brought his gun down hard on Jim's head again, this time knocking him unconscious. He slipped forward to the ground, his leg trapped between the wheel and the buckboard.

Emily cried out and struggled to get off the horse.

"Sit still, Mrs. Drummond, or I'll do the same to you."

"He might be dead," she pleaded. "Please, let me go to him."

The masked men laughed and started to leave. As they passed Jim's contorted body, Emily tensed with the realization that she was in grave danger. The third man came abreast to where she was being held against her will by the man behind her.

"Fine lookin' gal," he said to his companion. "Lots of money and lots of woman, huh, Jake?"

Emily could feel the man behind her pull off his mask. "Hands off, Luke. Our instructions are to bring her back—untouched."

The Stuarts were having dinner when Jack arrived at their ranch. He was shown into their dining room and wasted no time in demanding to know what their letters were about.

Slightly flustered, Ben Stuart got to his feet, saying, "Your divorce, of course. Darla has explained the entire situation and we understand. We'll be happy to help . . . finance . . . your legal fees. As soon as you can make it final, you and Darla will have that wedding you asked for last year. Sit down, Jack. Have something to eat with us."

Jack glared at Darla and asked, "What wedding?"

She looked nervous and flushed, standing at her place at the table. Her eyes darted from Jack to her father, then to Jack again. "You know, when you asked me to marry you. I refused you then because of what you had gone through . . . but I realize now that I was wrong."

Darla drew a deep breath. "I explained to Father . . . he knows we belong together, especially now." She walked to Jack and took his arm, her eyes begging him to play along.

Jack shook her from him and turned to Stuart. "I never asked your daughter to marry me, Ben. Even in a drunken stupor, I'd know better than that. I don't want a divorce from my wife, and I don't want to marry Darla. I can't make it any plainer than that. I believe you should take your . . . financial help . . . and commit her to an asylum."

Turning to Darla, whose face was bright red, he said, "Now you listen to me. I don't want to marry you. I was never enchanted with your company. You've pushed yourself and thrown yourself at me—at every man you've ever met—and now it's time to stop. I don't want to hear from you again. Is that clear?"

Without another word, Jack turned and left the dumbstricken Stuarts and proceeded to the nearest saloon to quench his anger—at both Darla and Elizabeth—in several glasses of strong liquor.

Jack sat alone in the corner of the saloon, depressed and sullen. He had come to the painful decision that when he went home to the ranch, he'd tell Elizabeth to leave. He knew she wanted to go back to David, she had revealed as much in her eyes when he had asked her the day before. That revelation brought him another: without Liz nothing was important—not even River Pines.

Jack kept delaying his return to River Pines. He stopped at every town on the way back, putting off the inevitable. He was no stranger to pain and loss, but he was afraid that this new grief was going to destroy him, for it was born out of a joy and passion he'd never expected to feel.

Five days later, Jack sat astride his stallion on the hill over looking his ranch. The time had come for him to let go of the only happiness he'd known as a man. He rode slowly toward the barn, dispirited and joyless. Then, like a flash of lightning, it occurred to him that he just couldn't do it. No . . . he *wouldn't* do it.

I'm not giving up all that I've worked for , all that ever made any sense to me. And by God, I'll not give her up that easily either. She's mine and by the time I'm finished with her, she'll know it, too.

Jack spurred his stallion to a pace where man and horse seemed to glide through the air. When he reached the courtyard, he swung down to the ground, bounded into the house, anxious to see Elizabeth, to hold her, even if it were against her will.

Calla was pacing in the kitchen. "Mr. Jack . . ."

"Where's my wife?" he demanded, excited and smiling.

"Mr. Jack, it's terrible bad. She ain't here."

The smile left his face and he glared at Calla. "Where is she?"

"It's been days . . . the day her sister left . . ."

Jack turned on his heel, left the house, and started to mount the stallion. Calla ran after him. "Mr. Jack, wait, let me finish. I gotta tell you . . . where you goin'?"

"To get my wife!" he threw back at her over his shoulder.

Calla tried to run after him. "You don' understand, Mr. Jack. Stop and hear me out. *Mr. Jack . . . ,*" she cried, falling to her knees. Jack didn't hear her or see her kneeling in the dirt, sobbing and calling for him. He set a course for Cherryton and never looked back.

Calla ran to her house where Jim lie on the bed with his head bandaged. "Jim," she said, tears streaking her face, "Mr. Jack's been here, and when I started to tell him 'bout Miz Liz, he just rode off. You gotta get him back and explain."

Jim stood up, but dizziness overcame him and he slumped back onto the bed. "I can't ride. Get Little Ben. Tell him to ride to town and find Mr. Jack. Tell him, if he can't find Jack, to go get Rone. But he got to go now!"

Little Ben rode to town and searched for Jack. He tried the hotel, but was told that he had just missed Mr. Drummond, and to try the stagecoach station. He went to the station master, who said he hadn't seen the man Little Ben described. Ben couldn't know, of course, that Jack, upon hearing where the young Miss Gerard had gone, didn't wait for a train, but rode straight to Ogallala himself.

Elizabeth, disguised as Emily, sat in the hotel room with her aunt. She had been there for three days. Although she had received searching looks from Catherine, she had not been suspected. Not quite sure how to act with David, Elizabeth was warm and genuinely pleased to see him, but avoided any private conversations with him.

Elizabeth knew it couldn't last much longer, for that morning at breakfast, he had asked, "For God's sake, Emily, what is going on?"

She looked at her plate, trying to decide how to answer him. What was it he wanted to know? The charade would be impossible to continue, but she wanted to buy some extra time.

"David, give me a little more time."

"Is Elizabeth happy or not? Did you explain to her about us? Did she give you her blessing and tell you we can finally be married and go on with the rest of our lives?" David leaned across the table and took her hand. "Please, Em, I need to know if this calamitous trip was worth it."

Elizabeth understood then. Emily had been denying him all these months, refusing to marry him until she knew Elizabeth had forgiven her and was happy. Tears filled Elizabeth's eyes at the thought of these two people, so right for each other, so miserably in love, and she'd been separating them the entire time.

"David, I can tell you one thing. You and . . . I will not be apart much longer. Just let me have a little more time to think. Once I explain everything, I know you'll be happy."

Now, as she sat talking quietly with her aunt, she decided that it was time for the truth. She had been acting like a child long enough, and David and Emily were the victims in this little pretense.

Elizabeth realized her absence from River Pines did not solve her problems, and she was more confused than she had been before. She did know one very important thing; she missed the ranch, and all the people she had come to love there, most of all Jack. The thought of him with Darla Stuart devastated her, but being away from him hurt more. She'd have to return and confront him, and all the problems that went along with him.

David walked in, and she stood up. "David, come sit with us. I have to speak with both of you."

He smiled at her and she felt warmed by it. Before she had reached Ogallala, she had wondered how she'd feel when she saw David again after all these months. She had expected her heart to jump at his smile as it once had, but instead, what she had felt was sisterly affection.

David came to her now and kissed her lips very gently and unexpectedly. Elizabeth stepped back and looked at him in surprise. The kiss had brought her no sensations—no dizzy, strangled tension. She didn't feel starved for more, wanting to throw her arms around his neck, silently demanding his lips, as she had again and again with Jack; and, suddenly, Elizabeth was elated.

She closed her eyes and a smile curled her lips as she thought, *I love Jack. I love him, and in my heart, I know he loves me, too. We'll have to work it out, because I can't go on without him. He'll have to decide between Darla and me, and I'm going to have to make sure it's me he'll choose.*

David's voice interrupted her thoughts. "You aren't Emily."

Elizabeth looked at him and could see his face was bewildered. He grabbed her arms in an angry grasp.

"No, David, I have to explain something to you. I just needed some . . ."

The door flew open and Jack stamped into the room. His eyes fell on the couple before him, David's hands holding her arms, a surprised look on both their faces.

"I've come for my wife." Jack's glare took them all in.

Elizabeth was frozen in place. *He knows, and he's going to kill me.*

Catherine's voice was puzzled. "But, Mr. Drummond, she isn't here. Isn't she at your ranch?"

"No," he said, taking off his hat now. "Are you sure she isn't here?"

David's eyes bore into Elizabeth's, but she found her voice and asked, "Where is she?"

"Calla said she's been gone since the day you came back here to Ogallala. I figured she left with you."

Elizabeth ran over to him. "Did Jim say where she was? He was with her when I left."

Jack frowned and shook his head. "Calla didn't mention Jim."

"What did she say exactly?" insisted Elizabeth, very alarmed now, as she twisted his coat lapels in her fingers.

"I guess I didn't let her finish. I just rode here as fast as I could."

Angry and upset, Elizabeth glared at him. "No, of course you didn't let her finish. You never let anyone finish what they have to say. You and your damned temper!"

Recognition grew in his eyes and Elizabeth knew she'd made a mistake tearing into him that way. His hands came up and broke her grip on his coat, twisting her wrists as he said between clenched teeth, "You!"

David, who had been silent up until then, spoke up, "Jack, let her go."

Looking down into Elizabeth's face, Jack said, "I don't believe you did this, Liz."

Catherine said, "Liz?"

"Yes," Jack said, turning her toward them roughly. "May I present my wife, *Elizabeth*," he said, shoving her at David.

"I know who she is, but I don't know what this is all about, Jack," David said, catching Elizabeth before she stumbled.

"Tell them, Liz. Go on, tell them how you've come here in your twin's place."

Elizabeth covered her face for a moment, then she cried, "All right, yes. I talked Emily into changing places with me so that I could get away from you for awhile. But we're wasting time. We must find her. David," she said, turning to him, "we have to go back and find Emily. She should have been at the ranch days ago. Something must be terribly wrong."

David stared into space, trying to grasp what he was being told. Beth looked at Catherine who, belying the anger which showed in her eyes, said very calmly, "I hope you will be able to explain yourself eventually, Elizabeth." Then turning to Jack, continued, "In the meantime, she is correct. You must find Emily."

David jumped into action. "We'll leave immediately."

Still glaring at Elizabeth, Jack told David, "I need a new horse."

"I'll have two fresh horses sent over from the livery." David said, starting for the door.

"What about me? I'll need one too."

David looked at her. "You'll slow us up."

"David, you know I can ride just as well as both of you can, and you aren't leaving without me."

David looked at Jack then. Pushing between them to move through the doorway, Jack snarled, "Get her a horse."

Elizabeth changed quickly into britches and a shirt and jacket. When she reached the lobby, Jack was waiting for David to come with the horses. She took a step toward him. "Jack, I . . ." But his eyes stopped her. She had seen this look before. It went beyond anger and deeper than hurt.

"You wanted to be away from me so much, you would even try a trick like this. "

"Let me explain, Jack."

"Why not just leave? Were you afraid I'd turn you in to the authorities because of what happened in New York? Or is it that you thought you could dupe David into making love to you, thinking you were Emily?"

"No, that isn't why, I just . . ."

"Forget it, Liz. There isn't any need to explain. I understand now. When this is finished and we find your sister, you can go home to stay. I won't bother you again."

"That isn't what I want, Jack."

"Don't say anymore, Elizabeth. In a way I'm relieved that it's settled. Get the divorce as soon as possible. If you don't, I will."

Elizabeth searched his eyes. "Do you mean that? Tell me the truth."

He looked away from her. "Don't worry, I won't disappoint you. You can go back East—with my pleasure."

He left the hotel just as David rode up leading two fresh horses and Jack's stallion behind him.

They sat huddled in blankets against the cold night. David stared into the fire, his eyes clouded with worry. Jack leaned against a tree, with his rifle over his thigh. He avoided Elizabeth's gaze, but when their eyes did meet, hers pleaded for understanding, his smoldered with anger.

She leaned her chin on her drawn up knees and joined David in staring at the flames. *How could I have done such a stupid, mind-less thing? How could Emily have gone along with it? My Lord, Em, where are you? What could have happened to you?*

Elizabeth covered her eyes with her hands. *Oh, please,* she prayed silently, *let her be all right.*

"How could you do this?" David asked, as if reading her mind.

"David, I know how wrong I was and there are no words to describe how sorry I am. I can't explain why, because it's much too complicated. For now, we have to find her, and we have to keep believing she's all right."

Putting her hand on his shoulder, she added, "She may be at the ranch when we get there, and this nightmare will be behind us."

"And if she isn't?"

"Don't say it, don't think it."

She turned to Jack then. "Why aren't we riding? Why do we just sit here?"

"Don't be a fool, Liz," Jack said. "Even if we could keep our-selves on horseback, the horses couldn't carry the pace. Sit down and be quiet for a change."

"That's right, Jack, attack me. It makes it easier for you to avoid owning up to your part in this."

Jack stood up and took several long strides closer to her, deliberately holding back from touching her. "Shut up, Liz. Just shut up."

"I wish you'd both shut up," David said quietly. "Whatever problem you have is unimportant to me right now, and I don't feel like bearing witness to your battles. I'm going to try to sleep and I suggest you both do the same." He turned his back to them and put his head on the saddle.

Elizabeth wrapped her blanket around her shoulders and walked way from camp toward the trees.

"Where the hell do you think you're going?" Jack asked.

"None of your business," she shot back.

"True, nothing you ever do again is any of my business."

When she was deeper into the trees and could no longer hear the crackle of the fire, she dropped to the soft ground. She needed time to be alone, away from the accusing eyes of the man she loved. Elizabeth tried to put her thoughts into some order as she listened to the eerie call of an unseen owl in the trees above her. Her chest hurt from the anguish and fear she was feeling. It was her fault Emily was missing, and that David was suffering because of it. The pain she felt because Jack was so angry was almost unbearable.

Slow, bitter tears came finally, and she wept. She wept only as a young woman can, heart-stricken and abandoned. She cried out of frustration that at the moment when she had decided to return to Jack, he would find her pretending to be Emily. The cold, accusing look in his eyes was unendurable and the fact that he wouldn't let her explain, frustrating.

"Are you finished now?" Jack's voice asked through the darkness.

Elizabeth stood up, still sobbing. "Is there no such thing as privacy with you? How long have you been watching me?"

When he didn't answer, she asked, "Did you enjoy it? Seeing me cry?"

"You're an idiot, Elizabeth. If you're feeling better, I'd like to go back to camp and get some sleep."

"I want to be alone. Why can't you just go back and leave me?"

"I'd like nothing better, but if something happened to you, it would waste time finding your sister—who does matter."

She wanted to spit back fighting words at him, but she felt overwhelmed by the desire to be held by him, comforted by him.

Her body trembled as she stood staring at the dark shadow he made against the moonlit trees.

"Jack, please, can't we talk for a moment? I need to talk. I need . . ."

"You need. *You* need. You needed to get away from me, so you placed your sister in my house and went away. You needed to get away because you and your sister want the same man, so you left, never thinking about how it would affect the lives of other people . . . people who trusted you. Now you need me to pat you on the back and tell you, it's all right, it doesn't matter what you've done, how you've hurt everyone. It makes me sick, Elizabeth. *You* make me sick."

She ran to him and fell against him with her arms around his waist. She buried her face in his coat against his chest. She could feel his heart beating against her tear-stained cheek. He stood guarded for a long time, then tried to pry her away, but she held tightly, murmuring that he had to listen.

"Elizabeth, get a hold of yourself. Let go of me."

Her face lifted to his and the moon shone on it. "Why, Jack? I only ask that you listen to me and let me explain. Are you so cold, so hard, that you can't put aside your anger for a moment?"

"What difference would it make, Elizabeth?"

"You are partly to blame for my running away, Jack."

He looked down at her distressed face and softened for a moment. "Only in your stubborn, foolish mind, Liz," he said.

Elizabeth needed his strength, his comfort, his arms around her.

He tried to pull away from her.

Elizabeth's lips found his throat just below his Adam's apple. His hands tightened on her shoulders and he threw his head back. She pulled him closer, holding herself against him. They swayed and he picked her off the ground, crushing her in a hungry kiss.

Then he dropped her and stepped back, away from her.

"Jack . . . ," she said, her hand held out toward him.

"No, Elizabeth." His voice was thick and he turned away.

She ran in front of him and blocked his way. "Some day you're going to be alone, completely alone. You're going to alienate every living person from you with your bitterness and your hatred and your anger."

Jack pushed her aside, "It wouldn't be the first time," he told her, resignation heavy in his words.

In the morning, David saw the dark circles under Elizabeth's eyes and knew that she had been crying during the night. He wanted to feel sorry for her, but she wrought her own problems. Now Emily had fallen into one of them, and damn it, he only had the time and strength to worry about her.

He wondered why Emily had ever agreed to stay in her sister's place, and again, as he had many times, decided it was because he had been pushing her too hard to marry him.

If I get her back, I'll set her straight about it all. She doesn't have to marry me, he thought, *but she has to learn that Elizabeth's life is her own, and Emily is not responsible for it.*

Elizabeth rode in silence and dared not look at Jack; she felt bruised and betrayed by his indifference the night before. She hated herself for begging him to love her, trying to force the kind of love from him he obviously didn't feel for her. She knew there was no way of going back to the way it was between them, but she longed for it nonetheless.

She noticed Jack kick the horse under him, urging it to go faster and move in front of her. Elizabeth had thought that he couldn't bear to look at her. She had no way of knowing that through the unrelenting anger that he felt for her and for what she had done, he was also relieved—relieved that it was Emily who was missing and not Elizabeth.

CHAPTER EIGHTEEN

They arrived at the ranch to find a thinner Calla and a worry-worn Jim. "Lord above, Mr. Jack," Calla cried when she saw Beth, "you found her."

Calla put her arms around Elizabeth and rocked her. Beyond the black woman's shoulder, Jack's eyes met Elizabeth's "Well, Calla," he began, anger still in his eyes, "I guess you could say that. Then again, no, I haven't."

Calla stepped back away from Beth. "What's he mean?"

Elizabeth touched the woman's arm. "Calla, I'm not the person who is missing. My sister Emily is. It's a very long story, and a very embarrassing one," turning to Jim, she said, "but first tell us what happened."

Jim told them everything, explaining that when he regained consciousness, Emily was gone, and he managed to get himself back to the ranch.

"Near death, he was, Mr. Jack," Calla said.

"Did they say what they wanted?" Jack probed.

"No, sir, they did not," Jim said, shaking his head slowly as if trying to recall.

"And you haven't heard anything?" Elizabeth asked.

When Calla and Jim shook their heads no, she looked at Jack. "This is even worse than I had imagined."

David said, "It's been days since they abducted her. She could be . . ." Unable to go on, he left the sentence hanging in the silence of the yard.

"The town got together a search party, but so far, nobody's brought her back," Jim told Jack.

By late afternoon Jack had rounded up his own search party. They split up, three different groups going west, south, and into the mountains. Barnes led one party, Ted Manning the other. David would go with Jack, as he didn't know the territory. The rest of their group consisted of three men, one of the regular ranch hands, a line man named Jenkins, a man called Dodger, and Calla's oldest son, Nathan. When they were ready to leave, Elizabeth came out of the house, freshly dressed for riding. Jack looked at her and said, "What do you think you're doing?"

"I'm going with you."

Dodger laughed. Jenkins, who knew the determined Miz Liz, was very serious. Jack dismissed her, annoyed.

"Get back in the house, Liz."

"I'm going."

Jack walked toward her, with his green eyes dark and threatening, as he said very slowly, "You are not going, do you understand me?"

Jack then picked her up in his arms, carried her to the shed, and threw her into it. Closing the door and catching the lock, he told Jim, "You keep this door closed and don't let her out. I don't care of she breaks her neck trying."

He mounted his horse and the group rode away. Elizabeth's screams could still be heard a half a mile away. David stopped and turned to look back where the tall black man and his wife stood watching, looking at odds.

"David," Jack called to him, "keep moving."

After a last glance back to where Elizabeth was imprisoned, David started after Jack.

Jack and his men rode quietly into the town of Peak's View. It was the last town before they would approach the mountain in the distance. Once a fur trading depot, it had swelled with the arrival of miners and pioneers headed west, who either moved on or staked claims. Though there were some farming families nearby, the town consisted mostly of men grown weary of empty mines and gun slingers who drifted through on their way south or west.

Jack and David dismounted and tied their horses to the hitching posts. As they entered the saloon and ordered whiskey, Jack's eyes covered the entire room. He picked out the men who would be of no help, and the men who might. David and Jack downed their drinks and ordered another round.

"You men passin' through?" the bartender asked.

David pushed his hat to the back of his head. "Yep," he drawled in imitation of the locals.

"You lookin' for a little action? Got a poker game planned for later on."

"No, thanks, don't think we have enough time for cards."

David leaned over the bar a little, and lowering his voice, taking the bartender into his confidence, said, "We *are* looking for a little information, though. Wonder if you've heard of a few men taking a woman a week back. Thought maybe someone would know where they're hiding out."

The legal profession had David well trained to see a look of understanding in the bartender's eyes a split second before the man hooded them.

"Sorry, don't know nothin' about it."

Jack's and David's eyes met, Jack raised his eyebrow, letting David pursue it.

"Well, now, I thought maybe there might be someone in this town that would. Know anyone like that? There's a hefty profit in a good memory."

For a fleeting second the bartender's eyes went to a cowboy sitting in the corner. David continued to study the bartender, but Jack took note and watched the man who sat leaning forward over his glass.

"Can't help you, Mister," continued the man behind the bar as he wiped the rough wood with a stained cloth.

"Well, that's okay. We're sure to find someone who can. Why don't you pour me another drink, and one here for my cousin?"

They took their glasses and sat at the table next to the cowboy's.

"Seems like you could use another drink there, friend." David said.

The cowboy looked up and took them in with his dark eyes. His voice was a low growl when he answered, "Why would you want to buy me a drink?"

"Just trying to be friendly," David said pleasantly.

"Well, I ain't your friend."

"Barkeep, give us a bottle over here," David called.

Once the bottle was on the table, David leaned over and poured the amber liquid into the cowboy's glass, then raising his own glass, toasted, "To your health!"

The cowboy took a swallow and put the glass down hard, asking, "What d'ya want?"

"We were wondering if you knew anything about a woman being kidnapped by some riders just southwest of Denver."

"Don't know nothin'."

David smiled his brightest smile. "I think you may be hiding something. There's more money in it for you, if you think twice."

The cowboy's eyes narrowed and he looked directly at Jack. "Seems I may have heard somethin'."

"That's good. Very good," David said. "What have you heard?"

"I heard she's somethin' to look at," the cowboy said, still staring at Jack, his mouth curling into a sneer.

"Where do you think she is now?" David continued, smoothly.

"Underneath, I s'pect," he said, completing the insinuation with an obscene laugh.

David's chair flew back. He had his gun cocked and pointed at the cowboy's temple, taking him completely by surprise as the man had expected Jack to respond.

"Where is she, friend?" David asked between his teeth.

"I don't know." The man's dark eyes flashed around the saloon, looking for help, but none was coming. The bartender had disappeared, the other patrons were ready to hit the floor at the first sign of shooting.

David pushed the cold metal of the pistol's barrel deeper into the cowboy's skin, leaving an impression. "I asked you a question and now I want an answer."

The cowboy held up his hands, "Look, all I know is that this guy came to town lookin' to hire some men for a kidnapin'. It ain't my type of work. Three drifters hired on, and they were talkin' the night before they left. Said they were goin' to pick her up and bring her into the mountain, then send a note to her father-in-law. That's all I know."

"Good," David said, pulling the gun back, but not putting it in its holster that hung on his hip. He threw two bills on the table and poured another drink for the cowboy.

Jack and David left the saloon. When Jack reached his horse, he hesitated. They heard the click at the same time, and David and Jack both spun around and fired their guns, hitting the cowboy in the chest, streams of blood dripped side by side within a half inch.

The surprised cowboy looked out at them from the saloon door. He had not even had a chance to shoot the gun, which still hung from his finger, before he fell forward.

David and Jack looked at each other. "Where the hell did you learn to shoot like that?" Jack asked his cousin.

David smiled back at him. "Pure fear. I knew I was going to get it in the back, and my instincts took over. Not bad for a city fellow, is it?"

"You've been holdin' out on me, Dave."

The small group of men turned their horses west toward the mountain. The golden sun was just setting behind it. But the beauty of the sunset escaped them, for now they knew it was where Emily was being held captive.

She felt numb inside and out. Emily's hands had very little feeling in them from the tight leather thongs that tied her wrists, and her legs ached from inactivity. Her body was bruised from being thrown around in the unpadded wagon.

She knew she had lost weight and she felt weak, yet she couldn't bring herself to eat the greasy food they put in front of her. She would be hungry, but as soon as *he'd* walk over to her, his hands and bearded face grimy, his body reeking with odor, Emily's appetite would leave and she could eat very little, only enough to keep herself alive.

She deliberately tried to keep her mind on other things, avoiding the terrifying situation she was in. At times, she'd allow herself to feel hatred for Elizabeth. In that hatred, she'd find the strength to get her through another hour. But soon the anger would dissipate, and she'd be lost in the terror of the wagon and the men who kept her there.

The wagon stopped and she sighed with relief. Then, the familiar wave of fear crept up from her stomach into her throat, for she knew he'd come into the back of the wagon to torment her and threaten her. Until now he hadn't carried out the threats, but she wondered just how long it would be until he did.

Emily jumped when the canvas flap flew back and he climbed in. "That was some bumpy ride, wasn't it, Miz Liz? I'll bet you're bruised all over that curvy body of yours. Shall I take a look and see if I can make you feel better?"

He put his hand on her hip and moved it slowly across her abdomen. This was familiar to her now as he did it whenever he could, but it never became easier for her to endure. She turned her head away, pinning herself closer to the side of the wagon.

What's wrong, honey? Still don't like me? Don't like me touchin' you?"

"Get your filthy hands off me. You make me sick," she said.

"Sick, huh? Miz Liz doesn't like me? Don't like the smell o' me." He lie next to her and rubbed his pelvis against her. "Come on, give me a kiss. You'll forget the smell."

"Stop it!" she cried as he rolled on top of her, his mouth on hers, the putrid odor of his breath assaulting her nostrils. She struggled against the binds on her wrists, but his hands held her firmly against the floor of the wagon.

"You're gonna get yours now, bitch," he said into her ear. "You're gonna find out what it's like to have a real man."

"I'm not Elizabeth! How many times must I tell you, I'm her sister. You have no fight with me. Please let me alone," she pleaded, sobs cutting off her breath.

She managed to get her knees up to her waist and pushed him off her. His laugh was cruel. "You're a fighter, all right, but I'll tame you, you little she-bitch."

He grabbed her hair, pulling hard and Emily cried out. He pulled again and she felt hair tear from her scalp. Emily turned her head and spat in his face, making him draw back for a second. Then she saw his fist come down from midair and her head exploded with pain.

In a second, she could taste the blood dripping in her throat and she thought her nose must be broken. Choking, she pulled her head up and droplets of blood fell from her nostrils and onto her clothing.

She sensed, rather than saw, his fist rise again for another blow, but this time she lurched aside and his fist hit the wagon with a terrific force. He cried out in pain as he grabbed his injured fist with his other hand.

"You whore. You rotten, whorin' bitch. I'll kill you."

He looked at his knuckles which were swollen and bleeding and tried to move his fingers. "It's broken," he moaned.

He rocked on his feet, holding his hand against his chest, his face distorted in pain. All Emily could think was that the last blow would have killed her had she not moved. She stared at him, and panic overwhelmed her. *He'll kill me for certain.* Instead, he crawled away and jumped from the wagon, leaving her huddled in a corner.

She heard him yell to the other men who sat around the campfire, and from the way one of them grunted, Emily knew he had been kicked.

Her body trembled uncontrollably and she spat out the blood that poured down her throat. It dripped constantly from her face and she held back her head to try to stop it, swallowing hard, becoming nauseated from the taste of the blood.

Emily felt the wagon move and one of the men climbed in. She went cold as she was certain he had been sent to murder her. He knelt in front of her and held a dirty cloth to her nose gently.

"Don't look so scared. I ain't gonna kill you. Not yet anyway," he said, as he ministered to her nose.

"Is it broken?" she asked.

"I don't think so. Just bloody and swollen. You broke his hand, though."

"I wish his neck were broken," she hissed.

"I wouldn't go around sayin' that, lady, especially to him."

He reached around and untied her hands. "Here, you hold this tight against your nose like this, and tilt your head back. That's it. Hurts like hell, don't it? Well, you'll have two black eyes for sure in the mornin'. I'll go get some water."

He started to leave, then turned back. "If I were you, lady, I wouldn't try to get away. You don't have a chance. Better for you if you just stay quiet. I'm takin' a chance myself by just tendin' you."

When he returned with the water, Emily washed her face and hands. The bleeding stopped, but she winced when she touched her nose. Her head ached and her eyes kept tearing.

"You'll be all right," he said, picking up the water which had turned red with Emily's blood. "I'll get you food."

"No, I don't want to eat . . . thank you . . . for being kind to me."

"Yeah, well, tomorrow I'll probably be puttin' my gun to your head and blowin' your brains out, so don't thank me." He had the leather straps in his hands and Emily pulled back.

"Please don't tie me up. I'll stay quiet. If my nose starts to bleed again, I'll need my hands. Please," she begged in a whisper, "Please."

He looked out of the wagon and then back at her. "I'll be right outside this wagon, lady, so if you were to get it in your head to run, you'll be dead before your feet hit the ground. Got that?"

She nodded and her head felt as if it would burst.

"You just be a good girl," he said and left her.

Emily lie back down on the wagon's floor and tears streamed from her gray eyes, though she cried silently, trying not to call attention to herself. Relief came in the way of sleep until later that night when Emily heard them talking.

"We gotta get rid of the bitch, Wilkes," she heard one of them say.

His name is Wilkes, Emily thought.

"Not until we get our money," Wilkes answered.

"Look it's been two weeks already. Either they don't care or they didn't get the message."

"They care," Wilkes said. "We just gotta give 'em more time."

"Just kill her and leave her. We'll head for old Mexico. I don't like it, it's too quiet."

"We'll wait, like I said. They'll come or they'll give the money."

Emily recognized the next voice as the man who had helped her earlier. "Maybe Wilkes is right. The old man will pay."

"The old man left town—no money—nothing—and he got the message."

"I said we're waitin' and that's what we're gonna do."

They were silent then, and Emily stared at the ceiling of the wagon. *What old man?* she asked herself. *Why haven't they come for me? Perhaps Elizabeth was right. Perhaps Jack doesn't care about her. He thinks I'm Elizabeth and he's glad they took her . . . me.* "Oh, God," she prayed aloud, "don't let him hate her that much. Please make him come for me."

Emily tried to quiet her rising hysteria to no avail. *Grace Dawson said Jack was crazy. How crazy? Crazy enough to let Elizabeth die?*

"I see her," Jack whispered to David from where they hid, watching the camp where Emily was being held in the wagon.

For two days they had followed the trail of four riders and a wagon. The trail was too unmistakable—too easy to follow—to suit Jack. He kept his search party as far back as possible.

"They're too anxious to be trailed," he told David. Although David had been keeping his patience in check, Jack could feel a mounting tension and knew his cousin wouldn't be able to hold back much longer.

"I trust you, Jack, and I'm willing to defer to you as long as necessary. But we don't know what they're doing to her, or even if she's alive, and a day—a night—could make a difference."

Jack shook his head. "Dave, there's something wrong here. They're making it too easy, and that makes me nervous. They want to be found."

"As I said, I'll leave it to you. I wonder, though, if it were Elizabeth with them, would you be as cautious?"

Jack looked at his cousin a long time, then said, "I'd do everything I'd need to save you, those men over there, and my own neck, while trying to decide how to get her out safely."

The question David had asked him bothered Jack and made him uneasy. Would he be as prudent if Liz's life was in jeopardy? He was unsure, and for that reason, they left their horses with Nathan that night and followed the trail on foot until they could see the encampment below them in a clearing. They waited for a view of Emily. Jack wouldn't make a move until he knew where she was and how well she was guarded.

It was obvious to Jack she was in the covered wagon because of the activity around it. One man, rifle across his lap, sat guard beneath the wagon all night.

"What are we waiting for?" Jenkins asked.

"We're waiting for that son of a bitch to fall asleep," Jack said casually.

"And if he doesn't?" David asked.

Jack studied the camp again. "I don't like it, Dave. I got a bad a feeling about this whole thing."

"Let's just rush them," Dodger said anxiously.

Jack looked at each man, they wanted to get it over with, for more than likely, one of them would be hurt—or killed—and the waiting was worse than the action.

"We'll wait until we see her. They have to let her out of there sometime."

In the early morning light, Jack saw the guard stand up and stretch, then climb into the wagon. Within seconds, Emily appeared and the guard walked her to a clump of trees outside the camp. After several long minutes, she reappeared.

Jack and David exchanged glances while Emily was being pushed roughly toward the wagon again. They could see her hands were bound behind her back. It was too dark to see her face, but the blood stains on her dress were unmistakable, and she walked as if in a trance.

"That's it, Jack," David said, checking his pistol. "I'm going in to get her."

Jack jumped toward him. "Then you might just as well take that gun and shoot her from here. We haven't got a chance in hell and more than likely she'll be the first victim."

"I'm not waiting any longer."

"Nightfall."

"No, now."

"Dave, I've always known you to be the wiser man in most cases, but this time you're being a fool."

David's eyes flared, but he took a deep breath. "Nightfall, Jack. No longer."

They made plans, Jack whispering orders to each man in turn. Jack knew there were four men in camp, two of whom kept coming and going, obviously acting as scouts or lookouts.

They would wait until all four men below could be seen at one time, then draw their guns and charge from different directions. Jack hoped David would have enough time to kill the guard and get into he wagon with Emily.

"It's almost time," Jack said when the sun had moved to the other side of the mountain. As each man in Jack's party started to move into position, they heard the snapping of rifles behind them.

"Move and we'll blow your heads off."

The four men froze. Jack heard footsteps coming closer and then felt the cold of a gun's muzzle against the top of his spine. "Nice and easy now, you throw your gun away."

The pressure increased against his neck. "Nice and easy, remember."

Reluctantly, Jack did as he was told. "Right. Now you other men do the same."

Jack saw Dodger's rifle fly to the left, and expected to see David's next, but David swung out, hitting the knee of the man who was holding the gun to Jack's neck, bringing him down to the ground in an excruciated cry.

Before any of them could react, another rifle was pointed in David's face. "You won't be so pretty without a head. That's it, you just sit there nice and quiet." Calling to the other man, he asked, "Jake, you all right?"

Jake lie on his side with his knee drawn up into his hands. He swore and moaned. "Son of a bitch, it hurts like hell."

Luke motioned to Jenkins. "Help him up." But Jake was balancing on one leg already and grabbed David. "I'll kill you . . ."

"Not now, Jake!" Luke said quickly. "Get 'em down there."

As the men walked out of the line of trees and into the clearing, Jack whispered to David, "They think she's my wife. Don't say anything different."

"Shut up, Drummond," Luke said, pushing Jack's shoulder with his gun.

Wilkes came from around the wagon with his pistol drawn in his left hand. When Jack saw who it was, he stopped short. Wilkes laughed. "That's right, boss man, it's your old cow poke. Come for your wife, have you? We been waitin' on you a long time."

"Where is she?" Jack asked calmly. Wilkes struck him across the jaw with a pistol.

Emily jumped from the wagon when she heard what was going on, but was grabbed by Bill, the man who had been guarding her. David started toward her. "I wouldn't," said Wilkes, pointing his gun at him.

Then he walked over to the trembling woman. "She's quite a gal, your wife." He put his arm around her shoulders and hugged her against his chest, letting his hand fall on her breast. She closed her eyes, unable to look at David.

"What's this about, Wilkes?" Jack demanded.

"My scar for one thing, Drummond. The one you gave me. Oh, yeah, and a little back pay you owed me."

Jack indicated Emily. "She has nothing to do with this. Let her go. We'll settle up between us."

"No, sir, I don't think so." Wilkes said as he took Emily by the hair cruelly. "I got better plans, boss man. And you're gonna have lots of fun watchin'."

Elizabeth reached down and picked up Jenkin's gun which had been inadvertently left behind by Wilkes' men a few hours before.

She had been watching from a tree higher up on the mountain, and she had seen the trap being set for Jack and David. Longing to be able to warn them, but unable to do so without being caught herself, Elizabeth had watched as they were led to the clearing and tied up. Except for Rone's old knife hidden against her ankle, Elizabeth was unarmed and knew she couldn't help.

Once the sun was down, she had climbed from the tree and had run to the spot where Jack and David had been waiting previously. She knew the gun was there and felt for it, found it and checked to see if it was loaded.

A hand came from behind and covered her mouth. She struggled to get free, then heard Rone's voice very close to her ear. "Quiet, Liz."

He let her go and she started to speak to him, but he silenced her again with his hand. She nodded and he pulled her down beside him. They waited until it was completely dark and the song of the insects would hide their voices. Rone spoke first, "You've done a good job tracking them."

"You've been here all along?"

He smiled in answer.

Elizabeth looked down the hill into the clearing where the fire burned brightly against the dark. "Do you think we'll be able to get them out of there safely? My sister's down there with them, Rone."

He was very serious and she knew he meant it when he looked at her directly and said, "I don't know."

They kept vigil through the night. Liz huddled into her jacket for warmth and dozed. When she awoke with a start, Rone was gone. She took her knife from its shield and knelt forward to look down at the camp.

It was barely audible, but she heard a sound behind her and turned to see Bill coming at her with his gun drawn. She brought the knife in her fist up and plunged it into his throat. He fell to the ground beside her, and she backed away, closing her eyes to the sight of the dying man's hands as they struggled with the embedded knife, blood pouring from the wound, already puddling on the dirt by his shoulder.

Elizabeth put her hands to her ears to block out the gurgling noise he was making. When it was quiet again, and she opened her eyes, he was dead.

Frantically, she searched for the gun she had found earlier, but it was gone. She knew her only option was to take back the knife. A shiver ran through her as she reached down and pulled out the bloody blade and wiped it on her pants.

Wilkes squatted down beside Jack. "I didn't count on you bein' stupid, boss man. I was afraid you'd see through our little trail leavin'. That's why I had two of my men followin' you." He laughed and Jack turned his head away from the stench of Wilkes' breath. "Only one I worried about was that injun bastard friend of your. That's why I waited 'til he was gone from the ranch."

Jack stared at the fire when he said, "I should have killed you that night, Wilkes."

Wilkes' good hand went up to his face and traced the scar Jack had left there. "Yep, you shoulda'. Now I'm gonna fuck your wife and kill her right in front of your eyes."

He called to Emily, and when she appeared at the opening of the wagon, he pulled her to the ground and dragged her over to where the bound men leaned against a tree.

"She sure is a lot of woman," he said, mauling her in front of them. Jack could feel David tense, and he quickly intervened, "Wilkes, let her go. Your fight is with me, not her. You used her as bait to get me here. It worked. Now let her alone."

Wilkes laughed and Emily struggled to push away from him. He grabbed the front of her tattered dress, tearing the material to her waist. Her breasts showed beneath the thin fabric of her chemise. She cried out and fell to her knees, desperately trying to cover herself with the ripped dress. Her face was twisted with fear and embarrassment.

David tried to crawl to her, but Wilkes kicked him in the face, sending him backward.

Jack yelled, "Stay out of this, Dave."

David turned to his cousin, "You know I can't." Then looking at Wilkes, he said, "She isn't his wife. She's his sister-in-law. For God's sake, man, leave her alone."

Wilkes' eyes narrowed and he said, "She tried to tell me the same thing, but . . . ." He pulled Emily's chin up with his bandaged hand and looked into her face.

He swore, pulled his gun, and shot David in the side. "You son of a bitch liar. You think I'm a fool. I know her well enough." Then pulling the terrified Emily to her feet, he said, "Yeah, this is her, all right. And I'm gonna kill her."

Wilkes was interrupted by the sound of a rider, and Jake, Luke and the other two men, jumped to their feet. The rider called out, "Hey, Wilkes, it's me, Evans."

He dismounted and said, "Wilkes, there's riders coming, 'bout a half day from here."

Wilkes let go of Emily and she ran to David, putting her hand on his side, trying to stop the bleeding.

"How many?" Wilkes asked Evans.

"Ten, fifteen maybe."

Wilkes spat, "You were followed."

"No," the other man said. "They were ahead of me. I circled around them."

"Don't lie to me. You were followed."

"I swear it, Wilkes. I wasn't." Evans' face was red and he started to walk to Wilkes, but was stopped when Wilkes pointed his gun at him. "Did you get the money?"

"Yeah, Wilkes, it's right here on the horse," he said, pointing to two bags tied around the horn of his saddle.

"All there?"

"Yeah. Listen, Wilkes, put away the gun. We have to split the money and get out of here."

Wilkes smiled. "You shouldn't of let yourself be followed," and, without further warning, he fired two shots into Evans' stomach. Emily screamed and buried her face in David's shoulder.

Luke said, "Wilkes, come on, let's get the hell out of here."

Wilkes turned back to him. "Go on, ride out. I'll follow later."

"The money . . ."

"I'll take the money. Now get out of here."

"Wilkes, uh, maybe we should split it now."

Wilkes pointed his gun at Luke now, "I said get out of here."

Jake, Luke, and the others rode out leaving Wilkes behind with Emily and the four men.

"Sorry, little lady," he said, kicking Emily away from David. "I guess you're outta luck. I only got time to kill you after all." Wilkes put the barrel of the gun to Emily's temple and cocked it. He turned to Jack with a vicious sneer, "You watchin', boss man?"

Elizabeth ran from the shelter of the trees and leapt up, kicking Wilkes' back full force with both feet. The shot rang out, and the bullet just missed Emily as the gun whirled through the air falling a few feet away from Jack.

Wilkes spun around and snatched Elizabeth around the waist as she came to her feet again. With the heel of her boot, she ground down on his foot as she grabbed his broken hand and twisted it in both of hers. He screamed and let her go.

With one hand pushing the other, her elbow shot back into his ribs, and she could hear a bone crack with the force, but as she turned, his fist flew out, caught her chin and she fell to the ground again. She was unable to move quickly enough to avoid his lunging on top of her. They struggled and rolled, but no matter how hard she fought, Elizabeth was still pinned to the ground.

Her fingers reached down to pull her knife from its shield in her boot. Wilkes fought to get it away from her, but she cut the palm of his good hand, causing him to sit up momentarily, giving her time to raise her leg and topple him. As she shifted to escape him, he grabbed her and pulled her back. Wilkes slapped her hard, she lost balance, and suddenly he was on top of her again.

The others watched helplessly as Wilkes slammed Elizabeth's hand down hard on a jagged rock. Again and again, her knuckles crashed against the stone until the knife was loosened from her fingers. She cried out as she felt it fall, unaware that at the same moment, Emily had taken the coffee pot from the fire and brought it down hard on Wilkes' head, spilling its boiling contents on his back.

He reared up in pain. Elizabeth grabbed the knife from the ground, and for a second time that day, plunged it into a man's chest. Wilkes grabbed the hilt, and slumped forward over her.

Elizabeth squirmed out from under him and got to her feet. There was an eerie stillness in the camp. Then the sisters looked at each other. Elizabeth held out her arms and Emily entered the embrace.

"What the hell are you doing here?" Jack shouted angrily.

"Saving your life," Elizabeth answered over her sister's shoulder. She held Emily at arm's length and pushed a strand of her sister's hair back from her face. "Are you all right, Em?"

Emily nodded, tears streaming through the dirt on her battered face.

Jack's voice demanded, "Untie me, Liz."

"Later," she said, watching as Emily went to David to untie him. Then Beth started toward Jenkins.

"Liz," Jack said, almost desperate. "Untie me *now!*"

As he said it, he could see Wilkes move, turning slowly, the knife in his hand now, aimed at Elizabeth's back. Jack lurched sideways and grabbed the gun Wilkes had dropped a few minutes earlier. Hands tied, without taking aim, he pulled the trigger, leaving a bloody hole between Wilkes' surprised eyes.

Elizabeth started and turned back to see Wilkes drop back. She said, "I thought he was . . ."

"You thought wrong, you idiot. Now get the hell over here and untie me."

Elizabeth ran over and cut the leather straps from his wrists and ankles without another word. "I ought to wring your neck," he said, grabbing her shoulders and shaking her.

"I should have let him kill you," she snapped, pulling away from him.

Jack went to David and looked at the wound. "The bullet went right through," he said. Then looking back up at Elizabeth, he asked, "Where's Rone?"

"How did you know he was here?"

Jack ignored the question. "Where is he?"

"I don't know. He disappeared during the night. I was looking for him when I saw what Wilkes was going to do and I . . . couldn't stay there and watch."

Jack's eyes narrowed as he searched the mountain around him.

"Back here, Jack."

Jack turned to see Rone climbing out of the tree that he had been leaning against while tied up during the night.

"You there all along?" Jenkins asked.

Rone nodded.

"Why didn't you do something?" Elizabeth screamed.

"I was going to until you got in the way, Liz." He gave her a crooked smile. "You didn't seem to need much help, though."

She was furious. "I could have been killed!"

Jack smiled at Rone and said, "I don't think so, Liz. Wilkes was a dead man even before you came out of those trees." He shook Rone's hand. "I could feel you out there."

Rone nodded again, then went to David. "How are you, old friend?" he asked.

David's smile was pained. "Not as good as I was the last time you saw me, Rone."

Rone squatted down and gently pulled Emily's hands away from David's side, smiling at her reassuringly. "I'll take care of him now, Miss Emily."

Nathan arrived with the horses and Jack asked, "Where've you been, kid?"

"Heard the shootin', Mr. Jack, and thought I'd take a look."

Elizabeth went to the horses and told Nathan to check the saddle bags for any clothes that could be used as bandages. She took a clean shirt from Jack's blanket roll and walked over to Emily.

"Here, Em, put this on," she said, extending the shirt to her sister.

Rone held his knife out to Elizabeth. "Put this in the fire."

She did what she was told. When she returned with it, she brought along water, handing both to Jenkins. Then she put her arm around Emily's shoulders and led her toward the wagon and away from the group of men.

Emily stiffened when she heard the searing of David's skin and new tears formed in her eyes when he stifled a moan.

Elizabeth searched her sister's face, deeply concerned. "It's all right, Emily. Rone knows what he's doing."

Elizabeth couldn't control her own tears when she looked at Emily's bruised face. "God, Em, what have I done to you?" Emily's only answer was a shake of her head.

Jack watched his wife and Emily carefully bandage David's side when Rone was finished cleaning it. "Can he ride?"

"No, he can't ride," Elizabeth said.

David started to argue, but Emily put a gentle hand on his shoulder to still him. "She's right, David. You're badly hurt." Looking up at Jack, she said, "I agree with Elizabeth. He can't ride."

Jack smiled kindly at his wife's twin. "Well, that settles it then. How long should we wait to move him?"

David answered this time. "If it's all the same to you, I'd like to leave right now. Get me in the wagon."

When Rone nodded that it would be all right, Jenkins and Dodger helped David to his feet and brought him over to the wagon, leaving Jack and Elizabeth alone.

He noticed her hand was swollen and scraped where Wilkes had battered it against the rock. He took it and examined it carefully. She winced and he said, "It's pretty bad. You're lucky it isn't broken."

She didn't answer and looked away from his green eyes.

"Well," he said finally, "you can put up with the pain, I guess."

She pulled her hand away from his angrily, and he laughed, taking it again. "Don't be so touchy, Liz." He took off his neckerchief and wrapped it around her hand.

"You want to ride in the wagon?" he asked her.

She shook her head, "No, let Nathan drive it."

"It's a long ride," he started.

"Jack, I made it here on horseback. I'll make it back." Then looking up at the mountain, she added, "If I can find Rusty."

"How *did* you get here, by the way? I told Jim to keep you in the shed."

"I found an axe and tore a hole through the side of it. There was nothing poor Jim could do to hold me, Jack. I saddled the bay and followed your tracks. Now, if you'll excuse me, I'll go find my horse."

Jack grinned at her and she was surprised to see what resembled respect in his glance. "Have it your own way," he said. "You always do."

CHAPTER NINETEEN

They pulled away from the camp where Jenkins and Dodger were burying Wilkes and Evans. The ride was slow and torturous for David as the wagon moved over the craggy terrain. Whenever the wheels would hit a ditch or rock, he'd wince, and at times a moan would escape his throat. Emily wiped his brow, and he squeezed her hand to reassure her.

"We're quite a sight, you and I," David said, touching her blackened eyes. "How often did they beat you, Emily?"

She kissed his palm. "Just once, but I'll tell you about it later, when we're all calmer and I have a chance to think."

As the day turned into night, they camped in a clearing beneath fragrant evergreens. Jack helped David from the wagon and they made a comfortable bed for him on the soft, browning pine needles. David laughed as Emily and Elizabeth fussed over him, and winked at Jack when he said, "It may take me a little longer to heal than I first thought."

Rone checked the wound and administered an ointment that came from a tiny bottle he kept in his saddle bag. Emily held the bottle for him as he applied its contents to David's side.

"What's that, Rone?" David asked him.

"Comfrey root," Rone answered. "It will relieve the pain and heal the skin."

Dave smiled as he looked at Rone's serious face. "I'd forgotten how good it is to have an Indian for a friend. You always were handy to have around in an emergency. But I see you still don't smile much."

Rone wrapped a clean bandage around David, allowing a small grin to form on his face, "I remember smiling often when you were around, Dave."

Emily listened to the warm exchange, and she asked, "How do you know each other?"

David answered, "My mother sent me to Colorado twice after my father died so that Jack's father could scare the daylights out of me when I got to be too much for her to handle. Little did she know I got into more mischief under the influence of Jack and Rone than I ever did in Benton."

He laughed then, grabbing his side and wincing. "Of course, Uncle Dan did scare the devil out of me whenever he caught us, which wasn't all that often, since Aunt Amelia covered up most of our wrongdoings."

Emily noticed Rone's face soften when Jack's mother was mentioned. His black eyes drifted aside in a secret memory, and a gentle smile tamed his features.

When they had eaten, they hovered near the campfire for warmth, and Emily's quiet voice told them of the ordeal she had withstood after Wilkes' men took her from Jim.

There were moments when Emily would not be able to speak for a few minutes while she regained composure, and then she would continue telling them of the constant threats which ended with the beating in the wagon.

Jack stared into the fire as Emily spoke, though occasionally he would glance at Elizabeth, his eyes unreadable. Elizabeth covered her face at times, as if to block out the scenes Emily described. She cried silently, sometimes wiping tears from her cheeks, at other times letting the drops fall onto the blanket that covered her.

"It isn't fair, Emily. It should have been me—was supposed to have been me, not you."

David's voice was harsh when he said, "If only you hadn't pulled that damned switch." When Emily looked at him, her eyes pleading, he said more gently. "I'm sorry, Beth. You didn't know it was going to happen. It's over, let's leave it behind us, if we can. Thank God, Em is all right, and you're both safe."

"I'll never forgive myself, David . . . for all that has happened this year." A sob caught in Elizabeth's throat. "What has happened to Emily is most terrible, but the fact that I've killed men— can it be possible?—what kind of person have I become?"

"Men?" Emily questioned her sister.

All eyes were on Elizabeth when she answered, "I killed one man earlier, when I was hiding. He came up behind me with his gun drawn, and I stabbed him. Then Wilkes . . . and . . ."

Emily interrupted, "Elizabeth, I never knew a human being could be so vile, so filled with evil and hatred, and as horrifying as murder is, I'm happy he is dead and can hurt no one else again. As for the other man, had he taken you, you would not have been able to help us."

David agreed, "Besides, you didn't kill Wilkes, Jack did, and if he hadn't, we would all be dead now. What you did, you had to do. Forget it."

Elizabeth looked at Jack and he knew that she was thinking of New York and what had happened to Tom Blackwell. He ached to go to her, to hold her in his arms and comfort her.

Had she been any other kind of woman, she would have been a casualty in each instance, but because of her strength and intelligence, she did not allow herself to be vicimized.

He had watched this woman—not much more than a girl—develop into a person able to handle herself fearlessly, fighting to save the lives of others, while risking her own life, yet the travesty in all of it was that she agonized over the death of the men who would harm her.

He knew that he must share in that guilt, for if it hadn't been for him, she would still be in Pennsylvania, far out of harm's way.

In order to keep from taking Elizabeth in his arms, he kept reminding himself that he had found her posing as her sister in order to be near David. This was a fact that tortured him, but did nothing to lessen his desire and need for her—for her love.

It was obvious to Jack that Elizabeth would never have David. Certainly it must be clear to her, as well, how in love David and Emily were. He thought about her going back with them, always loving the one man who would never love her, while another man burned with a passion she could not return. In the past, Jack had come to know the irony of life's cruelty, but, as Jack looked through the firelight at the beautiful woman he loved, he decided that he would never understand it.

Rone, who had also been studying Elizabeth through the glow of the fire, handed the bottle of ointment to Emily, and announced, "I must leave. Keep applying this to David's wound. Once you're back at River Pines get the doctor." Emily gave him a grateful smile.

He stood and as he left the camp, touched Elizabeth's shoulder and smiled down at her tenderly. "You did nothing wrong in using your abilities to save yourself and those you love."

Jack followed Rone and stood near him as he saddled his horse. "Thanks again, Rone," Jack said quietly.

"I didn't do much. Liz took care of saving your lives."

Jack didn't comment and Rone stopped working long enough to face him. "When I left the ranch, you were happier than I had ever seen you. I have no idea what has happened, and I don't care to know, but whatever it is, work it out with her, Jack."

Jack looked down and away from Rone's eyes.

"You're both miserable, you're both stubborn, and you both have to change," Rone told him.

Jack's eyes rested on Elizabeth who was still sitting near the fire. "You're right, old friend, but I don't know how, or even that it's worth it."

Rone touched Jack's shoulder. "It's worth it." Then he pulled himself into the saddle and, with one more look at Jack, rode away into the darkness.

Later, when Elizabeth was sleeping and Jack and Nathan sat watch outside the camp, Emily took her blanket and lie close to David. He had been staring at the stars through the branches above him and he smiled and put his arm out for her to rest her head against his shoulder.

"I love you," he said into her soft hair.

"I love you, David."

"I've been afraid to ask you why you switched places with Elizabeth. Was it because of me?"

Emily pulled up and looked into his face. "No, David, that wasn't the reason. It was to help my sister. She seemed so desperate and told me this was the only chance she had of getting away for awhile. I thought it may have been because Jack was cruel to her and I wanted to help. It was only going to be for a short while."

"Why did she have to leave you in her place if she wanted to get away? Why didn't she just leave with you?" he asked.

"I'm not sure," Emily said looking toward where Elizabeth slept. "She's in love with Jack, isn't she? I think he loves her, too. They're both so proud and stubborn that the love they feel is actually keeping them apart." She sighed as she looked back at him. "What fools they are."

"Is that so?" David asked, smiling.

Emily smiled back and placed her head against him again. "I know that you're thinking that they are no more foolish than I have been all these months. You're right, David. I have been terribly foolish."

She kissed his lips lingeringly. "Now I'm completely over that insanity. All I want to do is plan our wedding and be your wife."

"No more identity switches?"

Emily laughed and kissed him again. "No, never again."

As they approached the ranch, Elizabeth rode up beside Jack, who had stopped to look over his land. She studied him while he squinted against the sun from under the brim of his hat.

His skin was darkly tanned, and she could see a tendon in his neck stretch up through the opening of his black shirt. Elizabeth looked away from him, afraid of what might show on her face.

"It's a rich, beautiful land," she said, reading his mind.

Jack turned to her. "You do love this ranch, don't you?"

She nodded and breathed in the cold autumn air.

"You're a hell of a woman, Liz."

She was astonished by his words and her eyes met his.

"You aren't only beautiful, but you're intelligent and strong, with unshakable integrity. Don't misunderstand, I also think you're distrustful, deceitful, and stubborn."

Elizabeth glared at him now. "Do you realize what a contradiction that is?"

"You *are* a contradiction."

She looked away again. "I don't care what you think of me, Jack."

"One moment you're as soft as the water in a lake, and the next moment I feel like I'm drowning in a waterfall," he said.

"You're arrogant."

"You speak to me of love and give yourself completely in lovemaking, and then turn around and return to your former lover."

She was genuinely angry now. "How dare you speak to me this way, Jack! I did not return to my former lover, as I never had one, unlike you."

"But I must say," he went on as though she had not spoken, "you are quite a woman."

Elizabeth kicked her horse and galloped away, sending him one last scathing glance.

When she entered the yard, she saw a strange buggy. Jim stood beside it and when he realized who was riding toward him, his sad face suddenly brightened with a smile.

She jumped down off the horse and threw her arms around the tall, broad man. He looked embarrassed but delighted. "Miz Liz, I ain't seen nothin' so good since the first time I laid eyes on my Calla. Welcome home, Miz Liz, welcome home."

"Thanks, Jim. It's good to be back. Where's Calla?" She didn't wait for him to answer and ran into the brown house and the warm kitchen she loved. "Calla, we're back!"

Calla appeared in the doorway between the kitchen and living room. "Thank our Lord almighty, Miz Liz," she said as she folded Beth into her arms. "Where's the rest?" Calla asked, pulling away slowly.

"They're coming. Jack's cousin is hurt very badly and needs a doctor. Send Little Ben to town, and tell him to hurry."

Just then, as she looked beyond Calla's shoulder, she saw her aunt walk into the kitchen.

"Aunt Catherine, what are you doing here?"

Catherine kissed her niece's cheek and embraced her. "I've been so worried, Beth. Is Emily . . ."

"She's well enough, considering what she's been through. They're on their way in. How did you get here?"

"Did you really expect me to stay in Ogallala, half insane with worry? As it is, if it wasn't for Mr. Drummond, I would indeed be mad by this time."

"Mr. Drummond?"

At this, an older man stood up from a chair and turned to look at Elizabeth. She knew who he was immediately, even in the distance, for there were the same green eyes smiling at her, the same black hair, graying slightly at his temples.

So this is what Jack will look like in twenty years, she thought as she went to him.

Daniel Drummond took her hand in both of his, and said, "You must be my daughter-in-law."

CHAPTER TWENTY

The first meeting of Elizabeth and Daniel Drummond was interrupted by a whirl of confusion as Jack and Emily entered the room with Calla following behind, telling everyone what to do and where to put the injured man. Catherine and Emily readied the bed, and Elizabeth went to get fresh bandages, but not before exchanging a warm smile with her father-in-law. She liked him immediately and knew instinctively that he felt the same about her.

David was put into the room Elizabeth had slept in when she first came to the ranch, and Emily and Calla went about changing his dressing, which was stained with blood again.

The rest waited for the doctor in the living room, being warmed by the fire Daniel had prepared in the huge stone fireplace. He turned to look at his son, and their eyes met when he said, "I've been damned worried, Jack."

Jack took four glasses and a bottle of whiskey from his den. He poured the liquid into each glass, handing one to Beth, one to his father, and a third to Jim, saying, "Bring this into my cousin. He could use it." Then looking at Elizabeth and Daniel, lifted his glass and downed the liquid.

"What are you doing here, sir?" he finally asked Daniel.

"When I received the ransom note, I decided to come here and see what the hell was going on."

Jack looked at him in surprise. "What ransom note?'

The older man handed him a sheet of paper. "This. It says," he explained to Elizabeth as Jack read it silently, "that my daughter-in-law had been kidnapped and I was to pay Five thousand dollars for her return. I did as it said, notified the marshal to arrange for a posse, and then came here, where I found Miss Gleason waiting also. She explained what she knew about it to me."

Jack turned to Elizabeth and said, "Liz, go out to the wagon and get the bags."

Elizabeth was annoyed that he had ordered her and hesitated. "Please," he added, smiling. She went out to the wagon as he had asked, and while she was gone, Daniel said, "She's beautiful, son. I must admit, I thought your marriage was a guise to get the deed to this ranch. Now that I've met her, I'm not surprised that you've fallen in love.

"I'm sorry she thought I wouldn't understand that she wanted to see her aunt and left her sister in her place so that I wouldn't misunderstand and sell River Pines." He smiled and shook his head, "To think that she went to all that trouble to save your ranch for you, now that's a woman worth keeping."

Jack said nothing. He wasn't ready to tell his father the truth—that he was indeed in love with this wild, unreasonable woman, but that the marriage was a pretense in the long run and that what his father thought was the reason for her switching places couldn't have been farther from the truth.

Elizabeth reentered the room and handed the two bags of money to Daniel. "This is yours," she said, smiling, "and thank you for trying to save my life with it."

Daniel kissed her cheek. "I can see that it's a life worth saving."

Little Ben brought the doctor to David, who told him, "You're a lucky man. An inch or less, the bullet would have hit your lung. Those broken ribs don't look too bad either. You'll be up and about in a few days. In the meantime, stay quiet. No roughing it up." Although she tried to refuse, the doctor proceeded to check Emily's face and nose where the remains of the beating she sustained from Wilkes were still evident. He declared she'd heal and be as beautiful as ever.

They held hands when the doctor left, and David said, "You are beautiful, Emily, with or without black eyes."

After they had all washed and dressed for dinner, they sat in the living room again, the ladies drinking sherry, except for Elizabeth who joined the men in another glass of whiskey.

"One would never know you were reared in my home, Elizabeth Gerard, although nothing you do should surprise me," Catherine said in disgust as Elizabeth put the glass to her lips.

Jack leaned forward, his face very serious. "Speaking of homes, I think it's time we discussed this ranch, Sir."

Elizabeth looked apprehensively at her husband. Earlier that evening, while she was bathing, Catherine had explained that Daniel described the situation to her during those long days of waiting. He told her how he had been unwilling to relinquish the mortgage he held on the land to his unhappy son until he was sure Jack had settled down. Catherine also knew that Daniel had stipulated they must be married for one year, and that Elizabeth was expected to stay on the ranch during that time.

Elizabeth had taken her aunt's hand, saying, "Now you understand why I had to switch identities with Emily when I went away. No one could suspect I had left Jack before the year was over. This ranch is the only thing that means anything to Jack. I can't imagine him not owning it, or losing it for any reason. Jack is this ranch, and, oh, Aunt Catherine, what would happen to Calla and Jim and all the others if he were to lose it?"

Catherine had shaken her head and wiped her hands on the towel that lay across her lap. "It doesn't explain why you wanted to leave in the first place, dear. I know it wasn't just to see me, even though I've allowed Mr. Drummond to think so."

Elizabeth hadn't tried to explain, for her aunt would not understand. Elizabeth, herself, did not understand. In Ogallala, Jack had told her to leave, to get the divorce immediately, or he would.

Yet if she were to leave, he'd lose River Pines, which she could not bear to think of, nor could she think of the empty void living without him would leave in her heart.

There were still seven months until they were married one year. So much had happened in the last five, that she could only imagine what more lie ahead in living with Jack.

Elizabeth knew what had to be done before Jack told his father the truth, and she said to her father-in-law now, "Perhaps it would be better to discuss business after dinner. You'll feel more like talking after one of Calla's wonderful meals."

"On the contrary, my dear, Liz," Dan said, "I'm ready for bed after one of Calla's meals."

They all laughed and could hear Calla chuckling to herself in the kitchen. Then Elizabeth said, looking at Jack, "If you don't mind, I would prefer you wait."

He looked confused, but nodded at her. They chatted quietly during dinner, and when they were finished, Emily said, "If you'll excuse me, I think I'll go to David." Elizabeth took the opportunity to say to Jack, "Would you mind taking a walk with me?"

His brows knitted together, and she continued quickly, "You can speak to your father later."

Dan smiled, "Quite so, Jack. When your wife wants you to herself, you'd better learn to snap to it." He laughed, and his sparkling eyes looked at Catherine as if to take her in on this wisdom.

Then he said, "Miss Gleason and I will sit in the living room and talk awhile."

Jack eyed Elizabeth suspiciously, but he took her hand, placed it in the crook of his arm, and led her outside.

When they were near the barn, Jack opened the door and flung her inside. "What's this all about, Liz? You'd rather walk with a rattler than with me."

"Look, Jack, I . . . wait, let's calm down. There's no reason to start tearing at each other. I wanted to speak with you privately, before you had that talk with your father."

His eyes were still suspicious. "Don't worry, Elizabeth. I have every intention of telling him the truth. You'll be free to leave with your family when the time comes."

"Shut up for a minute, will you," she shouted. "Don't say another word until I have finished. I'm sick to death of your rude manners and your interruptions every time I have something important to say." Then taking a deep breath, she went on, "Now see, you have me all worked up again! I want you to promise me you'll stay quiet until I'm finished."

He stared at her.

"I said, promise, Jack," she warned.

He leaned back against the barn wall and folded his arms across his chest. This time he smiled faintly as he nodded his promise.

"I know all about the ranch—how your father holds the mortgage and . . . all. I love this ranch almost as much as you do, and I won't stand by and let you lose it. He told Aunt Catherine that he had planned to sell it to a stranger if our marriage hadn't taken place. I won't have that, Jack."

She found the courage to look at his face. The smile had disappeared, and his look was dark and brooding. She went on quickly, "So what you're going to tell your father is that we have a very . . . happy marriage—Jack, you promised not to say anything until I've finished! All right, I also want to say that I have money of my own, from my father's estate. You may use it to expand the ranch and whatever else you need to do with it. I'd like the house to be a little larger, and we'll use my money for . . ."

Jack swore loudly and glared at her. "I don't want your God damned money, Elizabeth."

She stopped speaking and straightened her shoulders. "What you really mean is that you don't want *me*. You'd rather lose your ranch than live with me any longer." She could barely finish the sentence, her throat ached so painfully.

"What I really mean is that I don't want *your money*. I want you, Liz."

They were both surprised by his words. With his face red from anger, Jack started to open the door of the barn, but she ran past him and threw herself against it. "Do you mean that, Jack? Tell me the truth, do you?"

His face came down close to hers and his voice was a whisper when he said, "Yes, you infuriating witch, I mean it. But I don't want to."

Elizabeth's hand touched his face, and Jack closed his eyes, willing himself not to return her touch, for all of his strength and conviction would crumble if he did. Her fingers caressed his jaw and moved to his neck. He deliberately placed his hands against the door of the barn, capturing her between them, while he tried to gain control of his emotions.

His eyes opened slowly when she took her hand away. He saw her fingers go to the buttons of her dress, and she slowly and deliberately unbuttoned each one. She was wearing nothing beneath, indicating to him that she had intended this to happen, had intended to seduce him.

"Prove what you just said to me," she whispered.

"What are you doing?" he asked, while his jaw tensed.

"I asked you to prove to me that you want me," she said, continuing to undress.

The gown fell from her shoulders, while she leaned against the wooden door between the confines of his arms. Jack looked down at her, at her lovely body, and she felt his hands move to her hips. A gasp caught in her throat when he pulled her against him, still withholding his kiss, his eyes smoldering into hers.

As they clung to each other, she delivered burning kisses to his face and shoulders. They fell to the floor of the barn, their mouths touching, exploring, rediscovering the sweet arousal they'd known once before in each other's passion.

When they could stand no more, they allowed the shuddering release to leave them spent and sated. She buried her face in his neck and he stroked her back. "What have I proven?" he asked, almost sadly.

"More than I had asked for, Jack," she answered.

"Meaning?"

"It's for you to tell me," she said, her finger tracing his chin. He leaned his head on his hand and cupped her breast with his other, but he still said nothing.

"All right," she said, after a long silence, "then *I* will say it. I love you. I don't want to stay because I want to save the ranch for you. Jack, I want to save *you*. You told me once that I was your balm. If that is true, then I shall spread myself over you and save you from yourself—from the pain you keep locked inside."

Jack kissed her lips, her neck, and finally her breast where his hand had rested. "I can't speak of that pain . . . not yet, Liz."

"I know and I don't expect you to. I just want you to know that I'll be here when you are ready, if that ever happens. I made you happy once, though it was only for a short time. Please let me try to make you happy again, Jack. Maybe with me, you won't have to search for it elsewhere." She wanted to add that she could make him forget Darla Stuart, but was afraid that the mention of the name would break the wonderful spell they were under.

He rested his cheek on her soft stomach, while she combed her fingers through his hair in a gentle caress. "The reason I was going to tell my father the truth wasn't only to release you from our agreement, but because I didn't want the damned ranch without you on it."

Very suddenly, he sat up, pulling her with him, his hands gripping her shoulders until his knuckles were white. "Elizabeth, you must tell me one thing, and you cannot lie to me. Are you still in love with David?"

Elizabeth put her hands on each side of his face when she answered, "I have never been in love with David. Only you, Jack . . . only you."

He closed his eyes, and his lips found the palm of her hand. Slowly, as if consuming her, he left a path of tiny, fiery kisses on her arm, until, once again, their lips met urgently.

"This has been a day of revelations," Jack said, pulling her on top of him.

"Would you like another one?" she asked coyly. "I want ten children, five girls and five boys. What do you say?"

Jack shook his head and gave her a crooked grin. "That's a lot of expanding on this house, Liz. I hope you have enough money in the bank."

They laughed as his mouth claimed hers and his body demanded more than she had ever given before.

Elizabeth opened her eyes and frowned slightly when she realized what day it was. The sun was beginning to show itself over the mountain and she listened as the birds began their morning litany. The last three weeks had been filled with a warmth and fullness Elizabeth had never experienced before. The presence of Catherine, Emily and David made River Pines all the more exciting.

She spent long days riding with Emily and Catherine, showing them the beauty of the ranch with its breathtaking surroundings. They helped Calla in the kitchen and shared meals that were filled with laughter and witty conversation. Each day, as David improved, he helped Jack and the other hands prepare the ranch for the coming winter months.

Now Elizabeth felt the heaviness of parting and closed her eyes again. Jack's arm came around her and she snuggled against him. His voice was thick with sleep when he asked, "What has you awake this early?"

She nuzzled his shoulder, enjoying the warmth from his body on the cold autumn morning. "They're leaving today," she whispered.

"Hmm, and then I'll have you all to myself again. We'll have all the time in the world to talk and laugh and make passionate love."

She smiled. "That does sound appealing, I'll admit."

Jack opened his eyes. "But, it's not the same, with your sister and aunt leaving, now, is it?"

Elizabeth sat up, gently unraveling herself from his arms. "I will miss them, Jack. These past three weeks have been wonderful, having all the people I love most around me. We've had such fun here on the ranch. Emily and Aunt Catherine have grown to love it as much as I do, and David has absolutely shone since he's been up and around." Elizabeth touched his cheek lightly, "and I've never seen you so relaxed and . . ."

He kissed her fingers. "Happy."

"Yes," she said smiling, "happy."

"That has nothing to do with them, Liz." He reached for her again and pulled her down onto the pillows once more, "it's you, beautiful lady."

"But being with David has been good for you, too. Admit it."

He lie back and put his arm under his head. "When I was a kid, some of the best times I had was when David came West to visit. Those times were few and far between but they were rich. The three of us were a handful, though. I remember my mother . . ."

"The three of you?" she interrupted him.

"Rone and Dave and me. My mother would stand on the back porch with her hands on her hips and shake her head. 'I don't know what to do with you boys,' she'd say. But she was smiling, always smiling, and we knew we weren't in as much trouble as we'd be if my father were home."

Elizabeth saw his face change gradually as the memory continued in his mind. Then he went on, "She was the gentlest, kindest lady I've ever known. We tried hard to be good for her sake. None of us could bear the thought of making her unhappy. Rone got into his share of trouble with us, but he'd always be the first to stop. Next thing we'd know, he'd be in the house, doing little chores for her, trying to please her, to make up to her for any mischief. They were very close. Rone hasn't been the same since she died."

Elizabeth brushed his hair from his forehead. "How did she die, Jack?"

He hesitated before he answered. "Diphtheria . . . a few days and she was gone. I wasn't there. I was at Princeton. Rone was with her, and my father, of course."

"That must have been very hard on you."

Jack closed his eyes for a moment. Then he took her in his arms again, and kissing her mouth hard, said, "That's all in the past, Liz. I've got you now, and together we have to go forward. I know you're going to miss them, Liz, and it will seem quiet around here at first, but the way I look at it is that this is our beginning, fresh and new and belonging just to us."

She smiled brightly now. "Oh, yes, Jack, you're right."

They heard horses approaching and then a knock on the front door. Within a minute, Calla tapped lightly on their bedroom door. "Mr. Jack, some men are here lookin' for Miz Liz," she whispered.

"Me?" Elizabeth asked.

Jack put on his pants and left the room. He walked into the living room where three well-dressed men stood looking around. Jack stiffened and the hair on the back of his neck lifted when he saw them. "I'm Jack Drummond," he said.

"How do, Mr. Drummond, my name is John Bellows. We are here to see your wife, Elizabeth Gerard Drummond."

"What do you want with her?"

By now David and Catherine were in the room, and Elizabeth entered just as the man named Bellows said, "We're here to arrest her for the murder of Mr. Thomas Blackwell of New York City."

PART III

CHAPTER TWENTY-ONE

The words echoed in Elizabeth's mind until she felt dizzy. She grabbed for the back of one of the chairs. For a brief moment, the room was silent as each person tried to absorb what had just been said.

Jack and Elizabeth exchanged glances, but Jack looked away quickly, and turning to Bellows, said, "What are you talking about?"

John Bellows smiled, "Your wife killed a man several months ago, Mr. Drummond. As agents of the Pinkerton Agency, we've been looking for her for quite awhile. We assume you didn't know about this little . . . mishap, shall we call it?"

Jack's face was set in a stony expression, and his eyes were black and dangerous. "She didn't kill him. Now get off my ranch," he demanded.

The agent smiled again. "I'm afraid I can't do that, sir. As of a few minutes ago, your wife is under arrest." Then turning to Elizabeth, he said, "If you'd be so good as to get dressed, we'll be leaving on the next train to Cheyenne. There's a train on Monday leaving for New York."

Elizabeth looked at Jack.

"She didn't do it, I tell you!" Jack said.

"Jack," whispered Elizabeth.

Bellows pulled his gun and pointed it at Jack, "I don't want trouble with you, Drummond, but you'll get it if you interfere any further. There are ten agents stationed around this house, ready and waiting for my orders. If necessary, we'll take your wife by force."

Calla walked over to the window and pulled aside the curtain. Four men on horses were visible, each with a rifle positioned toward the house.

Bellows' voice went on, "Your wife was with Thomas Blackwell the night he was murdered. There's an eye witness willing to testify to seeing her murder him."

"Who? Who could testify to a lie?"

"Stop it, Jack!" Elizabeth cried.

"Shut up, Liz," Jack warned her.

"No, Jack, I won't let you do this. They know I did it."

Jack grabbed her shoulders, "You didn't, Liz. Listen to me, you didn't kill him."

She turned to Bellows, "It's true that I killed that man. I'll go with you, just don't hurt anyone."

"My dear, Mrs. Drummond, we don't intend to hurt anyone at all," Bellows said graciously, then looking at Jack, he added, "unless it's necessary."

Jack raked his fingers through his hair and said to her, "It will be all right. We'll have this settled in no time. When we get to New York, we'll . . ."

"No, Drummond, she's coming with us alone."

Emily said, "But we were planning to leave on the same train to return East."

Bellows indicated Jack with his gun, "Not him."

David stepped forward now, "By, God, man, you can't take a young woman from her home and expect her husband to stay behind."

"She can take someone if she wishes, but not her husband. He has a reputation for being troublesome."

Catherine walked over to Elizabeth now and took her niece's hand. "I'll be with her, Jack. You can join us later in New York."

Catherine led Elizabeth down the hall and into the bedroom. Once behind the closed door, she asked her, "What is this all about, Elizabeth?"

Elizabeth couldn't seem to concentrate on any one thought that passed through her mind. She sat on the bed and cried into her aunt's lap. "Oh, God, oh dear God," she keened.

Catherine held her. "Elizabeth, this can't be true. You couldn't have murdered this man."

"I did . . . I did." Great sobs wrenched her thin body.

Catherine shook her head, "How? Why, Elizabeth?"

"He was going to rape me. He was beating me and going to rape me, and I knew only that I had to get away from him . . . away from the pain. I grabbed a letter opener and stabbed him, but I didn't mean to . . ." Elizabeth was unable to go on.

Catherine placed her hand on the crying woman's head gently. "My poor, impetuous Elizabeth. What did you do to yourself by running away that night?"

Calla entered the room with two large mugs filled with coffee. She placed the tray on the chest of drawers and carried one of the mugs to Elizabeth. "You drink this coffee now, Miz Liz. You'll feel better with somethin' in your stomach." Her rough, work-worn hand gently brushed Elizabeth's fair hair away from her flushed, wet face.

When Elizabeth and Catherine were dressed, they joined the others in the sitting room. Emily and David were dressed for travel, while Jack paced like a coyote around the room. Emily's eyes were large with worry, and she went to Elizabeth as soon as she entered the room. Elizabeth managed a nervous smile. "Don't worry, Em. It will be all right."

Emily said sadly, "Does trouble follow us everywhere?"

Jack turned to Bellows again, "Won't you listen to reason?"

Bellows shook his head. "My job is to find the accused and take her back, not decide her guilt or innocence. That's for the judge and jury to do."

"It was self-defense," Catherine tried.

"Then let her prove it in a court of law."

Elizabeth walked over to her husband and placed her hand on his arm. Their eyes met for a long moment, then she turned and said, "I'm ready, Mr. Bellows. Let's get this over with."

CHAPTER TWENTY-TWO

The car was empty except for an elderly couple and the five Pinkerton Agents who were escorting Elizabeth and Catherine. On Bellows' orders, David and Emily were forced to sit in another car, where more agents were seated. Bellows sat across from the women and studied Elizabeth carefully. He had been an agent for almost six years, and this was the first woman he had ever arrested.

Men were easy to read. Most of the time, Bellows could tell if they were innocent or guilty within ten minutes. He decided this was different and he looked at the beautiful profile of the young woman sitting across from him. Her hands trembled incessantly, yet her face was serene, showing no signs of her initial shock and fear when he had taken her into custody two days before. He knew she had murdered Blackwell, she admitted it freely. But was it self-defense as her aunt had insisted, or a lover's quarrel as the witness had testified?

He smiled to himself when he noticed she was smoothing the skirt of her dove gray traveling suit. She knew he was staring at her, musing over her, and she was uncomfortable.

Elizabeth's large gray eyes rose to meet his and defied him to continue to stare. Without a word, she reproached his rudeness.

Beautiful The word kept coming to him while he looked at her. *Beautiful.* Dangerous? *This kind of woman is always dangerous,* he thought. *Proud, determined and beautiful . . . definitely dangerous. But a murderess*? Now, that he couldn't answer.

Elizabeth saw them first, hooded men on horseback, before the deafening squeal of the train's brakes threw her and

Catherine over into the lap of the Pinkerton Agent. Struggling against the impact, Catherine and Bellows found themselves falling into the aisle with Elizabeth on top of them. Then there was a moment's pause.

Bellows pushed the women off him, shouting orders to the other agents to draw their weapons. It was too late. The door of the car crashed open and two hooded men bounded in, their pistols drawn.

"Get down on your stomachs," one of them commanded.

One of the agents reached for his gun and was shot.

"Get down on your stomachs," the bandit said again.

Elizabeth could hear the elderly woman weeping, and edging over, placed her arm protectively around the woman's shoulders, with her eyes daring the outlaws to stop her.

The woman raised her face to Elizabeth's. "My husband . . ."

Elizabeth saw the old man was unconscious. One of the bandits leaned over him, then turned back to the old woman. It surprised her when he said in a soft, polite drawl, "He's okay, Ma'am. Just a bump on his head, is all. Now don't you be worryin'. He'll be just fine."

He started to touch the old woman, but Elizabeth slapped his hand away. "What is this?" she demanded to know.

"Why, it's a robbery, Ma'am."

"Well, go ahead and rob us and be done with it."

Elizabeth could see his eyes crinkle in a smile, though his mouth was hidden by the hood.

"We'll do just that, Ma'am, but we'd appreciate y'all getting off the train first."

He guided the women off the train. Elizabeth looked around and saw that there were at least twenty outlaws on and surrounding the train. Each of the men who were passengers on the train descended single file with their hands on their heads. Beth saw Emily and David and wondered why David was shaking his head vehemently, but she couldn't understand what he was trying to tell her. Some of the bandits went around taking money and jewelry while the others held their guns on the group.

Elizabeth glanced at the front of the train. She saw three men on horseback, ropes trailing behind them attached to a huge tree trunk, which had been pulled across the tracks.

Another group of hooded men rode forward, leading two saddled, empty horses behind him. As they approached the group, the bandit with the southern drawl took Elizabeth's elbow. "Ma'am, we'd sure appreciate your gettin' up on that horse over there."

"Whatever for?" she asked, pulling her elbow from his grip.

"Well, we usually take a hostage or two to insure gettin' away. I decided it might as well be a beautiful one as an ugly one."

Elizabeth heard Catherine and Bellows issue surprised "No!" in unison.

"This woman is under arrest and in my custody. I will not allow you to take her," a red-faced Bellows declared.

The southern bandit laughed and shook his head, "Don't look to me like you got much of a choice, now. How you gonna stop us lawman? It's gonna be 'specially hard with a Winchester up your backside. I hear one more word outta you and that's just exactly the position you're gonna be in . . . sir."

Elizabeth looked from one to the other, then stepped forward, hands on her hips. "I won't go with you," she said.

The Southerner stood close to her, looking down into her defiant eyes. "Would you rather go to jail with them?"

"At least they aren't criminals."

"'Scuse me, Ma'am, but considerin' they have you in custody sounds an awful lot like you're a criminal yourself."

"She most certainly is not!" Catherine interjected.

He looked at Elizabeth's aunt as if noticing her for the first time. "Who might you be?"

"I'm her aunt."

"You under arrest, too?"

"I am not. I'm accompanying her."

"Well, all right then, Ma'am. You can just hop up on that other horse."

"What?" Catherine gasped.

Elizabeth stood in front of Catherine now as if to shield her. "No, you can't do that. You've robbed us, you've shot an innocent man—an agent, I might add, of the Pinkerton Agency—you've frightened the daylights out of us, especially those poor elderly people. You've done enough. I will not go with you under any circumstances, and I will not let you take my aunt. Go away. No one will follow you."

The bandits looked at one another and the southern man walked over to the group of men on horseback. They exchanged words. When they were finished, four of them dismounted and quickly apprehended Elizabeth and Catherine, but not without a fight.

Elizabeth used every ounce of strength to get away from the hooded men. The cumbersome traveling skirt and petticoats she wore prevented her from using the techniques Rone had taught her, and within minutes, the men had her arms pinned to her sides. She continued to struggle until she heard the cocking of a gun and saw one of the men hold it to her aunt's temple.

Elizabeth stopped immediately. "Don't hurt her," she said.

"You just calm down, pretty lady, and no one will get hurt. Get up there on that horse."

"Leave my aunt," she said first.

"I don't think so, Ma'am. I've decided to take her along with us after all."

The women were forced up onto the horses, their skirts pulled up to the calves of their legs. Bellows, still standing with his hands on his head, shouted, "You'll regret this. I'll hunt you down until I find you."

"You do that, Pinkerton Agent," the Southerner said. Then he rode to the front of the train and cut the ropes that were attached to the tree which lay across the tracks. The riders laughed and rode away.

The Southerner tipped his hat to the old woman who stood crying quietly. "I am most sorry for upsettin' you, Ma'am. I truly regret your husband gettin' hurt."

He took two pieces of jewelry from the bag of contraband— the woman's wedding ring and watch pin—and handed it to her. He turned and led the large party of bandits away from the train, Elizabeth and Catherine with them. Emily tried to run after them but David grabbed her, watching helplessly.

They rode through the night, resting only a few minutes at a time. Elizabeth studied the sky and knew they were riding southwest. She tried to memorize the terrain, but it was impossible, for every mile looked just like the mile before it. Her mind never rested as she struggled to think of an escape, but she knew it would be too easy to become lost on these desolate plains, and she couldn't leave Catherine.

Every now and then she would glance at her aunt. Catherine was tiring quickly, and her terrified expression alarmed Elizabeth.

When it was dark again, they stopped and made camp. Catherine and Elizabeth were kept close together but unbound.

Catherine sank to the ground exhausted, and Elizabeth sat beside her.

All but one of the men had removed their hoods as soon as
they were out of sight of the train, but as they rode furiously
throughout the night, Elizabeth had not had time to look at any
of them. Two men stood guard over the women, rifles always in
clear view. No one had spoken to them during the ride, and even
now the men avoided them.

She studied the leader of the group, the Southerner. She
knew from hearing the others address him that his name was
Jessop. He was tall—taller than most men—and walked with an
easy gait, carrying himself erect. Twice he found her looking at
him and flashed her a pleasant smile. Had she not seen how dangerous he was at the train, she would have thought him harm-
less.

His hair was the color of honey, and when he walked over to
her and stooped down beside her, she noticed his eyes were the
same color as his hair. His liquid voice and slow lingo were surprisingly appealing.

"Well, now, Ma'am, you must be right tired."

When she refused to answer him with anything but a glare,
he went on in the same pleasant tone. "We thought it time you
and your chaperon here rested awhile. Won't be long before we
have some grub ready. You and your aunt will be the first fed, I
promise you that."

Looking back over his shoulder, he indicated one of the men,
a Mexican, who stood nearby. "That man over there is in charge
of you ladies."

The young Mexican gave the women a toothy grin and nodded politely and enthusiastically.

Jessop went on, "You need anything, you just tell him and
he'll get it for you. He'll be your own personal . . . guardian, shall
we say . . . while you're our guests."

"Hostages, you mean," Elizabeth said angrily.

"Please don't look on it that way, Ma'am."

"What exactly do you intend to do with us?"

"At this point, I don't rightly know, but when I decide, you'll
be the first to hear of it."

"I'm sure I will. I just want to make it very clear that I do not
like being kidnapped by a gang of . . . of . . . lawbreakers, and I
will be as uncooperative as I possibly can. Please remember—
and make it clear to all your friends—that I will not tolerate any

one of them putting a hand on me or my aunt. Is that understood, Mr. Jessop?"

"Understood, Ma'am. 'Course I must just mention that should any one of us get to hankerin', there ain't much you could do about it, now, is there?"

"You'll have to kill me, Mr. Jessop . . . if I don't kill you first. Don't ever underestimate me."

He laughed heartily now. "You are somethin'. Well, consider the warnin' well taken, then. Truth is, we ain't out to assault ladies—just stealin' money."

Jessop put his hand on Catherine's shoulder. "We'll take good care of you. You have no cause for worryin'."

She smiled at him. "Thank you, sir."

Elizabeth was outraged. "Sir? Really, Aunt Catherine, how can you smile at him and call him 'sir'?"

Catherine was about to answer, but stopped when she looked up and saw the Mexican standing over them. He held clothing in his hands and extended them to Elizabeth. She stood up and took them, noticing they were men's clothing.

"Obviously, he wants us to wear these clothes." She looked around and said, "Well, I don't intend to undress here in front of you."

The Mexican looked puzzled a moment and he, himself, took a good look around to find some cover for the women to change behind. Then he said, "Over zere, behind ze horses. Do not worry, Edelberto weel keep watch." He placed his right hand across his chest and gave them a look that promised his trust-worthiness.

With a glare, Elizabeth took Catherine's elbow and led her away to change in whatever privacy the horses gave. When they were dressed, she turned to see Catherine looking exceedingly uncomfortable in the oversized pants and shirt. Elizabeth giggled at the sight.

"Elizabeth, what is so funny?" Catherine asked. "Under the circumstances, I can't think of anything humorous."

Elizabeth tried to control herself. "Oh, I know, but you look so . . . unlike yourself."

"What do you mean?"

"Well, I've never seen you in britches before, for one thing. You look so . . . different. You don't look a year older than I, Aunt Catherine."

Elizabeth took her aunt's shoulders in each of her hands. "We might as well laugh at something," she said. Then looking beyond the horses at the pack of men who had robbed the train and had taken them for God knew what reason, she added, "It may be the last time we do."

Chapter Twenty-three

During the next few days, they rode before the sun was up and long after it had set. Most of the men ignored Elizabeth and Catherine. It was Jessop and Edelberto who seemed to guard them and bring them their food.

Occasionally, Jessop would sit down with them and accompany them during the meal. He carried on pleasant conversation with Catherine and his infectious friendliness warmed Elizabeth slightly, and she found herself looking forward to the few times he ate with them.

One evening, the man who had remained hooded brought their dinners to them. He did not address them as he handed each woman a tin plate filled with food. Elizabeth could feel his eyes on her from the shadow of his sackcloth hood. It sent a chill up her spine. He turned and walked back to the other men and began to eat through a hole that had been cut around his mouth.

Jessop collected their plates when they had finished eating. Elizabeth said, "May I ask you a question, Mr. Jessop?"

He smiled, gratified that the usually sullen young woman initiated the conversation this time and it was enough to invite him to sit beside her, his unusually long legs stretched out in front of him.

What is it you'd like to know, Ma'am?"

She indicated the hooded man. "Why hasn't that man taken off his hood?"

Bill Jessop took a long time to answer and then he said, "A deformity. He's got a deformity of the face." Jessop was very serious when he added, "It makes him meaner than any mad dog I ever seen, too."

"What sort of deformity?" Catherine asked.

"It's hard to describe . . . but it's ugly. None of the other men can stand lookin' at him. He wears that hood day and night. Says people have tried to kill him just because of his face."

"The poor man," Catherine said, sympathetically.

Elizabeth huffed, "He's an outlaw, Aunt Catherine, not a poor man."

Jessop leaned closer to them so that he could speak quietly. "A word of advise, ladies. Stay away from him. He ain't the sort fine women like you would want to be alone with, if you know what I mean. His name's Carver—it's a nickname—because of what he does with his knife, especially when he's drunk. So don't ever be alone with him."

Elizabeth straightened her back and looked at Jessop. "I trust you'll see to it that we never are, Mr. Jessop."

"I'll try my best, Ma'am."

As the days wore on, Elizabeth became more cross. She had expected Jack to find them by now—or at worst, the Pinkerton Agents. The long hours of riding and the hot sun made her tense and irritable. Even Bill Jessop's amiability got on her nerves, and she no longer enjoyed his company at meals.

Edelberto sensed her aggravation and tried to be polite and sweet to no advantage. When he placed her dish before her one evening, she threw it back at him.

"You know, you'll never get away with this," she shouted. "You think you'll make it to Mexico, but you won't. The agents you took me from are after you right now, and if they don't catch up with you, my husband will. Yes, Mr. Jessop," she yelled out to the men who had turned to listen to her, "my husband. When he learns of this kidnapping, and I'm certain that he has already, he'll find us. When he does, he'll cut your heart out."

Edelberto wiped the beans from his shirt and pants and shook his head. "What ees wrong weeth you, Señora? You are so mad at us."

Elizabeth got to her feet and her face was red with anger. "You're damned right I'm mad. How dare you do this to me and my aunt. I demand to be released . . . now . . . tonight. I will not tolerate being your hostage for another minute."

Bill Jessop approached her. "Now, listen here, Ma'am, there ain't no reason fo' you to be goin' on so. We ain't done nothin' to you."

"Oh, really, Jessop? Well, for your information, I didn't want to be here with you. Neither did my aunt. Don't you come one step closer to me."

"I'm not goin' to hurt you . . . ," but he didn't heed her warning and she leapt at him, kicking him hard and beating him with her fists. Jessop pushed her away roughly several times, but she always charged back, striking out harder and more viciously. "Ow, stop biting me," he shouted, as Elizabeth's teeth sank into his side when he tried to pin her down. Two other men came to assist and each of them received a kick that sent them sprawling.

Catherine stood, shocked at the violent scene. Two more men were trying to still her niece, but Elizabeth was literally beating them and they were virtually allowing it.

Catherine expected them to kill Elizabeth at any second, but they laughed or howled in pain when her fist, boot or teeth found them.

At last they had her on the ground, and Jessop quickly tied her hands and feet, shoving a thick cloth into her screaming mouth. The men stepped back, sweating and looking exhausted from the fight. Jessop looked down into Elizabeth's angry eyes.

"Who the hell taught you how to fight? I thought you were a lady! Now you just settle down. There ain't no reason for you to try and kill us."

He pulled up his shirt to look at the teeth marks on his side. Elizabeth had drawn blood, and a red welt was rising on his forehead where she had kicked him. He looked at Catherine. "She's a savage; for two cents I ought to let Carver kill her."

One of the other men laughed and said, "Maybe you better clean that bite, Bill. She might have rabies," and the group laughed again, drifting back to the fire to finish their dinners.

Beth lie on the ground, tied and gagged by the dirty tasting rag. Her rage was subsiding, but her frustration was at a peak. Edelberto walked over to her and looked down. Elizabeth tried unsuccessfully to push the gag from her mouth with her tongue.

Catherine came to sit beside her. "Honestly, Elizabeth, you could have been killed. I don't understand why they didn't kill you. Be careful, for God's sake."

Then she sighed and tenderly brushed Elizabeth's hair from her eyes. "Are you hurt, dear?"

Elizabeth shook her head no. Catherine looked up at Edelberto. "I think she's calmer now. Couldn't you take the gag out of her mouth?"

He watched Elizabeth for a long while, then reached down and pulled the rag away from her face roughly. "You be nice, *si*?"

"I be nice, no! Untie me this minute you little Mexican pile of horse dung. I . . ."

Edelberto shoved the rag back in her mouth, shrugging at Catherine, who shrugged back.

They kept Elizabeth tied up the entire night. It grew cold and she was shivering and couldn't sleep even though Catherine had covered her with a thin blanket. Carver was on guard and she knew his eyes were watching her.

Elizabeth stiffened when he started to walk toward her. Bile rose in her throat. He was staring at her threateningly behind the brown sack. Her chest constricted in fear and she tried to pull back, straining against her bonds.

A flash caught her eye and she saw that his knife was in his hand. When he drew closer and bent down, a strangled cry, too strangled to be heard by the others, escaped her. She recoiled when he brought the knife up and pushed her on her side. He cut the ropes that were holding her wrists together, then, in a silent warning, put the pointed tip to her chin. After a long moment, he stood up and threw another blanket at her.

The next morning, Jessop awakened her, and when she jumped up, startled, he fell back with his knees bent, his hands ready to defend himself. "Now, I'm trustin' that you'll behave yourself, Ma'am. I don't want none of that stuff you showed us last night."

Elizabeth stretched her legs and gave him a sideways glance. "Don't worry, Mr. Jessop, I am sufficiently chastised for my rude behavior," she said, sarcastically.

He smiled at her now, patted her shoulder and said, "That's better. We've got a lot of miles to go today and we don't need trouble from you."

They rode through the heat of the day, and Elizabeth felt herself slipping into a bored trance. The land was brown and drab and she couldn't seem to concentrate on anything for very long. The constant movement of the horse beneath her, the heat and the boredom made her sleepy and she would doze, then awaken with a start.

She had fallen into one of these dozes when she felt the horse tense and rear up. Before she could react, the horse was racing away from the group. As she sped away, she could hear Catherine's scream echoing in the canyon around them.

For the first time in Elizabeth's life, she could not control her horse. She gave him his head and leaned forward, her cheek against his neck, hoping he would tire and slow down. He resisted all her machinations to control him. He jumped boulders and cacti in his way and almost unsaddled Elizabeth several times. She knew riders were behind her, trying to catch up to help, but the spooked horse wasn't reachable.

Then she saw it coming. The land dropped off into another canyon ahead. Elizabeth knew with certainty that in his panic, the horse would not see it and they would both be killed.

Elizabeth's mind was racing. If she were to slip off the horse, she would be trampled by his back legs or would break her neck with the impact. She looked down at the ground swiftly passing under her, trying to decide what to do, how to save herself.

The cliff was closer . . . closer . . . until finally she could see beyond it to where it dropped down. She wanted to scream, and though her mouth was opened, no sound came. Then, as the horse's front legs were in midair, over the edge, she felt the sting of rope whip around her shoulders and her body pitched backward.

Suspended in air, she could see the horse's long tail sail between her legs just before the animal disappeared beyond the cliff.

Elizabeth landed solidly on the earth. She felt as though she were being hit bottom-side with a pillow rather than pain as she had expected. It surprised her even as she sank into unconsciousness.

Elizabeth felt herself swimming up out of a darkness unfamiliar to her, and then wanted to go back down into the comfort of that blackness, but a voice was calling her—a man's voice—a voice not to be refused.

It called her name and asked her questions she could not understand. Only the voice she understood. It stopped when she saw light beyond her eyelids and she spoke, she knew she spoke, but did not know what it was she was saying.

Elizabeth reluctantly opened her eyes and there she saw the hood—the hated sack of Carver—above her. Bill Jessop's face appeared in its place suddenly.

"Ma'am, you just lie still a minute. I want you to slowly try to move your legs and arms, not too fast, that's it. Good. You feelin' any pain? Your back hurtin' you?"

"Everything hurts me, Mr. Jessop," she answered.

"Does your neck hurt, Ma'am?" Jessop continued.

She closed her eyes to shield them from the blinding sun. "Mr. Jessop, I just this minute told you everything hurts me . . . and will you please stop calling me 'Ma'am.' I find it infuriating. My name is Elizabeth."

Bill Jessop looked up at the group gathered around them. "Sounds like she's all right to me," he said, laughing.

Elizabeth felt arms move under her knees and shoulders and knew she was being lifted. She opened her eyes and saw that Carver was carrying her.

"You're trembling," she said to him.

He didn't answer her, but their eyes connected, and there was something palpable in that glance. She wanted to ask questions, but she couldn't form words. All she seemed to be able to understand was that this man who held her in his arms and carried her toward her aunt was shaking uncontrollably.

CHAPTER TWENTY-FOUR

They approached the Mexican border a week after being taken from the train, and Elizabeth wondered what would happen to her and Catherine now. She doubted Jessop would keep them. Was death the only alternative?

Elizabeth looked for her aunt on the horse several feet abreast. Feeling guilty that Catherine was in this predicament, she wondered what life for all of them would have been like now if she had not run away from Benton. The only good that seemed to have come out of it was that she knew Jack and knew what loving him was like. And now she wondered if she would ever see him again, for surely, if he were going to find them, he would have by now.

She became aware of Carver behind her when his leg moved and his thigh touched hers. Weary and sore, she allowed herself to lean back against his chest. Since the death of her own horse, she had been forced to ride with him. It was as if she belonged to him now that he had saved her life.

When she had protested privately to Jessop, he had shrugged and looked embarrassed. "I'm sorry, Ma'am. He has decided you're his now, and to be truthful with you, I don't want to mess around with that mean bugger."

Catherine, on the other hand, showed Carver respect and gratitude for having saved her niece's life. When Elizabeth had chided her aunt for it, Catherine had reminded her how Carver had lassoed Elizabeth to safety just as the horse plummeted down to its death on the canyon's floor.

"Over and over he tried to catch up to you, but always fell back slightly. I'll never forget the paralyzing fear I felt when I watched him trying to save you. Then, I saw him twirling the rope in the air, and," at this point Catherine had closed her eyes and shivered, "it just fell around you as the horse went over the edge."

Catherine had let out a long breath. "You fell with such a force, I thought surely you had been killed anyway. I think Carver thought so too. He jumped from his saddle and attended to you with such gentleness. I can't believe you weren't hurt, Elizabeth."

Elizabeth had moaned, "I am hurt. Every inch of me aches." She had adjusted herself on the ground with a wince as if to verify it. "Really, you talk about him as though he were a hero. This man uses human beings as whittling wood when he's drunk, for heaven's sake, Aunt Catherine. If they hadn't robbed the train and taken us hostage, I wouldn't have been in that danger to begin with."

Catherine had nodded her head, but Elizabeth could see she was unconvinced. "I know, dear, but he did save your life."

"I don't care. I don't like him. He frightens me. I wish he'd take off that hood. Anything would be better than that damned hood."

"He did, Beth. When your horse bolted, he pulled it off and went after you."

Elizabeth had sat up quickly, wincing again with the effort. "What did he look like?"

"I don't know. I was so frightened and worried about you I didn't look at him. As soon as he saw that you were regaining consciousness, he put it on again. Then, he lifted you in his arms. At first, he seemed not to know where he was going. It was as if holding you and getting you away from the cliff was the only thing important to him."

After thinking it over, Elizabeth asked, "Why doesn't he speak to us?"

Catherine had known the answer. "Mr. Jessop said he can't talk well because of his facial deformity, so he doesn't speak at all if he can help it." Catherine's eyes filled with tears. "It's really very sad when you think of it, Beth. Perhaps those are the circumstances that has made him become so . . . strange."

Now, as Elizabeth leaned against his chest, she could feel his heart beating against the rough material of his shirt. *What will he do with me when we get to Mexico?* she wondered. *Has he saved my life just to end it when he is safely out of the country?*

She felt weary and tired then, as they crossed the border, Elizabeth didn't notice his arm tighten around her as she fell asleep against him.

The night was hot and she awakened slowly. Her eyes focused on the stars in the clear sky above her. She couldn't remember when the day ended and the night began. She sat up and pushed the blanket away from her. Jessop was guarding the camp and saw her sit up. He walked over and said, "Never saw anybody sleep like that before."

"Where are we?" she asked him.

"Just the other side."

"Mexico," she confirmed.

He nodded and asked, "You hungry?"

"A little." She looked around for Carver.

Jessop smiled. "He's sleepin' over there. Come on over to the fire, Ma'am, and I'll get you some beef strips and coffee."

She looked around as she drank the hot, bitter coffee. There were only a few men in camp. "Where is everyone?" she asked.

"Split up," Jessop answered. "They each got whatever was comin' to them, and then they went on their way, until next time."

"Next time?"

"Next time there's some robbin' to do up north."

Elizabeth looked at him for a long time, then said, "You're hard to figure out, Mr. Jessop. You aren't a typical thief."

He smiled a warm, gentle smile. "That's very nice of you, Ma'am."

"What do you intend to do with us now, Mr. Jessop?"

"That's hard to say."

"Are you planning to kill us?"

"You're an awful pretty lady, Mrs. Drummond. It'd be a shame to kill you. I don't think I got that in mind atall."

He offered her another cup of coffee, but she shook her head. "No, thank you. I think I'll go back to sleep now."

She walked back to her blanket and picked it up. Catherine was sleeping soundly. Elizabeth's eyes sought Carver, and he, too, appeared to be sleeping peacefully. Then she dropped down slowly and covered herself and fell into a restless sleep.

Elizabeth did not feel Carver's eyes watching her through the night.

When dawn broke, Elizabeth awakened to see Jessop, Carver, Edelberto, and another man gathered in a circle talking. She strained to hear what they were saying, but it was impossible to understand the words. Then she saw Carver hand Jessop money and they shook hands.

Jessop mounted his horse and started to ride away. Elizabeth sprang up and ran towards him, shouting, "Wait! Where are you going? What is this?"

Jessop turned his horse around to face her. "Well, Ma'am, we're splittin' up. Carver will take care of you now."

He lifted his hat in a courtly gesture. "It was a pleasure, Ma'am, a real pleasure."

"Don't, Jessop. Please don't leave me with him. You have no right to sell me. What kind of a person are you?"

"I'm a thief, Mrs. Drummond. Maybe I'm a typical thief after all. I'm sorry."

Tears stung Elizabeth's eyes and she was about to cry for the first time since being abducted.

"You don't need to worry, Ma'am. I got me a funny kind of sense of humor, so don't be worryin'," was all Jessop said. He flashed an apologetic smile at her and rode away.

Slowly she turned to face the silent, hooded man who had just purchased her and, obviously, her aunt, as well. The thought that their lives were in the hands of this man filled her with terror.

"Now what?" she asked him, with bravado she didn't feel.

Catherine stood watching. Edelberto, who seemed to be staying with them, brought the horses to the group. The men mounted and then Catherine climbed silently onto her mare. Carver extended his arm to assist Elizabeth.

She stared at him for a long moment, then her hand gripped his forearm and his fingers closed around her elbow as he pulled her up behind him.

They rode north, back over the border. Elizabeth asked questions that went unanswered. "Why are we going back? Where are you taking us? Why won't you answer me?"

Catherine, tired and annoyed, said, "For heaven's sake, Elizabeth, hold your tongue. He isn't going to answer you."

They rode for several days until Elizabeth recognized that they were heading back into the Rocky Mountains. Her heart beat faster with the idea that maybe they were taking her home to the ranch. She dared to hope, as Carver seemed different, kinder, but she asked no more questions.

Disappointment enveloped her when she realized they were headed in a different direction from River Pines. They climbed mountain passes, which were cold in the late autumn. Trees were almost bare the higher they climbed. They rode with blankets over their shoulders, and in the mornings when they awakened, frost lay heavily upon their covers.

It was just after noon on the coldest day when they came to a small cabin. Smoke billowed out from the stone chimney. There were some horses in the corral behind the cabin, and Elizabeth noticed a cow grazing lazily in the grass.

She felt Carver dig his spurs into the horse and it trotted toward the little house. When they drew up in front, he dismounted and tied the horse to the post along the porch. He lifted his covered head to Beth, his dark eyes searching hers from behind his hood.

There was no mistaking his look—he was bidding her farewell. Elizabeth allowed him to help her down, and he held her a second longer than was necessary. She walked to the door of the cabin and opened it. Her eyes tried to adjust to the darkness within it, and then her mouth fell open and she gasped.

"Well, it took you long enough to get here, Liz," said Jack, who was sitting at a rough wooden table with an open bottle of whiskey and six glasses in front of him.

"Jack," she breathed, then cried out his name louder, "Jack!" Elizabeth ran into his open arms, allowing his hungry mouth to cover her lips.

Then she pulled away and spun to look at the other man. Carver stood alone in the doorway, still hooded.

Her eyes narrowed and her anger nearly choked her when she growled, "How could you do this to me, Rone?"

He slowly lifted the hood away. Elizabeth felt a black rage, the culmination of frustration and betrayal, and she walked over to him and slapped him hard across the face.

"How could you be so cruel to me?" she demanded.

Jack pulled her back but she pushed him away. Her eyes never left Rone's, nor did his leave her face.

"You are no friend to me, Rone Daniels," she said, and the words delivered a more severe blow than the slap had.

"Liz," Jack started, "he couldn't tell you. If you knew who he was, you wouldn't have gone with him. You had to be kept in the dark."

"The entire time?" Elizabeth asked.

"Would someone please tell me what is going on?" Catherine asked.

Jack answered her, "Catherine, I don't believe you've met my friend, Rone."

A slow recognition came into her eyes and she inclined her head to him. "I knew I liked you, hood and all."

Rone's frown lightened slightly. "I'd like to welcome you to my home," he said, then looking at Elizabeth, "both of you."

A very angry Elizabeth sat down at the table. Then she asked, "Jessop?"

Jack held a chair for Catherine and he took a seat beside his wife. "Bill Jessop's a friend of mine."

Elizabeth was aghast. "But they robbed those people and . . ."

Jack looked at Rone and grinned. "So, he couldn't resist?"

Rone nodded. "It was for the best. It would have been obvious what we were doing if we had just taken the women."

Jack tipped his hat back on his head. "Was it worth while?"

Rone smiled now, "Very."

"Like old times, eh, Rone?"

Elizabeth looked at him sharply. "What do you mean?"

"Just that Rone and I rode with Jessop's gang once, a long time ago."

She was dumbfounded, "You don't mean you were . . ."

"Yep, you might say it was in our wild days, before the ranch. Rone wasn't a very good outlaw, though. I suspect he went along to keep me out of too much trouble. Was that it, Rone?"

Rone looked at Jack a long time, then leaning against the wall, he stared out through the window.

"Yeah," Jack continued, watching his friend closely, "Rone and I go back a long way."

Edelberto walked in and smiled sheepishly at Elizabeth. "And who are you?" she asked.

"I work at ze Double D, Señora Drummond. I am so sorry to fool you like that."

Jack poured out the whiskey into the glasses and Elizabeth took one, gulping down the fiery liquid. Catherine also lifted a glass and sipped. Tears sprung to her eyes and she coughed, but took the rest down in one swallow.

"What happens next?" she asked, licking her lips.

After a few minutes, Jack said, "Well, ladies, it may be awhile before we leave here. There's another room in there with a bed." He indicated a door and Elizabeth could see a straw bed covered with blankets.

"You can have that room Catherine. Liz and I will sleep in the loft."

"What about Rone?" Catherine asked.

"I'll be going to River Pines, Miss Gleason," Rone answered. "Edelberto and I will leave later."

"Where exactly are we?" Elizabeth asked Jack.

"Well hidden in the mountain. No one will find us until we're ready to be found. Especially with winter coming, although I expect we'll be able to leave before then. I'm hoping we will, because once the snow comes, we'll be bound here 'til spring."

After they had eaten the stew Jack had cooked in the pot in the fireplace, Catherine went to bed, while Rone, Elizabeth and Jack took a walk around the small homestead.

Jack held Elizabeth's hand while he explained what had transpired after Bellows had taken her and Catherine away, and how Rone and Bill Jessop agreed to go along with his plans.

"I have reason to believe there's more to this story in New York than we were told, Liz."

"Jack, I was prepared to go to New York and face what I had done. I should have stayed when it happened. It was crazy for me to leave then. It won't be long before they realize this . . . this kidnapping was a pretense. Now I'm not only a murderess, but a renegade as well."

"Elizabeth, listen to me," he said, swinging her around to face him, "you are not a murderess."

She shook her head sadly, "I am, Jack. I did kill that man whether or not it was self-defense."

"Liz, the truth is . . ."

"The truth is that you are trying to protect me and I love you for it. I wish I hadn't killed Tom Blackwell, but I have and not owning up to it will not give me back those agonizing moments throughout the last months when I've thought of it and hated myself for it. Maybe standing trial will ease my conscience."

Jack looked away from her eyes. Then he said, "First we have to find this eyewitness and find out what he's up to. How could anyone have seen you that night, Liz? You were alone in that suite, and I was alone when I broke into it. There was no one in the corridor; I'm sure of it. So, who is this eyewitness and how did he know who you were?"

"Jacob Riis? He helped you that night, Jack."

"No, Jacob didn't see anything in your suite. David and Emily are going to try to find out exactly what's going on. When they feel confident you'll receive a fair trial, they'll wire my father and he'll send for us."

Elizabeth's eyes shown in the dusk and he could see she wasn't convinced. "Trust me, Liz. I won't have you going to prison—or worse—for this. You committed no crime that night, remember that. You were defending yourself."

"Then why did you take me away? Why did we steal away in the middle of the night and . . . and . . ."

Jack swore under his breath. "Just forget it for now. You'll be cleared eventually."

She sighed heavily and started walking again. The two men followed her. Then she turned to Rone. "You still owe me an explanation. Do you have any idea how frightened of you I was?"

Jack started to answer her, but Rone held up his hand to silence him. Then he spoke to Elizabeth. "At first it was to prevent being recognized by you as Jack had said. Then it was important that none of Jessop's men identify me and connect me with you in any way. A man will tell anything for a reward. Not all of his men could be trusted, and I took no chances that the law could trace us back here. Until your aunt mentioned it at dinner, I had no idea Jessop had told you that story about me . . . Carver, I mean." Rone smiled at Jack then, "Bill has a strange sense of humor, I guess."

"After we separated from Jessop, why didn't you show yourself then?"

Rone's eyes met hers but he didn't answer. It wasn't necessary, for in his eyes, for one brief, fleeting moment, she saw the answer.

There had been something different in Carver's manner from the day he saved her life. He was more protective, more possessive—loving.

The hated sack hid what his face would have told her each time Rone looked at her, and his anonymity behind the hood allowed him a vestige of intimacy.

"It doesn't matter why," Jack said, pulling her gently to him, possessively placing his arm around her shoulders. "All that matters is that you are here, safe from the hangman's noose. Rone owes you no explanation, Liz. We, on the other hand, owe him our thanks. Rone was there—as he always has been when I needed him."

Elizabeth was shaken by the momentary unveiling in Rone's dark eyes. "I'm so desperately tired," she mumbled, closing her own eyes.

"Go back to the cabin and sleep, Liz," Jack said, kissing her cheek gently.

She started for the cabin, then turned and looked at Rone once more. Gone was the look she had seen in his eyes not a minute before.

When Jack and he were alone, Rone announced, "I'm leaving now, Jack."

Jack smiled but his eyes were sad. "Somehow I knew you were about to say that. Take care of River Pines for me. I know I'm leaving it in good hands."

With a quick glance at the cabin, Rone extended his hand and Jack took it. "And I know that all I care about is in good hands, as well, Jack."

In their friendship, in the all encompassing trust between them, it was understood what Rone meant.

CHAPTER TWENTY-FIVE

Although they anticipated receiving a message from David before winter set in, they harvested Rone's neatly planted garden, and Elizabeth and Catherine bottled whatever they might need in case they were there longer than expected.

Jack spent hours cutting wood and stacking it against the side of the little cabin. He taught Elizabeth how to attend to the few chickens in the coop by the barn, and despite her protests, made her watch when he cleaned and butchered a buck he'd brought home. "You might need to do this someday, Liz. I want you to be able to take care of yourself."

"I can take care of myself without killing and butchering the most beautiful, graceful animal on this earth. It's bad enough having to kill the chickens. Can't we just eat vegetables, Jack? I hate doing this."

Snow had begun to fall and left a shawl of white on their shoulders. "We're a week into November, and it's snowed every day. I'm worried that we won't hear from my father before winter. It's going to be a bad one, and it worries me that we aren't prepared," Jack said, looking at the sky.

Every day, as Jack instructed, Elizabeth and Catherine milked the cow, churned butter and did other chores they had never had to do before. They worked from early morning to evening, surprised to find that, despite the hard work, they were enjoying themselves.

At night they read books from the shelves of Rone's impressive collection, familiarizing themselves with the classics once again, and Elizabeth would run her finger over passages in books that Rone had marked for himself. She was learning more about

Rone through his favorite literature than she had through personal contact with her shy, quiet friend.

Once in a while, her mind would drift back to the days when she had been Rone's captive, and the memories would confuse her. Very deliberately, careful not to dwell on them, Elizabeth would put those thoughts from her mind, and eventually the anger she had felt went away.

In the dark, she and Jack would make love in the loft of the warm cabin, whispering each other's names, losing themselves in the joy of being together. Elizabeth had never known such contentment.

Like children, they played in the snow, and Jack taught them how to snow shoe, and he made a rough sled for them to use on the hills behind the cabin, joining them whenever possible.

He instructed them on the way to prepare sourdough biscuits, just the way he liked them, and they relished a dish he called, apologizing to Catherine, son-of-a-bitch stew, telling them it was a favorite of the cowboys on the trail.

They roared with laughter when he entertained them with stories from his past as a cowboy and while he was a member of the Jessop gang. They in turn made him laugh when they related the mischief Catherine and her household endured at the hands of the mischievous twins.

Jack was relieved that the women seemed content in the cabin in the mountains, comfortable in each other's company. They shared happy, quiet moments. Jack and Catherine became better acquainted, establishing a warm bond of friendship. He knew that it was important they all get along well in the small confines.

But as the winter of 1886 enveloped the West with the worst blizzard and cold in the history of the area, Jack became more and more unnerved by the severe weather. He worked before the sun came up and after it went down, chopping wood, storing fodder, placing as many chicks as possible in the brooder.

The snow was too deep for the lambs to find their own food, and Jack watched as they rubbed their noses raw in desperation to break through the ice to the dead grass below.

Jack foraged in a chest Rone kept in the barn. There was a buffalo skin jacket and a pair of woolies, which he knew would get him through the winter whenever he needed to go out hunting, as the fur chaps would protect his legs.

There was a sheepskin coat for Elizabeth that she could use when she needed to milk the cow or collect eggs.

He was relieved to find a stock of coal-oil and a warming lamp for the chicken coop. If they could keep the chickens alive and laying, they had a better chance of surviving the unexpected freeze.

Jack kept up a jovial front with Elizabeth and Catherine, not wanting to alarm them, but late in December, he knew he was going to have to warn them to be more careful with the food and the wood.

He was pulling on his buffalo jacket one morning, when Elizabeth asked, "Where are you going?"

"To find one of the lambs."

"Do you know what today is, Jack?" she asked, smiling.

He shook his head. Elizabeth put her arms around his waist under the warm coat. "It's Christmas, my love."

He kissed her lips tenderly. "Merry Christmas, beautiful lady."

"Aunt Catherine and I are fixing you a special dinner today, so don't stay away long."

His eyes clouded over. "Don't over do it, Liz. We may have to start rationing the food."

Elizabeth shook her head and frowned. "You worry too much, Jack."

He kissed her one last time and left the cabin. Bitter cold air assaulted her, but she went out onto the porch with him. She shivered when he stepped into the snow. "Jack! Be careful." He waved back to her as he followed the stretch of rope from the cabin to the barn, and disappeared inside to saddle his horse. Elizabeth looked at the trees where the elk and deer had already eaten most of the bark and then had moved on.

When he returned to the cabin later, he was white. Catherine placed a platter of fowl on the table and looked up at him. "What is it?" she asked, alarmed at the expression on his face.

"They're gone."

Elizabeth had been in the loft changing into one of the dresses Jack had brought for her from the ranch, and she stopped half way down the ladder, and asked, "Who?"

"Sheep . . . game . . . there's no food out there."

He sat down heavily in a chair, and they could feel the coldness radiating from his clothing.

Elizabeth went to him. "Darling, take off your coat and come to the fire. We've roasted a chicken and some potatoes. You'll feel better after you've eaten."

Jack moved slowly, as though he had difficulty maneuvering. He ate dinner moodily and didn't finish it all. The women exchanged disappointed glances.

When Catherine placed a white cake, beautifully iced with raspberry preserves, on the table in front of him, Jack saw her expectant eyes search his for approval.

He tried to smile. "I'm sorry, Catherine. Here it is Christmas, and I've done nothing but sulk and worry."

She patted his hand. "We'll get through this winter, Jack. You wait and see—God will see us through this."

Elizabeth cut the cake and gave him a large piece. "Let's forget the weather now, Jack. It's Christmas. We can start worrying again tomorrow."

Jack laughed and said, "Well, it can't be Christmas without a Christmas tree." He put on his coat again and went outside. Within minutes, he opened the door of the cabin and stood holding a young sapling, roots and all. "How's this?"

Catherine laughed, "Well, it's a tree."

They placed it in a pot and decorated it with biscuit cutters and pieces of yarn. They carefully hung anything that was colorful enough and small enough to fit on the tiny branches. When they were finished, Jack gave them a crooked smile. "Now that's the prettiest Christmas tree I've ever had."

Then he got out the half-filled bottle of whiskey he had opened the first day they were in the cabin and they toasted one another and took a drink.

"I've got an idea," Jack said, pushing the table against the wall and moving the chairs aside. "We'll have a Christmas dance."

"But there's no music, Jack," Catherine laughed.

He thought a moment, then announced, "I'll hum—sure, I'm a good hummer." He proceeded to hum Christmas music as he took Catherine in his arms and swung her around the cramped dance floor, while Elizabeth clapped her hands.

Catherine took her turn humming when Jack danced with his wife, but after a few turns, he grabbed his head and stumbled. "You ladies have worn me out 'til I'm dizzy," he said, grabbing for a chair, his face becoming very pale.

After they had sat before the fire, reminiscing about Christmases past until it was very late, Catherine went to bed. Elizabeth put herself on his lap and they chuckled when the chair creaked noisily with the extra weight.

"You must have eaten too much for dinner, Liz," he said, putting his head against her shoulder, as his arm went around her waist.

Elizabeth put her cheek on his dark hair. They stared into the fire in silence for a long time, and finally she asked, "You're desperately worried, Jack, aren't you?"

He sighed. "It's a bad winter, Liz. The worst I've ever seen. I'm worried about River Pines. A winter like this could destroy the richest ranch, and the crops we harvested might not be enough to keep it going through January. God knows, Rone will do his best, but some things are beyond man."

"And us?"

He looked up into her eyes. "With this snow, it won't be easy to cut wood. I'm worried about food. I didn't think we'd be here this long, and to tell the truth, it scares me."

"The pantry shelves are still half full, Jack," Elizabeth offered.

"You'll be surprised at how fast those shelves will empty."

Elizabeth put her lips on his forehead to kiss him, but stopped. "You feel so warm, Jack."

"It's the heat from the fire."

She was uneasy. "You look tired, too. Let's go up to the loft."

A sensuous smile curved his lips. "Ah, but you are a tempting little seductress."

Elizabeth gave him a stern look. "I meant to sleep."

He cupped her breast over her dress. "What? No Christmas present, beautiful lady?" He nuzzled her neck and eventually their lips touched. She stood and pulled him from the chair and he followed her up the ladder.

Two weeks later, in the middle of the night, Elizabeth found Jack sitting up in bed, his head in his hands.

"What is it, Jack? Are you ill?"

"Just a headache."

"How can I help you?" she asked, reaching for him. His skin was hot. "You're warm again. You've had fever on and off for days, Jack."

He pushed her hands away as she tried to touch his forehead. "It's nothing, Liz. Leave me alone."

"Jack, please . . ."

He stood up and started for the ladder. "I said I'm all right."

She lie awake listening to him moving in the room below. Beth knew he hadn't been well since Christmas, though he wouldn't admit it. He left the cabin each morning to tend to the horses, and what was left of the chickens. Day after day, things looked worse. Except for jars of herbs, carefully labeled by Rone, the pantry shelves were almost bare, and there were few potatoes left.

After a restless night, Beth went down to the kitchen to start coffee, and she found Jack asleep in the chair, wrapped in his buffalo coat. His face was pale and gaunt; dark circles ringed his closed eyes.

He muttered in his sleep and she touched his shoulder. They both jumped when he yelled out, "Stop!"

"I'm sorry, Jack. I didn't mean to startle you," she said, nervously.

Jack was disoriented for a moment, then taking her in his arms, his breathing labored, he kissed her face. "Jack," she said, tears springing to her eyes, "you're sick, aren't you?"

"Elizabeth, listen to me. This is very important. You must be very frugal with the wood and the oil in the lamps. Understand? We must eat as little food as possible."

"Jack . . ."

"I'm going out now. I won't come back until I've found some game. You must save the wood, though. You and Catherine can stay warm by lying together in the bed, under the blankets. Keep the chickens alive. They won't lay any more eggs, but when we need to, we can cook them."

"I won't let you go out there, Jack. You can't. Please, darling, don't do this . . ."

He pushed her away gently, and put his arms through the sleeves of the coat.

She followed him. "It's snowing, Jack. You won't find anything, and you need to rest." She tried to stop him, pleading, "Jack, listen to reason."

He shook his head and pushed her away again, leaving the warmth of the cabin, and she saw him disappear toward the barn. She closed the door against the wind and leaned her head against it, as a dark foreboding cold crept into her soul.

Four hours later, she stared through the glass in the window of Rone's cabin. The snow was falling so thickly she could see nothing. The fire had almost burned out and a damp cold permeated the room. Catherine stared into the dying fire, too cold and listless to move about.

"Where is he, Aunt Catherine?"

"That's the fifth time you've asked that question, Elizabeth."

"He's not coming back."

"Hush, girl."

Elizabeth looked around the room and saw her jacket hanging on the hook beside the door. "Something is very wrong." She left the window and took the sheepskin coat from its peg.

"What in heaven's name do you think you're doing?" Catherine asked alarmed.

"I have to find him."

"That's a blizzard, Elizabeth. You won't make it past the front porch without being lost yourself. Don't be a fool." Elizabeth would not heed the words her aunt threw at her, and the wind blew the door back when she opened it.

The snow had drifted against the front of the house, and Elizabeth could feel the frigid wetness through her boots. She bent into the gusts of wind trying to find the end of the porch while Catherine reluctantly closed the door behind her.

She heard the faint neighing of a horse through the squealing wind, looked up and could barely distinguish the shadowy outline of Jack's stallion as it pawed the snow near the barn door.

Desperate to find Jack, Elizabeth stepped into the depths of snow, lost her balance and fell. She struggled to raise herself above the drifts, and once she was up again, could only move a few more inches towards the horse's silhouette. Each step took every fiber of strength she had to move against the biting wind and snow. Ice formed on her eyelashes, making it almost impossible for her to see.

Each time she inhaled, her nostrils burned from the assault of the freezing air. Her feet were becoming numb. She pushed herself forward—several inches, a foot—until she stumbled and fell against an impenetrable mound.

Elizabeth brushed the snow away frantically, and there beneath it lie Jack. She shouted his name and pulled at his jacket, but he was unconscious, face down. Again and again she tugged at him, calling, begging him to move. Again and again she fell down, on to the mass that was his body, the snow burying him once more and her with him.

Gasping for air now, she found his hand. She tugged at it, but his glove fell off and blew away in the wind. A sob caught in her throat, and she lie down on the bitter cold blanket of white, exhausted.

I won't give up. I will not give up. Elizabeth left Jack and struggled towards the porch. There was a rope kept on a nail on the side of the house. When she reached it, she took it down and unrolled it. She tied the end to the porch rail, her gloved hands so cold she had trouble moving her fingers.

She slogged through the snow toward Jack again, all the while dragging the rope. Her body ached with the effort and she winced with each movement. When she found him again, she tied the rope around his legs, knotting it as many times as she could.

Using him as a weight, she pulled herself back along the rope to the porch and banged on the door. Catherine opened it with a frightened expression.

"Come help me," Elizabeth sobbed. "Put on your coat, and help me."

Catherine grabbed her woolen jacket, barely warm enough to protect her from the biting wind and snow that surrounded her when she stepped out. She followed the staggering Elizabeth to the rope.

"Pull with me," Elizabeth shouted above the howl of the wind.

Catherine grabbed the rope and pulled, as did Elizabeth. They strained against Jack's weight, each one of them bending and pulling, but it was almost futile with the buffalo jacket and snow weighing him down. The rope gave a little and Jack's body moved slightly, but the effort had exhausted them both.

"It's no use, Beth. He's too heavy," Catherine shouted, her hands aching with the cold.

Elizabeth trudged over to him again and pulled his arms from the heavy jacket, then half way back to the porch, she began to pull at the rope again. Catherine followed her lead.

They tugged harder, this time successfully, and drew him closer very slowly, until finally, he was close enough for them to drag into the cabin.

"Make a fire, Aunt Catherine," Elizabeth demanded.

"But he said we shouldn't . . ."

"Do as I say," Elizabeth snapped. His face was ghastly and his hands had turned white. She grabbed a blanket and rubbed his skin with it, then made a bed by the fireplace for him.

Catherine fetched more blankets from the bedroom and covered Jack. "He's burning with fever," Catherine said, touching Jack's forehead. His teeth chattered and his body shivered incessantly.

Elizabeth and Catherine sat near him on the floor through the night. They took turns warming him with their own bodies. In his delirium, he alternated between mumbling and shouting.

Catherine tried to quiet Elizabeth's fears, but the young woman had never seen anyone so ill before and she was terrified that he was going to die. Catherine herself had never taken care of anyone who was sick and felt ill equipped to help.

They piled blankets and coats on him to try to keep him warm. His temperature climbed. Elizabeth held his head in her lap and stroked his hair. After awhile, he lay very still.

She leaned her back against the fireplace and dozed, but Jack awakened her when he started moving violently again, thrashing around on the floor, shouting words and names that made no sense to her. She struggled to calm him and keep him on the bed by the fire.

When the fire burned out, they didn't relight it; the fuel bin was nearly empty. Elizabeth had never known such cold, and her body ached with it.

The snow fell constantly and the wind never gave up its haunting cry. Catherine took in some snow to melt and then wiped Jack's brow with it while Elizabeth tended to the horses.

Two days went by, and Catherine and Elizabeth lit fires at sundown and burned them long enough to cook a chicken or heat the broth. Elizabeth had relinquished her loft to the two chickens that were left—her only way to keep them alive.

Still, Jack's fever remained constant. "This isn't right, Aunt Catherine. He can't go on like this much longer. If only we knew how to help him. I read something, I know I did. Something about fever and what to do. Where? Where did I read it?"

She looked up at Rone's shelves of books. "Here—it was here in the cabin. I was looking for something else, and . . ." She ran to the shelves, pulling the books down and onto the floor, searching for the right title or cover, anything that would remind her.

"Elizabeth, are you mad? What are you doing?"

"It's here, I know it is."

More books tumbled down, and then she yelled, "This is the book."

She thumbed through it, searching for the information she had read once before when she didn't need to. Finding the passage, she reread it, tearing the paper as she turned it to finish reading the following page.

She put the book down on the table. "Get all these covers off him. Hurry," she said to Catherine.

"But Elizabeth, it's so cold."

"We've been going about this all wrong. He's too warm. We need to cool his body. Hurry up, take it off him." They pulled at the pile of covers. "Take the bucket and get snow, lots of snow, and bring it in. We have to surround him with it," she said to her aunt, as she stripped off Jack's clothing.

Catherine was incredulous but did as Elizabeth asked. They worked together, scooping the snow around his naked body. His teeth chattered until Elizabeth thought they would break. He shouted and tried to move, but she pushed him down to still him, and he went easily because he was so weak.

In minutes, his head was cooler, and by nightfall, when the snow had melted, he was only warm to the touch. Catherine made a fire, while Elizabeth sopped up the puddles and dressed him lightly. Elizabeth was placing a blanket on him gently, when she heard him whisper, "Darla."

A lump formed in her throat, and she looked away from him. Catherine asked, "Who did he call?"

Elizabeth took a long time to answer. "Someone he knows. A rancher's daughter. Someone I couldn't make him forget."

Catherine searched her niece's face, then said kindly, "He's still delirious."

Elizabeth frowned, "It's not important."

She slept on the bed with her aunt that night. The cold was almost unbearable. Ice had formed on the ceiling and walls of the cabin. She dreaded getting up from the bed but knew she had to check on Jack, who was sleeping by the embers in the fireplace. She felt weak and sore and had trouble putting her feet into her cold-stiffened boots.

The chickens were gone, as were the potatoes. She looked in the pot over the ashes and saw that only a plateful of broth was left. She wondered what they would do now, with no food and very little wood.

She hadn't been to the barn in days. Today she would have to go and see if the horses were still alive. If they were, she knew she'd have to kill one for food.

Beth looked through the window. It was barely dawn, the snow had stopped and there was no wind. Then she saw it. At first she believed she imagined it, but it was unmistakable. A six-point buck looked up at her through the window.

Elizabeth took the rifle down from its place above the door. She loaded it clumsily with numbed hands, leaned the weapon against the wall, and put on her coat. She readied herself for the cold blast of air that would attack her when the door was opened, but she was surprised that it was not as bitter as she had expected.

The buck faced her. She raised the rifle to her shoulder and took aim. Slowly, silently, she closed her finger on the trigger, and the deer went down even before the noise of the blast reverberated through the mountain. She knew she had shot him right between the eyes, for he never wavered while he stared at his hunter.

Elizabeth went back inside to get her knife. Catherine came out from the bedroom to ask, "What's happened? What was the shot?"

Tears poured from Elizabeth's eyes. She looked at the older woman, saying in a childlike voice, "I've killed a deer."

The venison kept them alive and Elizabeth carefully rationed what meat she did get from the lean animal. They kept it frozen on the porch and took only what they needed to keep from starving.

With the blizzard gone, Elizabeth was able to chop some wood and replenish the bin in the cabin.

Elizabeth studied Rone's medical book in order to find a way to keep Jack's temperature from rising again. The names of the herbs looked familiar to her and she went to the jars on the pantry shelves. Her fingers traced each label, until she found the one she wanted. "Boneset," was printed in Rone's even handwriting.

They melted snow and boiled the water over the evening's fire. Elizabeth proceeded to make a tea with the boneset and spoon fed it to Jack. His face twisted and he tried to push the spoon away, but Elizabeth persisted, dropping the bitter tasting liquid into his mouth, murmuring to him as she would to a child.

Jack awakened once and looked up at her. A weak smile touched his lips and he whispered, "Beautiful lady." She kissed his cheek in answer, and he fell back to sleep.

"Elizabeth!"

She opened her eyes in the darkness and listened. When she heard nothing, she decided she had dreamed the calling of her name. She turned over and moved closer to her aunt for warmth.

"Liz, where are you?"

She sat up, but Catherine seized her arm. "He's ranting again. Perhaps the fever's back."

Elizabeth took one of the blankets and wrapped it around herself. "Well, at least he's dreaming of me this time," she said, wearily. She left the bedroom and looked toward Jack's place by the fire. He wasn't there. Dread welled up in her and she called, "Jack!"

There was a momentary pause, and then she heard him in the loft. "Liz, is it you?"

She started up the ladder and he met her at the top, his arms clutching her.

"Thank God . . . thank God," he whispered. "You're all right."

"Jack, darling, what are you doing up here? Why aren't you in bed? You've been very ill."

He kissed her face and held her tightly against him. "I thought you were gone—dead."

"But I've been taking care of you, Jack. Don't you remember?"

He shook his head and his grip loosened as his knees buckled slightly. "No . . . no . . . I can't seem to remember anything. I . . ."

"Here, Jack, lie down on our bed. I'll get blankets."

She helped him to the straw mattress, left him for a short time, then returned to cover him.

He took her hand. "Lie beside me," he pleaded quietly.

She lifted the blanket and stretched her body out against his, her head resting on his shoulder, her arm across his chest. It felt so good to touch him and know that he was cool. She could feel his heart beating normally under the delicate skin of her wrist for the first time in days.

"I can't believe we've survived," he whispered.

Elizabeth tightened her arm over him, but could not speak, for her throat ached painfully with unshed tears.

Chapter Twenty-six

Three mornings later, while Jack lie in a deep sleep, Elizabeth left the loft and started a fire, being careful to use only enough wood to boil water. She broke the thin layer of ice that lay over the bucket filled with melted snow, and scooped water into the coffee pot, filling it. She put more into a basin, then washed in the cold water and dressed quickly by the warmth of the fire. When the coffee was finished, she boiled fresh water to brew boneset tea for Jack.

Catherine came out of the bedroom and looked questioningly at Elizabeth.

"He had another good night," Elizabeth said, happily. "I think he'll be fine now."

Catherine gave Beth a relieved smile and said, "He seemed much stronger yesterday—and full of the devil again."

Jack whistled. Elizabeth recognized it immediately as the one he always used to call the stallion to him. Elizabeth was bent over the basin of water she was warming in the morning's fire. Again, he whistled.

She smiled to herself, put some rags over her arm, and taking the warm water in one hand and the tea in the other, she gingerly climbed the ladder.

"So, you would call me as you do your horse, Jack Drummond?" she admonished him.

He was sitting up against the wall, the blanket over his lap. The neck of his long johns was open slightly, and Elizabeth could see a tuft of hair just above the buttons. He looked thin and his face was still pale beneath several weeks' growth of beard, but his smile was warm and his eyes sparkled again.

She suddenly felt shy, and turned away, busying herself with the basin and the mug of tea. He chuckled. "What's this? Are you blushing?"

She handed him the mug. "Don't be ridiculous."

Jack took the tea and his fingers closed around her hand at the same time. "But you are, Liz!"

"Drink that and be quiet," she said, pulling away.

He smelled the potion and winced, "What is this poison you've been pouring down my throat?"

"Boneset tea."

Jack put the mug down on the floor beside him, "Ugh!"

Elizabeth became agitated. "Now, Jack, it saved your life. I read all about it—how it helps to bring down fever—and had the good fortune to find it in Rone's pantry. I fed it to you on a spoon for hours, and it worked."

Jack frowned, "Leave it to that Indian medicine man to have it around. It stinks, and now that I'm better, I refuse to drink it. I'd like coffee."

She frowned at him, while she dipped one of the clean rags in the water.

"What's that for?" he asked, suspiciously.

"This is how I've been bathing you while you've been ill." She could feel a flush burn her cheeks again.

There was amusement in his eyes when he said, "There you go blushing again. By God, you're acting like a new bride, Liz. I must say, I find it rather appealing."

She bit her lip and didn't answer him, so he continued, "Well, whatever you've been doing while I was unconscious, I might as well enjoy while I'm awake, so by all means, have it your way." He pushed the blankets away and chuckled again.

Elizabeth hesitated between the basin and the bed. Her hands shook involuntarily, and it greatly annoyed her, as did his attitude. How dare he make fun of her this way.

"Here, you can do it yourself now!" She threw the rag at him. It wrapped itself around his face and clung there. The back of her fingers flew up to her mouth in surprise. Very slowly his hand came up, and he gingerly pulled the cloth down, while his beard dripped with water.

Elizabeth waited for a tirade from him, but instead his face broke into a smile and he started to laugh heartily. Amazed, she stared at him. Then, like a bubbling spring, she felt the laughter stir in her, too, and she was suddenly bent over, holding her side, cackling and gasping for air.

It wasn't until he leaned toward her, his face serious and alarmed, that she realized her laughter had turned to sobs and tears, and he said, "What is it? Why are you crying, Liz?"

Elizabeth buried her face in her hands and rocked, while deep, aching sobs overcame her body. Jack pulled her hands down and asked again, "What's wrong, love?"

She took several long gulps in order to speak. "Oh, Jack, I'm so disappointed in myself. You were so ill—so very ill—I thought you were going to die. And it was so cold, and we were hungry and it was all my fault. My stomach would growl, and I'd cook a chicken. I wasted the wood and the food, and the brooder wouldn't work, and there were no chicks, and there were no eggs. I almost shot the horses. I did shoot a deer, and I said I never would, and then I had to butcher it. And you had such bad dreams, and you called for . . ."

Jack took her shoulders and pulled her across his lap and cradled her in his arms. "Hush, baby, hush. It's all right now. Don't cry, don't cry."

"I'm such a spoiled, stupid, inept idiot, Jack," she cried, wiping her nose on her sleeve. "I can't do anything right. We could have starved to death—could yet—and it would be all my fault. I'm so ashamed, Jack, I'm so sorry that . . ."

"That's enough, now, Elizabeth," he said sternly. "Stop and listen to me. If it weren't for you, we *would* be dead. I have only myself to blame for being ill. I knew it was coming, yet I didn't take care. *You* saved my life."

His own eyes filled with tears, but he continued, "And as for food, you did the best you could. As well as I would have done. We're alive, and it's due mostly to you."

Elizabeth quieted, though a sporadic sob would escape her. He stroked her hair, and his voice became tender when he went on, "You're just a girl, really. You should be back East, wearing pretty dresses, going to fancy balls, dancing and flirting with handsome young men. Yet, you're strong and capable and do what has to be done to survive. You fight like a tigress, and bust broncos, and kill deer and butcher it for food. Is there anything you can't do, beautiful lady?"

Jack took the corner of the cover and wiped her face as he would a child's. "If that isn't enough, you're the most exquisite looking woman God ever made."

His words and tenderness filled her with desire she hadn't felt in a long time.

Reaching up around Jack's neck, she kissed his mouth hard. Her hips arched toward him and he tried to pull away, saying, "Hey, your aunt is just downstairs . . ."

She silenced him with smothering kisses and moved until she was astride him. "Liz," he protested against her lips. "I'm still as weak as a . . ." But she ignored him, her hands reaching, touching, her body's desire beyond self-control.

They were alive and this was the way she wanted to celebrate it, to consummate the fact that they had survived—and would continue to survive.

Elizabeth felt Jack quiver and moan beneath her as she took command of their lovemaking and his resistance dissolved.

The winter had not subsided yet, and while Jack recuperated slowly, the inhabitants of the tiny cabin in the mountain still faced an angry, relentless nine weeks of bitter weather.

When the blizzards let up, and it was safe to leave the cabin, Elizabeth saddled the bay and hunted for food. Most days she came home empty handed, but the little food she did find kept them fed until a more successful hunt. She became adept at cutting wood and her already slender body became firm and taut with sinewy muscles. She stopped menstruating because of the lack of food and the hard, unrelenting work she did to keep them alive.

Elizabeth worried that she looked less feminine, but Jack reassured her constantly in the privacy of their bed that she was more beautiful than ever.

However, he was worried about her, and even before he was fully recovered, Jack took over the chores of providing food and fuel again. He never stopped worrying about River Pines and the effect the harsh season was having on his ranch, and he prayed that it would be salvageable when he returned to it. More than anything else, Jack worried about the people who he'd left behind there.

They noticed the snowfalls were coming less often and lasted a shorter amount of time. They rejoiced when the grass started to peek out from under the blanket of white until eventually there were only patches of snow. There was still very little food, but Jack was able to find fowl returning from the south and awakening wild life coming out of hibernation. The sun grew warmer and the days longer, and they knew the worst was over.

It was on an unusually warm spring day in the mountain when Elizabeth and Jack looked up from the garden where they were replenishing what they had taken the previous fall, and saw a rider in the distance making his way up the side of the mountain. They looked at each other, and Jack asked, "Are you ready?"

Elizabeth smiled at him, dropped her rake, and they stood hand in hand, with the breeze lifting Elizabeth's shining hair, waiting, as Rone approached them.

Jack walked to the horse, grabbed its bridle, and smiled at Rone. "You're a damned good sight, Rone Daniels."

Rone dismounted and they shook hands. The bronze-skinned man's voice was heavy with affection when he said, "And so are you, Jack." His eyes rested on Elizabeth's face and a muscle twitched in his cheek. "I wasn't sure what I'd find when I got here."

"It was rough, but we managed," Jack told him, knowing that Rone had anticipated finding them dead. "Come on in and eat," Jack said, slapping his friend on the back, trying to lighten their moods. "You'll find your cabin exactly as you left it. I fought the ladies hard, though. They wanted to put up lace curtains and frills, but I wouldn't let them."

The three of them laughed, and Elizabeth said, "Don't believe him, Rone. We love the cabin just the way it is. Even though you weren't here, we could feel your presence and it was reassuring and comforting." She took both his hands in hers and kissed his cheek. "We've missed you, Rone."

"You've forgiven me, then?" he asked her, shyly.

Taking both men's arms and leading them toward the cabin, she answered, "How could I not?"

"How did River Pines fair, Rone?" Jack asked now.

Rone's face darkened. "Not good, Jack. We're still counting, but we know we've lost one hundred fifty head and eight horses. We expect that count to go up, I'm afraid."

"The hands?" Jack asked as they stepped on the porch.

"We lost one man," Rone answered, avoiding Jack's eyes.

"Who?"

"Barnes . . . I'm sorry, Jack."

Elizabeth's breath caught in her throat. "Oh, no," she said sadly, "he was such a gentle man. I can't believe what you're saying is true."

Jack exhaled, leaning his arm against the post, his brow lined and his eyes hard. "How?" he demanded to know.

"The blizzard in January," Rone answered. "Must have been riding the line and got caught in it. We found him right next to his horse . . ." Rone put his hand on Jack's shoulder, and said again, "I'm sorry, I know it isn't easy to lose one like him."

"He was a good man—one of the best hands I had—and a friend." He looked at Rone's face, asking, "Anything else?"

Jack saw a flash of warning in his friend's eyes and tensed with the understanding that there was indeed more, and it wasn't good.

Later, alone by the barn, Jack asked, "Is the news bad from New York?"

"Actually, there's very little to offer as far as that's concerned. David, who is working with Reginald Smythe, is in contact with your father, but they still know very little."

Rone turned to face in the same direction as Jack was facing, their back's to the cabin. "The news I bring concerns Darla Stuart."

"Now there's a name that chills the heart," Jack mulled. "I had a nightmare when I was sick. Darla had a knife and was about to plunge it into Liz's chest. I wanted to scream her name to stop her, but all I could get out was a whisper." He shuddered at the memory.

Having Jack tell him about the dream made Rone all the more reluctant to go on, but after a long pause, he said, "Darla's had a son; claims you're the father."

Although Jack continued to stand with his elbow leaning casually against the rail of the corral, his eyes were shining with anger, his body taut and ready to spring. Rone readied himself. It wouldn't be the first time he saw his friend lash out at anyone nearby when pushed to a blinding temper.

"Your father wants to know what to do about this."

"Well, of course, he'll go to her immediately. After all, she just gave birth to his child."

Both men started at the sound of Elizabeth's voice. They turned to look at her and her eyes were black with rage and accusation as she glared at her husband. An icy sensation crept through Rone as he looked at the furious woman, her fists clenched at her sides, her white teeth glimmering in the sunset in a bitter smile.

The dangerous anger drained from Jack for the moment as he tried to explain to his wife, "Liz, it's not mine."

"Liar," she hissed.

"I haven't touched her in almost two years."

"Pig!" she screeched.

"Listen to me, the child is not mine, damnit."

"How could you be such a coward to deny it, Jack? You're a disgusting, foul, rutting animal, Jack Drummond."

Rone saw the anger return to Jack and he stepped between the couple. Jack spoke over his friend's shoulder at his wife.

"So, I'm guilty! No questions asked. After spending months with me, knowing me as you do, you can actually believe this story? Oh, you're a fine woman, Liz; a real good wife. Is that how I can expect you to stick by me? You're supposed to find out the truth before condemning a man. I guess that's not a lesson you've learned, even after all we've gone through together."

"I don't want to hear an explanation. I saw you with her with my own eyes, right in our own garden. You were lovers!"

"One night—one stupid, drunken night—long before you came into my life."

"You're a black-souled liar," she screamed at him, vividly remembering how he had called for Darla in his delirium..

"Elizabeth," he shouted back, "I've been accused of many things, much of it true, but no one ever had the gall to call me a liar."

She pushed around Rone and said, "Have you ever lied to me, Jack? Tell me, have you ever lied to me?"

He hesitated for a moment, but it was too long, and she said, "Well, *I'm* calling you a liar now!"

Jack picked her off her feet and shook her hard, then released her quickly. Rone pulled her away, holding her arms tight, as she struggled to get back to her husband, kicking out, trying to hurt him any way she could.

Jack stepped toward them, but halted at Rone's voice, "Settle down, Jack."

"Get out of here, Jack. Just go away—go to the mother of your child," Elizabeth said.

"She is not the mother of my child—it is not my child."

"Get out of here!"

Jack shook his finger at her. "I'm leaving, all right. I'm going to take care of this business in New York, and when it's over, I'll make damned sure you're planted safely in your aunt's home in Pennsylvania. One thing I don't need is a wife like you!"

"Nor I a cheating, lying husband like you," she rejoined, turning on her heel, and slamming the cabin door behind her when she had entered it.

Jack stormed into the barn and saddled his horse while Rone watched. After a while, Rone said, "I don't believe the child is yours."

"I don't care what you believe."

Rone continued, undisturbed. "I'll talk to her. You know Liz has a quick temper but gets over it when she sorts out the truth."

"Don't bother, Rone. She's just ruined everything we ever had together. If she can't believe me when I tell her the truth, then there is nothing between us. I'm going to take care of this nonsense and be rid of her once and for all. The one thing our marriage was not based on was trust."

Jack led the horse out of the stall and into the open. "Have you ever known a more infuriating, unreasonable individual? I've been a fool. I actually believed that she loved me. But a woman doesn't turn on her husband like a rattler—or call him a liar—when she ought to know . . . What's the use? Twice burned, eh, Rone?"

"Jack, when are you going to realize that she's not Kristina? Liz does love you . . ."

"Shut up, Rone, I don't want to hear it." Jack pulled himself into the saddle and rode away without looking again at his friend or at the house where his wife sat crying at the table.

Rone walked into the cabin and saw her there, her face down on her arms, her long curly hair covering her shoulders and back to her waist. He listened to her sobs for a long time, then touched her shoulder gently. She ignored his presence and continued to give in to the waves of hurt and rejection that overwhelmed her.

Rone squatted down by her chair and stroked her silky tresses, still not speaking, letting her vent the pain she was feeling through tears.

Catherine appeared at the bedroom door, where she had gone to nap after they had eaten. "What's wrong, Beth? Where's Jack?"

Elizabeth lifted her face and said, "Get ready, Aunt Catherine. We're going home."

Catherine's mouth fell open, but Elizabeth did not see, for her eyes were locked with Rone's and understanding passed between them. He nodded and left the cabin. In the barn, he saddled three horses.

Chapter Twenty-seven

David and Emily sat in the handsomely decorated parlor of Mr. and Mrs. Reginald Smythe, talking softly. David reached for Emily's smooth, warm hand and said, "I'll be happy when this is over, darling. I can't wait much longer. It's unbearable being with you, yet without you. We should have been married months ago." His lips rested on her fingers.

"I know, David, and I feel as you do. How long do you think it will take?"

"It all depends. She won't see Reginald or me, and the prosecutor insists we stay away from her. They explain nothing. Em, I just don't know how long this could drag on. Won't you reconsider and marry me now?"

Her eyes were pained. "No, David, I can't. When this is settled, the very next day, we'll be married and we'll go away for a long, exciting, happy honeymoon."

"And where will that be?" he asked, the dimples in his cheeks deepening.

"It doesn't matter, my love. Anywhere you'd like, just as long as we're together."

"I was thinking of Europe," he said thoughtfully.

"That sounds wonderful. I'd love to see Paris."

"And then to England?"

"Oh, yes."

"Spain, Germany, Switzerland?"

"Definitely."

"By the time we get back, the house should be completed. You won't mind living in Philadelphia, will you, love?"

"Not at all. I'm looking forward to it, David."

She saw the smile vanish from his face as he left her, walked over to the mantle and stared into the fire. "But first we have to clear Elizabeth. I can't figure out how Mrs. Blackwell could have seen what happened. From what Jack told me, there was no one in the hall, or in the room, certainly. Reginald and I have been to the hotel dozens of times, and except for a balcony which is almost inaccessible, there is no other way to enter the room. It does not make sense."

Mrs. Smythe opened the door of the parlor and called in, "Someone to see both of you."

"Jack!" Emily said as he walked into the room. He was unshaven and his hair hung long around his collar.

"My God, man, you look awful," said David.

"Never mind how I look. Just what the hell is going on? How long do you expect us to wait?" he stormed, ignoring the extended hand of his cousin.

"Calm down, Jack," David said.

"Have you found the bastard who is claiming to have seen Elizabeth murder Tom Blackwell?"

David and Emily looked at each other. "It's his wife, Terese Blackwell."

"What?" Jack was taken aback. He sat heavily in one of the Smythe's elegant tapestry chairs and considered this news. Then he asked, "Have you spoken to her?"

"No, they won't let us within a mile of her."

"Why not?" Jack asked loudly. "There must have been a hearing of sorts, why didn't you question her?"

"We've only seen her deposition. Apparently she is in delicate health and has not left her home since the night of the murder. She claims she went to the hotel to look for her husband and somehow—none of us know how exactly—she witnessed Elizabeth stab Blackwell."

Jack shook his head, "No, it's impossible."

"Her butler has submitted a statement that he took her to the hotel that night, Jack."

"Did she see me also? Has she said?"

"No, as a matter of fact, there was no mention of you."

Jack stood up again. "If she saw Elizabeth stab Blackwell, then she had to have seen me. I walked in right at that moment. Why didn't she show herself at that time? Why didn't she scream and bring the hotel employees?"

"These are all questions we've been asking, Jack," Emily said calmly. David continued then, "She claims she is very ill and cannot see or talk with anyone about the incident until the trial. Naturally, the prosecutor is protecting her, as are her servants."

"There's a hole in this story, David, and I can assure you she's lying. I'm going to see her myself."

"Now, Jack, you stay out of this. It's bad enough without you interfering. She wouldn't see you anyway. You could be arrested for harassment, not to mention that you were an accomplice and disposed of the body."

"There was no body, David. Elizabeth stabbed Blackwell, but he wasn't dead and it wasn't a serious wound. I disposed of a *living* Blackwell."

Emily and David were shocked by this disclosure. David went over to Jack. "Why didn't you tell me this before?"

Jack met his cousin's eyes when he answered, "I didn't want Liz to know—for my own reasons. I thought that by this time you'd have the truth and it would be over."

David's face was red with anger. "It would have helped to have the whole story. We've wasted months . . ."

Jack paced the room like a tormented animal. Emily said to him, "Jack, you haven't told us how you've come to be here. Where are Elizabeth and Aunt Catherine? Is there something wrong?"

Jack glared at her, then looked away. "They're fine, or at least they were the last time I saw them."

"Something's wrong; I can feel it," she said, her face becoming pale.

"It's none of your damned business," he threw at her.

David could keep his temper under control no longer. "Jack, I'll remind you that you are speaking to my fiancee, and I won't allow you to treat her this way. Either calm down or get out of here. We're trying to help you. For once, realize who is on your side."

Jack sat down wearily beside Emily on the settee then, leaning his head against the back of it and closing his eyes. "I beg your pardon, Emily. You are a gentle, sweet lady and David is correct, you do not deserve to be subjected to my bad temperament."

She took his hand, "We're all upset over this situation. Jack, you look exhausted. Shall I ask Mrs. Smythe if you may rest in David's room awhile? Afterward, we can talk, and then you can explain everything to us. I'm sure you must have had a good reason not to tell Elizabeth and the rest of us about Tom Blackwell." She sat forward, "Perhaps you'd like something to eat?"

"No . . . thank you, Emily . . ." He looked into her gentle eyes and wondered why Elizabeth couldn't be more like her trusting, reasonable sister. Then, looking at David, he asked, "Could I borrow some clothes from you, Dave?"

David, though still annoyed, relaxed. "Certainly, I'll have a bath drawn for you right away."

As Jack stood to leave the room, he looked down at his sister-in-law once more and touched her cheek tenderly. "Your sister and aunt are fine, and I am sorry that I was rude to you, Emily."

She smiled and nodded. "Go rest awhile, Jack."

Jack bathed quickly and took a pair of black trousers from the wardrobe and donned a white shirt. This he covered with a black jacket. Within the hour he left the house again.

The brownstone was in darkness except for a window on the top floor. Jack could see a silhouette pass behind it as he stood across the avenue, hidden in the shadows of the trees in the park. He had socialized in this house many times—long, painful years ago. He had stood in these same shadows before, suspecting his wife and her lover were inside. So often, he had pictured himself barging in . . . alarming them . . . catching them . . . yet hoping that once he was inside, it would be another fair-haired wife of some other poor bastard that he would find.

While still on his honeymoon, before taking her to his ranch, Jack suspected she was here, and he had memorized the house and its facade. He knew each projection, each cubby where his foot would fit to lift him to the next protrusion. He knew the balcony where he could have looked into the bed chamber to see his beautiful wife and her lover consummate their adultery. Even though he had never done it, he knew how. It was a familiar sight, this house on the avenue across from the park.

In her nightly ritual, Terese sat at her mirror brushing her gray streaked hair as her mind wandered through a maze of memories. Her face was deeply lined and her eyes were an indistinguishable color, made all the more indefinable by the glassiness that covered them. Her lips were pulled into a thin line as she looked at her face, old and homely, though it had once been considered attractive.

She knew why Tom had married her, but it didn't matter. She had bought him with her father's money, then she had tried to make him love her. It hadn't worked. She suffered through the many beautiful women he found and kept. They meant nothing, and she could put up with them, as long as he stayed married to her and came home in the night.

Then *she* came, with her fair looks and her violet eyes. *She* slept with him in this bed—*my* bed. The little whore.

Terese stared at her reflection and said aloud, "I got her, though." It was then that she saw Jack's image reflected over her shoulder.

David finished his brandy and said to Emily. "I'd better check on Jack."

Emily agreed. "I'll have a tray brought up to him. He's in such a state, David, please be careful what you say to him."

"Don't worry, my love, I know him only too well."

David walked up the stairs to his room. On the bed lay the ragged clothes Jack had been wearing when he arrived, but not his cousin as he had expected. He looked in the wardrobe and saw the trousers and shirt missing. A suspicion formed in his mind and he ran from the room.

Downstairs, Reginald Smythe was just arriving home. As a servant took his hat and coat, he greeted his wife with a kiss and smiled at Emily, who carried a tray laden with food for Jack.

"He's gone!" David shouted from the top of the stairs.

"Who?" Reginald asked.

"What do you mean?" asked Emily, alarmed.

"He's not in the room, that's what I mean," David answered.

The servant, still holding her master's clothes, said, "Do you mean that gentleman who arrived this afternoon, sir?"

"Yes, Bessie," Emily answered for David.

"He left awhile ago, Miss Emily. I thought you knew."

David came down the stairs two at a time. "I think I know where he is," he said, taking the hat and coat and giving it back to Reginald. "We may still have time to stop him, but for God's sake, hurry."

Emily handed the tray to Mrs. Smythe. "I'm going with you."

"What do you want, Mr. Drummond?" Terese asked in a whisper.

"You've accused my wife of killing your husband." He walked into the room from the balcony. "I just want to know what happened, then I'll leave."

"No, I won't tell you. She won't get away with it this time. You helped her the last time, but I'll see to it she hangs for what she's done to me."

"She didn't kill him," Jack said calmly.

"Yes, he's dead and she killed him." Her voice turned to a whine when she continued. "How could you want to help her? She has hurt you as much as she's hurt me. We can't let her hurt us anymore. Go away and let me do what I have to do."

"He was going to rape her, Mrs. Blackwell. She was defending herself."

Terese stood up and her face burned red. "No! That is not the way it was. She wanted him to leave her alone so she could have other men. I know, I was there the first time."

Jack stared at her. "The first time?"

"You weren't there; you don't understand."

"What are you talking about? What first time?"

Terese Blackwell's face went blank. She turned away from Jack and put her brush on the vanity.

"What first time, Mrs. Blackwell?" Jack persisted.

"I don't know. I'm . . . I'm . . . not well. You have to leave. Tom will be home any minute and he'll kill you if he finds you here in my room." She seemed pleased by the thought, however, and closed her eyes and smiled.

Jack suddenly realized that the woman was mentally ill. "Mrs. Blackwell . . ."

"Do you think I'm pretty, Mr. Drummond?" she asked, looking like a hideous caricature of an ingenue when she cocked her head to one side and smiled at him.

Elizabeth's life lies in the hands of this insane woman, he thought.

"Yes, of course, you're pretty, Terese," he answered.

"As pretty as she is?"

He started to move toward her. "Prettier."

"Why did you bring her back, Mr. Drummond?"

"I don't know what you mean. Who did I bring back?" He walked over and took her shoulders gently. "Explain to me what you mean, Terese."

"Will you like me if I tell you?"

Jack nodded and said, "I'll like you anyway, but I must know. Perhaps I can help you. I need to understand why you've accused my wife of murder."

"If I tell you, you'll go away and let me do what I have to do to her?"

Jack swallowed hard, but inclined his head.

Terese sat down at the mirror again, picked up the brush and resumed stroking her hair. "It wasn't bad before she came the first time. He always came back to me. Then when he met her, his 'golden woman' he called her, he didn't come in the night anymore. He sent me away so that he could be here with her. I knew, I knew it well. I know that you knew it, also. Sometimes he took her to Boston, and he'd leave me here all alone. I always waited for him. When she married you, I thought he was over her, especially when you took her to your ranch."

Jack heard the commotion in the hall downstairs, but he stood listening silently to the strange story being told to him. Terese didn't hear the footsteps in the upstairs hall or the knock on the door. She sat as if in a trance, reciting a memory.

"Madam, it's Johnson," Jack heard at the door of her room. "Are you all right? Madam, is someone in there with you?"

Terese kept speaking into the mirror. "Then she came back and he told me he was leaving me for her. At first I didn't believe him, but he did leave and took her to Boston again. I followed them. I had to convince him she was no good. He had to know the truth about her, but it was too late. She had already hurt him. I heard them talking in the room in Boston. My husband was begging her to marry him."

The door of the bedroom opened and a man in night clothes came in, followed by David and Reginald Smythe. Jack held up his hand to silence them, but the servant ignored him.

"Madam, you do not have to speak to these people. I will have them arrested," said Johnson.

"No, Johnson, it's all right," she said, "Mr. Drummond will like me if I tell him." Then turning from the mirror she looked directly at Jack. "You see, when he asked her to marry him, she laughed. She laughed at him and said, 'Don't be a fool. I'd never marry you. You're old enough to be my father, you fat, funny old man. I like the gifts you give me, and the places you take me. But marry you?' Then she laughed at him. I expected Tom to kill her with his own hands, but he didn't. He just cried. My wonderful Tom, crying over that whore."

The woman's face paled then and her eyes shone with tears. "So when she went riding later, I followed her. She rode like a wild animal, and I had trouble catching up. I called and she stopped and waited for me. Her horse was wild, too, mean and wild, and she was having trouble holding him still. When I told her that I knew about her and my Tom, she laughed at me.

"She was cruel. I lifted my whip and brought it down on her face. She tried to stop me, but I was too strong for her. I whipped and whipped until her horse's rein broke and it ran. There was a stone wall and I prayed the horse would stop, but it didn't, and she fell off when the horse's leg hit the wall and stumbled.

"She wasn't dead. So I took a rock and brought it down on her head until she stopped breathing." Terese closed her eyes, "They thought it happened when she fell off the horse."

Terese stood up and went to Jack and grabbed his arms, "But she wasn't dead. You brought her back to New York and he started seeing her again. I saw them together. Johnson found out where she was staying, and I went to her hotel and paid a maid to let me in her suite. Then I waited on the balcony of her room. I saw her stab him. Then I saw you carrying him out, and Johnson and I followed you. You left him on the park bench, didn't you? I went to him and held him in my arms, and he moaned. There was blood on his coat, and it got on my hands."

Terese held out her hands with her fingers splayed as though she could still see the blood. "Then he said her name. He called Kristina. When he opened his eyes and saw me . . . he . . . cried . . . he cried because I wasn't her."

Terese put her head down on Jack's chest and her arms encircled his waist. "So I killed him," she said very quietly.

There was no movement in the room. Each man stood in their own reverie as the confession was told. Then she lifted her head and her voice was shrill when she said, "But I've fixed her now! She'll hang now!"

The agonized cry hung in the air as the four men stared at the insane, tormented woman. Answers he had not expected, but that he had sought for years, were running wild through Jack's mind.

The anguish of finding out what had really happened to his first wife was mixed with the sheer relief that there were witnesses to the truth that Elizabeth was innocent.

Jack's head ached and he felt very weary. His eyes focused again on the woman who stood before him, her thin hands covering her face. He felt sympathy, and pity, and a need to comfort her. *Did I not agonize over what Kristina had done? I didn't lose my mind as this poor woman has, but I came close enough.* His arms went around her and he led her to the bed. She leaned her full weight against him as he half carried her.

David looked at the servant, who stood staring at the floor, tears glistening on his cheeks. "Have you known this all along?"

Johnson nodded and his voice was dull and lifeless when he spoke, "I tried to help her, to make her tell the truth, but she's so ill." His eyes lifted to the young lawyer. "You can see she is very ill. I have been with her family for many years, and I couldn't bear to see her put into an asylum. I didn't think they'd find the other woman."

David looked toward the bed and his eyes met Jack's, then he touched the old man's shoulder, "All right, Johnson, but as you say, she's very ill. She needs help which you cannot give her."

The man nodded and David went on, "Are you willing to testify to what you've heard tonight? Will you tell the truth?"

Johnson looked at Terese and answered, "Yes, I should have from the beginning." He walked over to the sobbing woman and patted her back. "Come now, Mrs. Blackwell, you must sleep."

Jack extricated her hands from his coat and stood away from the woman and her servant. After a last glance, he walked out of the room, down the staircase, beyond the waiting Emily, and out into the night.

David followed him and took Emily's shoulders. Her eyes searched his, and he said, "It's almost over, Em."

Jack climbed into the hansom that awaited them. He was silent on the ride back to the Smythe home as David explained the entire story to Emily. She sent furtive glances to Jack when his first wife was mentioned, and she ached to comfort him, but his cold silence forbade it.

Light shone from every window in the Smythe house when they arrived.

"What now?" Reginald asked as he approached the door and let himself in. The rest followed him and there, in the foyer, stood Catherine.

CHAPTER TWENTY-EIGHT

They gathered in the Smythe's parlor and Emily sat beside her aunt. "How did you get here? Where is Beth?"

"Rone brought us here right after Jack left us in Colorado. Elizabeth insisted upon turning herself in to the authorities. She's there now."

Emily gasped, "Oh, no," and looked at David.

David spun to Reginald and the older man sighed heavily. "Yes, yes, I'll go immediately. I do hope I'll have a chance to eat dinner sometime in the near future."

His wife's eyes opened wide. "Now where are you going?"

He patted her shoulder, saying, "To get the young Mrs. Drummond out of jail. Did you ever expect we'd have this much excitement in our later years—or this much company, for that matter?"

Mrs. Smythe shook her head as she looked around at the little crowd gathered in her parlor. "I dare say not." Then giggling, she added, "but it did break up the tedium, didn't it?"

David turned back to the women when Reginald was out of the house. "He'll be home with Beth shortly. It's over now."

Catherine listened attentively as David explained the story to her just as he had to Emily. "Amazing," she said, when he had finished.

There was a silence in the room for a short while, then Emily said, "I can't bear to think of Elizabeth in that horrible place. She must feel so alone and worried."

Catherine placed her hand over Emily's. "She has an inner strength that keeps her going, and she isn't exactly alone. Rone insisted upon staying in the building with her. He wanted to be there in case she needed him, not that they would let him do anything for her, but at least she would know he was there."

Jack turned from the mantle for the first time since entering the room and his eyes met Catherine's. She wanted to question him, but thought better of it.

"She won't be there long. They should be back within the hour." David assured them.

Jack poured himself whiskey and drank it down, then turning to David, he said, "I find it curious that none of you have asked me why I allowed Elizabeth to think she had killed that man."

No one spoke, so he went on, "If I were to tell you the truth, none of you would understand." He looked at David, "I would appreciate your allowing me to borrow your clothes a little longer, David, and I'll need a change of shirts."

"Of course, Jack," David said, "but tomorrow you can purchase . . ."

"I won't be here tomorrow.

All eyes turned on him and he explained. "I have some business at home to attend to. It can't wait. I'll be leaving early in the morning, and tonight I'll stay somewhere else."

Catherine stood up and went to Jack, placing her hand on his arm. "Jack, don't do this, it isn't right. You're exhausted and not thinking straight. Whatever the problem is, it can wait a few more days. You owe it to Elizabeth to stay."

"I'm leaving now, Catherine."

"I'm aware," Catherine argued, "that you and Elizabeth are having problems, but, Jack, she's going to want to be with you now. At least wait to see her and talk to her. If nothing else, you owe her an explanation."

He took her elbows in his hands. "Even if I wanted to, Catherine, Elizabeth will not want to see me after she learns that she did not kill Tom Blackwell and I knew it all along. There is nothing that can be done for us—there is nothing that can save our marriage. Liz has you and Emily . . . and Rone. She doesn't need me in her life. She made it clear to me before and will certainly feel that way now."

He turned and walked from the room with David in his wake, grabbing his arm angrily. "You've done many things that have surprised me, Jack, but I never knew you to be a coward."

"Let go of me, Dave. I'm in a dangerous mood, so don't interfere."

They glared at each other, but David released him, saying, "I'm disappointed in you. I'm ashamed of you, Jack."

Jack left the house without another word to anyone.

Elizabeth sat straight and proud on the narrow cot in her cell. She still wore her gloves, grimy now from the dirt surrounding her, and her skirt and cape were rumpled and soiled. She willed herself not to look around, though her nostrils flared at the odors that assaulted her. For two hours she had sat this way, unable to move, trying to contain the panic that kept rising in her chest. She felt nauseated and dizzy, then calm and controlled, then dizzy again.

She tried not to think about when she had first arrived at the jail and told them who she was, and how three policemen grabbed her to constrain her. Rone almost had been arrested himself when he had flung one of them across the crowded room, and was released only after she had begged them to leave him alone and promised it would not happen again.

Tears flooded her eyes when she remembered how they had forced her into a little room with a camera, and a few minutes later Jacob Riis walked in to take her picture. His eyes widened when he saw her, and she could not look at him, she was so ashamed. How grateful she felt toward him, when he pretended not to know her and just took the pictures and walked from the room quietly.

Elizabeth's head ached with fearful thoughts of what awaited her, a trial . . . a verdict . . . a hanging.

She heard locks being turned and low voices coming from a distance. Then she saw the guard with Rone and an older man, well-dressed, self-confident, papers in hand. She stood when they entered the cell. Reginald Smythe held out his hand to her. "Dear girl," he said kindly, "I am Reginald Smythe. You're free to come with us now."

"Am I going home?" she asked in a whisper.

"Your aunt and sister are waiting for you at our house."

She closed her eyes in relief, took Rone's hand, and said, "Thank God."

They led her out of the cell and down a long dark corridor. Words were exchanged between Smythe and a guard, and then they were out of the building and into fresh air. Rone helped her into a carriage and then climbed in after her. Once seated Reginald explained what had happened and how he had come to have her released.

"You are a free woman, Elizabeth. You may go on with your life, and leave this behind you."

"Won't there be a trial? I killed a man," she asked, bewildered.

"No, my dear, you only thought you did."

Confused, she shook her head, "I don't understand."

Reginald looked uncomfortable. He did not feel it was his place to explain to her—and indeed did not even know why—her husband had allowed her to believe she had committed the crime of murder.

"I believe that this will all be explained to you eventually. For now, just celebrate the fact that you are innocent."

She looked at him a long time, trying to understand, then finally said, "Well, I truly appreciate what you have done, Mr. Smythe. You have been a good friend to us—and a wonderful lawyer."

"I'm afraid I've done very little, really. It was your husband who did what David and I have been trying to do for months. It was he would made the truth evident."

"My husband was here? In New York?" She said nothing more and looked down at the coach's floor. Rone sat silent and aloof next to her. Smythe wondered what his association with her was. *Obviously not a servant*, he thought. The cab stopped and they alighted.

Elizabeth was smothered with embraces when she entered the house. She looked around for her husband, but in her heart knew he would not be there, and she did not ask for him. Emily cried and Beth gently chided her for it. Spirits rose with the talk of Elizabeth's freedom, despite the late hour.

"It's over now," David said, handing Elizabeth a glass of whiskey. She looked up at him without taking it. "This is what you drink lately, is it not?"

She took the glass in her fingers, and her eyes filled with tears when she said, "Thank you, David, for everything." When he took her hand reassuringly, she added, "I have so many questions."

"Tomorrow, Elizabeth. I don't know if I can even answer them then, but at least I'll have had a chance to think and reason it all in my own mind."

Catherine stood and pulled Beth to her feet. "We all need some rest. Come, dear, and we'll take you to Emily's room. It wouldn't be the first time you girls roomed together."

When Elizabeth had changed into Emily's night clothes, she sank into the soft bed and rested her head on the covered feather pillow. She protested that she would not be able to sleep, but her eyes closed, and she was vaguely aware of her aunt's and sister's kisses as she drifted into a black velvet sleep.

The ugly stench of the cell permeated the room and she was crying and begging to be let out. The bars led up into the unseen sky and she tried to climb, but slipped down onto the grimy floor. She lie sobbing, and when she looked up, Tom Blackwell was above her, his face accusing. She screamed for help, but they were alone, and he walked closer and closer. His hands came out and he held her down, his body fell on top of her . . .

Elizabeth jumped out of the bed and gasped for air. She tried to get her bearings as the blood drained from her face.

A dream—it was only a dream. She covered her face with her hands. Without warning, she was very ill and just had time to grab the chamber pot and vomit into it.

She lie down on the bed holding a towel to her mouth. Emily, who had been sleeping beside her, sat up. "Beth, what is it?"

Elizabeth felt her stomach turn and again retched into the porcelain bowl. Emily was on her feet then, her hand touching Elizabeth's forehead. She poured some of the cool water from the pitcher onto a towel and wiped Elizabeth's perspiring face with it.

Elizabeth pushed it away and on shaking legs walked to the window. She noticed dawn was beginning to break. Her heavy head leaned against the coolness of the brocade draperies as she looked out at the sleeping city.

Where is he? she wondered. *Why isn't he here?* Elizabeth looked at the street. *Is he out there—close enough to be seen?*

Emily put her arms around her sister from behind. "How can I help you, dearest? I can't bear to see you hurting this way."

Tears dropped from Elizabeth's eyes. "I've been a fool in so many ways, Emily. For someone who is supposed to be a woman, I tend to think and act like a child still."

"Is it Jack?" Emily asked her. "What's happened?"

How could her sister possibly understand this new disastrous complication? *I should have listened to him, let him explain. Is the child his? And if it is, can I go through life without him after loving him as I do. Are we to be apart forever now? Can I bear that?*

She turned from the window and looked at her sister. "I know one thing," she said. "I must confront him, Emily. Before I can let him go, I have to have some answers."

Several days passed as the Gerard sisters and their aunt allowed Mrs. Smythe to entertain them and introduce them to New York society. Much of the city reminded Elizabeth of Jack. It made her pain more intense. The fact that Jack had known all along that she had not killed Tom Blackwell didn't ease her desire to confront him, it only intensified it, made her realize there were too many questions to be answered before she could go on with her life.

Rone had purchased a dark suit of clothes for himself and accompanied Elizabeth to every function. He was treated with a politeness he had never known in the West. Here in New York he was a rarity, and considered alluring and mysterious. Elizabeth found this amusing, and teased him about the women who surrounded him at every gathering.

"I might as well enjoy it before I go back," he said, giving her his rare and special smile.

The white of his shirt made his skin look darker and his chiseled features more pronounced. He was surprising adept at small talk and seemed to enjoy the attentions he received from the beautiful, inquisitive ladies he met.

A week later, Catherine declared it was time to go back to Benton. "I for one intend to leave this city and go back to the peace and quiet of my home now that this nightmare is over. I have had enough excitement for one lifetime. It's time you girls were settled and for me to go about my old age."

David smiled and placed his hand on Emily's. "One of your nieces is going to be 'settled' right away." Turning to her, he asked, "What do you say we marry here, in New York, this week?"

"I'd love to, David, but, well, I . . ."

The smile vanished from his lips, "Now what?"

"If it's all right with you, I'd like to be married in Benton. After all, we owe it to your family. They should be allowed to attend your wedding; you are all your mother has. It is our home, after all."

His smile returned, "I've waited this long, I suppose I can wait a little longer. But I warn you, Emily, I won't allow much of a delay."

"As soon as we get home, we'll start the arrangements. It will be a small wedding, at the house."

Catherine groaned, "Will I never have peace?"

They laughed, "You don't mind, do you?" Emily asked.

"No, I don't mind. I'm thrilled for you," Catherine admitted.

"And Beth will be my matron of honor, and can wear . . ."

"I'm sorry, Em, I wasn't listening. What did you say?"

They all looked at her in surprise. "Haven't you heard anything?"

"About what?"

"We're talking about our wedding, Beth. I was saying you can wear . . ."

"I won't be here, Emily. I'm sorry."

Again she received shocked glances, but her face came alive for the first time in many days, and she looked at Rone. He smiled a broad white smile and she said, "Go on, Rone, you know what to do."

Without another word, he left the Smythe's house.

"What are you talking about, Beth?" Catherine demanded.

"I'm going home."

"That's just what we were saying."

"No, not to Benton. Home . . . to Colorado."

David found his voice first. "Beth, you're not going to Jack?"

"Yes . . . well, to his father."

David was astounded. "I don't believe it. After the way he left that night . . . and the fact that he had allowed you to believe you killed a man . . ."

"Beth," Emily started, "you couldn't stand that trip. You haven't been well lately. Every morning . . ."

"You don't understand. I hope you never have to understand anything as complicated as this. Please know that I wish you all the love and happiness in the world, but I cannot stay."

She looked directly into David's eyes when she added, "I must go back."

After a long pause, Emily said, "Go to him if that's what you need to do, Beth. We only want what's best for you."

A sad smile formed on her lips. "So do I."

CHAPTER TWENTY-NINE

Dan Drummond stood on the platform as the train pulled to a stop. His eyes scanned each person who stepped off the train until he noticed the young woman and the bronze-skinned man. He smiled warmly at them and kissed Elizabeth's cheek.

"I was elated when I received your telegram," he said, shaking Rone's hand.

"I had hoped you wouldn't mind, Father," she said, using the title they had agreed upon at the ranch when they had first met.

"No, not at all. It is a pleasure to have you with me, and at a very opportune time."

He ushered them to a coach. Beth noticed a gilded double "D" etched into the door just as the driver pulled it open for her. Once they were inside, Elizabeth brought him up to date on what had transpired in New York. He listened solemnly, then nodded when she finished.

"Thank God that's over," he said. "I would have been there myself, but I . . . had other pressing business to attend to here."

"I understand," she said, placing her gloved hand on his arm. 'I'm anxious to hear what has developed."

He wore a very serious expression when he said, "It's the stuff nightmares are made of. But we'll talk later. Tell me how your lovely aunt is?"

"She's in the midst of planning Emily and David's wedding. I do believe she can't wait until it's over."

They laughed and Elizabeth felt a pull at her heart when she looked into his eyes, which sparkled in emerald like Jack's and his hearty laugh reminded her of happier moments with her husband.

Not far outside of Denver, they approached a ranch, resplendent with clean, spacious buildings, even rows of crops and an orchard where fruit trees were just beginning to show pale green buds. Elizabeth was enthralled with the house which was three stories high and painted an immaculate white. A wide veranda surrounded the first floor, the gardens beneath it were beautifully landscaped. She noticed that a balcony bordered the upper story as well, and several sets of French windows opened out onto it from the bedrooms.

"It's a bit pretentious, I've been told," he said apologetically.

"Absolutely not," she told him, smiling broadly. "It's a magnificent house."

Pleased with her appreciative response, he said, "I wanted to build my wife a home she would feel comfortable in, a home she could be proud of. She decorated it herself. It took her many years."

The coach stopped at the steps leading to the veranda, and Rone, who had insisted upon sitting up with the driver, jumped down and helped Elizabeth out of the coach. Several servants piled out of the house, and Dan proceeded to introduce his daughter-in-law to them. When they entered the foyer, Elizabeth was overwhelmed. "It's breathtaking, Father."

Dan beamed at her. "It will be good having a woman in it again."

Colorful flowers from the ranch's hotbed had been placed in crystal vases throughout the house, creating a sweet bouquet mixed with the scent of polish and soap. A huge, winding staircase lifted high to the second floor.

Daniel showed her though the house, and she was awed by the beauty of each room she entered. The dining room was the largest, adequately filled with a huge cherry wood table. A smaller, round table sat in the bay window, as well, for intimate dinners or luncheon. A crystal chandelier adorned the ceiling, and bronze sconces hung on the light blue walls.

From the dining room, Dan took her into another large parlor and then into a smaller room, obviously a woman's sitting room, which was also beautifully decorated.

The seven bedrooms each had a fireplace inlaid with marble. The furniture in most of the rooms was hidden with dust covers from lack of use. Dan brought her into the last room which had been redecorated in light green and yellow.

"I hope this suits you, Elizabeth," he said hopefully.

"It's beautiful, Father."

"Would you like to rest until dinner, Liz?"

She nodded and he continued, "Good. Dinner is at seven. One of the girls, Justina, will call you and help you dress. I had Calla send some of your clothes here. You'll find them in the closet."

Elizabeth turned quickly. "Calla? But I didn't want Jack to know I was coming just yet."

He shook his head, "No, no, I swore her to secrecy. I assure you, my dear, he doesn't know you are here."

Reassured, she asked him, "Father, please be candid with me. I'd like to know how things are."

A minute passed until he said, "The Stuart woman still claims that the child is his and demands support for it, and Jack continues to deny it. He has never been one to socialize much, but he's been to every engagement and dinner party in the county. You would think that a scandal like this would make him shy away from public appearances. When I pressed him, he told me to mind my own business."

She frowned. "Sounds vaguely familiar."

"Frankly, it seems a waste of time. I don't think anything he does will make people believe he's not that child's father, and with River Pines suffering such great losses during the winter, I should think his time would be better spent concentrating on restoring the ranch."

Elizabeth sat on the edge of her bed. "How bad are his losses, Father?"

Dan leaned against the door jamb. "Not as bad as some, worse than others. I fared better, having a larger herd, and my ranch is better equipped to handle a winter like this last one. My other business holdings kept me going, too. I have the money to put back into restoring what I've lost. But small cattlemen like Jack lost everything. I hear of ranch after ranch sliding into insolvency."

"Not River Pines, Father?" Elizabeth asked, disturbed.

"Not yet, but he has to work to get it back to the way it was."

Elizabeth looked down at her hands. "I wish I could help him."

Dan walked over and sat beside her on the bed. "Your being here will help with one of his problems anyway. It's good for him to have his wife by his side at a time like this. It's a show of confidence."

"My only intention is to find out the truth, Father."

Daniel studied her. "If you should find that the child is his, will you leave him?"

The question pierced Elizabeth's heart, and she didn't know how to answer him. Then she said earnestly, "I don't want Jack to lose River Pines, no matter what the truth is."

Daniel understood what she was telling him and said, "He may anyway, but not because I'll sell it. I would have given the deed to Jack the day I met you, but he wouldn't take it. He told me he wanted me to wait the year."

This surprised Elizabeth, "Why?"

He shrugged. Then he said, "I know my son, Liz. If it means anything to you, I don't believe the story that girl is telling. Jack would admit it if it were true. He's a lot of things, but not a liar."

Elizabeth pursed her lips. "He let me believe I killed a man when he knew it wasn't true. You'll forgive me if I don't exactly trust him. To me, he has been a liar."

During the next few days, Elizabeth began to realize that her father-in-law was a very busy and important man. He spent days in his office in town, then came home, and greeted business associates in his study after dinner. Most of the visitors were ranchers in desperate trouble due to the winter that they were now calling the "Great Die-up."

Elizabeth spent much of her evenings in her favorite room in the house. It was a small sitting room, elegantly furnished with a distinctly feminine hand.

Dan explained to her that it had been his wife's favorite room also, and Amelia had used it as her office and library. It contained a delicate desk and chair, which Elizabeth learned had been two of the few pieces of furniture Amelia had brought with her from Pennsylvania.

While Dan conducted business, Elizabeth wrote letters to her aunt and sister on the desk, and each time she used it, she felt as though she was getting acquainted with the other woman.

She sat in an exquisite brocade chair and read wonderful novels and poetry from Amelia's collection, now and then looking up at the painting of her mother-in-law, which hung above the fireplace. Beth liked Amelia's gentle smile and admired her delicate hand which rested on the shoulder of a young boy Elizabeth knew had been Jack.

It was on an evening like this that she heard Dan's footsteps approach the door to the sitting room and men's voices raised in discussion.

"Liz," Dan said when he opened the door and saw her sitting there., "would we disturb you if we joined you in here?"

Dan was followed by another man, well dressed and distinguished, who raised an appreciative eyebrow when he spied Elizabeth. Rone, dressed in the suit he had purchased in New York, stood behind the stranger.

"Of course not, Father," Elizabeth said graciously, smiling at each of them in turn.

"Liz, this is a good friend of mine, Senator Henry Teller," and turning to his guest, added, "my beautiful daughter-in-law, Elizabeth Gerard Drummond."

"It is my most sincere pleasure, Mrs. Drummond," Senator Teller said over her hand.

"Won't you sit down with me, Senator?" Elizabeth asked, indicating a chair opposite hers. "Would you like some tea? Or there's sherry . . ."

"Senator Teller would prefer tea, Liz, as he doesn't imbibe." Dan said, patting the other man's shoulder. "Sit, Henry, and I'll get myself and Rone a glass of sherry while Liz pours for you."

Senator Teller leaned back against his chair and crossed his legs. His eyes shone and his face was pleasant. "Well, this is what I call comfortable, sitting in a lovely room with an even lovelier young woman. It tends to make the world and its problems disappear for awhile."

Elizabeth handed the cup to him, smiling, "Thank you, Senator."

Dan sat on the arm of Elizabeth's chair while they chatted, and after a while the conversation turned to a new bill that was being legislated.

"I was reading about he Dawes Severalty Act in the newspaper just today," Elizabeth said. "It sounds like a wonderful opportunity for the Indians, Senator."

For the first time, Elizabeth saw Henry Teller frown and his mood darkened. "Many things are not what they seem, Mrs. Drummond. I'm afraid I can't agree with you. Oh, certainly, it sounds fair and right to divide the reservations into individual holdings and give each Indian family their own land. But I don't have any faith in the land itself—it's too arid for farming. Even livestock would be difficult for them to raise."

He put the glass down and leaned forward, "There are too many loopholes in this law, and too many white men I don't trust. In the long run, Indian families may end up losing everything they have now, what little it is. No, Mrs. Drummond, there's too much to investigate first." His eyes drifted to Rone, who nodded.

Elizabeth was apologetic. "I'm sorry, Senator, I had no idea. Once your investigation is complete, I hope you come to find you are mistaken, for from what I've read, the bill will be passed, and if it is, I should hope it's a success. There is no reason why the Indians cannot farm their own lands or raise their own cattle and have more productive lives."

The older man stood up and took her hand again. "You're right about our brother Indians, but not unless they are dealt with fairly by the white man and not unless they are given good land and a fair chance." He looked at Elizabeth sadly and said, "I'm afraid I've become jaded as I've grown older."

Henry Teller bowed his head, saying, "Thank you for sharing your room and your excellent company with us, but I must be leaving."

Elizabeth smiled at him and said, "I hope we'll meet again, Senator Teller."

"Now that would be a great pleasure, indeed."

The next afternoon, while she was writing at the desk, Rone stood in the doorway, watching her. She felt his presence and looked up. "Come in, Rone," she called to him warmly. "I was just writing to Aunt Catherine."

"Will you give her my regards in your letter?" he asked. Then, taking her hands in his, he said very quietly, "I wanted to say good-bye."

"Where are you going?"

"I have some business to take care of."

They looked at each other a long time, then Elizabeth said, "How can I ever thank you? You are my dearest friend."

"There is no need for thanks. I hope I'll always be around whenever you need me."

"You've become such an important part of my life now, parting with you, even for a short time, is desperately upsetting." She swallowed back tears.

He smiled faintly but said nothing.

"It's easy to see why Jack is so fond of you," she said.

Dropping his usual reserve, he said, "We were like brothers once."

"Has that changed?" she asked, afraid of the answer, knowing that she had somehow interfered. He didn't answer her. She asked him, "When will I see you again?"

"If you ever need me, Daniel Drummond will know where to find me."

As they stood staring into each other's eyes, Elizabeth felt a strange melancholy. As if knowing, his arms reached for her and she went into them. With his face close to hers, their lips almost touching, Rone's shining black eyes seemed to search her very soul. Her throat constricted when she whispered, "Rone?"

"Good-bye, Elizabeth." He turned and left through the veranda doors.

Time started to drag for Elizabeth after Rone left. One day Daniel came home from town early and found her cooking with the kitchen staff.

"Liz, may I speak with you?"

She wiped her floury hands on an oversized apron and followed him into his office. "I think the time has come for you to have a social life. I've been invited to a party at Mrs. Abigail Bradley's next Friday evening and want you to accompany me."

Elizabeth studied the pattern in the Persian rug under her feet. "And Jack?" she asked.

"He will most probably be there."

Dan's answer elicited a mixture of excitement and dread. She sighed, "Well, I guess it's time. I'll attend the party."

"Good, Jack has told everyone you are visiting your family back East. They know, of course, about the episode in New York as it was in all the papers. I suppose it may be a bit uncomfortable at times. The other scandal is hot in every circle, as well. There's a whole lot of gossip surrounding you and Jack. Are you ready to face all this?"

"I have nothing to feel ashamed of any more."

He smiled again. "You're quite a woman, Elizabeth. I'm proud of you."

"Let's hope I don't disappoint you—or myself."

The day before the ball, Daniel brought home a box for Elizabeth. She opened it and lifted out a gown. It shimmered in the light, its material an unfamiliar iridescent.

"I have never seen a gown this beautiful," she said.

"I hope it fits. The material is from India, and as soon as I saw it, I thought of you. It's almost exactly the color of your hair. See," he said, stroking the long folds, "in one light it looks golden, then turn it slightly and it's silver, like moonlight. I had it made for you awhile ago, when I had first met you. I thought you might like to wear it on Friday."

"Yes, of course, Father."

"If it needs alterations, the dressmaker will come out to the ranch."

"I'm certain it will fit well. Shall I try it on for you?"

"No, I think I prefer to wait until Friday. It's been a long time since I took a beautiful young woman out on my arm."

The next day, Justina, a young Mexican woman, who was Elizabeth's personal maid while she stayed at the Double D, helped her slip into the gown. It was very plain in lines, with no adornments, but when Jussy fastened the tiny, covered buttons in back, the dress fell in long folds, shimmering and shadowing. It did match Elizabeth's hair uniquely. The neckline was very low and small sleeves fell over the edges of Beth's soft shoulders. The material gathered over a bustle and fell in gleaming folds into a train.

The delicate pink of Elizabeth's skin and flushed cheeks seemed heightened by the pale dress, and her gray eyes shown brilliantly. Her hair was pulled up, away from her face, and cascaded in long curls.

Jussy stood back wide-eyed as Elizabeth looked at her reflection. "Señora, I hab never seen anything that looked like you," the girl exclaimed in her exotic accent.

Daniel knocked at her bedroom door. "May I come in, Liz?"

"Yes, do," she called. Elizabeth turned for him and he said nothing for a long moment.

"My God, you are beautiful," he finally managed.

She laughed. "Thanks to this lovely gown, Father."

He held out a black velvet case. "I thought that you might like to wear these tonight. They were my wife's and I've had them locked away since her death. It would make me happy to see them being worn again."

She opened the box. Diamonds sparkled and winked at her. There was a choker and earrings and a single strand bracelet. Daniel said, "Let me help you," and he fastened the choker around her slender neck.

It reminded her of the fateful night of her eighteenth birthday, when Catherine and Emily gave her their diamond offerings. She swallowed back sad tears.

"They're perfect," she said, looking into the mirror. "You're so very kind to me."

"Nonsense, I insist you look as a Drummond woman should look."

"And do I?"

He smiled tenderly. "Elizabeth, I couldn't ask for more."

CHAPTER THIRTY

Jack Drummond stood by his hostess' chair and they eyed each other. "You've got gall, I must say, young man. Every tongue in this room is wagging. Doesn't this scandal bother you at all?" Abigail Bradley asked curtly, though her eyes shown with undisguised amusement.

He kissed her wrinkled, age-spotted hand, "Should it?"

"I should hope not," she answered, laughing. "I would have been very disappointed if you didn't show. It's the most excitement this town has had in years."

"That isn't saying very much for your entertainment, Madam."

"Jack, you *are* my entertainment, always have been, since you were hangin' onto your Mama's skirts. The devil was in you even then."

He laughed. "And *you* are a feisty woman, Abigail."

She tapped his arm. "I enjoy you, young man. Though if your poor mother were alive today, she'd be disgraced."

The smile slipped from his lips. "That would bother me," he said sincerely.

"Well, she's not around so you needn't worry," Abigail told him flippantly.

"Giving me free rein to do just as I wish," he agreed, the corner of his mouth pulled into his familiar crooked grin.

"Including fathering a bastard child?" she whispered.

His eyes met hers, and she smiled again, "Of course, I don't believe it," she answered the question in his eyes.

"Thank you, Ma'am, for you are the only one."

"Not true. Your father doesn't believe it either. Speaking of your father, there he is. Who is that glorious woman with him?"

Jack followed her gaze to find his father. Elizabeth stood, regally holding Dan's arm, with the light catching her iridescent gown and hair, her eyes sparkling as brightly as the diamonds at her throat and wrist. A lightning bolt of recognition pierced Jack's heart.

Abigail left her chair and tottered across the room to greet her newly arrived guests.

"Daniel, how good to see you. Who is this?" she asked, her eyes covering all of Elizabeth.

"This is my daughter-in-law, Elizabeth. Liz," he added, turning to her, "our hostess, Mrs. Abigail Bradley."

Elizabeth nodded politely but felt extremely uncomfortable under the old woman's perusal. "Is that so?" Abigail asked amused, looking back toward Jack.

Elizabeth spotted Jack then and saw that he had been staring at her with his brows drawn over his eyes. When he saw her look at him, he smiled—charming, sarcastic, condemning.

In several easy strides, he came across the room. Her heart raced as he took her in his arms and kissed her long and hard.

All eyes were on them, but she did not push him away. He released her, the smile still there, and she met the smile, as well as the look in his eyes, with a caustic one of her own.

"Darling," he said. "I didn't expect you."

"I've just arrived and wanted to surprise you, my love," she said sweetly.

At this, Jack's eyes turned on his father. "Good to see you, Dad, and thank you for the surprise. I'll have to repay you sometime."

Daniel cleared his throat, but Jack was already looking hard at his wife again. Abigail scrutinized them closely, a small smile touching her lips.

"Well, this is a surprise for all of us. She's a beauty, Jack," she said.

"Yes, isn't she," his eyes never left her for a moment, and she met them and held them, while they exchanged silent messages.

The music started and Jack's hand went to the small of Elizabeth's back. "If you'll excuse us, I've been longing for a dance with my charming wife."

"Of course, of course," Abigail said, while Daniel nervously watched the couple as they walked away, merging with the other dancing couples.

Jack swept her into the dance, swirling, holding her tightly against him. His head was bent, as though he were whispering endearments into her ear, but what he was saying was another story.

"What the hell are you doing here?"

Elizabeth wanted to flinch from his tone of voice. Keeping her own voice sweet, she smiled into his face. "Visiting my father-in-law."

"I told you I never wanted to see you again," he hissed.

"Since when do I care what you say or want?"

"I thought we agreed the feeling was mutual."

"I'm here, Jack."

"What do you want, Elizabeth?"

"Some answers . . . and the truth, whatever it is."

"I told you the truth."

"Really?" her eyebrows lifted, and she forget the pretense she had assumed, anger showing in her eyes then.

Jack knew she was referring to Tom Blackwell and he said, "If I told you the truth about that, you wouldn't believe me. I'm warning you, Liz, I won't put up with any games."

"And I intend to play none," she snapped back.

"Go back to Pennsylvania immediately," he said into her ear.

"I'll go back when I'm ready to do so."

"Be ready tomorrow," he warned her.

"You don't frighten me, Jack!"

They danced in silence for several minutes, then she looked up at him. "By the way, thank you for not allowing me to hang."

He ignored her sarcasm. "How long have you been staying at my father's."

"Two weeks."

Anger flared in his eyes and she spoke quickly. "Don't be angry with him. I asked him not to mention it to you. I needed rest before confronting you again. I wasn't feeling well."

"And Rone?"

"He left shortly after we arrived at the Double D."

"Elizabeth . . ."

"Yes?"

"I don't want you here. I'm asking you to go home and forget about all this . . . me. You have an opportunity to straighten out your life, why not take advantage of it?"

"I want to know if the child is yours, Jack. If it isn't, then having me here, a loving, dedicated wife, will put doubts in people's minds."

"What business is this of yours?" he asked, defeated.

"I am your wife, am I not?"

His laugh rang out, and his white teeth flashed in a bitter smile. Several people near them on the dance floor turned to look at them. "Yes," he said, "and a fine wife you are, too."

The music stopped and he released her as though burned by the touch of her. The inquisitive insisted upon being introduced and he spent time taking her around and greeting people. Their hypocritical smiles and newsy questions almost undid him, but he kept his temper in check, and soon men were surrounding Elizabeth, asking her to dance. Jack disappeared into the background and she didn't speak to him again.

When it was late, and many of the guests were leaving, Daniel took her arm and said, "I think we should be going now, my dear."

Jack appeared from nowhere and together they bid good night to their hostess. "It was a pleasure being here this evening," Elizabeth said to the old woman.

"It was a pleasure having you here, Elizabeth. Your presence turned an otherwise dull evening into a splendid one, I must say."

"That's enough from you, Abigail," Jack chided her while kissing her cheek.

"Are you coming with us?" Dan asked his son when they left the house.

"Yes, indeed, I am."

"Must you?" Elizabeth asked.

"Your desire to be with me warms my heart, wife," he said, sweeping his arm and bowing to her graciously as she stepped into the coach.

She was annoyed that Jack seated himself beside her, while Daniel sat across from them. The tension was thick when Dan asked, "What is this obsession with social gatherings you seem to have acquired, Jack?"

"Simply, I don't intend to hide myself away and let this lie embed itself in everyone's mind. I also intend to find out just who the father of that kid is and have him admit it openly."

"You think you'll find him among these fine families, do you?"

"Why not?"

"Why wouldn't Darla name him then?"

Jack lit a cigarette and exhaled the blue smoke. "Because she's wanted me from the time she was an ugly kid in pigtails. She's vicious enough to do anything to get what she wants."

Jack looked through the window of the coach and into the moonlit countryside. His mind drifted to the day he had ridden to the Stuart's ranch upon his return from New York.

The confrontation with Darla's father had been bad enough, and he had feared he would have had to defend himself, even if it had meant killing the old man. Jack remembered the way Darla had walked into the room, carrying the baby in her arms. The initial shock of seeing Jack standing across the desk from her father had quickly changed to a radiant smile as she had run to him.

"Oh, Jack, I knew you'd come when you'd heard. Look at him, Jack, our son . . . our beautiful son."

Jack had backed away from mother and child, insisting, "Don't go on with this charade any longer. This is not my child and I'm here to see that you admit it once and for all."

She looked worried and bit her lip. "How could you say that? You know there hasn't been any other man, Jack. You know the night you seduced me . . ."

"I don't know how many men there have been, but I haven't been one of them for a good long time."

Ben Stuart's voice had boomed, "You admit that you've been with my daughter? Here, in front of me, you admit it?"

Jack had felt trapped, but knew that the truth would be best. "I admit it, but it was over a year and a half ago. She's been with other men since."

"You are a liar, man, and you discredit all of us by trying to insinuate such filth. Darla has been in love with you for years. You are a scoundrel for having taken advantage of her love, and now you deny her and the child. I intend to see she is avenged for this."

Jack leaned over the desk that separated them. "And I intend to see you learn the truth about your daughter."

"Get out of this house," the old man said, his face swollen and red with rage. "When I'm finished with you there won't be a decent person in the West that will have anything to do with you."

Jack had started to leave and Darla's eyes followed him. "No matter where you go, I'll be there, Jack. You will admit this baby is yours."

Darla followed up on those words, for immediately after Jack's visit to their ranch in Pueblo, Benjamin had bought a house in Denver and had moved Darla and the child into it. She paraded the baby though the town, and played the wronged and deserted woman.

Jack, in turn, publicly denounced her and the child every chance that was made available to him, sowing seeds of doubt and making many young men, who had been seen in the company of Darla in the past, very nervous.

Jack looked at his wife sitting beside him now. Having Liz in Denver, by his side, would help his case, and she did do a good job tonight at Abigail's, acting the beautiful, devoted wife. He knew it was a farce and that fact hurt him more deeply than her absence would have.

When they entered the house, Elizabeth said good night and started for her room. Jack stood at the bottom of the staircase and called, "Elizabeth!" She continued to walk up the stairs, her shoulders straight, her head erect.

"I want to talk to you," he demanded. She continued to ignore him and went to her room, closing and locking the door behind her.

Elizabeth knew a confrontation was imminent, but she wasn't prepared for it yet. Any discussion would have to be on her terms, when she was fresh and rested, and not so shaken from the mere presence of him.

In the morning Jack was gone. Daniel told her that Jack intended to be home for dinner that evening, since he had decided to stay with them in Denver for awhile. Throughout the day, Elizabeth found herself rehearsing for the scene that was to come. She dressed in a rose colored gown and arranged her hair the way he liked it, annoyed with herself for doing so, but aroused when she imagined the response it would create in his eyes.

They had waited an hour for dinner, but he did not arrive, and Daniel insisted they hold dinner no longer. She picked at the food on her plate, each bite feeling like sawdust in her mouth.

"Aren't you hungry, Liz?" Daniel asked.

"Not very. I'm sorry, Father, I'm not very good company this evening."

"Are you upset that he didn't come home?" he asked her.

"Absolutely not!"

Daniel started eating again, smiling to himself. When he was finished and the plates were cleared from the table, they walked into the sitting room. He poured brandy for himself and handed a glass of sherry to Elizabeth.

Elizabeth felt restless and she picked up a book she had been reading earlier that day. Her father-in-law watched her through hooded eyes. She snapped the book closed, stood and paced, then sat down in the same chair, once again picking up the book.

"You would think," she said, "that he'd come home to eat after saying he would."

"Yes, you would think so, wouldn't you," Dan agreed.

"I don't think he ought to be given anything to eat when he does arrive," she continued.

"No, really, you are right. Though undoubtedly he'll have eaten before he comes in."

"*If* he comes in," she finished.

"If he comes in," he agreed again.

"Not that I hope he does."

"I don't blame you. He's in a black mood these days."

"Well, he should be," she said, and Dan detected defensiveness in her tone.

"Yes, that's true," he added, stifling laughter now.

Elizabeth paced some more, then they heard hoof beats on the drive. The door opened and slammed and Elizabeth fell into her chair.

Jack sauntered into the room, saying nothing to either of them, and poured whiskey into a glass. Elizabeth had opened her book and pretended to read.

Daniel nodded to Jack. "You missed a fine dinner, son."

"I wasn't hungry," he said, sitting heavily in a chair, his long legs stretched out in front of him.

"You could at least apologize to Elizabeth," Daniel said.

When she looked up, Jack's mouth was pulled into a smile. "I apologize to you, Elizabeth. I see you've become the lady of the house. What a cozy scene this is. Just the three of us, sitting with an after-dinner brandy, homey as you like . . ."

Elizabeth stood up. "I'm going to bed. I find this 'cozy' scene quite intolerable since you've arrived." She heard him laughing as she reached the staircase and she slammed her bedroom door loudly, throwing her book to the floor.

The raised voices of father and son downstairs let her know that Daniel was reprimanding Jack for his treatment of her, and surprisingly, it didn't please Elizabeth. She couldn't make out the words they spoke, but she knew it was a heated argument.

Shortly after, she heard quick, heavy footsteps in the hallway and Jack's bedroom door slam as hers had.

Beth brushed her hair angrily then lay on the bed wide awake, as she had done the previous night. Several hours later she was still tossing one way and another, unable to sleep. She listened at the door and hearing nothing, opened it, and walked down to the lower floor.

The house was in darkness, but she knew the rooms well, and going into the drawing room, she found the decanters of brandy and whiskey.

She lifted the brandy but decided it wasn't strong enough. She poured whiskey into a glass, then added more to it, and took a swallow.

"That should help you sleep," Jack said from the shadows.

She turned in the direction of his voice, startled. "What are you doing here?"

"I'm staying here, remember?"

"I mean in the dark."

"I couldn't sleep either."

Elizabeth put down her glass, unfinished.

"Please, don't let me stop you," Jack said. Then, in feigned concern, he asked, "Have you been drinking much lately?"

"I . . . just . . . I don't have to explain myself to you."

"Of course not. I felt responsible."

"You? Responsible? You take no responsibility for anything, Jack, including your own actions. Please do not feel responsible for mine."

They were silent for awhile, then he said, "I've never seen you look more beautiful than you did the other night, Liz."

"I'm going back to bed," she said, nervously.

Jack stood in her way. She backed up a few steps, saying, "Leave me alone."

"I want to talk, Liz."

"No, not now."

"Why did you come back?"

"I told you, Jack, I wanted to find out the truth."

"My word isn't good enough?"

Elizabeth turned her back to him, but his hand found her shoulder and he spun her around to face him again. "That child is not mine. I would admit it if it were. I haven't been with another woman since I've met you."

"Don't lie to me, Jack."

"I'm not, damnit," he said, bending to kiss her neck.

"Jack, please, don't do this . . ."

He ignored her and his arms tightened around her and his lips traveled up to the back of her ear, then her cheeks, and finally her waiting mouth.

"Why won't you believe me?" he asked her, sadness heavy in his voice.

Her face rested on his soft shirt and she said, "How can I be so weak? With just a kiss and a gentle word from you, I melt in your arms. Oh, Jack, I want to believe you. I'm afraid of being duped. Every time I close my eyes, I see you and Darla together as I saw you that night in the garden."

"Liz, nothing happened that night. Don't you remember? I took you for the first time that same night."

Elizabeth remembered and it stung her. She pushed him away. "Yes, I do remember. You're quite a man, being able to take two women the same night."

Jack's voice was cold now. "You refuse to listen to me then?"

"I can't trust you, Jack. You've lied to me before—did you not? All those months, you allowed me to believe that I had killed Tom Blackwell. You took me away, letting me believe I was a murderess. How could you do that, Jack? What kind of person are you? Have you no idea what that did to me?"

She was crying now, unable to go on, and he took her in his arms again, but she pulled away. He said, "I have no excuse for it except that I knew you wouldn't come with me any other way, and I wanted you, Liz. I didn't know it, but I loved you then, I needed you. It was stupid and cruel, and I will never forgive myself. I wanted to tell you. I tried many times, but always stopped for fear you'd leave me. I was afraid you'd never forgive me, Liz."

Elizabeth raised her face to his. "There was a time I may have forgiven you, and I even believe that you love me now, but I don't dare believe that you brought me to Colorado because you loved me then. I know you needed our marriage to keep your ranch. You used me, Jack."

Jack was defeated again for he could not deny that it was true, that in order to keep his ranch he needed to be married. There would be no way to convince her how much he loved her at the time, especially since he had fought against it for so long and treated her with such disdain. She wouldn't understand that there was no other woman he would have ever married—even to keep the ranch—except Elizabeth.

Elizabeth went on, "I understand your love for River Pines, and in a way, I can understand why you did what you did."

"Elizabeth, I am not the father of that boy. If you believe nothing else, please believe that."

"I want to, Jack, but . . ."

"You won't," he finished for her. Then he swore under his breath and said, "Our life together is over, isn't it? Even if you do learn the truth, what is the truth without trust? That has been destroyed. We both killed it. I wonder if there was ever any love between us. I think I must have dreamed it." He turned and looked at her again, "But I'm awake now."

The words he spoke and the pain in his voice, crushed her heart and diminished her resolve. She wanted to tell him it wasn't true, but she couldn't. Too much had been said. Too much had been done to crush whatever there was between them.

Jack left the room and in the morning he was gone.

CHAPTER THIRTY-ONE

The days passed slowly and Elizabeth no longer enjoyed the quiet solitude of the graceful house. She didn't revel in the early spring, as she had since she was a child, and she rarely went riding. Her father-in-law tried to lighten her spirits, to no avail. Elizabeth stopped reading, for she couldn't concentrate on the words. She didn't plan the meals any longer or take an interest in Dan's business. When he was home with associates in the evening, she drifted to her room and avoided contact with anyone.

On her birthday, Daniel insisted she accompany him to the Tabor Grand Opera House, and he tried to interest her in gossip about the man who had built it, H.A.W., and his young wife, "Baby Doe," but, although Elizabeth listened attentively, he knew it didn't interest her.

"You know, Liz," he told her, "when Tabor left his first wife to marry Baby Doe five years ago, it was a bigger gossip story than Jack's exploits are right now, and they survived."

"Somehow, Father, that doesn't help," she said, "but I appreciate your trying."

It was mid-morning one day shortly after that Elizabeth sat looking at Amelia's and the child Jack's portrait, when her depression became overpowering. She allowed burning tears to drop from her eyes and track uneven lines on her cheeks.

What am I doing here? she asked herself, and realized with bitter disappointment that her presence had proven nothing. Her last encounter with Jack had been more painful than she could have imagined.

He told her he had deceived her about Blackwell because he needed her and loved her, but that was unlikely since he actually acted as though he disliked her then. She wished she had never known that he needed to marry her to keep the ranch. At least then she could try to believe that much.

Elizabeth felt that he had been more cruel to tell her that he loved her than to tell her the truth. The truth—Jack said she wouldn't believe it. *God, how I want to believe it.*

She knew one thing. If he hadn't brought her to Colorado because he loved her, then somewhere along the way he had fallen in love with her, for she believed without a doubt that he did love her the night they had first made love and during the weeks following. He loved her most in Rone's cabin in the mountain.

Or did he? Whose name did he call out in delirium? Who haunted his dreams?

Elizabeth instinctively enclosed her arms around herself, and she retreated deeper into the chair. She was tortured by the thought that Darla's baby was his, whether or not they had been lovers while she and Jack were lovers themselves. *He had called her name.*

Standing up from the chair, her tears stopped. She glared at the face of the boy in the picture. *How can he blame me—how can he possibly be angry with me for doubting him?*

"I have no business here anymore. I don't know how I will go on without you, but I will go on. I may never know the truth, but I cannot—will not—subject myself to this torment for another day."

Elizabeth bolted from the room and ran up the stairs, past Justina who was polishing the already gleaming floors. Elizabeth opened her wardrobe and started throwing clothing onto the bed.

Justina appeared in the doorway and asked, "Señora, where are you going?"

"Get my trunk, Jussy. I'm going home to Pennsylvania where I belong."

When the trunk and several bags were packed, Elizabeth sat down at the desk in the sitting room and started to write Jack a note informing him of her decision to proceed with the divorce.

She heard Justina's agitated voice in the foyer but paid no attention as she struggled to compose the letter.

Seconds later the door flew open and Darla Stuart stood beside a very young woman who was holding a baby. Elizabeth was stunned by their appearance and she stood with her mouth open.

"I thought you might like to see your husband's child," Darla said.

Jussy ran around the two women, mumbling in Mexican, and looked worriedly at Elizabeth, "I try to make her wait, Señora Liz."

Elizabeth took a deep breath and ran her hands over the skirt of her dress. "It's all right, Jussy. Just leave us and close the door."

The girl threw a furtive glance at Darla, then left, obediently.

"I want to know why you came back. You know this child is his," Darla began as soon as the door was closed.

Elizabeth remained calm. "I know nothing of the kind, Miss Stuart."

"It's the truth."

Elizabeth shrugged. "My husband denies the baby is his."

"Then he is lying to you." Darla's air of superiority diminished slightly and the color in her cheeks drained. "He doesn't want you anymore. He told me himself. After all, he has found out you were a murderer. How could you expect him to stay with you?"

Elizabeth shook her head. "You don't have any idea what you're talking about, which proves to me that *you're* the liar, Miss Stuart."

"He will admit that this is his son when you leave. Why would you want to stay with a man who doesn't want you?"

"Because he is my husband and I love him." The truth of those words almost undid Elizabeth.

"He is my lover. He was mine long before you married him."

Elizabeth looked at Darla a long time. "If that is true, why didn't he marry you to keep his ranch?" It was a question Elizabeth had not asked before, not Jack, not herself. And the answer lie in Darla's eyes, as she had no idea what Elizabeth was talking about. Wouldn't he have married the woman he loved in order to keep River Pines? It was so simple . . . and at that moment Elizabeth realized with perfect clarity that he had indeed done that very thing.

"I think you'd better go now," Elizabeth said.

Darla was angry beyond control. Her eyes bulged and her hands clenched and unclenched. "I want you to leave Colorado, do you hear me? I will tear your hair out if you don't go away!" Darla snarled.

Elizabeth felt a surge of cold anger, yet an icy calmness settled on her. "Don't try it, Darla, you don't know who you're dealing with," Elizabeth warned, as the other woman started to approach.

The young girl, still holding the baby, stepped forward and pleaded with Darla. "Please, Miss, don't do this. What will happen to the baby? Please don't hurt anyone."

But Darla was beyond logic and reasoning. "Get out of my way."

The girl was trembling, but she held the baby close to her chest as she continued, "Think of the baby, Miss Darla. What will happen to him?"

"I don't care what happens to him," Darla said, pushing the girl away. She stumbled to the floor, and the baby, jarred from sleep, started to scream.

Elizabeth watched as the girl tried to stand, all the while comforting the child, and murmuring to it soothingly. The girl got to her feet, and Elizabeth could see wet stains spreading from her breasts through the light gray material of her dress.

The realization of what that meant shocked Elizabeth momentarily, putting her off guard, but she dodged away as Darla Stuart moved closer.

"Not only is that baby not Jack's," Elizabeth said to Darla, "but he isn't even yours!"

The other woman stopped walking toward Elizabeth then. Beth turned to the girl. "He's *your* baby, isn't he?"

"Keep your mouth shut," Darla said to the girl.

Elizabeth persisted, "You gave birth to that beautiful little boy, didn't you?"

"You think you have it all figured out, don't you?" Darla said angrily. "Well you're wrong. She's a wet nurse."

Elizabeth continued to address the young girl. "Did Miss Stuart pay you for the baby? She told you that you could be his nurse while she raised him as her own, didn't she?"

"No!" Darla screamed, and as she did, Justina opened the door to let in Daniel and Benjamin Stuart.

"Papa," Darla cried.

"What are you doing here, Darla? I told you to stay away from this house. When your mother told me you were coming here, I immediately followed to bring you back."

Elizabeth silenced him with her hand, and still looking at the girl, said to Darla, "Do you intend for me to believe you are the mother of this baby when the girl's breasts leak milk in answer to his cries? You are not this mother, Miss Stuart."

Then walking over to the girl, Elizabeth put her arm around her shoulders and asked, "Do you really want a woman like this to raise your baby? Tell the truth to us. We will help you, no matter what the answer."

The girl's brown eyes were large with tears. She looked from Elizabeth to Darla. In a shaking voice, she said, "Miss came to me and asked to buy my baby. She said they'd take good care of him and me. I couldn't take care of him by myself. Ma and Pa didn't want me around no more, and I didn't know what to do."

Darla Stuart's hand came out and slapped the girl's cheek. She started to strike out again, but Benjamin grabbed her wrist.

"That's enough, Darla. You've done enough harm here." He looked beaten when he added, "To think I followed you here to protect you."

"But, Papa, you don't understand," she whined.

Benjamin looked at Daniel. "Late last summer she told us she was going to have Jack's baby. When Jack made it clear he didn't want her—that his marriage was important to him—we sent her away to my sister's. She came back with them," Benjamin said, indicating the girl and the baby. "We owe you an apology, Dan."

Elizabeth answered him. "You owe Jack an apology, Mr. Stuart."

As if summoned, Jack walked in from the veranda through the French windows. His eyes rested on each person in the room, Elizabeth last, and he instinctively knew that whatever events had just transpired, his name was finally cleared.

That night there was an uncomfortable silence in the lovely blue dining room as Elizabeth, Dan, and Jack had dinner. When they had finished eating, Daniel asked, "You never told us why you came here today, Jack."

Jack's eyes glanced at Elizabeth. "I have something for Liz."

Daniel cleared his throat and said, "Well, if you'll excuse me, I think I'll take a walk."

He stood up and patted Jack's shoulder. "I'm glad this is over, son, not that I ever doubted you."

Jack smiled an unusually warm smile at his father. "You and Abigail," he said, looking accusingly at Elizabeth.

"Good night," Dan said, and as he left, he kissed Elizabeth's forehead.

When they were alone, Jack moved to a chair beside Elizabeth and faced her fully. "So now you have your proof, Liz."

"Yes," she whispered and took a drink of water nervously.

"Now you can go home and get that divorce we've been waiting for."

She stared at the white tablecloth.

"Well?" he prodded.

"Yes . . . yes, I can. I'm already packed."

He lifted his eyebrows.

"I had decided to leave today," she explained.

Jack nodded, "Good, I'll take you to the train tomorrow," he said lightly, leaning back in his chair.

Elizabeth's throat ached painfully. "I'm sorry, Jack. I'm sorry I doubted you and didn't believe you."

"Don't mention it, Liz," he said, and his tone was still light. "By the way," he went on, reaching into his pocket and pulling out an envelope which had been folded several times, "I came to give you this. It's a letter from David for . . . us. He says that their marriage will take place on the Twentieth and that they hope we can arrange to be there. They want us to be their witnesses. It seems you're leaving just in time."

Elizabeth repeated the date, as their eyes locked. To hide her discomfort, she said, "They should have been married months ago. It's my fault they weren't." Jack said nothing and she continued. "I feel guilty about so many things." Her eyes caught his again.

He quickly looked away from her saying, "Spare me."

"Please, Jack, I want to apologize."

"It's too late for recriminations—from either of us."

Elizabeth opened her mouth to speak again, but he stood, and leaving the room, said, "I'll send David a telegram in the morning telling him you're on your way home."

Elizabeth sat in the chair in her bedroom and ached with an emptiness almost too much to bear. Her hand rested on her abdomen where a firm mound was appearing, seeming to grow larger each day. It occurred to her for the first time that she would have this child and rear it alone. It would not know its father, or the joy of belonging to River Pines.

She would steal home to Pennsylvania, and quietly give birth. She and Jack would be denied all that they longed for— Jack, his child, and Elizabeth a life with him at River Pines.

Elizabeth searched her trunk for something to sleep in and found the blue velvet dressing gown Jack had purchased for her in New York. She put a thin white gown over her naked body, then the dressing gown over it, and left her room to walk to the door behind which Jack lie sleeping.

Elizabeth rapped lightly, hesitating, and started when she heard his surly voice answer, "Come in, it's open."

Jack was on top of his bed, clothed only in tight black pants. His head rested on an arm behind his head. His eyebrows lifted slightly and the corner of his mouth shifted into a smile. Jack's eyes moved over her and she was aware that the dressing gown had fallen open, showing the white night dress under it.

"I just wanted to tell you . . . ," she started, but hesitated.

"Well, I'm listening."

"I wanted to tell you that you needn't bring me to the train tomorrow. Your father and I discussed David's letter when he returned from his walk, and he has decided to join me for the wedding."

Jack shrugged his shoulder and looked at the ceiling.

"Good night," she whispered, turning to leave, but in a swift movement, Jack was off the bed and his foot was high against the door, barring her way.

She was close to his body, next to his arched knee, where his elbow leaned casually across it. He took a lapel of her dressing gown and pulled her closer between his legs, close enough that she could feel him harden against her thigh.

"You know, Elizabeth," he said, his mouth drawn tight, his brow furrowed, "I was just thinking that there is really no such thing as love between a man and a woman."

"Is that so?" she asked, breathless because of his closeness.

"Yes, that's so. It's just a mating ritual that calls us to each other, and we say those sweet little words to make it seem more civilized, to make us feel less like animals."

His hand reached up and played with a strand of her hair. "But there is no such thing as love," he repeated.

Elizabeth reached for the doorknob, but she felt herself being lifted into the air and flung upon the bed. Jack's body fell on hers, their lips touching briefly.

"Why are you doing this, Jack?" she protested, struggling.

"Because tomorrow you're leaving, but tonight you are still my wife."

Jack's mouth covered hers hard and she resisted. "Not like this, Jack," she said, yet knowing this had been her intent all along.

Jack's hands moved quickly as he pulled the dressing gown and night dress from her shoulders, and her struggling ceased when his lips found her breast. Her back arched when his hand pulled the night dress up her thigh and his fingers found her.

He pulled away from her, looking deeply into her eyes, "Tell me now, Liz. If you do not want this, tell me now."

Her gray eyes filled with tears, while her thighs opened to receive him. They joined together, matching each other's rhythmic thrusts, while he keened her name. "Liz . . . Liz . . . Liz . . ."

Jack breathed in the scent of her hair, her breath, the muskiness of their bodies. He wanted more and more of her, and still could not get enough. His thrusts became deeper, stronger, more demanding.

Elizabeth held him close with her arms, their legs entwined, as tears dropped from her lashes, falling down her temples and ending in dark circles on the sheet beneath her head. He tasted the salty wetness on her face and kissed it away. When their arousal was sharpened to the point where they could stand no more, Jack heard Elizabeth cry out into his shoulder, and they lay throbbing and exhausted in each other's arms.

Jack walked onto the veranda through the dining room and leaned against the white house with his back near the sitting room. He rolled a cigarette, lit it, and inhaled deeply.

He felt drained, and berated himself for having taken her that way, realizing with dismay that he could have hurt her. He blew a stream of smoke into the moonlight. *But how was I supposed to know?* He leaned his head back against the cool wood, wondering how he was ever going to let Elizabeth go, when the doors of the sitting room opened, and he heard his father's voice.

Daniel and Rone sat talking in the room. Daniel has been expecting him when Rone arrived late that evening and had gone out to meet him in the stables. Very quietly, so as not to disturb Elizabeth and Jack, they walked into the house, going directly to the sitting room.

"Did Henry Teller explain what he wants you to do in Idaho?" Daniel asked, as he opened the French windows to allow in the fresh night air. "It was I who suggested you be hired. There's no one I'd trust more."

"I see," Rone said, sitting in Elizabeth's chair. Her scent lingered against the cushion. He closed his eyes, breathing it in.

Dan explained to Rone what had happened earlier that day, and finished by saying, "Jack's still angry with Liz. It seems stubbornness runs deep in this family."

The men's eyes met and held, then Dan said, "Will it ever be right between us? Will you ever forgive me?" Leaning forward, he continued emotionally, "You know how I feel about you."

"How do you feel about me?" Rone's voice was almost a whisper.

"If you would only say the word, I'd acknowledge you . . . even now after all these years. It is you who has never wanted that."

Each of Dan's elbows rested on a knee. "I've never been ashamed of you, Rone, or of who you are. I was wrong in the beginning, I'll admit it. But it was a difficult time and I was young. I didn't know how my wife would take it, and—right or wrong—as much as I loved your mother, I loved my wife more."

The admission hung in the air between them. "When I did tell Amelia, and realized she understood, I tried to do right by you then, Rone. We both would have accepted you as our son."

"I was no longer your son, sir. I was Ute. If I could have chosen, I would have stayed with my mother's people."

Daniel shook his head. "I wanted you with me. You were as much my son as Jack was."

They were silent for a long while. Rone stood up and put his hand on the shoulder of the older man. "There is much that could have been different. We can't change the past. The years I spent with the tribe, waiting for you to come for us, taught me a hatred no boy could understand. By the time you came for me, I thought I could not feel love ever again."

Rone looked at the painting above the mantle and studied the face of the woman who smiled down into the room. "I was wrong. I could not help loving your gentle wife . . ." When his eyes rested on the face of the small boy standing against Amelia's chair, he added, ". . . or my brother."

Dan followed his gaze and said, "When you were boys, I would watch you playing from this window. I ached to join you, hoping you would let me in. I wanted to be included in the closeness you and Jack shared." Daniel's shoulders lifted in a heavy sigh.

"Once I almost went out to tell Jack the truth—that you were his brother—but Amelia stopped me. She said I would betray you, reminding me that I had promised you I would tell no one, and in turn you agreed to live with us. I was angry with her and accused her of not wanting Jack to know so that she wouldn't have to acknowledge you publicly. She never forgave me for saying that."

Daniel rubbed his eyes with his fingers, as he continued. "I know now that I wanted to tell Jack because I was jealous of your relationship. I'm glad Amelia stopped me. At least through all these years, he has had you . . . and you have had him."

Dan looked at Rone and saw that the younger man was moved, and he asked, "Have I done anything right by you or Jack?"

"You let us know each other. That was the most important gift you have ever given me."

Dan's green eyes were pained when he said, "And now you're faced with the torment of being in love with his wife."

Rone's eyes locked with his father's, and he finally understood why he had been asked to work for Senator Teller on a reservation two states away. Nothing else needed to be said between them.

Jack stood with his shoulder against the side of the house, his cigarette burning his thumb and finger, and stared in the direction of the French windows. The other men's voices had stopped, but he replayed their words in his mind.

He felt flogged by each new revelation he overheard, beaten with the disclosed knowledge. He had known for many years that his father had had an affair with another woman, and it was the reason why he had turned against his father when he was seventeen.

It had never occurred to him that the faceless woman he always hated passionately was Rone's dead mother.

Jack stepped off the veranda and strode, dazed and angry, to the stables.

CHAPTER THIRTY-TWO

Elizabeth awakened in Jack's bed. She knew he was gone even before she reached out for him. She started to rise, then lie back on the pillow. The morning nausea had stopped weeks ago, but she still felt weak and dizzy when she first arose each day.

This morning Elizabeth felt fatigued and sore. Jack had never made love to her the way he had the night before—urgent, savage, demanding. She had felt consumed by him, and knew she had responded with the same wild, earthy abandon.

When they had been sated, he'd fallen beside her, his hand resting on her stomach. She had wanted to tell him that beneath his palm lived the product of their love.

There's no such thing as love, he had told her.

So she had said nothing. Instead, she had closed her eyes and turned her head away from him, feigning sleep. She had felt Jack take his hand from her and leave the bed. She had heard him pace for a long time, and then muted noises as he had dressed. When he had gone to the door and opened it, Elizabeth was aware that he had stood looking at her for a few, very long moments before leaving the room.

In the morning light, as she lie in the aftermath of their most passionate night, she knew their life together was beyond hope. She got to her feet, covered herself with the dressing gown, and went to her own room. Her gray traveling suit was laid out on her bed, her trunk ready to be locked for the trip back to Benton.

She washed and dressed, carefully concentrating on every detail so that she would not think of Jack or River Pines, yet thoughts of him charged every one of her senses, pervaded every moment.

Elizabeth went downstairs and found her father-in-law having breakfast at the round table in the bay window of the dining room. He was alone, as she knew he would be.

"Liz, come join me. We'll be leaving very soon, and I think you should have something to . . ."

She left him and went into Amelia's sitting room. She looked at the portrait of her mother-in-law, and the eyes looked sadder to her than usual. The French windows were open and a breeze caught her skirt.

Elizabeth walked onto the veranda and then toward the barn. She opened the door and looked at the stall where the black stallion would be. It was empty—as empty as her heart.

"Elizabeth," Rone spoke from behind her.

She did not turn to him. He stepped closer and she could feel his presence within inches.

"Elizabeth," he said again, still closer.

Words would not form for her. Her depression didn't allow for conversation.

"Please," he whispered, and she could feel his breath in her hair. She leaned back against his chest. They stood that way a very long time, each in their own thoughts, their own misery.

Finally, Elizabeth said, "I will probably never see you again."

"Don't go back to Benton, Liz. Stay here. Fight for what is yours."

"He doesn't want me," she said, and Rone was bothered by the absence of life in her usually melodious voice.

"Get back up on the bronco, Liz," he encouraged her, gripping her arms tighter.

"I've been thrown too far and too hard this time. There's no white hat to gain."

"Jack needs you, even if he won't say it."

"Take care of him for me, Rone."

"I won't be here. He'll be alone."

Elizabeth turned and searched his face. "Where are you going?"

"It doesn't matter where. I don't know how long I'll be gone."

Elizabeth was lost in the darkness of his eyes, where she could see the beauty of his soul. She had always sought refuge in those eyes, but now she flinched at the pain she found in them.

Her fingers traced the hollow of his cheek and the width of his jaw and chin. He kissed her fingertips when they touched his lips.

Almost unable to see him through the tears in her eyes, she whispered, "Wherever I am, for as long as I live, I will think of you, my dearest friend, and remember."

Then, touching his cheek one last time, she walked around him, out of the barn, and into the sun. Before she reached the house, Rone caught up with her. "Elizabeth, if I were to give you a parting gift—anything at all—what would it be?"

"Jack," she answered simply.

Rone took her face in his strong hand. "Your white hat?"

She couldn't smile back at him. "It's hopeless."

"If it weren't hopeless and you could have another chance, what would you say?"

"I would say that there *is* such a thing as love, and that I love him. I want to live with him at River Pines and have his children."

Daniel walked onto the veranda and said very quietly, "It's time, Liz."

She closed her eyes and swallowed hard, pulling her face from Rone's grip. "But there are no more chances."

Rone tied his horse to the corral fence. The brown timber house was in darkness, and he decided to go to Calla's cottage where the windows shone brightly. He knocked and Calla opened the door. "I knowd you'd come, Rone."

He entered the warm, inviting kitchen and found Jim and their boys sitting at the table. The black man stood and pumped his hand. "Lord above, we got problems. Now you're here, maybe it be all right." Jim's jaundiced looking eyes filled with tears, and Rone felt an icy finger of dread touch him.

Rone sat down and accepted the cup of steaming coffee Calla put before him. He smiled at her, but her face was grim and her eyes were worried as she sat down at the table.

"He's real bad. Never seen him like this since the last time, Rone. He just sits in that house, mean as a Africa tiger. He drank all night until he passed out, then when he wakes up this mornin', he starts drinkin' again. I tried to talk to him and help him when he first came home, but he was just too far gone. Now I don't even go into the house, that's how bad he is."

Rone listened intently, then he said, "Sounds worse than the last time."

"Maybe so, Rone," Jim said, shaking his head and staring into his cup. "This place needs lots of work done on it from that winter and I'm too old to do it by myself with just Little Ben and Nathan. He keeps this up, he's gonna lose it all."

"I'll go talk to him."

Calla shook her head. "No, he won't listen, even to you, not tonight. He might . . . well, I jus' don' think you oughta go in there. Maybe he gotta work this out hisself . . . if he can."

Rone touched her shoulder reassuringly. "I've come up against him before, Calla. I can handle him."

"Not this time. You don' know what he's like. Whatever Miz Liz done, it's real bad. He ripped her curtains to shreds last night. Then I heard him cryin'."

"She didn't do anything, Calla. It's more to do with what's inside him," Rone told her gently.

He stood to leave and she took his arm, "I know you, and I know I can't keep you outta there if you're makin' to go in, but please, Rone, be careful."

The moon shone through the bare windows where, just a short time before, the pretty curtains Elizabeth had sewn were hung. Now they were torn and thrown in a corner. In the moonlight, Rone saw Jack slouched in a chair, his head back, his eyes closed. Two empty bottles of whiskey were broken on the hearth, and a half-full bottle hung from Jack's hand.

Rone waited a long moment, and when Jack didn't stir, he started walking over to him.

"Don't take another step closer," growled Jack.

Rone stopped.

"Who is it? What the hell do you want?" Jack squinted in the dark. Then a malicious smile crept to his lips. "So, it's you. My old buddy. Brother's keeper and all that."

"I just came from Liz," Rone said quietly.

"So you did. How is my lovely wife? Busy getting ready to go back to her God damned fancy home in Pennsylvania? Quite a woman, that gal is . . . but then you know. Who will be her next victim, I wonder? You? Has she enchanted you into her arms, too? You bed her yet, Rone?"

"Shut up." Rone's voice was barely audible.

Jack sat up and laughed. "Oh, so she has then. Well, you're welcome to her. You deserve each other . . . my beautiful wife-witch and my half-breed *brother*!"

Rone stiffened and his blood ran cold. He stood silently as Jack continued, "Do I detect surprise in that Indian face? Of course, you wouldn't think I knew the truth. Well, I didn't. Not until recently." Then lifting his bottle of whiskey, Jack said, "Let's have a drink to the family, buddy . . . excuse me . . . brother."

He brought the bottle to his lips and drank, his eyes never leaving Rone's face, then he extended the bottle to Rone who took it and flung it across the room. It crashed, making a tinkling sound as the pieces fell against one another.

"What's this? You don't want to drink to the family? To Elizabeth, then, the woman in our lives—after I get another bottle."

"You've had enough," Rone said.

"That so? I don't think so, half-breed brother o' mine."

"Which hurts you more, Jack, that your marriage to Elizabeth has failed or that I'm your brother?"

When Jack didn't answer, Rone continued, "I have wondered many times what it would be like if you knew the truth. I've pictured it in my mind. There were times when I could hardly hold back calling you my brother right out in the open.

"But there were times, like now, when I was almost ashamed and disgusted by that truth, and wished I never knew who the hell you were. For many years I've sat back and watched you. You've been given everything, taking all, and not knowing what to take next. I thought it didn't matter, you turned out all right in the long run. But now I see things differently." Rone pointed his finger at Jack, "Now I see that *you're* the bastard in this family."

Jack's hands came together in several loud claps and he said, "That was a fine speech, Rone. I do believe that's the most you've ever said at one time. I've taken everything, have I? Well, it's your turn. You can take whatever you want—including Liz. I don't want a damned thing from anyone anymore."

"When will you grow up?" Rone asked sadly.

"This is great," Jack said sitting forward, his face taught with anger, "you're sounding more and more like dear old dad. Please go on."

"I have no more to say. I don't waste my time talking to fools. I prefer the company of men."

Jack leapt to where the other man stood. They were inches apart, and Jack looked into the face of his bronze-skinned brother. "Why the hell didn't you tell me? All these damned years I could have—should have—known. Why?"

Rone didn't answer and Jack went on. "Did you think it would matter? Did you think I'd resent you? Were you afraid I would look down on you? What? There was some reason, and I want to know what it was!"

Rone's voice was hoarse when he said, "I wanted your friendship, not your blood. Your knowing the truth could not have made us closer, but it could have torn us apart. I didn't want it to matter."

Jack backed up a few steps and raked his fingers through his hair. "Well it would have mattered. But it doesn't anymore. I don't give a damn if you *are* my brother."

Rone shrugged. "I didn't come here to discuss my birth with you. I came to bring you back to Elizabeth. You're going to Dave's wedding."

Jack laughed with his head thrown back, and then he said, "The hell I am."

Rone was undaunted. "I'm going to get some strong coffee from Calla. Then you're getting dressed and coming with me."

"You'll have to kill me first," Jack threatened, all laughter gone now.

"Liz loves you, Jack. I won't let you throw her away." Rone's face lightened a little when he added, "She wants to come back to River Pines and start a family."

Jack put a hand on each of Rone's shoulders and said, "Take a message to her, Rone. Tell her she can still have Drummond children. Tell her that I send my best wishes for her marriage to you, and I hope your blessed union will be fruitful," his lips turned into a sneer, "if it hasn't been already."

Rone's fist caught Jack in the stomach, knocking him backwards a few steps, then his other fist collided against Jack's jaw, this time sending him down onto the wide planks of the floor. Within seconds, however, Jack was back on his feet, lunging forward and grabbing Rone by the throat.

They hadn't fought each other since they were young boys. As grown men, they were worthy opponents and well matched. Years of companionship had them trained in the other's style of fighting, and now as each one seemed to gain the advantage, the other caught up.

Blood splattered their clothes, the walls, and the floor. They tumbled and fell from room to room, until finally they went from the darkness of the house to he darkness of the night outside. The soft ground cushioned their falls, and they always got up again, throwing more punches, bloodying more of each other's faces.

When their knuckles were swollen and too painful to use, they kicked and wrestled, battling in a ancient choreography known strictly to men.

"Fall, you blasted Indian," Jack gasped as he threw a punch.

"You fall, you stubborn jackass," Rone answered, delivering a kick, almost knocking himself over in the process.

Again and again they picked themselves up and attacked, until, finally, when neither of them could stand straight, Jack fell forward, face down in the dirt, and Rone immediately followed.

Jim walked from the little porch of the white house and pulled water from the well, carefully pouring it onto their heads.

Jack opened his eyes first, his mouth was filled with blood and dirt. The water stung his eyes and he swore as he sat up. He looked around for Rone and saw him prostrate beside him.

"You okay, Mr. Jack?" The black man asked cautiously.

Jack spit grit and blood through his swollen lips, and asked, "Who won?"

Jim shook his head. "I ain't really sure. You fell first, though, if you're countin' seconds."

Jack pushed Rone with his foot, "Get up, Indian."

"No!" Jim interceded, "No more fightin', Mr. Jack. I don't think I could bear seein' the two of you goin' at it again. Calla's inside cryin' like a baby. I'll knock your heads together, you fight any more." Jim warned, uncharacteristically angry.

Jack wobbled to his feet, and found it difficult to stand on his legs. Rone still lay on his back, though they could see his eyes were opened and looking through narrow strips of swollen flesh.

"It don't matter who won this here fight, Mr. Jack," Jim continued angrily. "All that matters is that two friends . . ."

"It's okay, Jim," Jack said, leaning down to take Rone's wrist in his hand to help him up. "I don't want to fight anymore. I want to get washed and dressed. I got a wedding to go to."

Their horses sped into Cheyenne and Jack threw the reins of the stallion at Rone when he ran into the station house and inquired about the train.

"It pulled out a few minutes ago, sir."

"Was there a private car from Denver coupled to it?"

"Yes, sir, there was."

Jack went back out to Rone. "We missed it by a few minutes. What do you say? Are we up to the old 'catch up' game, Rone?" he asked.

Their eyes met with amusement, and Jack winced when he smiled, a smarting reminder of the fight from the evening before.

Without another word, the two men spurred their horses and galloped from town. Soon, they could see the train in the distance, and exchanging glances, eased into a race, their horses abreast, closing in on the black iron cars that steamed along the endless tracks.

The silky black mane of Jack's horse blew in the wind as he guided it beside the private car. His one hand reached out as his other gave the reins to Rone, whose horse's shoulder was almost touching the stallion's.

Faster and faster the horses' hooves hammered the soft earth. Jack balanced with his legs as his fingers closed around the cold projection of the car's handle. He released his thighs and the horse was out from under him, expertly being led away by Rone.

Jack pulled his dangling legs around and his feet caught on the step. He smiled, smoothed his jacket, and straightened his hat. He looked out and saw Rone bringing the horses to a gentle trot.

Jack raised his hand in a parting salute, and Rone responded.

Elizabeth and Daniel sat in his private car. He attempted small talk, and she answered politely, but her thoughts were elsewhere and her misery unending.

They had been traveling for a day and a half, and still Elizabeth stared out the window, silently watching the scenery. Daniel worried about her pale face and tired eyes. Fatigue seemed to plague her, and she ate just enough to give her what little energy she had.

Elizabeth saw it first. A man with two horses, racing beside the train. She sat up straight and pointed out the window, "Look!"

Dan put down his newspaper and his eyes squinted against the sun. Then he, too, sat up. "Rone . . ."

They saw Rone slow the horses and turn them around to look at the train, and watched as his hand came up in a farewell salute.

"What the hell are they up to now?" Daniel asked, just as the door of the car snapped open and Jack sauntered in grinning through his battered face.

"A friend of mine talked me into going to a wedding," he said. Then, reaching into his jacket, he remembered, ". . . oh, yeah, Rone sent this to you."

There in his hand, wrinkled from being stuffed against his chest, was Elizabeth's white hat.

CHAPTER THIRTY-THREE

With its multicolored stone, white shutters, and shining windows, the Gleason home was a beautiful sight to Elizabeth. She stood at the bottom of the stone steps leading to the aged oak door, and her eyes filled with tears. Had it only been a year since she had left in the night?

Yet, as wonderful as it looked to her, it was no longer home. River Pines was home in her heart now. Fate brought her back, supposedly to attend the wedding she had run away to avoid, but would she ever be able to call this her home while pining for the ranch, and the man who lived on it, that helped to create the woman she was now—so different from the girl who had run away.

She felt Jack's shoulder brush hers and he stood close beside her, also looking at the doors. They hadn't spoken much on the train. She didn't know why he joined them or what it meant, but it was enough for now to be near him.

Jack took her elbow now and asked, "Shall we go in together?" But the doors opened, and within moments, she was surrounded by her aunt and sister and the many servants she remembered from her childhood. Glorie stood at the door, her wrinkled, arthritic hands folded in front of her, her hazel-colored eyes bright, her mouth pouting at the prodigal Beth.

Elizabeth went to her and embraced the old woman who seemed more bony than Elizabeth had remembered.

"You been up to no good," Glorie said in her clipped brogue.

Elizabeth laughed, "Oh, yes, Glorie, do scold me. I've missed it. I've missed you."

With that they all laughed, and Glorie waved her hand at the group. "Ah, ye're too much for the poor old woman that I am."

Emily put her arm around Elizabeth. "Glorie's retired, you know, Beth. But she dresses in her uniform every morning and orders us all around, just like she always has. For the life of me, I don't know what she must think retirement means."

Glorie wagged a finger at the girls, "I'll keep me eye on this house and all that goes on in it 'til the day I die. Now go on up to your room and rest before dinner. And mind, I won't have any shenanigans while you're here."

Emily led Elizabeth to her old bedroom, and the two young women chatted affectionately for an hour. Emily brought her up to date on all that would take place in two days, the day of her and David's long awaited wedding.

"I'm wearing Mother's wedding gown, Beth, and each time I try it on, I can feel her presence. In my heart I know they'll be here with us."

Emily was so animated and happy that it made Elizabeth cry, which alarmed her twin. Elizabeth hugged her. "It's only that I'm so happy for you, and happy that I'm here to share it with you. I'm afraid I cry very easily these days. If I'm not crying, I'm sleeping."

"Are you ill?" Emily asked, her gray eyes round with concern.

Elizabeth laughed. "No, not ill." Changing the subject she said, "Please, tell me more about the wedding."

"No," Emily said. "I've been too selfish. You're exhausted from your trip. Rest now, Beth, and we'll talk again later. Do you need help changing?"

Elizabeth shook her head, afraid her voice would betray her again, and after another worried glance, Emily left the room.

A moment later, Jack walked in. "It seems we've been assigned the same room."

"Oh, dear," she whispered.

"Shall I go and explain to your aunt?" he asked her.

Elizabeth took his arm. "No, don't. Apparently they think we are . . . reconciled. It would be too upsetting to tell them the truth. I don't want anything to spoil the wedding, Jack."

He smiled and looked around the room. "Well, I can put up with it if you can."

"We must, Jack, for Emily and David's sake."

He looked at her seriously for a moment, then smiling again, said, "I'll sleep on the floor by the fireplace."

"No, that's all right, I'll sleep there. After all, you are a guest here."

"Please," he said, bowing, "allow me to be gallant."

"That would certainly be a unique experience for you," she threw at him. She expected an angry response, but he continued to smile.

Touching one of the bruises that still marred his face, he said, "It took a good whippin' to teach me that."

Then putting his hand on her cheek, he traced the dark circle beneath her eye. "The trip was too much for you. You're tired, Liz."

His touch made her heart beat faster than she thought it could. She fought the urge to throw herself in his arms, and backed away from him instead.

"Shall we go downstairs and join everyone?" she asked, more brightly than she felt. "I understand the Smythes arrived yesterday. I'd like to see them."

Jack smiled again and they both started for the door, bumping against each other. Laughing, Jack opened it and waited for her to exit.

That night, after an extravagant dinner held at the Dawson home, Daniel and Jack took David to Philadelphia to bid farewell to his unmarried life.

Elizabeth had been in bed a long while before she heard her husband enter the room. "Are you asleep, Liz?" he whispered. When she didn't answer, he began to whistle, at first a winsome little melody, but ending in his favorite call. Beth settled herself deeper into the bed, deliberately ignoring Jack.

She had left blankets and a pillow for him, and after much tossing, he finally found a comfortable spot. "Good night, Elizabeth," he said. "I hope you're enjoying the comfort of that bed. I don't know if I care too much for this gallant business."

"They say," she informed him from under her covers, "hard floors are good for the back and the soul." She laughed when he grunted in reply.

The wedding day was bright and sunny. The spring warmth was cooled by a gentle breeze as the beautiful bride and her anxious groom exchanged vows.

Elizabeth watched David put the ring on Emily's finger, and her heart ached with a poignant mixture of happiness and sadness. She looked down at her own wedding ring, borrowed from Calla one year ago. When she lifted her eyes, Jack was looking at her from over the heads of his cousin and her sister, and what Elizabeth found in their green depths seemed to resemble what she herself was feeling. She wondered if he remembered what day it was.

The wedding breakfast was a veritable feast. Elizabeth and Catherine were busy entertaining the guests, organizing the staff and preparing for the reception that evening. After they bid the bride and groom farewell, the dancing began, and Elizabeth, who had changed into the iridescent gown and diamonds from her father-in-law, found herself circling the dance floor continuously throughout the evening.

Jack danced with her many times, and she was excited by his attentions, though afraid to hope for more. For the first time in weeks, her eyes shone and her cheeks glowed a healthy pink.

They noted, conspiratorially, how often and how well Catherine and Daniel danced together, and Jack gave her a knowing wink from across the room when the older couple walked out into the garden together.

When it was late and the last of the guests had left—namely, Daniel—Catherine kissed Elizabeth good night at the foot of the staircase. "I've told the servants to wait until morning to finish cleaning up. I'm exhausted."

Elizabeth grabbed her aunt and hugged her. "I love you, Aunt Catherine," she said.

Catherine held her at arm's length after the embrace. "Are you all right, dear?"

Elizabeth nodded. "I just wanted you to know."

She watched her aunt climb the stairs, and when she was no longer in view, Elizabeth walked back into the large drawing room that had been cleared of its furnishings in order to accommodate the dancing.

She knew Jack was there, and when she joined him, he poured two glasses of champagne and handed one to her. They toasted silently.

Jack took the glass back and placed it beside his on the table. "Shall we have one last dance?" he asked, his arms extended to her.

"But there isn't any music," she said.

"I hum, remember?"

Elizabeth laughed and went into his arms, and they danced close together. He hummed a reel and swung her around the dance floor as he had in his barn the night they first made love.

Then he slowed to a waltz, gracefully twirling around the perimeter of the empty room. His mouth was close to her ear. "We've had some very bad times, Liz."

"Yes," she answered, sadly.

"But there were good times. You were happy at the ranch, weren't you?"

He felt her nod.

"We've said some cruel things to each other, yet there were sweet words always mixed in."

Again, Elizabeth nodded, and again he whirled her around the dance floor.

"There could have been many more happy times if we had given ourselves the chance."

"If only . . . ," she bit her lip and swallowed hard.

"Liz, do you remember what today is?" He stopped dancing, but still held her in his arms.

She nodded, "The year is up, Jack."

"Happy anniversary, beautiful lady."

Elizabeth couldn't answer, and he swayed with her again, turning and waltzing this time, then stopping to bring his lips down, almost touching hers. He said, "I lied to you, Liz. There *is* such a thing as love, and I knew it all along. I'm insane with it."

Her hand clung to his back, tears formed in her eyes.

"Start over with me, darling," he begged. "River Pines is ours now, what's left of it, but we can rebuild it together. We'll start fresh . . ."

She allowed the tears to fall on her cheeks then. "Oh, yes, Jack, yes. I've been so afraid that you wouldn't . . ."

She stopped speaking as he swept her up into the dance again, this time laughing, his eyes a sparkling emerald.

"Do you have anything to tell me?" he asked her.

Elizabeth looked at Jack in surprise, not sure what he meant, and uncertain of what his reaction would be.

Jack stopped abruptly, wondering if he had been mistaken. Though disappointed, he decided it didn't matter, because now that Liz had just agreed to go back to River Pines with him, they'd have plenty of time to fill the ranch with children. He tenderly kissed her forehead and danced again.

"I've been told you want children," he said, his cheek against her hair. His voice was like a sensuous caress when he continued, "So do I, Liz, and when we're finished dancing, I'm going to take you up to our room and make love to you—probably all night long because I never seem to have enough of you—and who knows, we might be lucky and start this family we both want."

Elizabeth said nothing for a long moment, then, "Jack?"

"Yes, beautiful lady," he murmured.

"We already have begun our family," she said into his shoulder, afraid to look at him. She felt his body tense. Then, lifting her off her feet, up to his face, his mouth found hers, and he began to dance again, around and around the empty room, as invisible musicians played only for them.